POKÉMON™ ADVENTURES BLACK & WHITE

**Pokémon ADVENTURES
BLACK AND WHITE**
Volume 2
VIZ Kids Edition

Story by **HIDENORI KUSAKA**
Art by **SATOSHI YAMAMOTO**

© 2013 Pokémon.
© 1995–2013 Nintendo/Creatures Inc./GAME FREAK inc.
TM and ® and character names are trademarks of Nintendo.
POCKET MONSTERS SPECIAL Vol. 44
by Hidenori KUSAKA, Satoshi YAMAMOTO
© 1997 Hidenori KUSAKA, Satoshi YAMAMOTO
All rights reserved.
Original Japanese edition published by SHOGAKUKAN.
English translation rights in the United States of America, Canada,
the United Kingdom and Ireland arranged with SHOGAKUKAN.

Translation/Tetsuichiro Miyaki
English Adaptation/Annette Roman
Touch-up & Lettering/Susan Daigle-Leach
Design/Shawn Carrico
Editor/Annette Roman

Printed in the U.S.A.

Published by VIZ Media, LLC
P.O. Box 77010
San Francisco, CA 94107

10 9 8 7 6 5 4 3 2 1
First printing, November 2013

www.vizkids.com

www.viz.com

POKÉMON
ADVENTURES
BLACK & WHITE

2

VOLUME TWO

Story by
**Hidenori
Kusaka**

Art by
**Satoshi
Yamamoto**

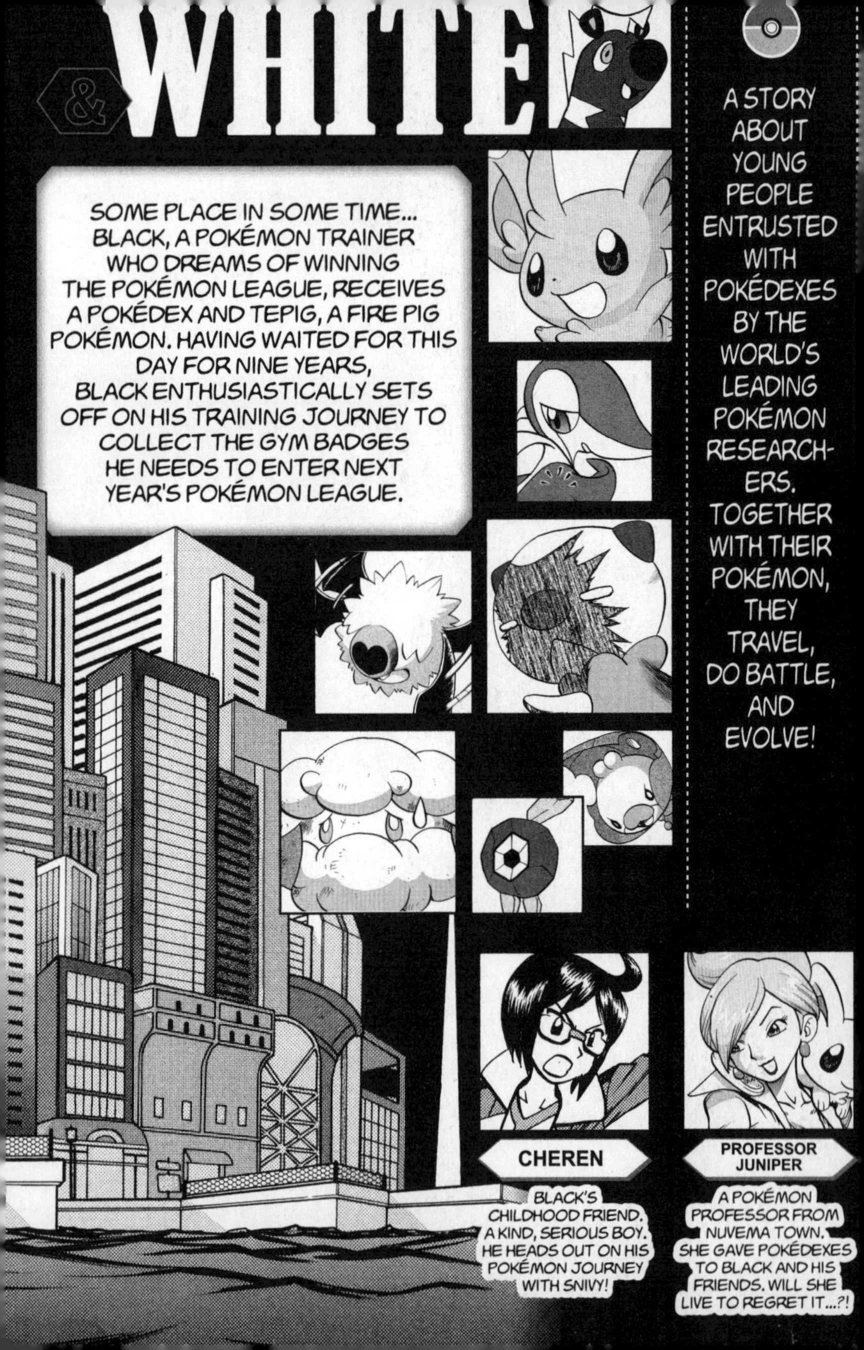
& WHITE
A STORY ABOUT YOUNG PEOPLE ENTRUSTED WITH POKÉDEXES BY THE WORLD'S LEADING POKÉMON RESEARCHERS. TOGETHER WITH THEIR POKÉMON, THEY TRAVEL, DO BATTLE, AND EVOLVE!
SOME PLACE IN SOME TIME... BLACK, A POKÉMON TRAINER WHO DREAMS OF WINNING THE POKÉMON LEAGUE, RECEIVES A POKÉDEX AND TEPIG, A FIRE PIG POKÉMON. HAVING WAITED FOR THIS DAY FOR NINE YEARS, BLACK ENTHUSIASTICALLY SETS OFF ON HIS TRAINING JOURNEY TO COLLECT THE GYM BADGES HE NEEDS TO ENTER NEXT YEAR'S POKÉMON LEAGUE.
PROFESSOR JUNIPER
A POKÉMON PROFESSOR FROM NUVEMA TOWN. SHE GAVE POKÉDEXES TO BLACK AND HIS FRIENDS. WILL SHE LIVE TO REGRET IT...?!
CHEREN
BLACK'S CHILDHOOD FRIEND. A KIND, SERIOUS BOY. HE HEADS OUT ON HIS POKÉMON JOURNEY WITH SNIVY!

POKÉMON ADVENTURES

The Tenth Chapter

10 BLACK

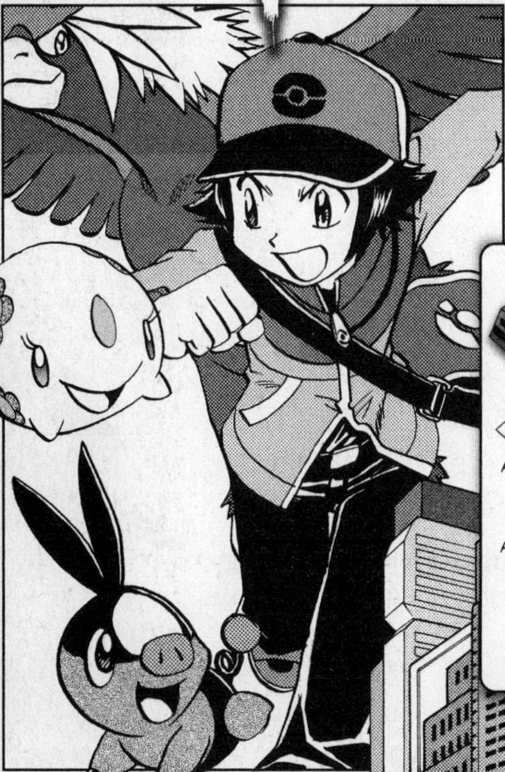

PLACE: UNOVA REGION

A HUGE AREA FULL OF MODERN CITIES. MANY OF ITS TOWNS ARE CONNECTED BY BRIDGES. IN THE CENTER OF THE REGION RISE THE TOWERING SKYSCRAPERS OF CASTELIA CITY, THE SYMBOL OF UNOVA.

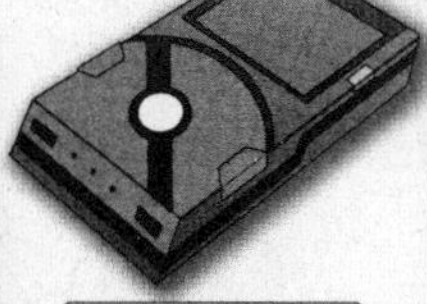

BLACK

A TRAINER WHOSE DREAM IS TO WIN THE POKÉMON LEAGUE. A PASSIONATE YOUNG MAN WHO, ONCE HE SETS OUT TO ACCOMPLISH SOMETHING, CAN'T BE STOPPED. HE ALSO DOES HIS RESEARCH AND PLANS AHEAD. HE HAS SPECIAL DEDUCTIVE SKILLS THAT HELP HIM ANALYZE INFORMATION TO SOLVE MYSTERIES.

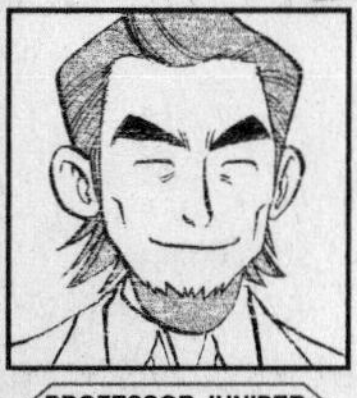

PROFESSOR JUNIPER (THE ELDER)

PROFESSOR JUNIPER'S FATHER, A RENOWNED POKÉMON RESEARCHER IN THE UNOVA REGION.

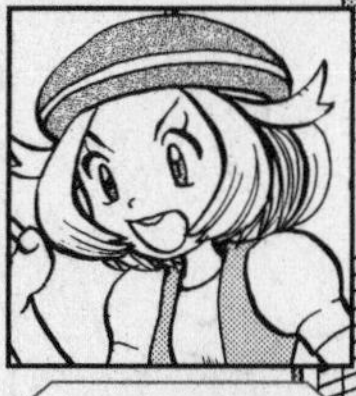

BIANCA

BLACK'S CHILDHOOD FRIEND WHO LIKES TO TAKE THINGS AT HER OWN PACE. SHE DEPARTS ON HER TRAINING JOURNEY WITH OSHAWOTT!

POKÉMON
ADVENTURES
BLACK & WHITE

2 VOLUME TWO

CONTENTS

Pokémon™ Adventures Black & White

GALVANTULA

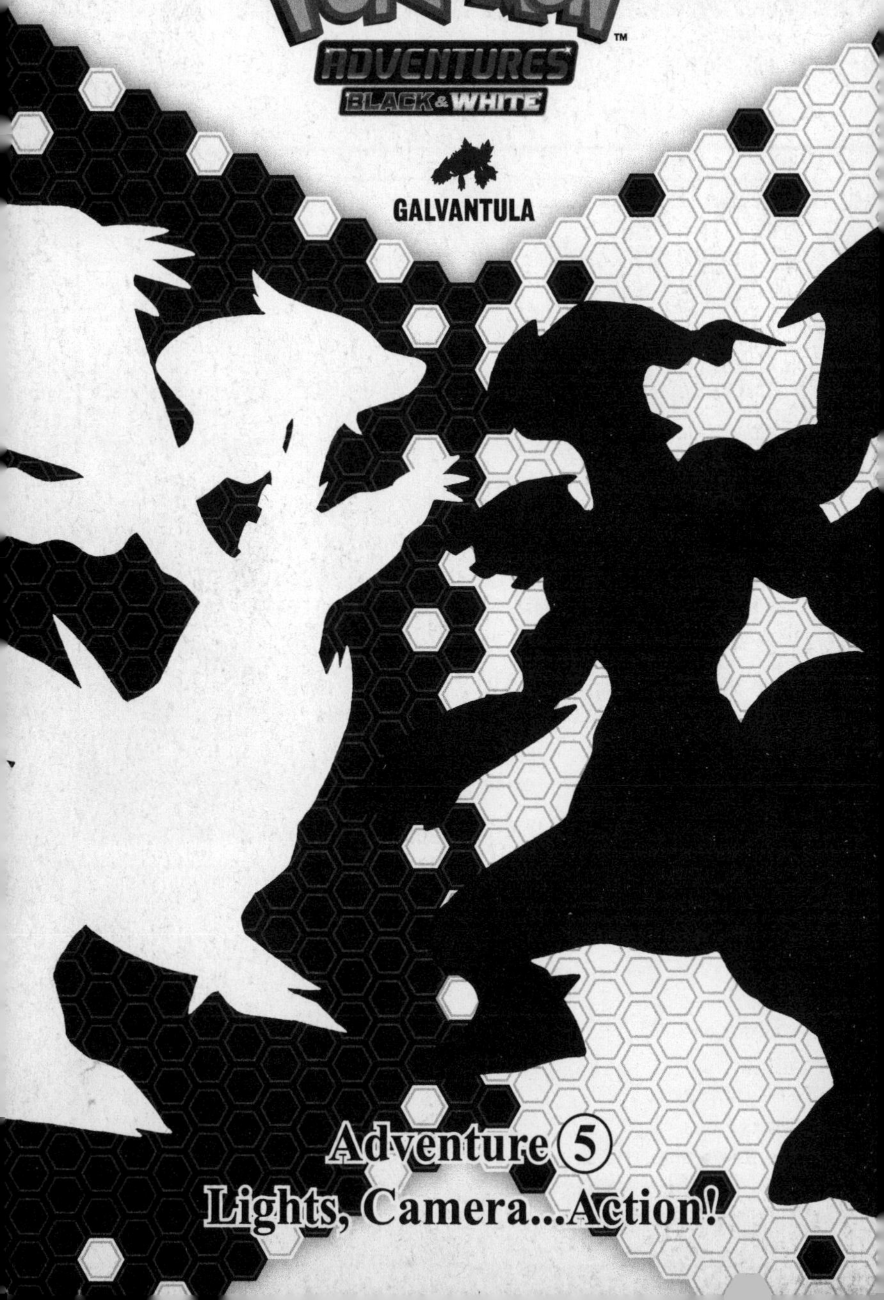

Adventure 5
Lights, Camera...Action!

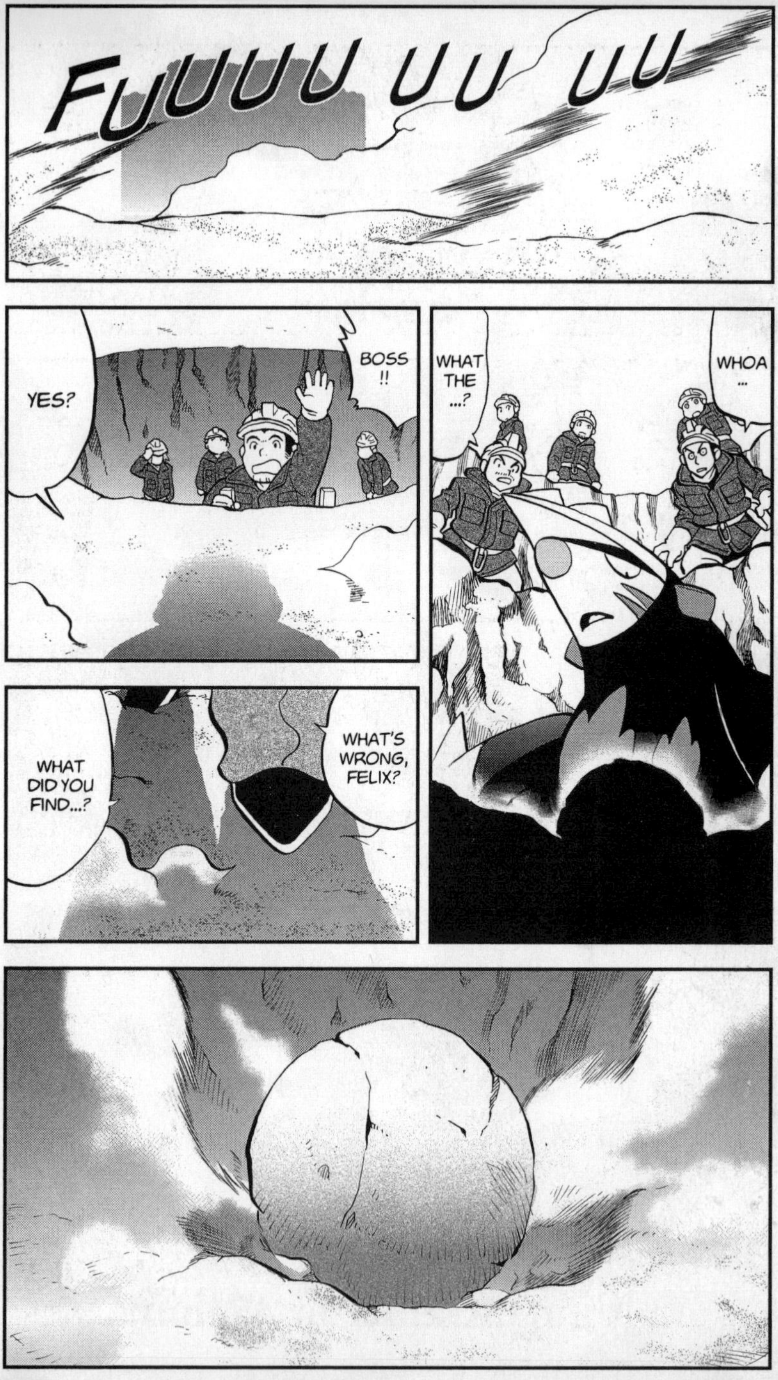
FUUUUU UU UU
WHOA ...
WHAT THE ...?
BOSS !!
YES?
WHAT'S WRONG, FELIX?
WHAT DID YOU FIND...?

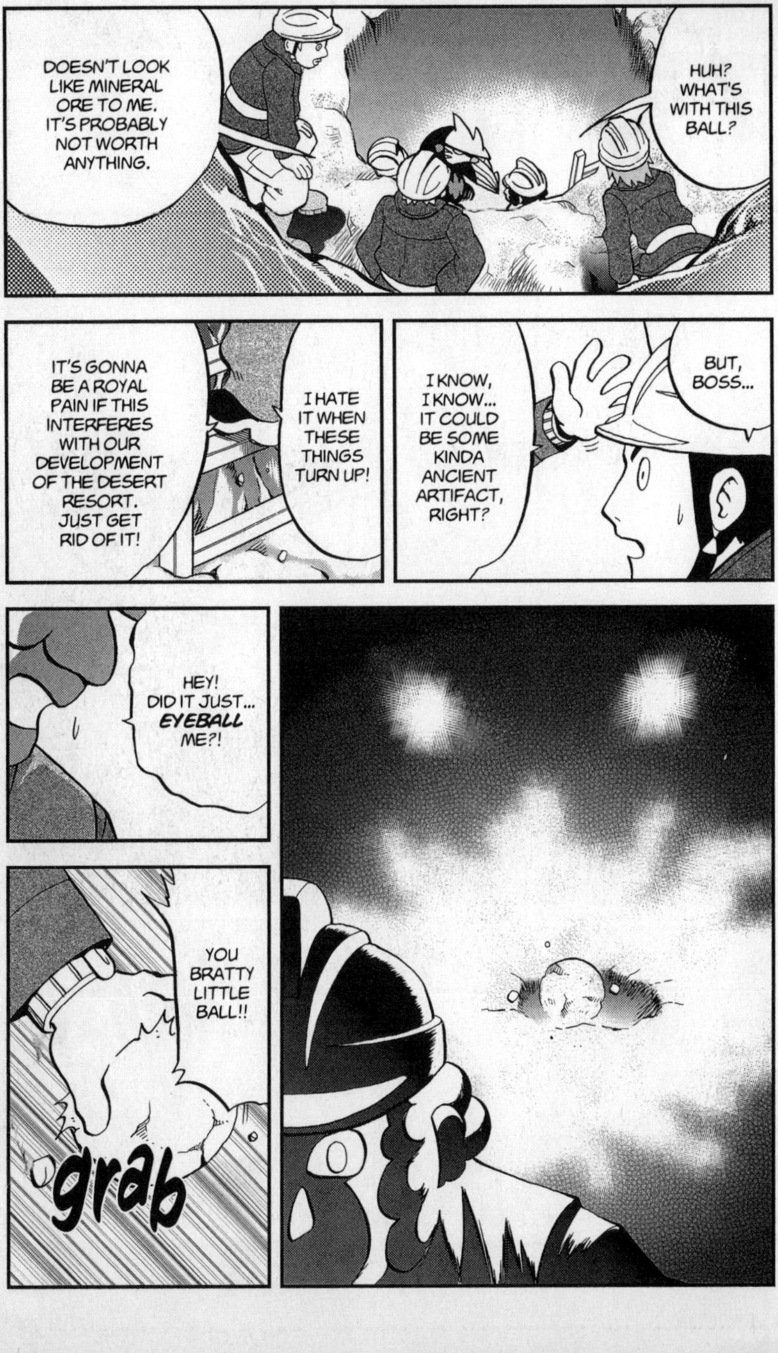
HUH? WHAT'S WITH THIS BALL?
DOESN'T LOOK LIKE MINERAL ORE TO ME. IT'S PROBABLY NOT WORTH ANYTHING.
BUT, BOSS...
I KNOW, I KNOW... IT COULD BE SOME KINDA ANCIENT ARTIFACT, RIGHT?
I HATE IT WHEN THESE THINGS TURN UP!
IT'S GONNA BE A ROYAL PAIN IF THIS INTERFERES WITH OUR DEVELOPMENT OF THE DESERT RESORT. JUST GET RID OF IT!
HEY! DID IT JUST... ***EYEBALL*** ME?!
YOU BRATTY LITTLE BALL!!
grab

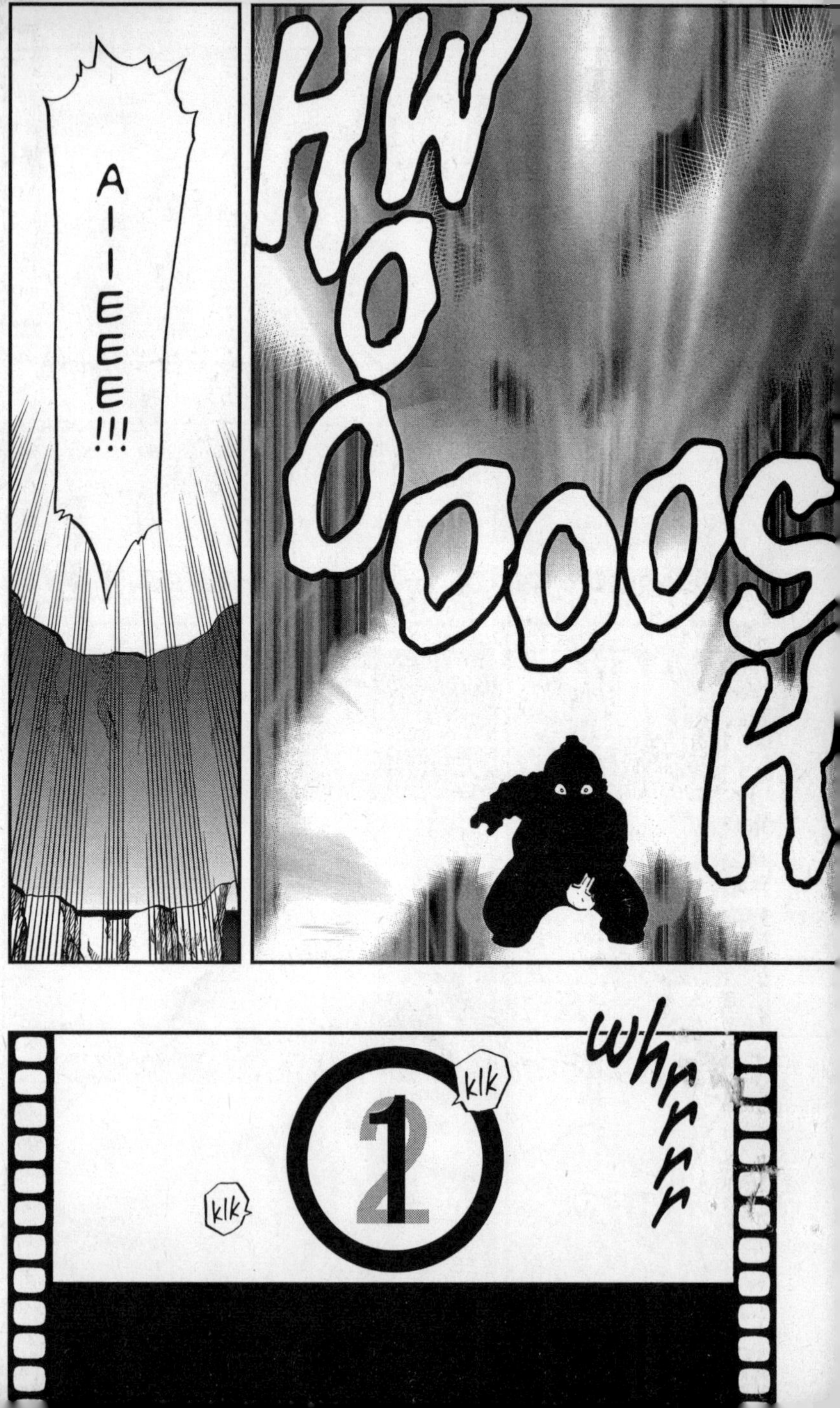
HWOOOOOSH
AIIEEE!!!
whrrrrr
klk
klk

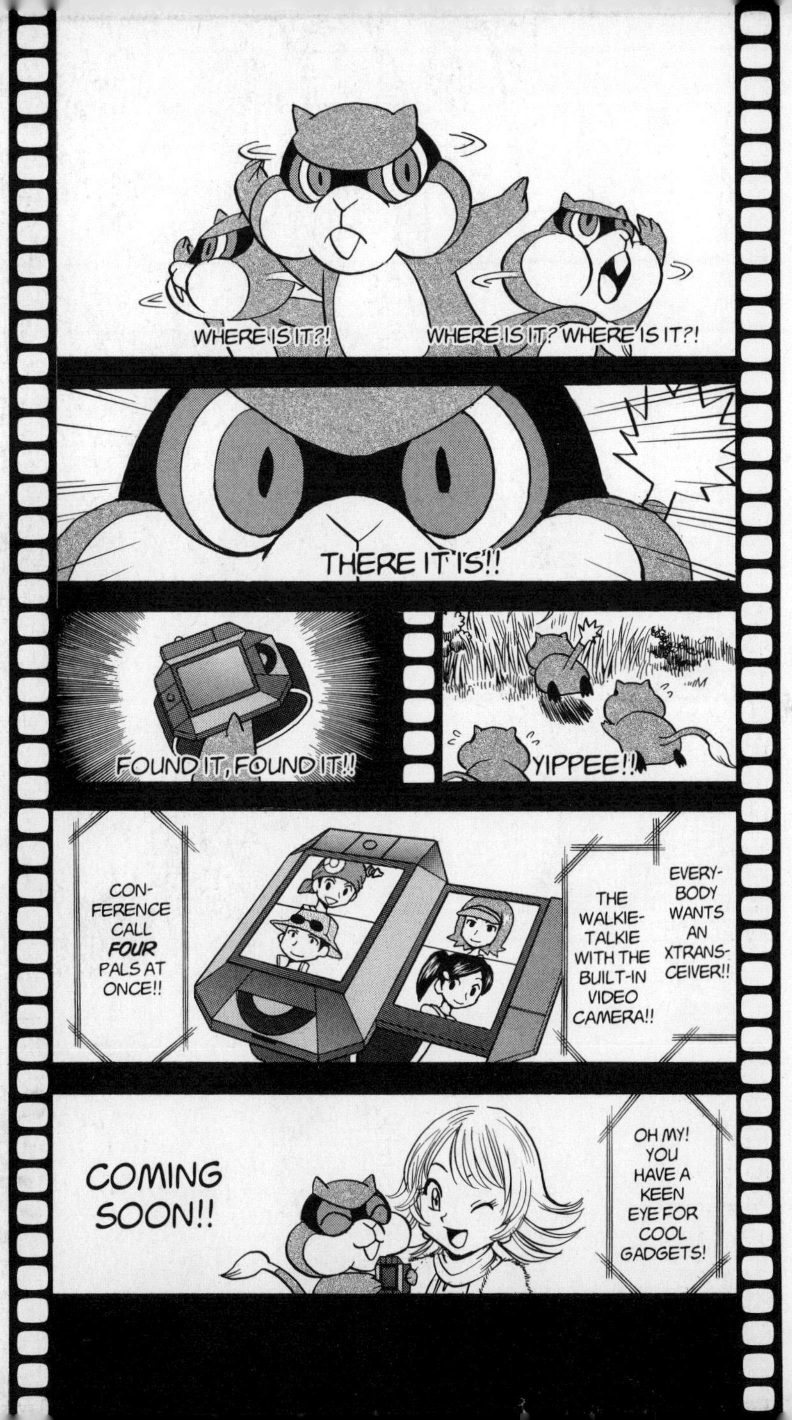
WHERE IS IT? WHERE IS IT?!
WHERE IS IT?!
THERE IT IS!!
YIPPEE!!
FOUND IT, FOUND IT!!
EVERY-BODY WANTS AN XTRANS-CEIVER!!
THE WALKIE-TALKIE WITH THE BUILT-IN VIDEO CAMERA!!
CON-FERENCE CALL **FOUR** PALS AT ONCE!!
OH MY! YOU HAVE A KEEN EYE FOR COOL GADGETS!
COMING SOON!!

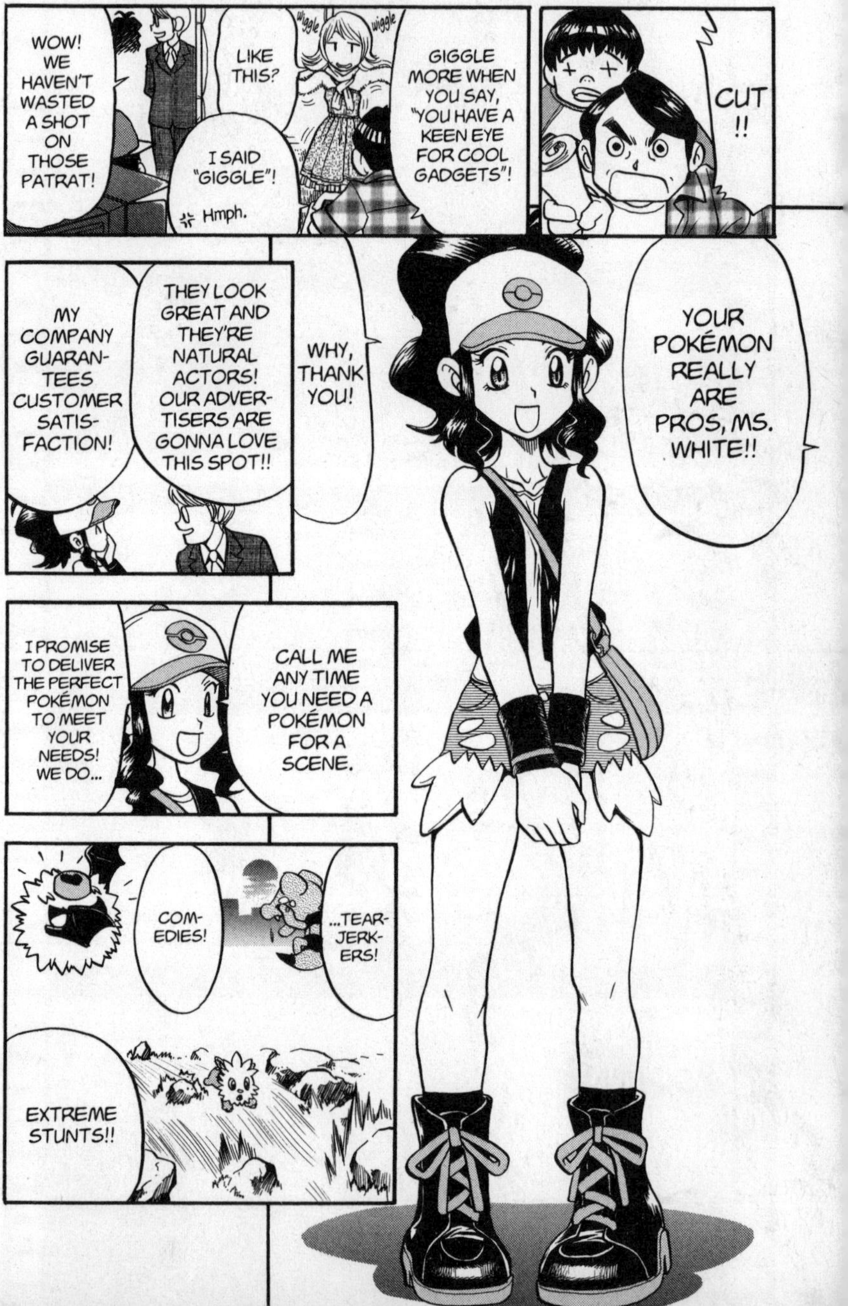
CUT !!
GIGGLE MORE WHEN YOU SAY, "YOU HAVE A KEEN EYE FOR COOL GADGETS"!
wiggle wiggle
LIKE THIS?
I SAID "GIGGLE"!
Hmph.
WOW! WE HAVEN'T WASTED A SHOT ON THOSE PATRAT!
YOUR POKÉMON REALLY ARE PROS, MS. WHITE!!
WHY, THANK YOU!
THEY LOOK GREAT AND THEY'RE NATURAL ACTORS! OUR ADVERTISERS ARE GONNA LOVE THIS SPOT!!
MY COMPANY GUARANTEES CUSTOMER SATISFACTION!
CALL ME ANY TIME YOU NEED A POKÉMON FOR A SCENE.
I PROMISE TO DELIVER THE PERFECT POKÉMON TO MEET YOUR NEEDS! WE DO...
...TEARJERKERS!
COMEDIES!
EXTREME STUNTS!!

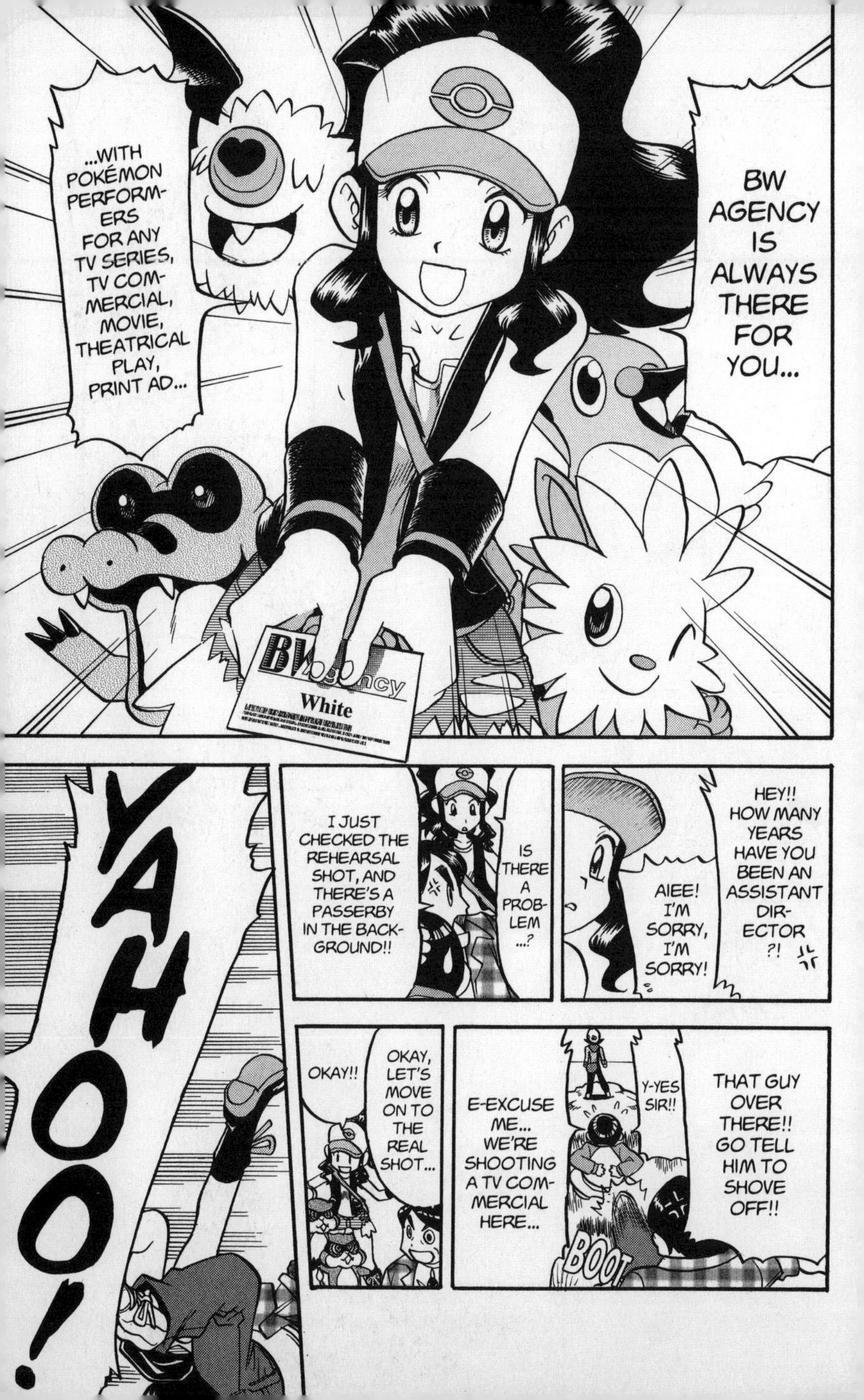
BW AGENCY IS ALWAYS THERE FOR YOU...
...WITH POKÉMON PERFORMERS FOR ANY TV SERIES, TV COMMERCIAL, MOVIE, THEATRICAL PLAY, PRINT AD...
BW Agency
White
HEY!! HOW MANY YEARS HAVE YOU BEEN AN ASSISTANT DIRECTOR?!
AIEE! I'M SORRY, I'M SORRY!
IS THERE A PROBLEM...?
I JUST CHECKED THE REHEARSAL SHOT, AND THERE'S A PASSERBY IN THE BACKGROUND!!
THAT GUY OVER THERE!! GO TELL HIM TO SHOVE OFF!!
Y-YES SIR!!
E-EXCUSE ME... WE'RE SHOOTING A TV COMMERCIAL HERE...
BOOT
OKAY, LET'S MOVE ON TO THE REAL SHOT...
OKAY!!
YAHOO!

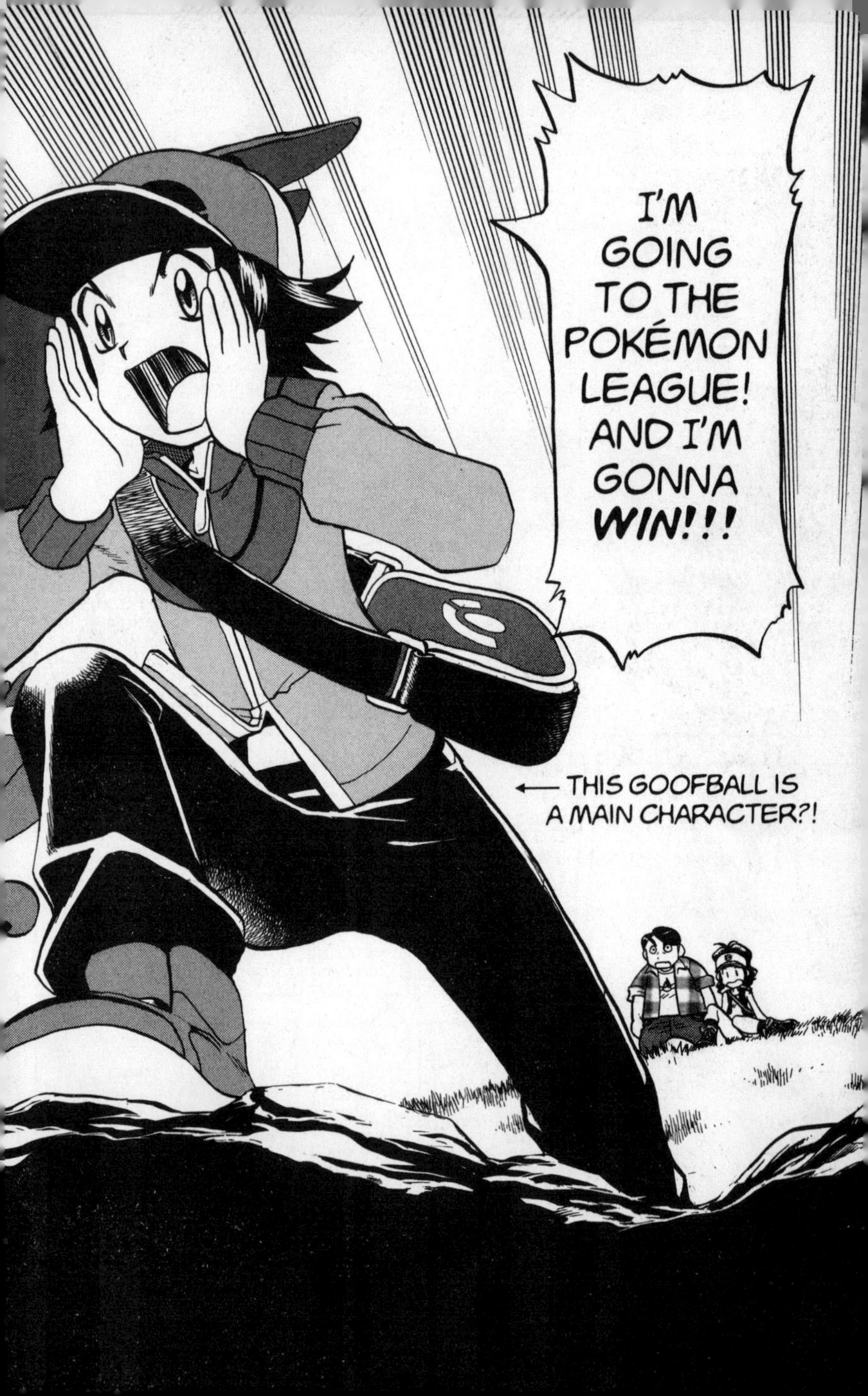
I'M GOING TO THE POKÉMON LEAGUE! AND I'M GONNA **WIN!!!**
THIS GOOFBALL IS A MAIN CHARACTER?!

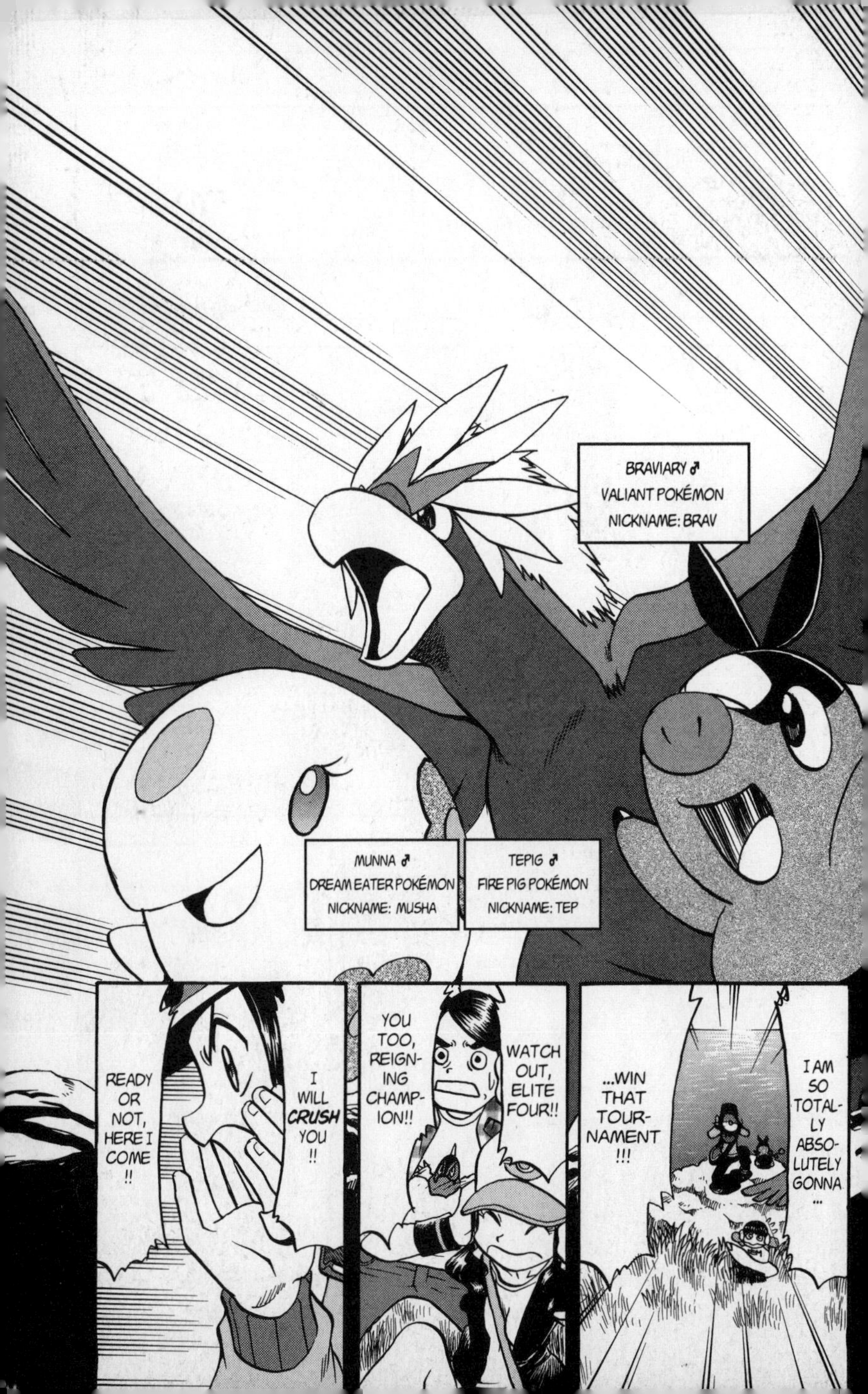
BRAVIARY ♂
VALIANT POKÉMON
NICKNAME: BRAV
TEPIG ♂
FIRE PIG POKÉMON
NICKNAME: TEP
MUNNA ♂
DREAM EATER POKÉMON
NICKNAME: MUSHA
I AM SO TOTALLY ABSOLUTELY GONNA...
...WIN THAT TOURNAMENT!!!
WATCH OUT, ELITE FOUR!!
YOU TOO, REIGNING CHAMPION!!
I WILL **CRUSH** YOU!!
READY OR NOT, HERE I COME!!

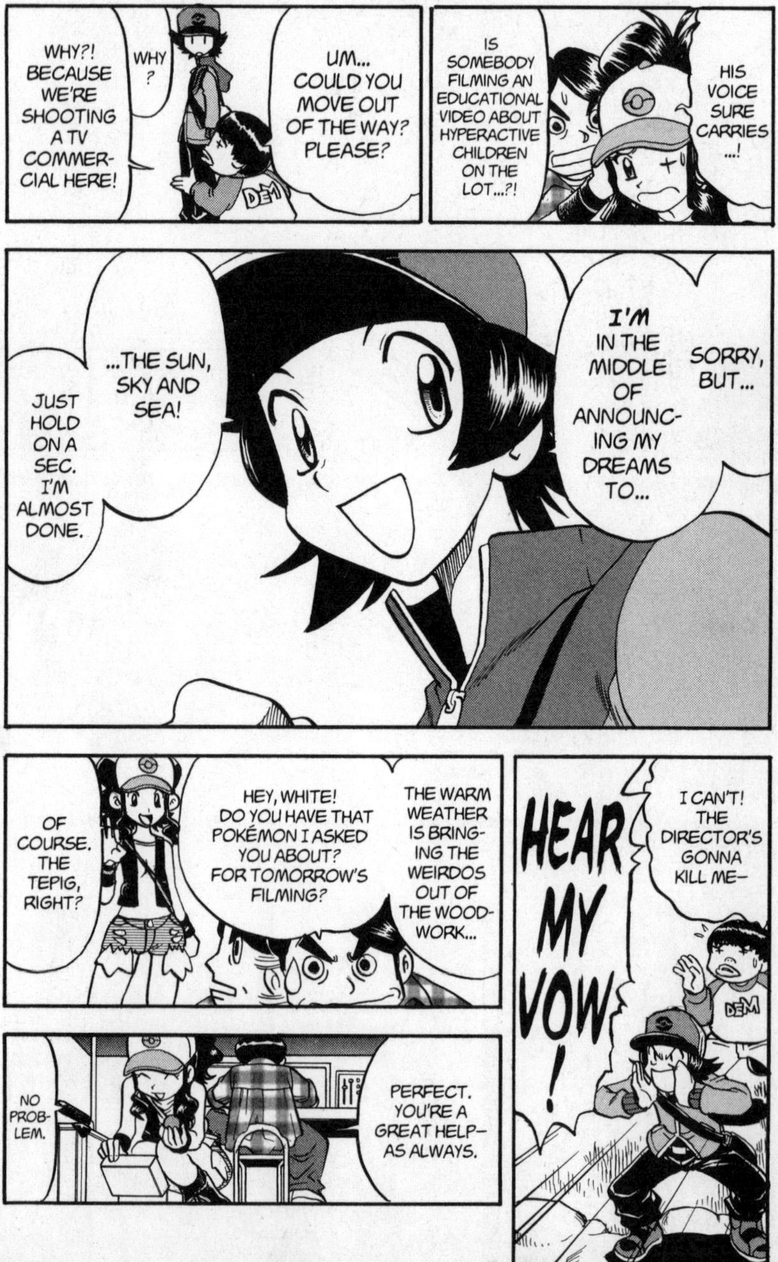
HIS VOICE SURE CARRIES ...!
IS SOMEBODY FILMING AN EDUCATIONAL VIDEO ABOUT HYPERACTIVE CHILDREN ON THE LOT...?!
UM... COULD YOU MOVE OUT OF THE WAY? PLEASE?
WHY ?
WHY?! BECAUSE WE'RE SHOOTING A TV COMMER-CIAL HERE!
SORRY, BUT...
I'M IN THE MIDDLE OF ANNOUNC-ING MY DREAMS TO...
...THE SUN, SKY AND SEA!
JUST HOLD ON A SEC. I'M ALMOST DONE.
I CAN'T! THE DIRECTOR'S GONNA KILL ME—
HEAR MY VOW!
THE WARM WEATHER IS BRING-ING THE WEIRDOS OUT OF THE WOOD-WORK...
HEY, WHITE! DO YOU HAVE THAT POKÉMON I ASKED YOU ABOUT? FOR TOMORROW'S FILMING?
OF COURSE. THE TEPIG, RIGHT?
PERFECT. YOU'RE A GREAT HELP— AS ALWAYS.
NO PROB-LEM.

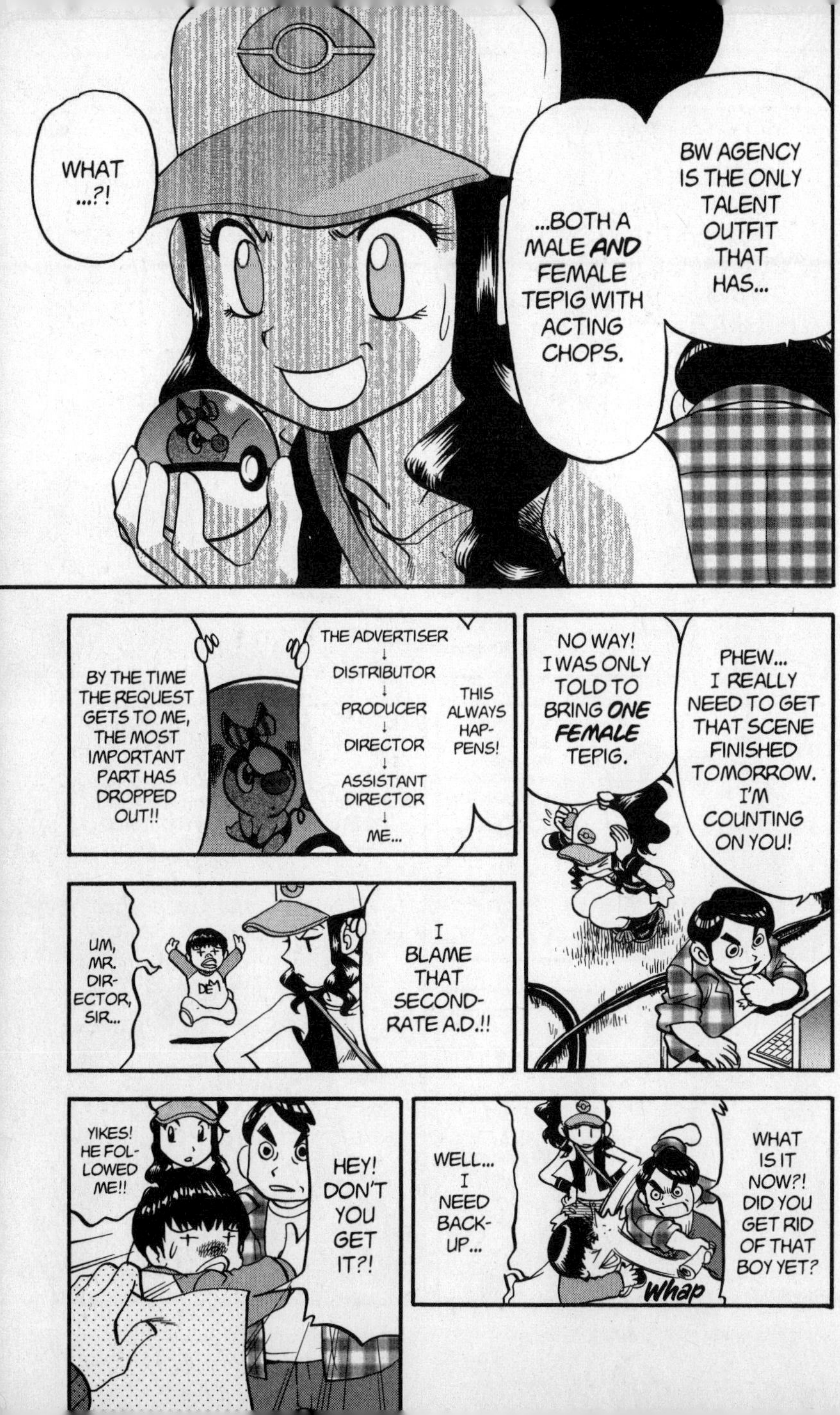
BW AGENCY IS THE ONLY TALENT OUTFIT THAT HAS...
...BOTH A MALE **AND** FEMALE TEPIG WITH ACTING CHOPS.
WHAT ...?!
PHEW... I REALLY NEED TO GET THAT SCENE FINISHED TOMORROW. I'M COUNTING ON YOU!
NO WAY! I WAS ONLY TOLD TO BRING **ONE FEMALE** TEPIG.
THE ADVERTISER ↓ DISTRIBUTOR ↓ PRODUCER ↓ DIRECTOR ↓ ASSISTANT DIRECTOR ↓ ME...
THIS ALWAYS HAP-PENS!
BY THE TIME THE REQUEST GETS TO ME, THE MOST IMPORTANT PART HAS DROPPED OUT!!
I BLAME THAT SECOND-RATE A.D.!!
UM, MR. DIR-ECTOR, SIR...
WHAT IS IT NOW?! DID YOU GET RID OF THAT BOY YET?
Whap
WELL... I NEED BACK-UP...
HEY! DON'T YOU GET IT?!
YIKES! HE FOL-LOWED ME!!

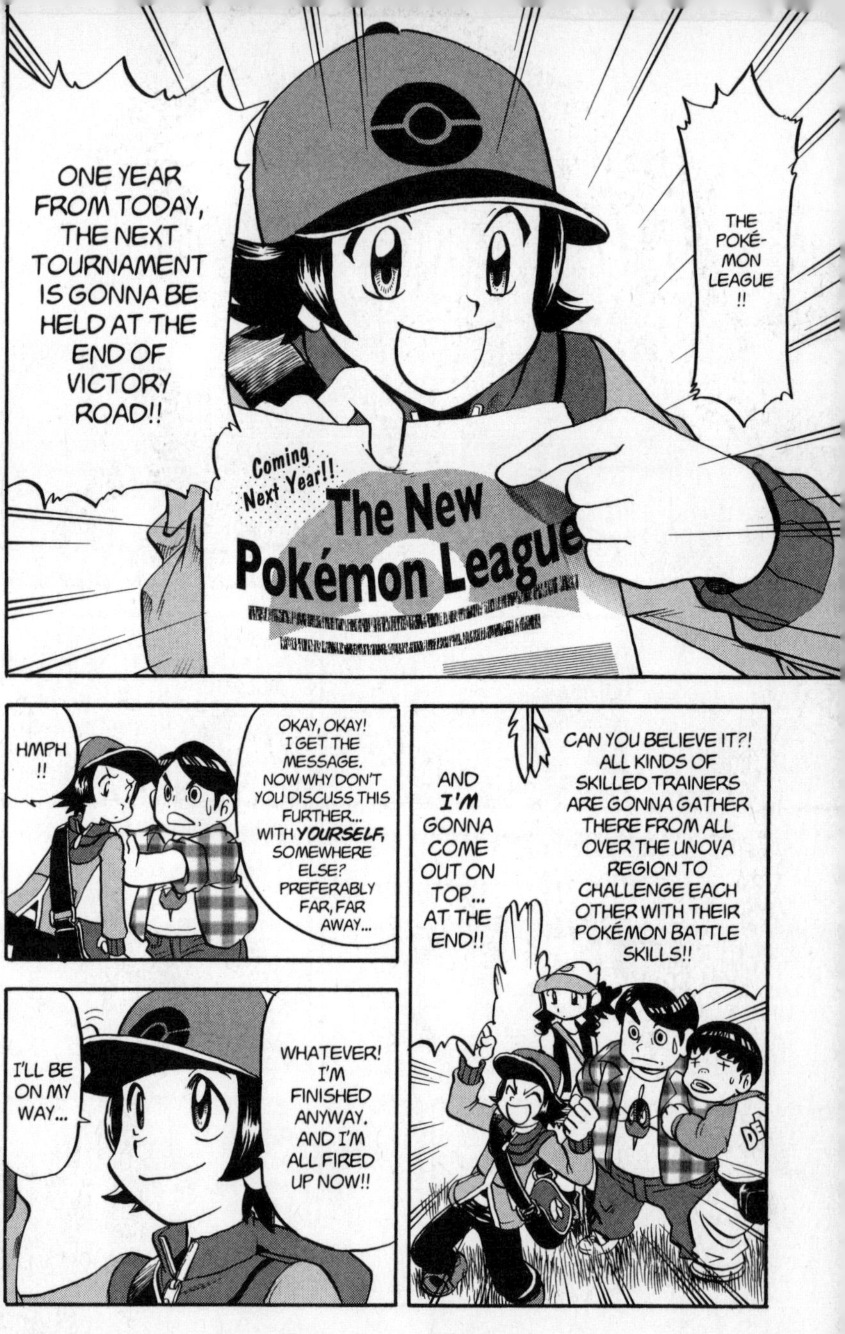
THE POKÉMON LEAGUE !!
ONE YEAR FROM TODAY, THE NEXT TOURNAMENT IS GONNA BE HELD AT THE END OF VICTORY ROAD!!
Coming Next Year!!
The New Pokémon League
CAN YOU BELIEVE IT?! ALL KINDS OF SKILLED TRAINERS ARE GONNA GATHER THERE FROM ALL OVER THE UNOVA REGION TO CHALLENGE EACH OTHER WITH THEIR POKÉMON BATTLE SKILLS!!
AND ***I'M*** GONNA COME OUT ON TOP... AT THE END!!
OKAY, OKAY! I GET THE MESSAGE. NOW WHY DON'T YOU DISCUSS THIS FURTHER... WITH ***YOURSELF***, SOMEWHERE ELSE? PREFERABLY FAR, FAR AWAY...
HMPH !!
WHATEVER! I'M FINISHED ANYWAY. AND I'M ALL FIRED UP NOW!!
I'LL BE ON MY WAY...

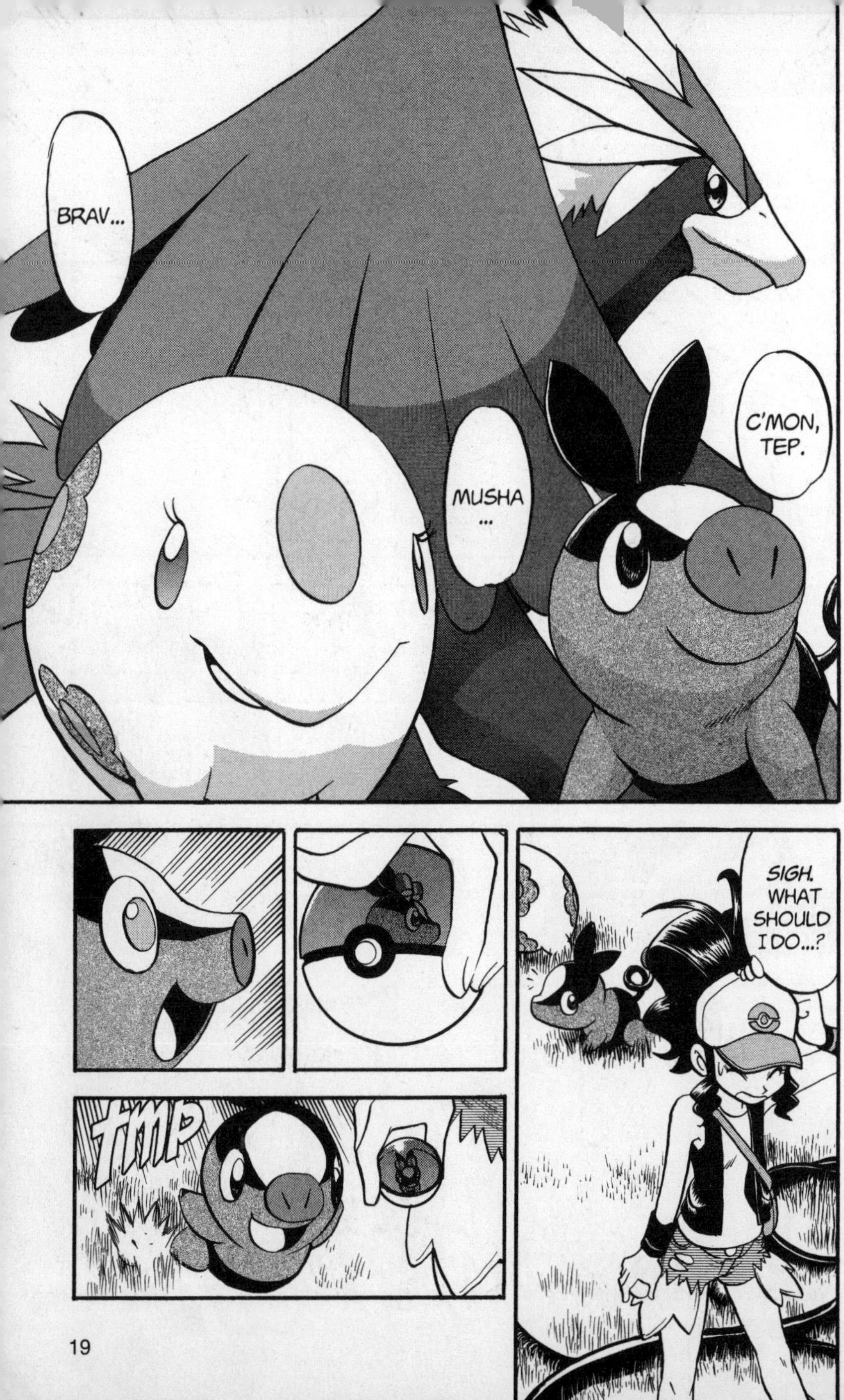
C'MON, TEP.
MUSHA ...
BRAV...
SIGH. WHAT SHOULD I DO...?
TMP

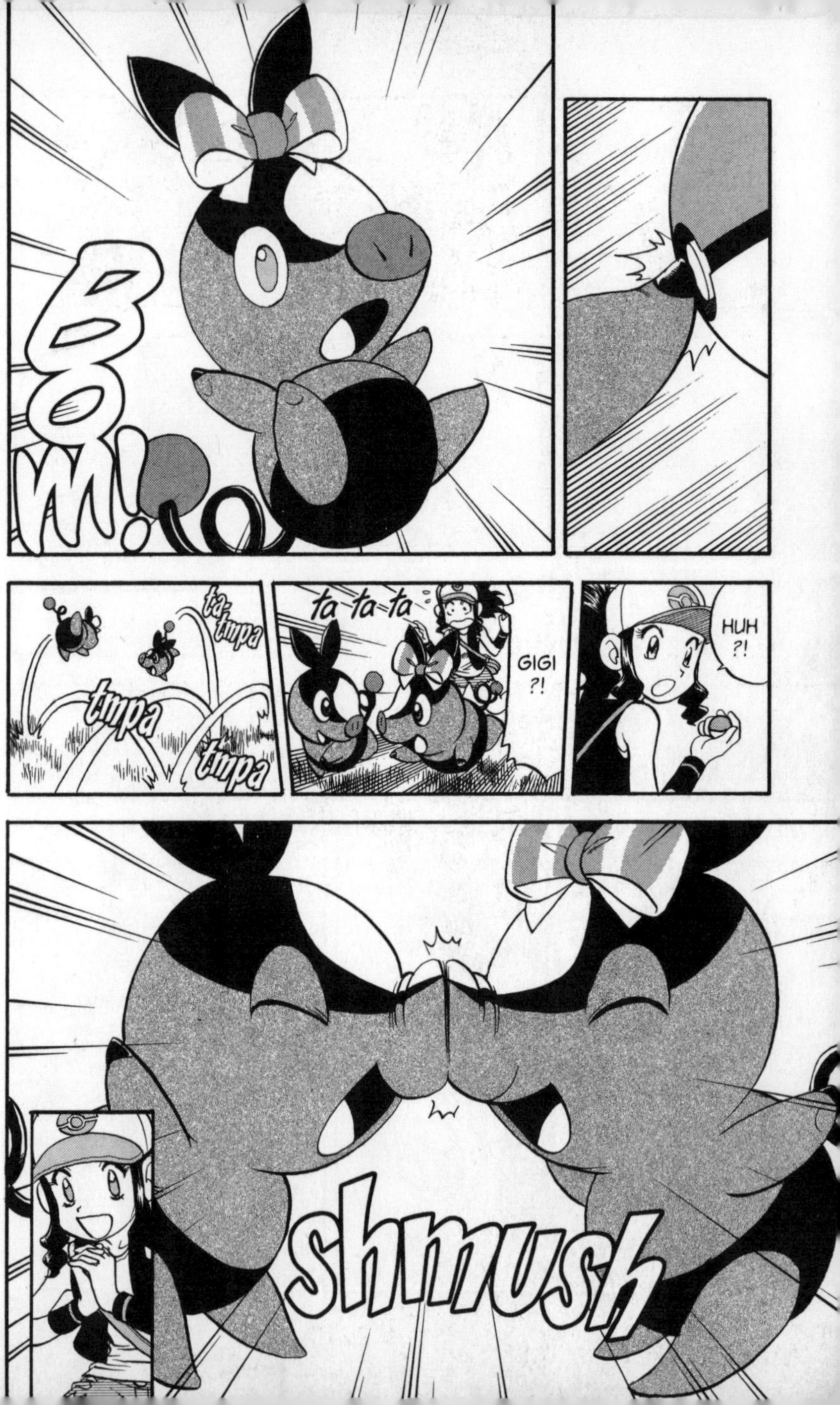
BOOM!
HUH ?!
ta-ta-ta
GIGI ?!
ta-tmpa
tmpa
tmpa
shmush

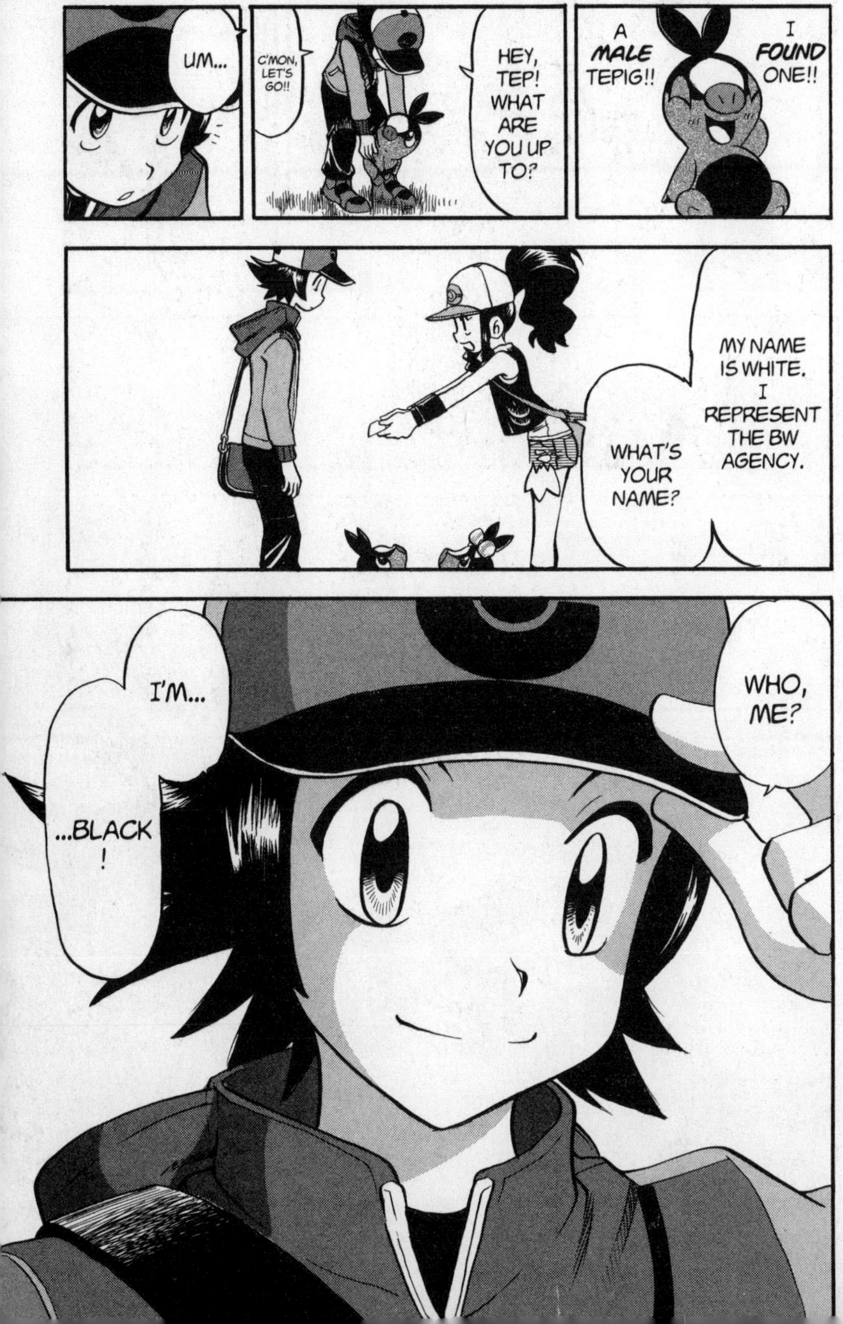
I FOUND ONE!!
A MALE TEPIG!!
HEY, TEP! WHAT ARE YOU UP TO?
C'MON, LET'S GO!!
UM...
MY NAME IS WHITE. I REPRESENT THE BW AGENCY.
WHAT'S YOUR NAME?
WHO, ME?
I'M...
...BLACK!

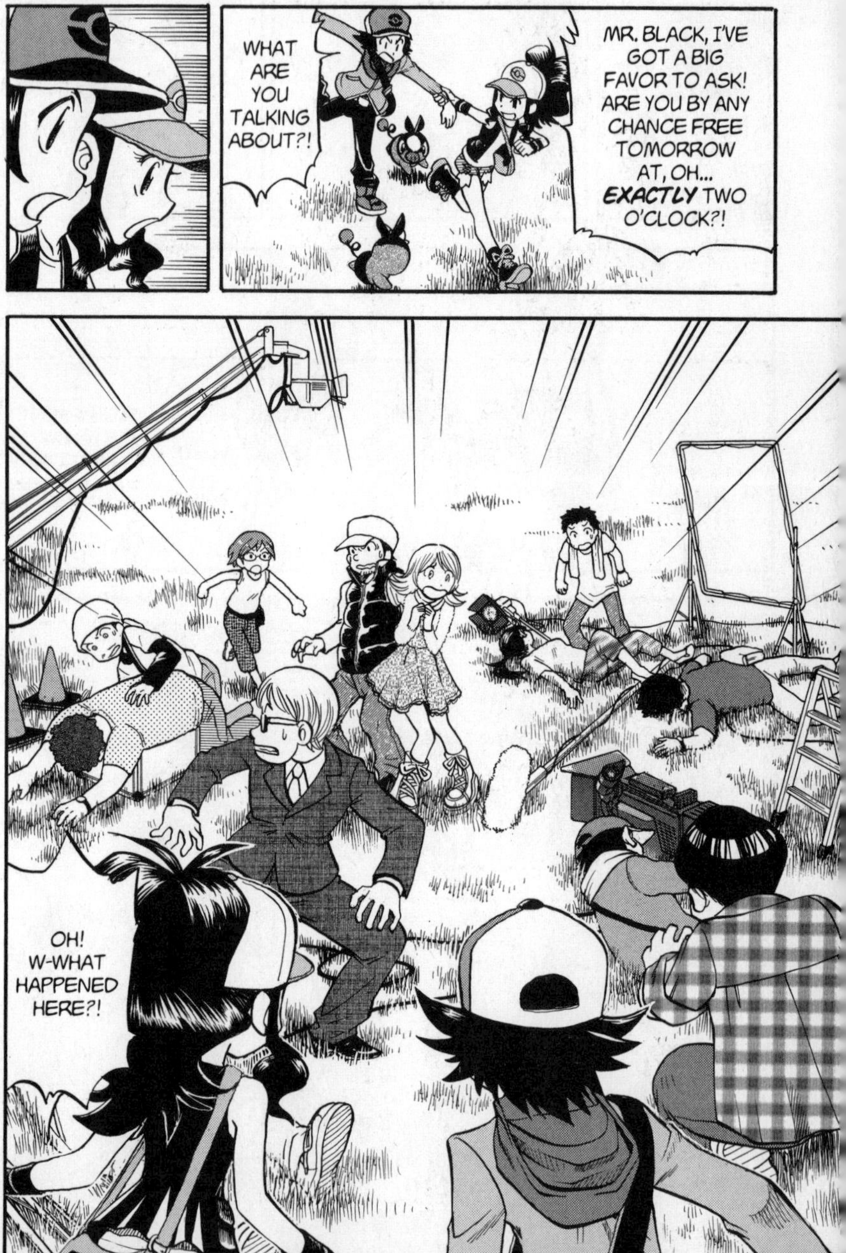
MR. BLACK, I'VE GOT A BIG FAVOR TO ASK! ARE YOU BY ANY CHANCE FREE TOMORROW AT, OH... **EXACTLY** TWO O'CLOCK?!
WHAT ARE YOU TALKING ABOUT?!
OH! W-WHAT HAPPENED HERE?!

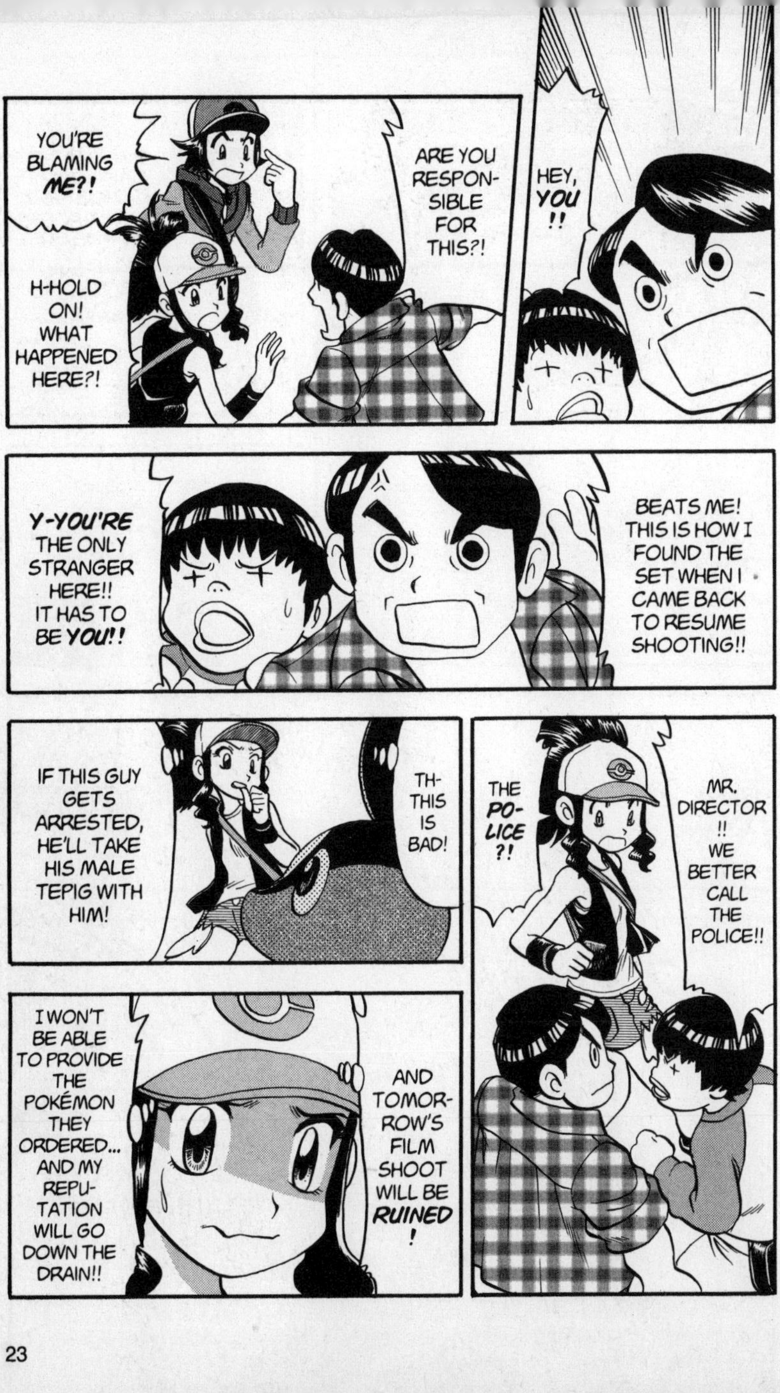
HEY, YOU!!
ARE YOU RESPONSIBLE FOR THIS?!
YOU'RE BLAMING ME?!
H-HOLD ON! WHAT HAPPENED HERE?!
BEATS ME! THIS IS HOW I FOUND THE SET WHEN I CAME BACK TO RESUME SHOOTING!!
Y-YOU'RE THE ONLY STRANGER HERE!! IT HAS TO BE YOU!!
MR. DIRECTOR!! WE BETTER CALL THE POLICE!!
THE POLICE?!
TH-THIS IS BAD!
IF THIS GUY GETS ARRESTED, HE'LL TAKE HIS MALE TEPIG WITH HIM!
AND TOMORROW'S FILM SHOOT WILL BE RUINED!
I WON'T BE ABLE TO PROVIDE THE POKÉMON THEY ORDERED... AND MY REPUTATION WILL GO DOWN THE DRAIN!!

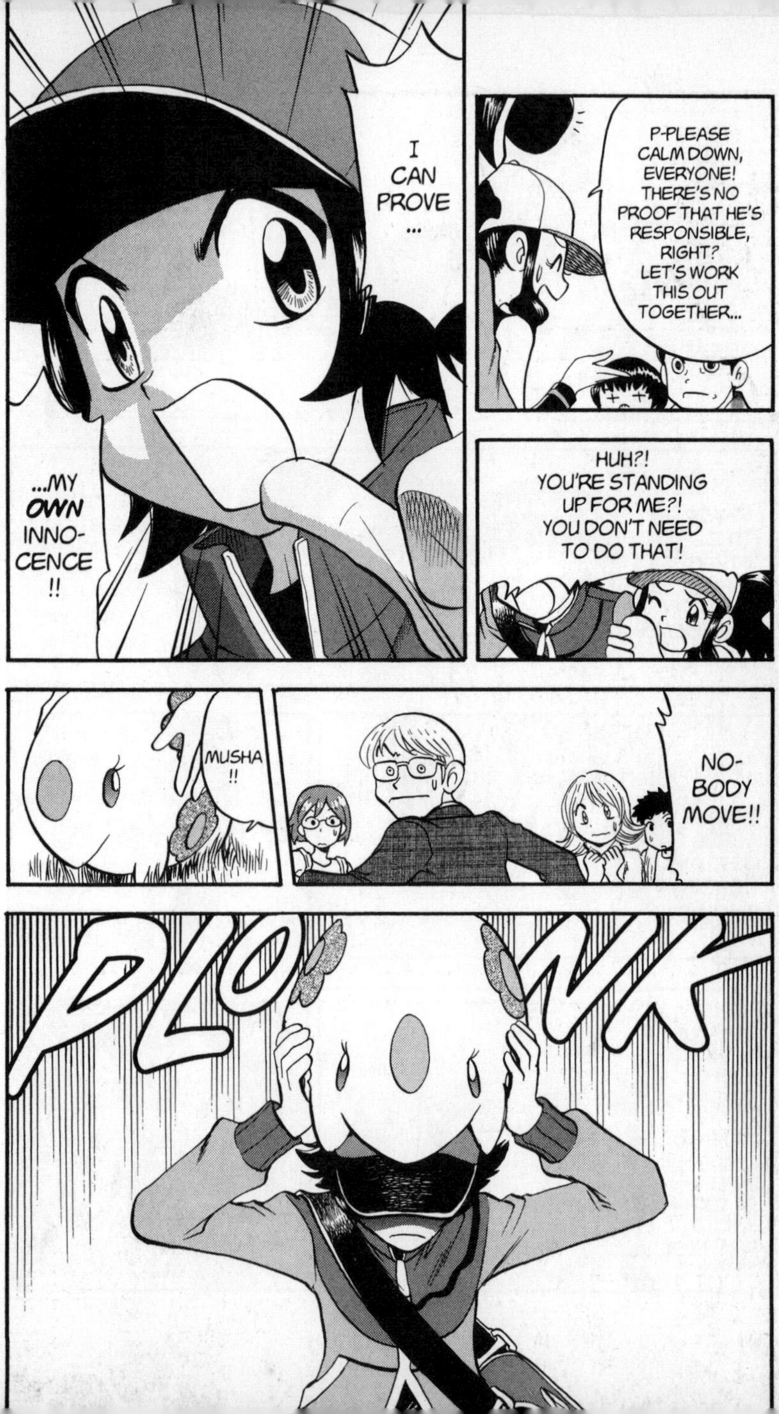
P-PLEASE CALM DOWN, EVERYONE! THERE'S NO PROOF THAT HE'S RESPONSIBLE, RIGHT? LET'S WORK THIS OUT TOGETHER...
HUH?! YOU'RE STANDING UP FOR ME?! YOU DON'T NEED TO DO THAT!
I CAN PROVE ...
...MY *OWN* INNO-CENCE !!
NO-BODY MOVE!!
MUSHA !!
PLONK

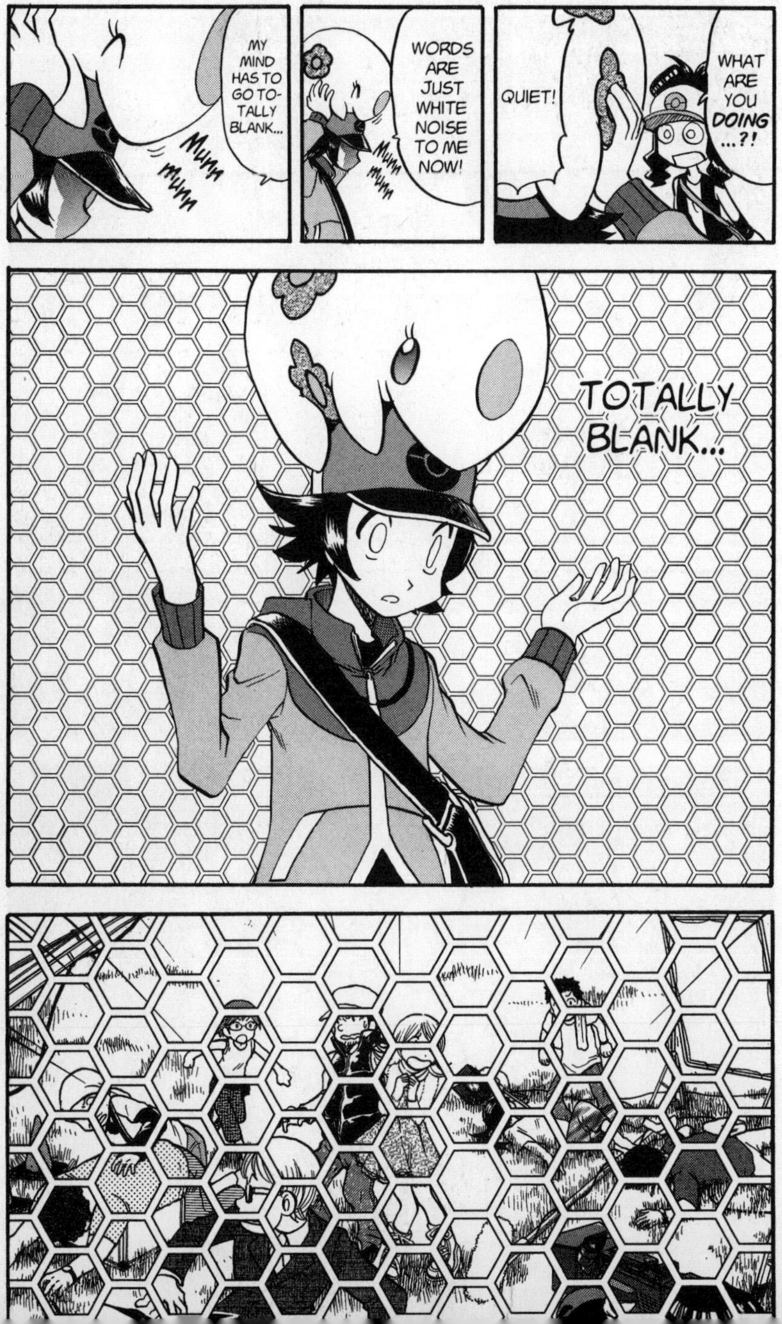
WHAT ARE YOU DOING...?!
QUIET!
WORDS ARE JUST WHITE NOISE TO ME NOW!
Munn munn
MY MIND HAS TO GO TO-TALLY BLANK...
Munn munn
TOTALLY BLANK...

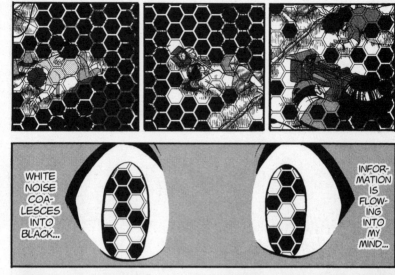

INFORMATION IS FLOWING INTO MY MIND...
WHITE NOISE COALESCES INTO BLACK...
THE CULPRIT IS...
I'VE GOT IT!!

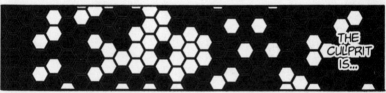

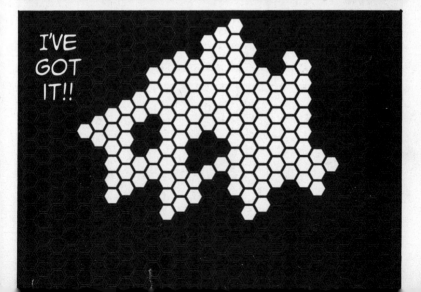

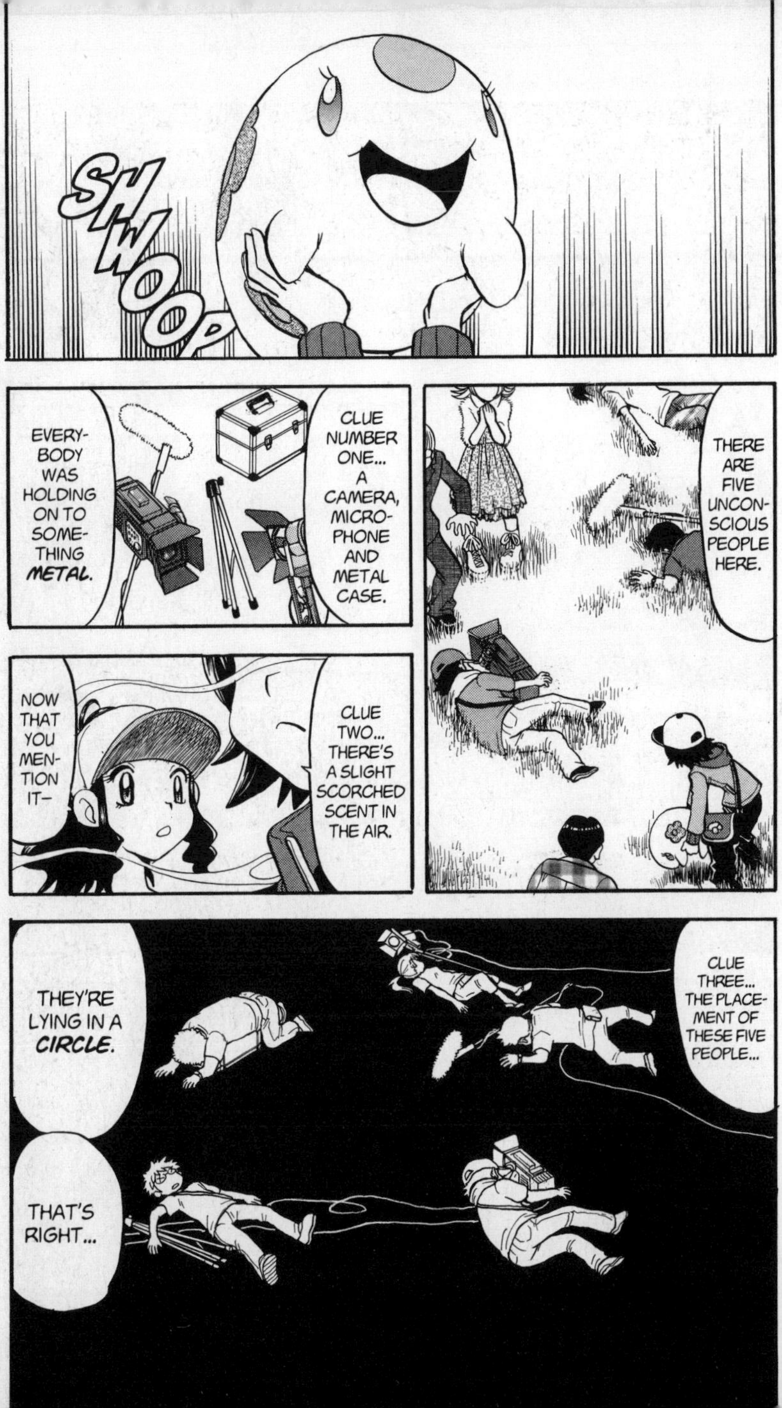
SHWOOP
THERE ARE FIVE UNCONSCIOUS PEOPLE HERE.
CLUE NUMBER ONE... A CAMERA, MICROPHONE AND METAL CASE.
EVERYBODY WAS HOLDING ON TO SOMETHING **METAL**.
CLUE TWO... THERE'S A SLIGHT SCORCHED SCENT IN THE AIR.
NOW THAT YOU MENTION IT—
CLUE THREE... THE PLACEMENT OF THESE FIVE PEOPLE...
THEY'RE LYING IN A **CIRCLE**.
THAT'S RIGHT...

AND LAST BUT NOT LEAST...

I JUST SAW SOMETHING *SHINY*.

SNAP

TEP!

FWWW

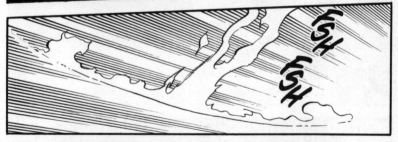
FSH
FSH

ELECTRICITY IS FLOWING THROUGH THIS "WIRE"!!

KZZT

DON'T TOUCH IT!!

WHAT'S THIS ...?!

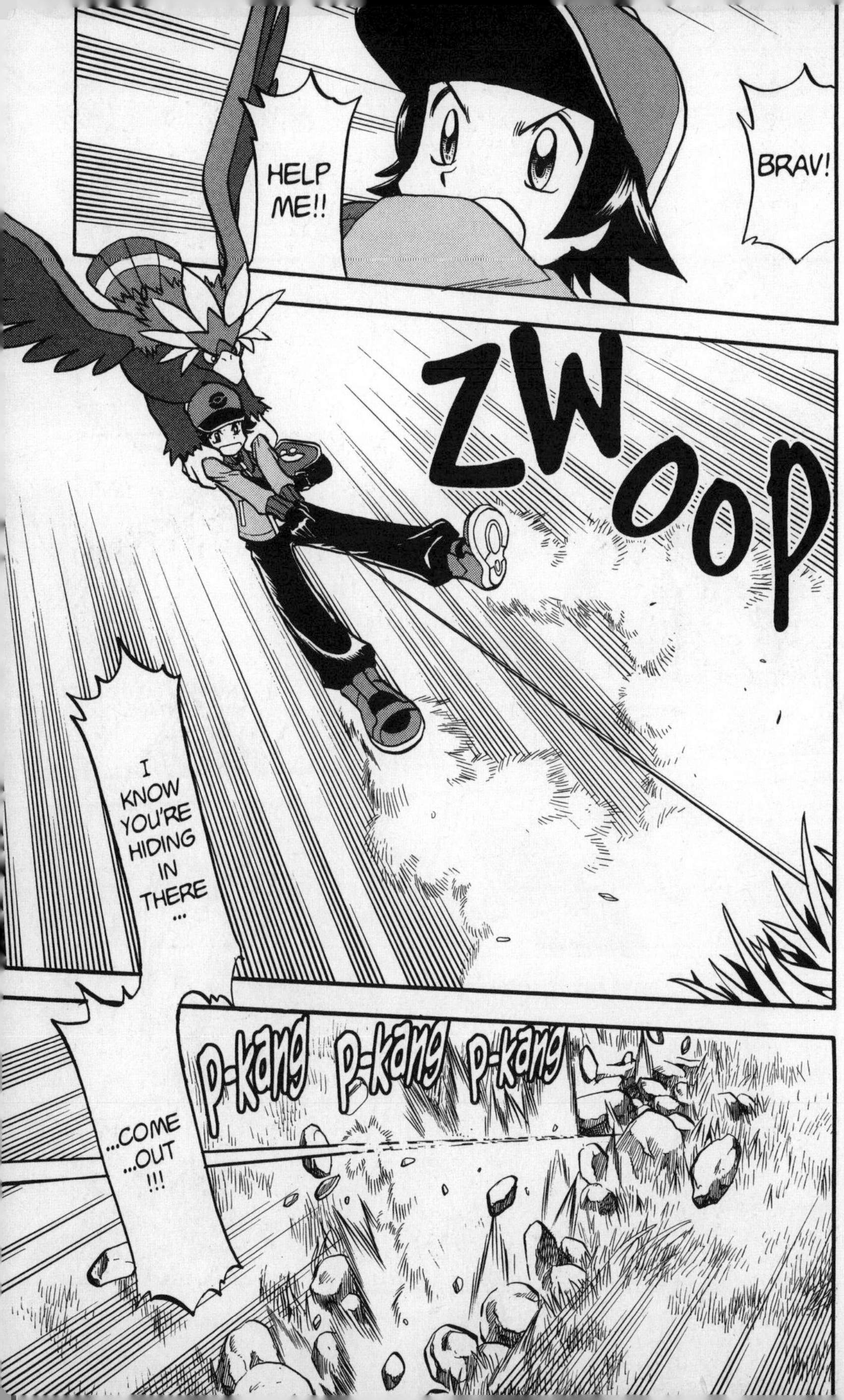
BRAV!
HELP ME!!
ZWOOP
I KNOW YOU'RE HIDING IN THERE ...
p-kang p-kang p-kang
...COME ...OUT !!!

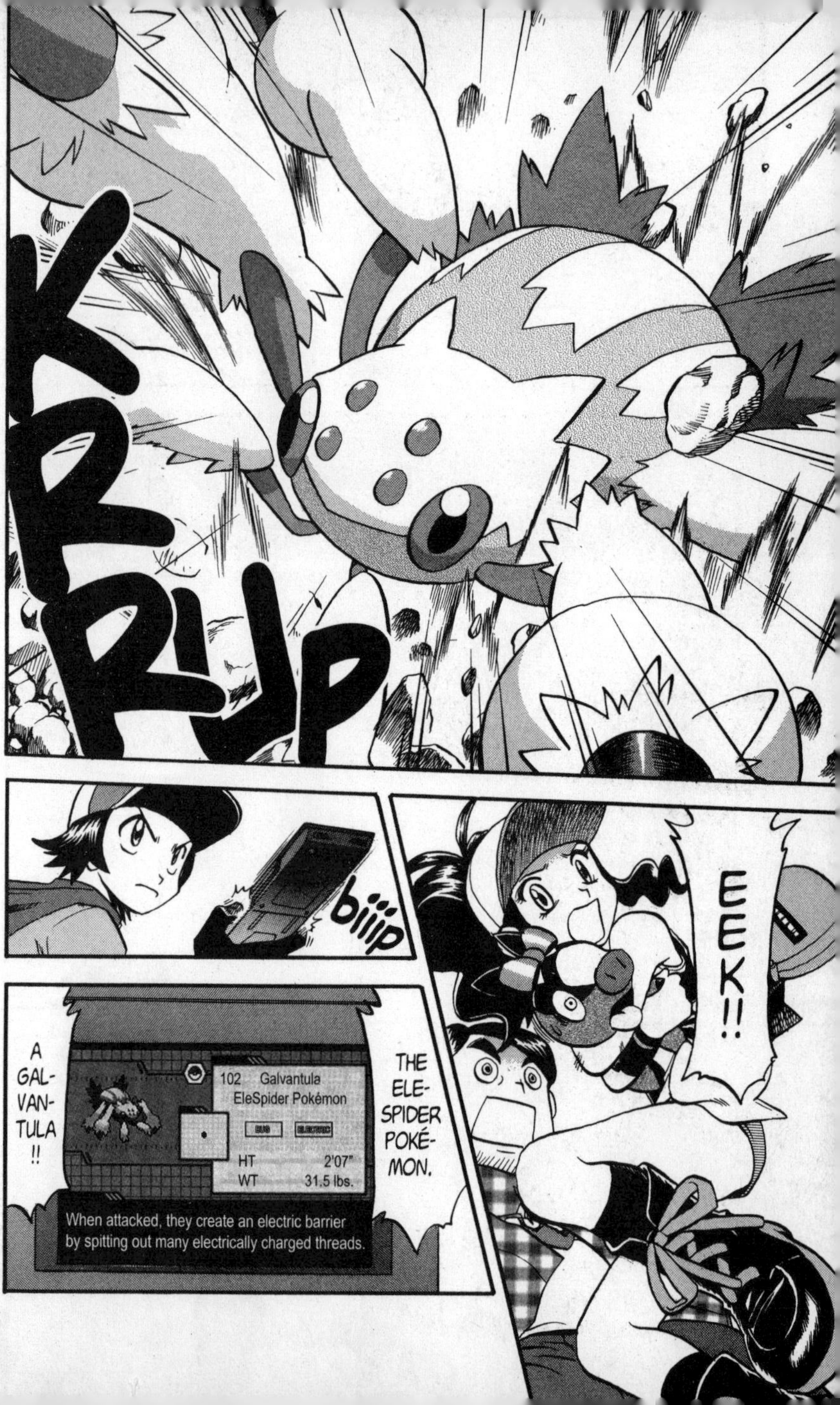
KRRUP
EEK!!
biiip
THE ELE-SPIDER POKÉMON.
A GALVANTULA!!
102 Galvantula
EleSpider Pokémon
BUG
ELECTRIC
HT 2'07"
WT 31.5 lbs.
When attacked, they create an electric barrier by spitting out many electrically charged threads.

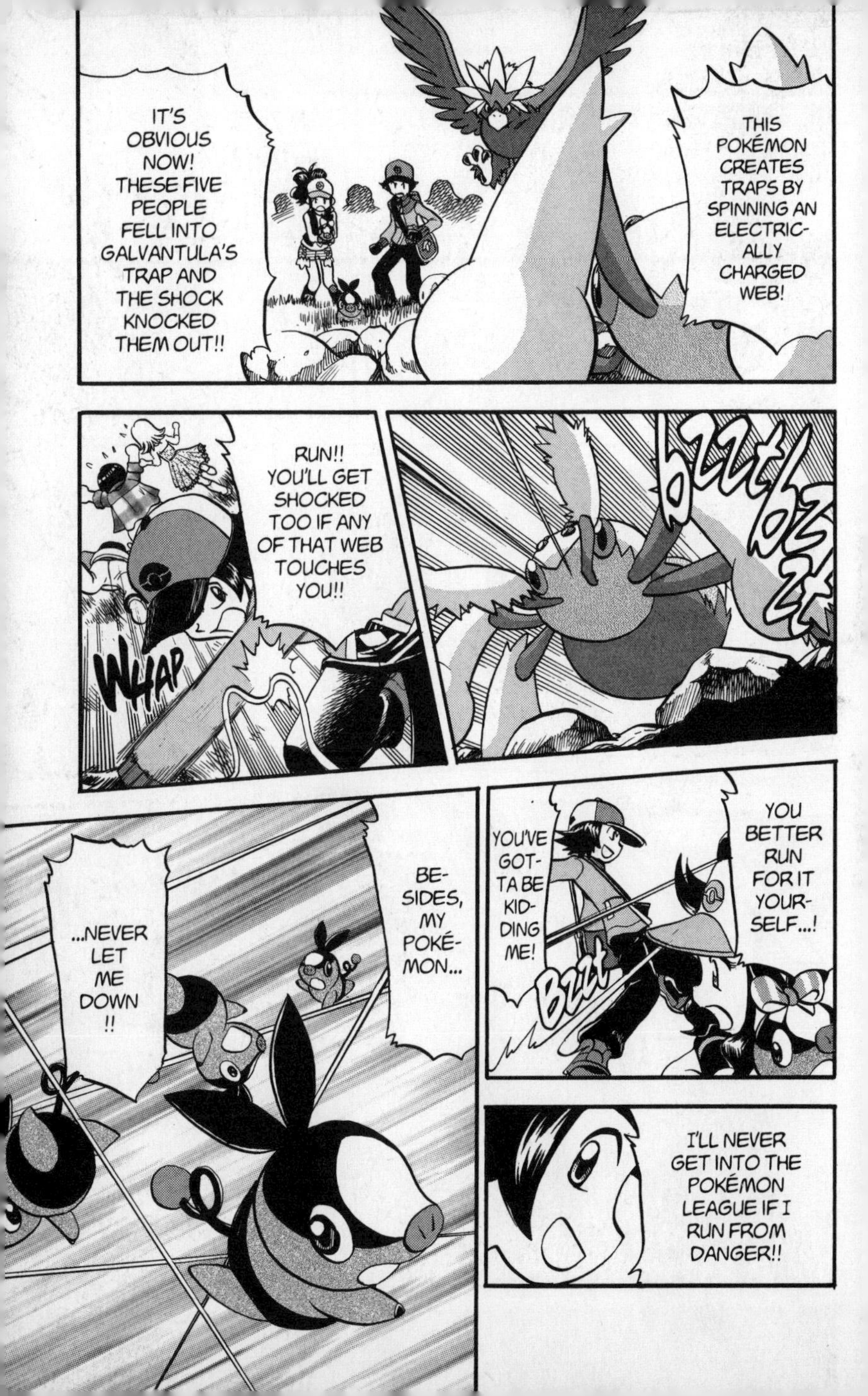
THIS POKÉMON CREATES TRAPS BY SPINNING AN ELECTRIC-ALLY CHARGED WEB!
IT'S OBVIOUS NOW! THESE FIVE PEOPLE FELL INTO GALVANTULA'S TRAP AND THE SHOCK KNOCKED THEM OUT!!
bzzt
bzzt
RUN!! YOU'LL GET SHOCKED TOO IF ANY OF THAT WEB TOUCHES YOU!!
WHAP
YOU BETTER RUN FOR IT YOUR-SELF...!
YOU'VE GOT-TA BE KID-DING ME!
Bzzt
I'LL NEVER GET INTO THE POKÉMON LEAGUE IF I RUN FROM DANGER!!
BE-SIDES, MY POKÉ-MON...
...NEVER LET ME DOWN !!

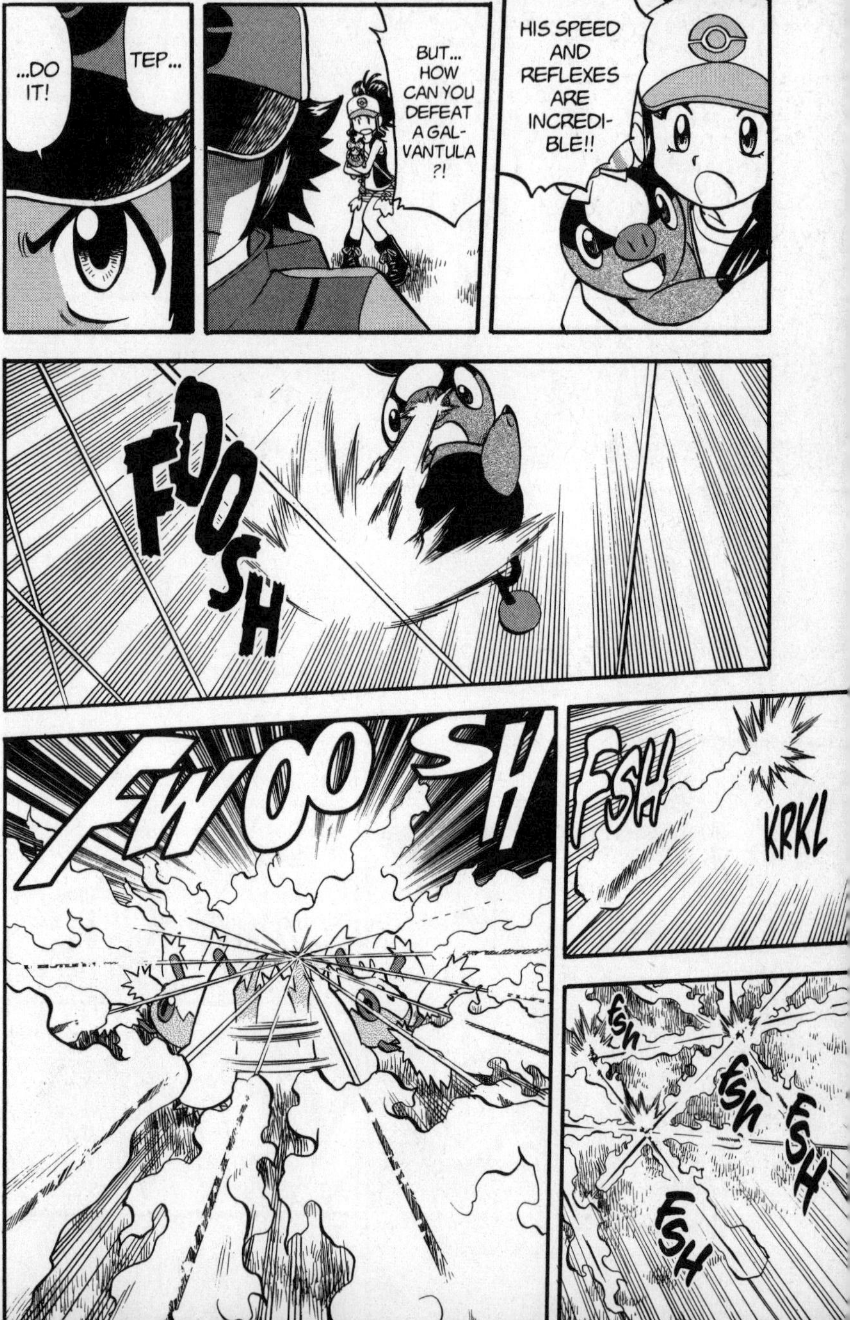
HIS SPEED AND REFLEXES ARE INCREDIBLE!!
BUT... HOW CAN YOU DEFEAT A GAL-VANTULA?!
TEP...
...DO IT!
FOOSH
KRKL
FSH
FSH
FSH
FSH
FSH
FWOOSH

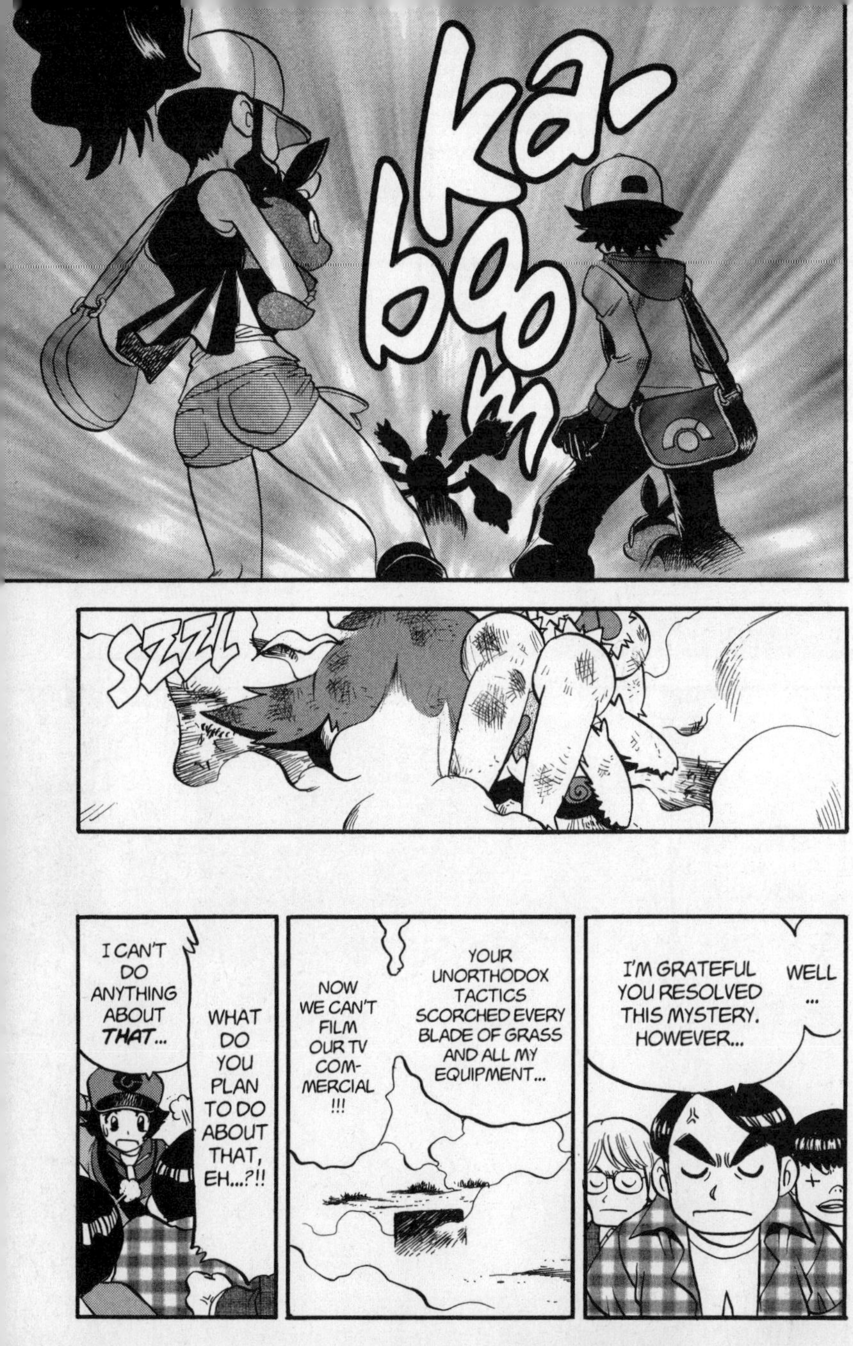
KA-BOOM
SZZZ
WELL...
I'M GRATEFUL YOU RESOLVED THIS MYSTERY. HOWEVER...
YOUR UNORTHODOX TACTICS SCORCHED EVERY BLADE OF GRASS AND ALL MY EQUIPMENT...
NOW WE CAN'T FILM OUR TV COMMERCIAL!!!
WHAT DO YOU PLAN TO DO ABOUT THAT, EH...?!!
I CAN'T DO ANYTHING ABOUT *THAT*...

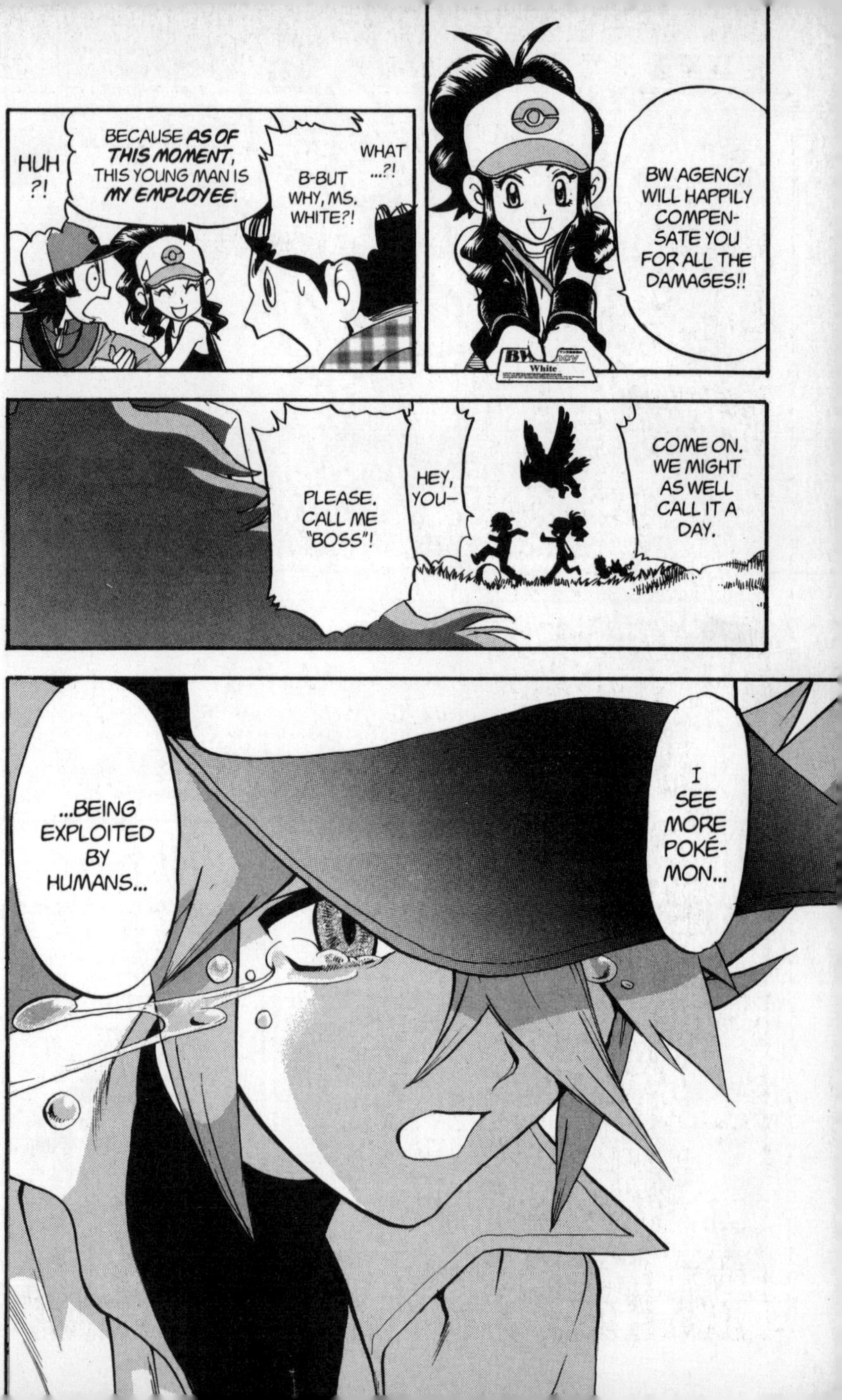
BW AGENCY WILL HAPPILY COMPEN-SATE YOU FOR ALL THE DAMAGES!!
White
WHAT ...?!
B-BUT WHY, MS. WHITE?!
BECAUSE ***AS OF THIS MOMENT***, THIS YOUNG MAN IS ***MY EMPLOYEE***.
HUH ?!
COME ON. WE MIGHT AS WELL CALL IT A DAY.
HEY, YOU–
PLEASE. CALL ME "BOSS"!
I SEE MORE POKÉ-MON...
...BEING EXPLOITED BY HUMANS...

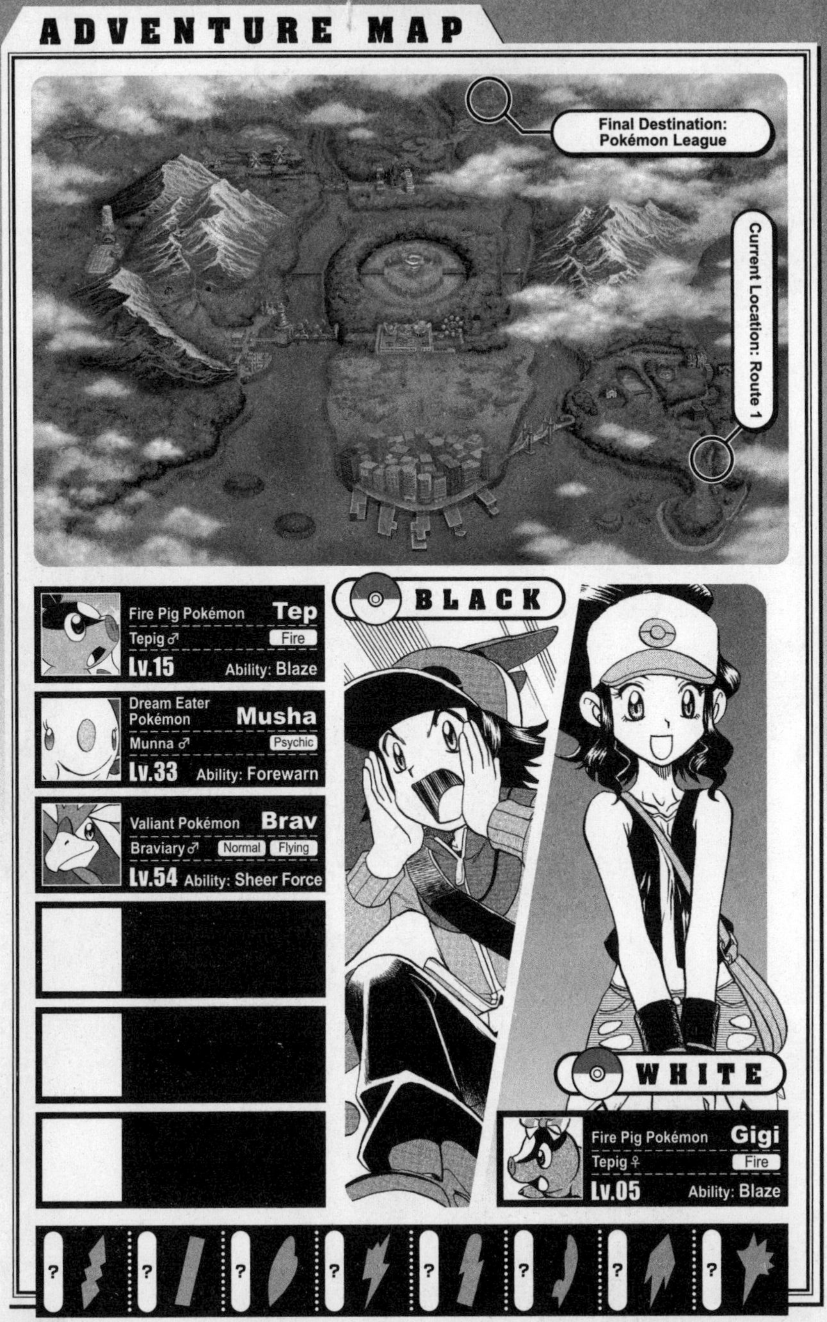
ADVENTURE MAP
Final Destination: Pokémon League
Current Location: Route 1
Fire Pig Pokémon
Tep
Tepig ♂
Fire
Lv.15
Ability: Blaze
Dream Eater Pokémon
Musha
Munna ♂
Psychic
Lv.33
Ability: Forewarn
Valiant Pokémon
Brav
Braviary ♂
Normal
Flying
Lv.54
Ability: Sheer Force
BLACK
WHITE
Fire Pig Pokémon
Gigi
Tepig ♀
Fire
Lv.05
Ability: Blaze
?
?
?
?
?
?
?
?

Pokémon Adventures Black & White

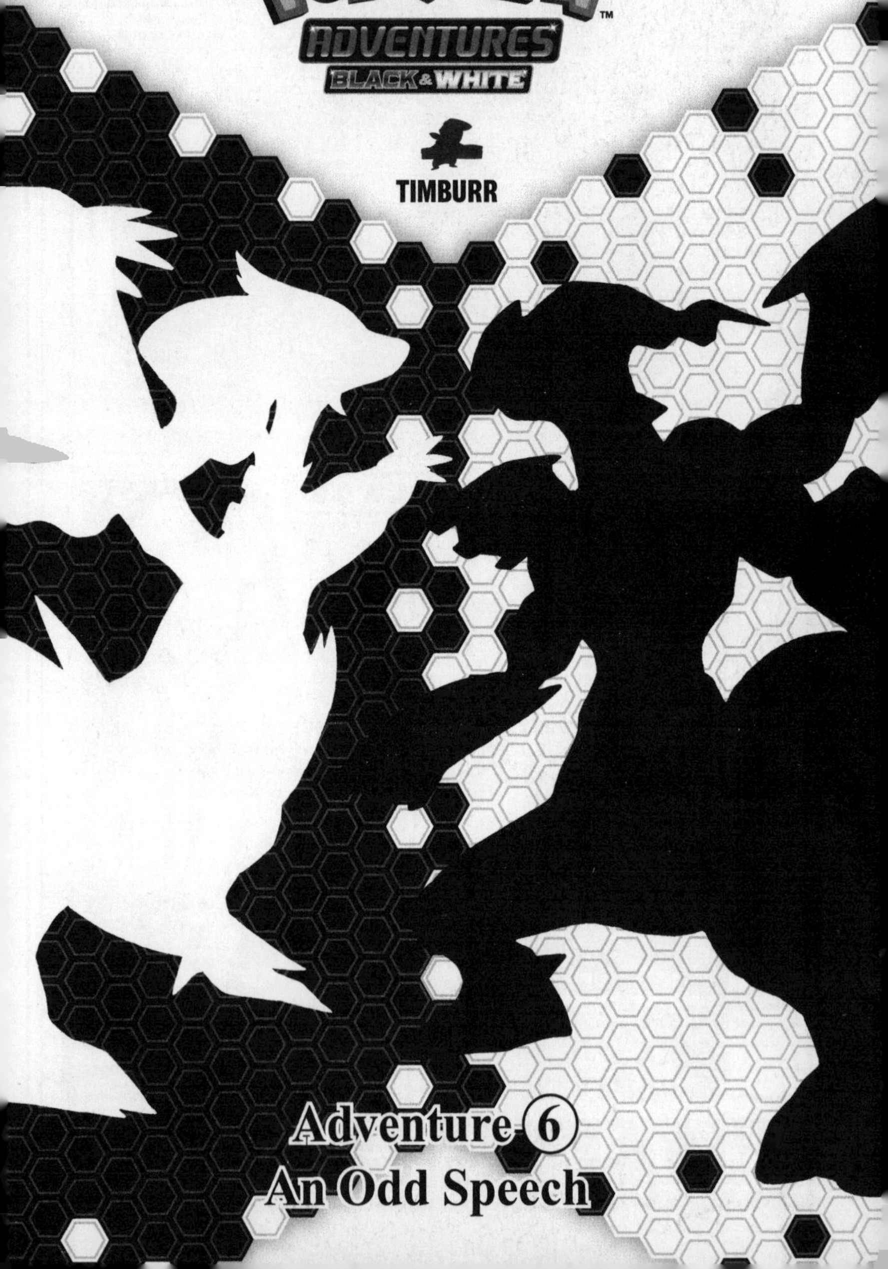
TIMBURR

Adventure 6
An Odd Speech

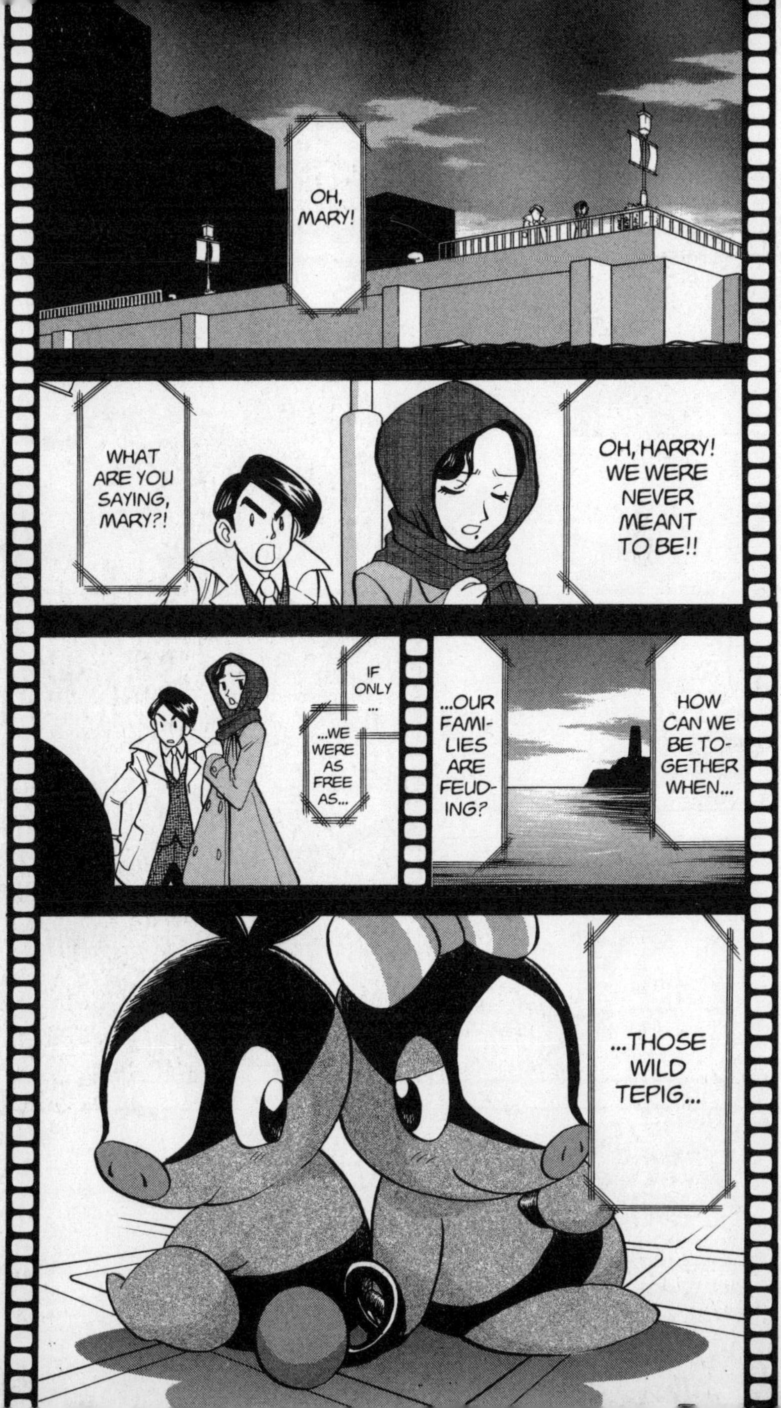
OH, MARY!
OH, HARRY! WE WERE NEVER MEANT TO BE!!
WHAT ARE YOU SAYING, MARY?!
HOW CAN WE BE TO-GETHER WHEN...
...OUR FAMI-LIES ARE FEUD-ING?
IF ONLY...
...WE WERE AS FREE AS...
...THOSE WILD TEPIG...

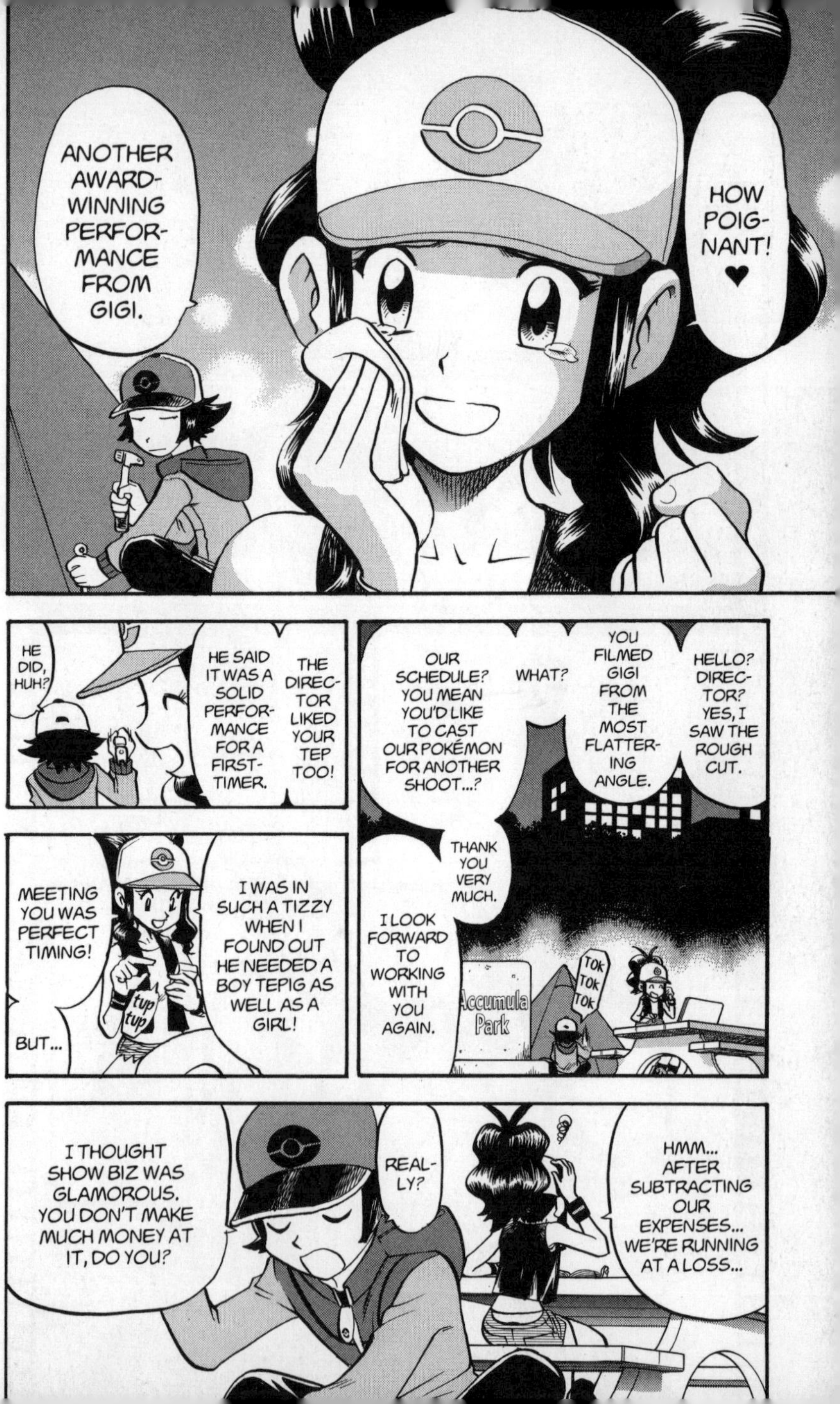
HOW POIGNANT! ♥
ANOTHER AWARD-WINNING PERFORMANCE FROM GIGI.
HELLO? DIRECTOR? YES, I SAW THE ROUGH CUT.
YOU FILMED GIGI FROM THE MOST FLATTERING ANGLE.
WHAT?
OUR SCHEDULE? YOU MEAN YOU'D LIKE TO CAST OUR POKÉMON FOR ANOTHER SHOOT...?
THANK YOU VERY MUCH.
I LOOK FORWARD TO WORKING WITH YOU AGAIN.
TOK TOK TOK
Accumula Park
THE DIRECTOR LIKED YOUR TEP TOO!
HE SAID IT WAS A SOLID PERFORMANCE FOR A FIRST-TIMER.
HE DID, HUH?
I WAS IN SUCH A TIZZY WHEN I FOUND OUT HE NEEDED A BOY TEPIG AS WELL AS A GIRL!
MEETING YOU WAS PERFECT TIMING!
tup tup
BUT...
HMM... AFTER SUBTRACTING OUR EXPENSES... WE'RE RUNNING AT A LOSS...
REALLY?
I THOUGHT SHOW BIZ WAS GLAMOROUS. YOU DON'T MAKE MUCH MONEY AT IT, DO YOU?

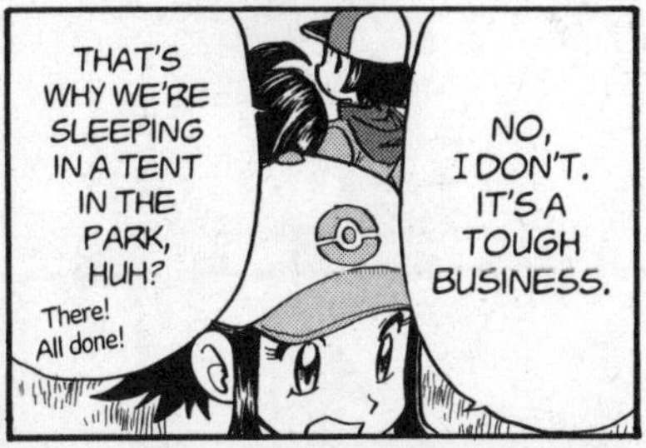
NO, I DON'T. IT'S A TOUGH BUSINESS.
THAT'S WHY WE'RE SLEEPING IN A TENT IN THE PARK, HUH?
There! All done!

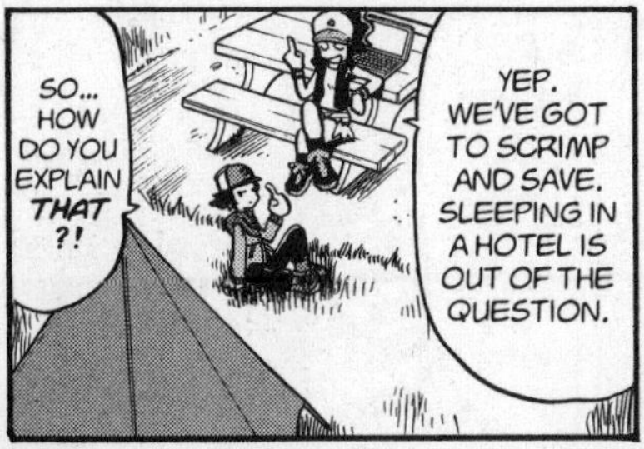
YEP. WE'VE GOT TO SCRIMP AND SAVE. SLEEPING IN A HOTEL IS OUT OF THE QUESTION.
SO... HOW DO YOU EXPLAIN ***THAT*** ?!

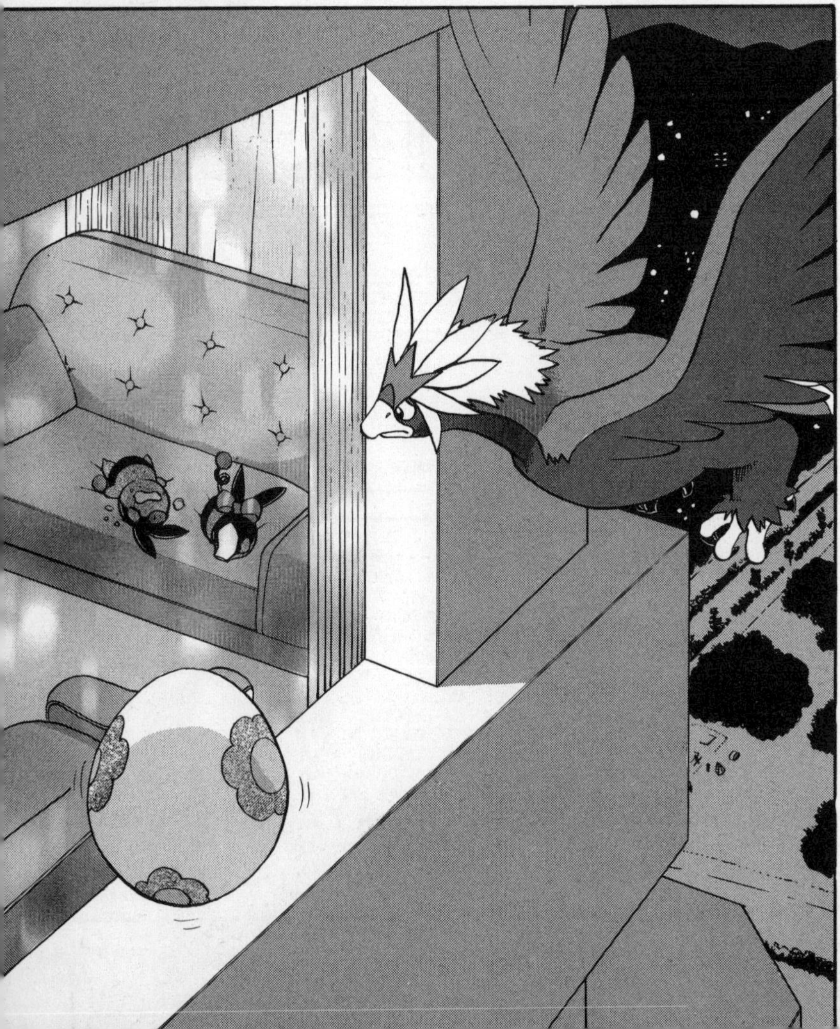

SHE'S...

...AN *ARTISTE!*

PEOPLE SLEEP OUTSIDE? WHILE POKÉMON STAY IN A HOTEL?

WHAT? YOU MEAN GIGI'S HOTEL ROOM...? AT THE BW AGENCY, WE ALWAYS BOOK A ROOM FOR THE TALENT.

NATURALLY.

GIGI DEBUTED JUST ONE YEAR AGO! ISN'T IT AMAZING?

Gigi

BW Agency

Filmography

Movies
Titles: *Holding the Moon Stone*
Sunny, Followed by Hailstorms

TV
Titles: *Surfing IV*
Touring Unova with Tornadus
Calcium Man: The Movie

LOOK!

HERE'S GIGI'S RESUMÉ.

...GIGI LIKES TO BE OUTSIDE IT FOR EXACTLY EIGHT HOURS A DAY.

THE POKÉ BALL IS FINE, BUT...

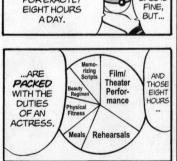

...ARE *PACKED* WITH THE DUTIES OF AN ACTRESS.

Memorizing Scripts	Film/ Theater Performance
Beauty Regimen	
Physical Fitness	
Meals	Rehearsals

AND THOSE EIGHT HOURS...

THAT'S WHY I PUT SO MUCH EFFORT INTO MY WORK AS GIGI'S TALENT AGENT. I WANT GIGI TO BE AS COMFORTABLE AS POSSIBLE, TO FOCUS ON THE ART OF ACTING.

GIGI HAS REAL TALENT!

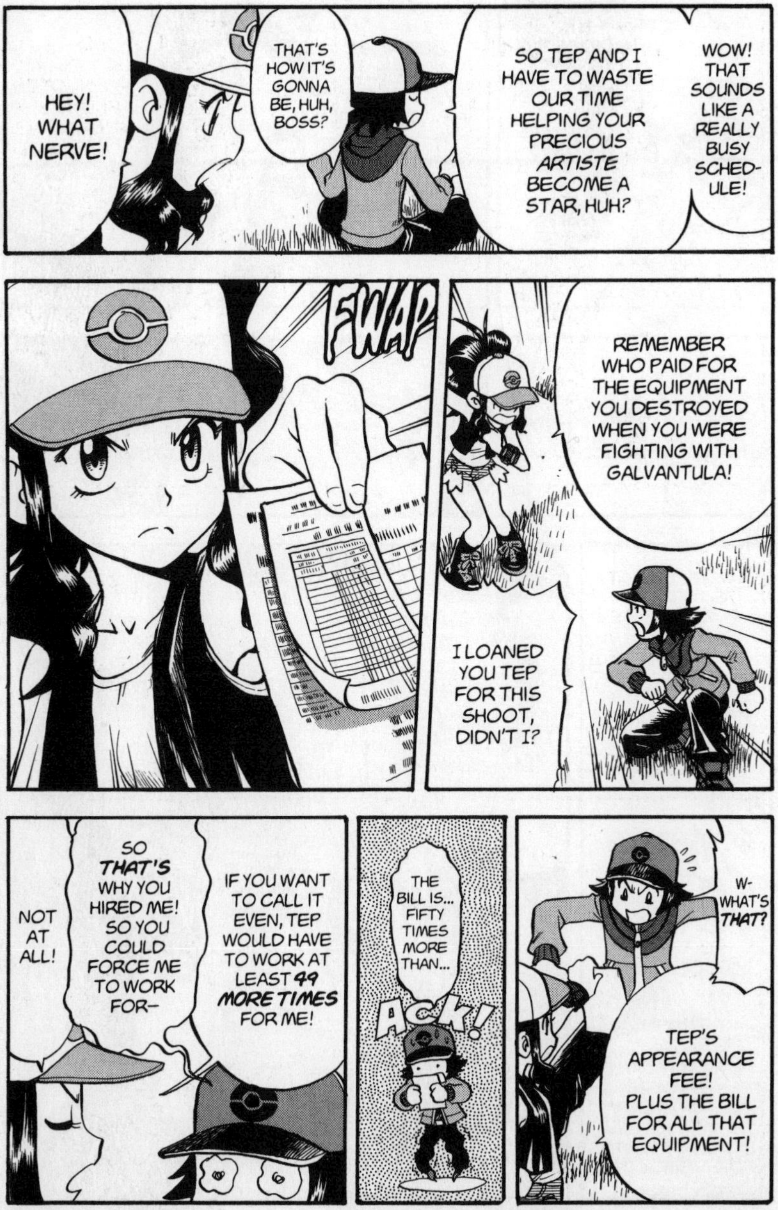
WOW! THAT SOUNDS LIKE A REALLY BUSY SCHEDULE!
SO TEP AND I HAVE TO WASTE OUR TIME HELPING YOUR PRECIOUS *ARTISTE* BECOME A STAR, HUH?
THAT'S HOW IT'S GONNA BE, HUH, BOSS?
HEY! WHAT NERVE!
REMEMBER WHO PAID FOR THE EQUIPMENT YOU DESTROYED WHEN YOU WERE FIGHTING WITH GALVANTULA!
I LOANED YOU TEP FOR THIS SHOOT, DIDN'T I?
FWAP
W- WHAT'S *THAT?*
TEP'S APPEARANCE FEE! PLUS THE BILL FOR ALL THAT EQUIPMENT!
THE BILL IS... FIFTY TIMES MORE THAN...
ACK!
IF YOU WANT TO CALL IT EVEN, TEP WOULD HAVE TO WORK AT LEAST **49 *MORE TIMES*** FOR ME!
SO ***THAT'S*** WHY YOU HIRED ME! SO YOU COULD FORCE ME TO WORK FOR–
NOT AT ALL!

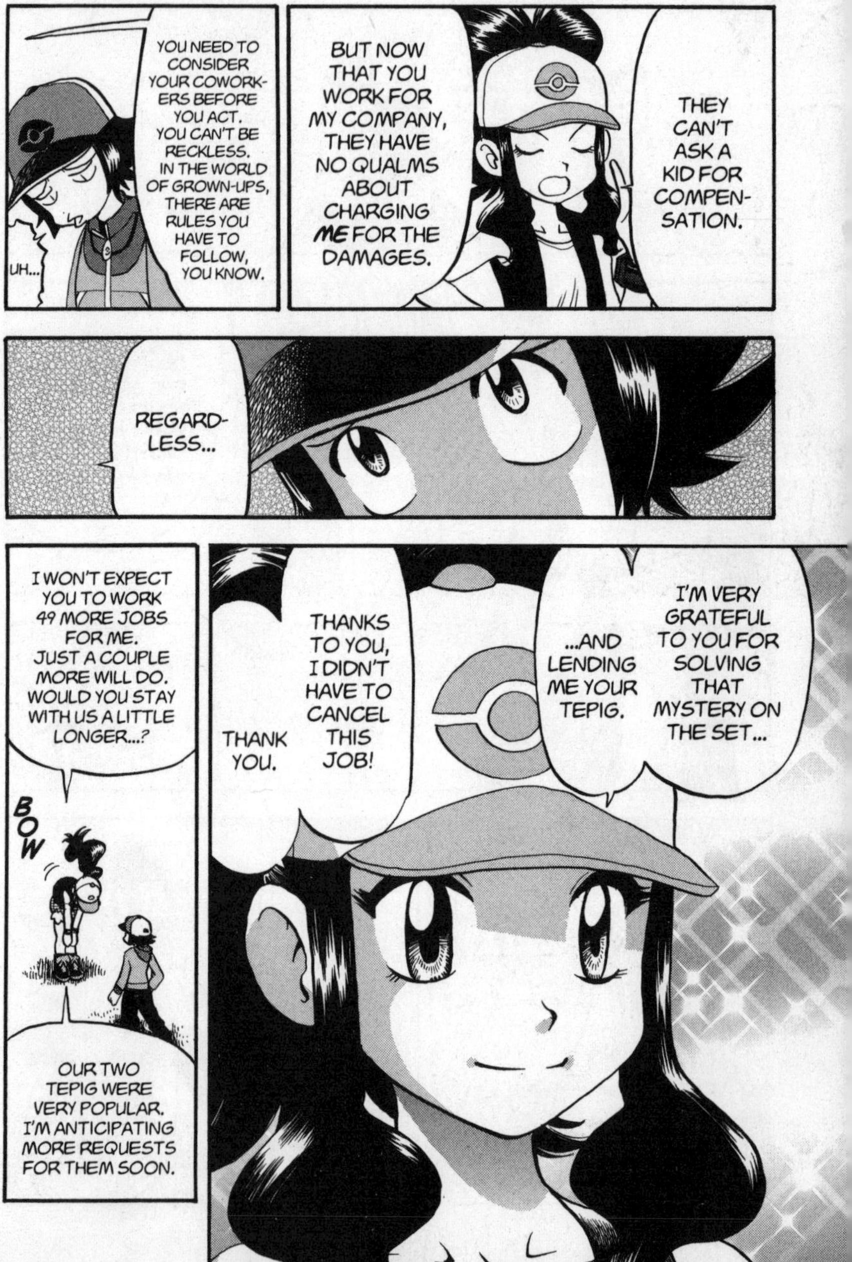
THEY CAN'T ASK A KID FOR COMPENSATION.
BUT NOW THAT YOU WORK FOR MY COMPANY, THEY HAVE NO QUALMS ABOUT CHARGING *ME* FOR THE DAMAGES.
YOU NEED TO CONSIDER YOUR COWORKERS BEFORE YOU ACT. YOU CAN'T BE RECKLESS. IN THE WORLD OF GROWN-UPS, THERE ARE RULES YOU HAVE TO FOLLOW, YOU KNOW.
UH...
REGARDLESS...
I'M VERY GRATEFUL TO YOU FOR SOLVING THAT MYSTERY ON THE SET...
...AND LENDING ME YOUR TEPIG.
THANKS TO YOU, I DIDN'T HAVE TO CANCEL THIS JOB!
THANK YOU.
I WON'T EXPECT YOU TO WORK 49 MORE JOBS FOR ME. JUST A COUPLE MORE WILL DO. WOULD YOU STAY WITH US A LITTLE LONGER...?
BOW
OUR TWO TEPIG WERE VERY POPULAR. I'M ANTICIPATING MORE REQUESTS FOR THEM SOON.

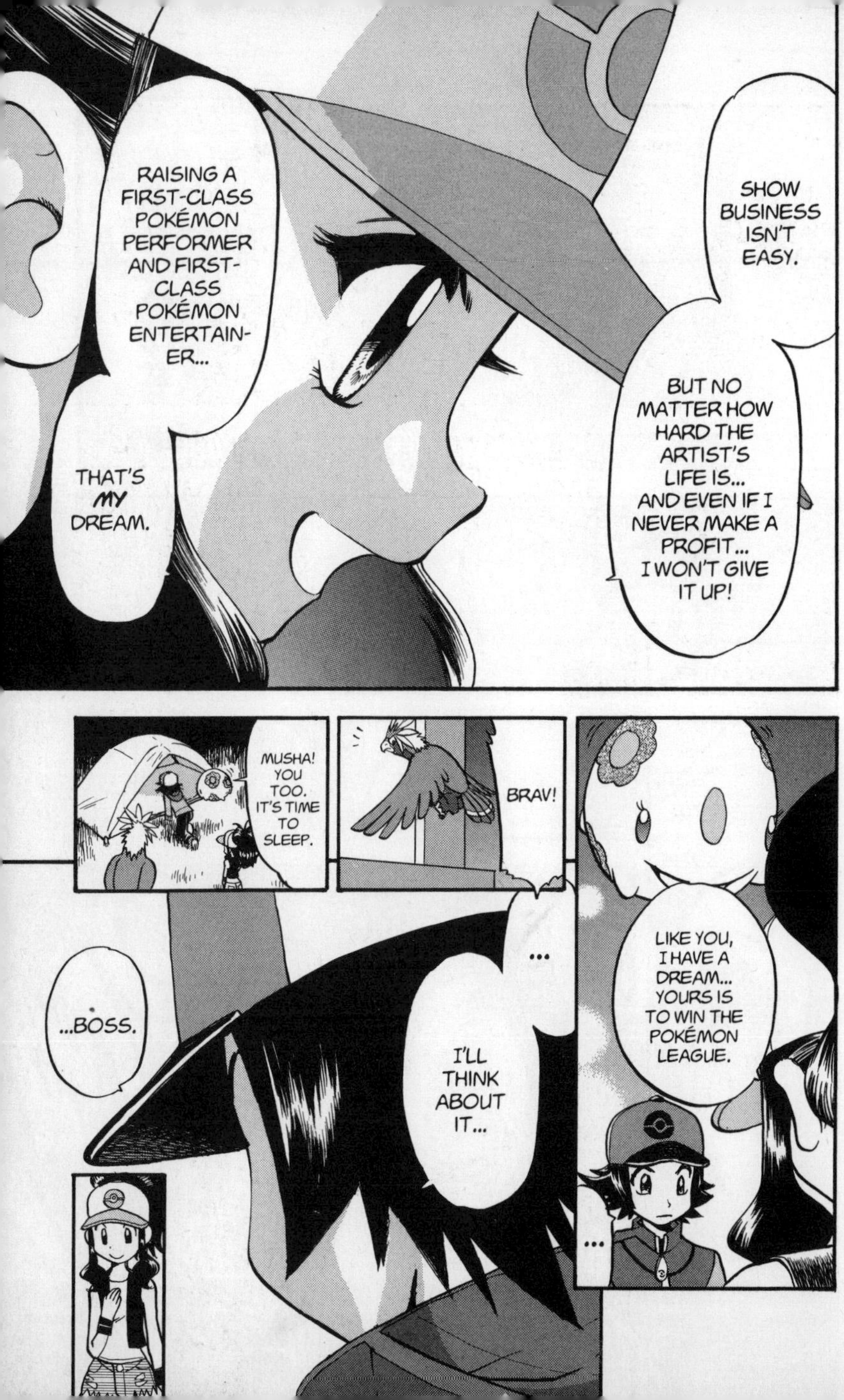
SHOW BUSINESS ISN'T EASY.
BUT NO MATTER HOW HARD THE ARTIST'S LIFE IS... AND EVEN IF I NEVER MAKE A PROFIT... I WON'T GIVE IT UP!
RAISING A FIRST-CLASS POKÉMON PERFORMER AND FIRST-CLASS POKÉMON ENTERTAINER...
THAT'S *MY* DREAM.
LIKE YOU, I HAVE A DREAM... YOURS IS TO WIN THE POKÉMON LEAGUE.
...
BRAV!
MUSHA! YOU TOO. IT'S TIME TO SLEEP.
...
I'LL THINK ABOUT IT...
...BOSS.

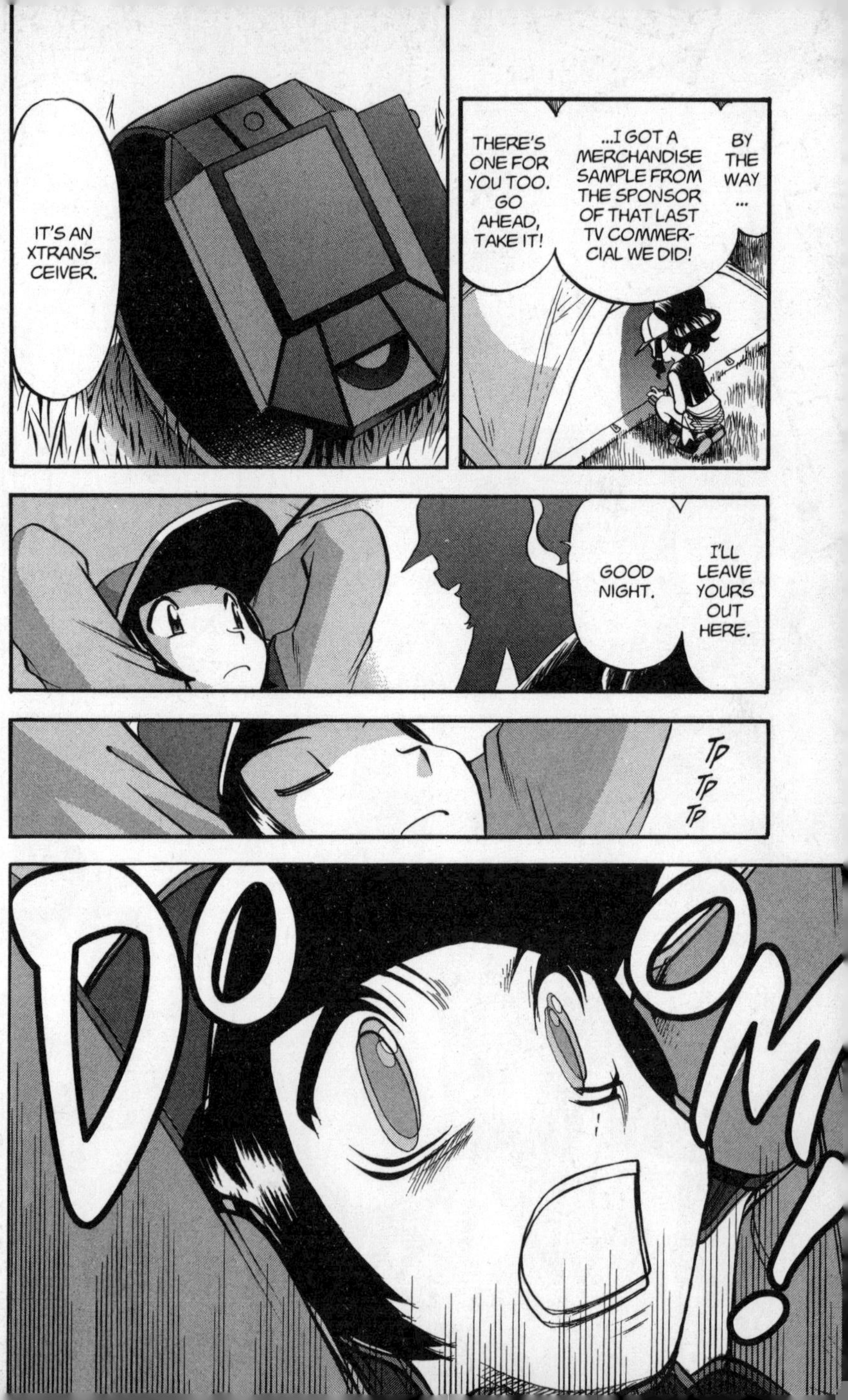
BY THE WAY ...
...I GOT A MERCHANDISE SAMPLE FROM THE SPONSOR OF THAT LAST TV COMMERCIAL WE DID!
THERE'S ONE FOR YOU TOO. GO AHEAD, TAKE IT!
IT'S AN XTRANSCEIVER.
I'LL LEAVE YOURS OUT HERE.
GOOD NIGHT.
TP TP TP
DOOM!

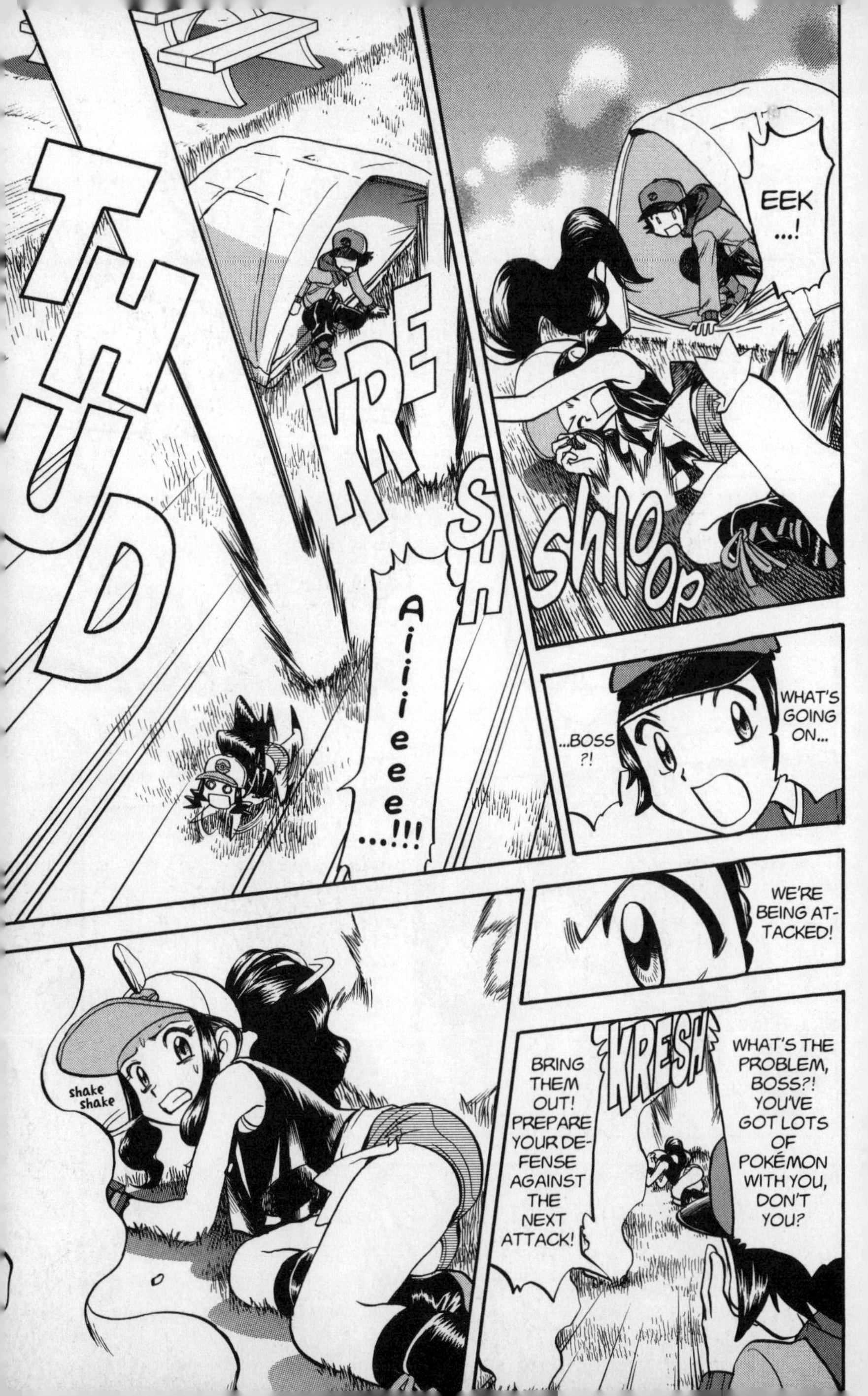
EEK ...!
SH
SHOOP
...BOSS ?!
WHAT'S GOING ON...
WE'RE BEING AT-TACKED!
THUD
KRE
Aiiiieee...!!!
KRESH
WHAT'S THE PROBLEM, BOSS?! YOU'VE GOT LOTS OF POKÉMON WITH YOU, DON'T YOU?
BRING THEM OUT! PREPARE YOUR DE-FENSE AGAINST THE NEXT ATTACK!
shake shake

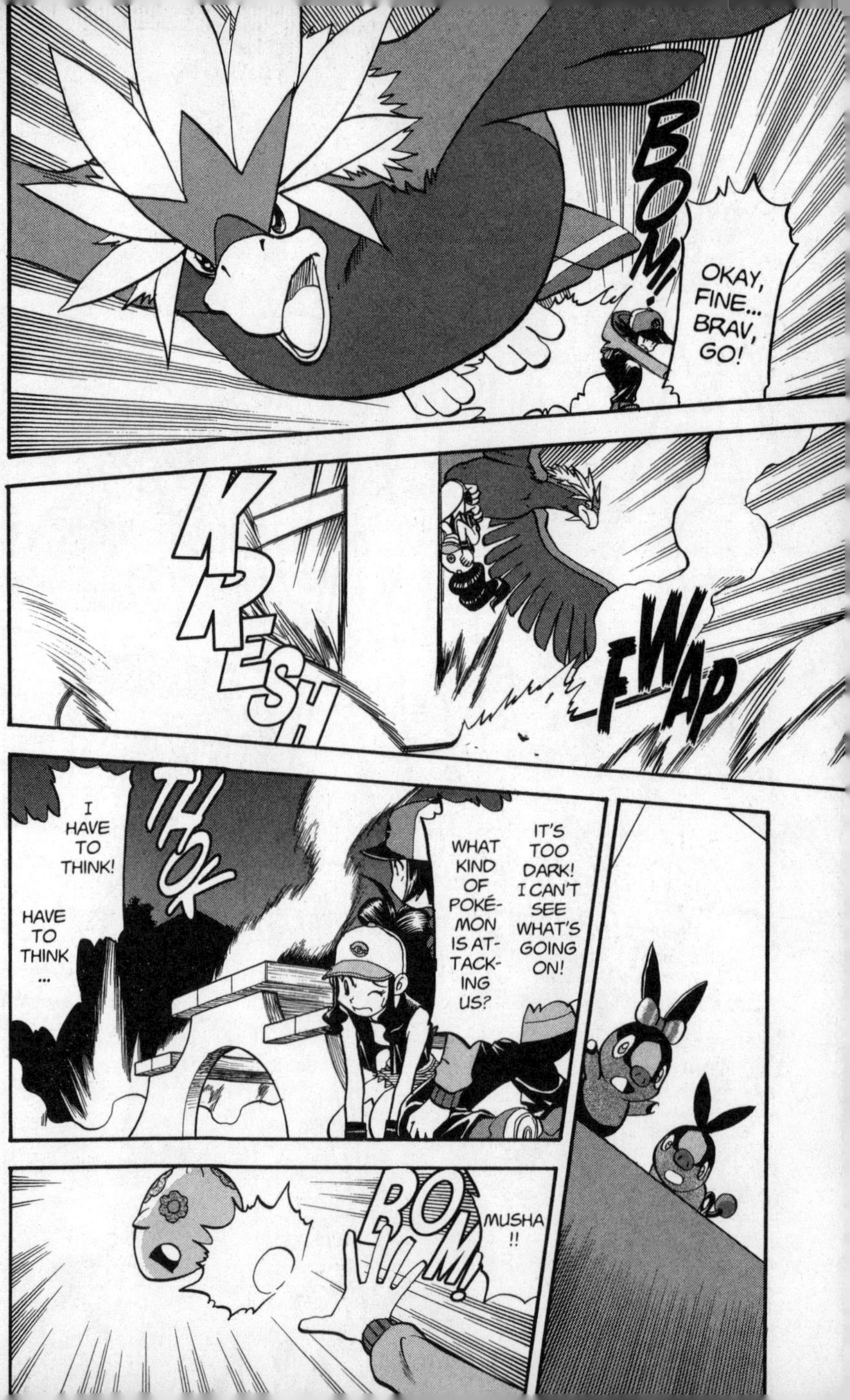
BOOM!
OKAY, FINE... BRAV, GO!
FWAP
KRESH
IT'S TOO DARK! I CAN'T SEE WHAT'S GOING ON!
WHAT KIND OF POKÉ-MON IS AT-TACK-ING US?
THOK
I HAVE TO THINK!
HAVE TO THINK ...
MUSHA !!
ROOM!

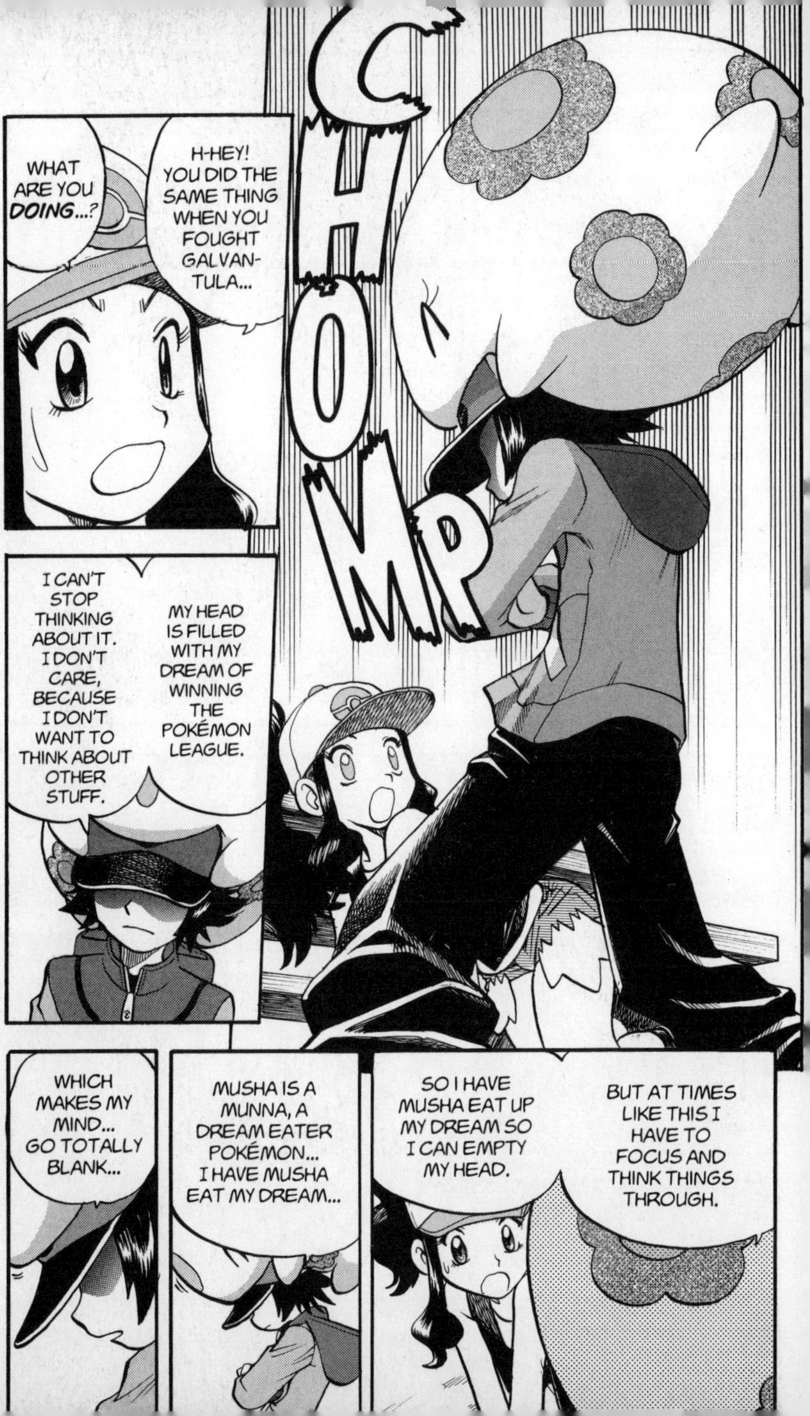
CHOMP
H-HEY! YOU DID THE SAME THING WHEN YOU FOUGHT GALVANTULA...
WHAT ARE YOU **DOING**...?
MY HEAD IS FILLED WITH MY DREAM OF WINNING THE POKÉMON LEAGUE.
I CAN'T STOP THINKING ABOUT IT. I DON'T CARE, BECAUSE I DON'T WANT TO THINK ABOUT OTHER STUFF.
BUT AT TIMES LIKE THIS I HAVE TO FOCUS AND THINK THINGS THROUGH.
SO I HAVE MUSHA EAT UP MY DREAM SO I CAN EMPTY MY HEAD.
MUSHA IS A MUNNA, A DREAM EATER POKÉMON... I HAVE MUSHA EAT MY DREAM...
WHICH MAKES MY MIND... GO TOTALLY BLANK...

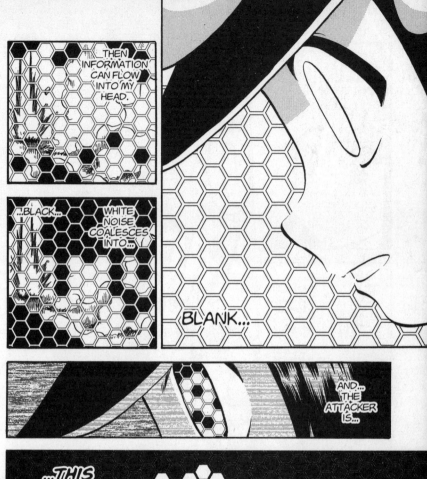

...THEN INFORMATION CAN FLOW INTO MY HEAD.

...BLACK... WHITE NOISE COALESCES INTO...

BLANK...

AND... THE ATTACKER IS...

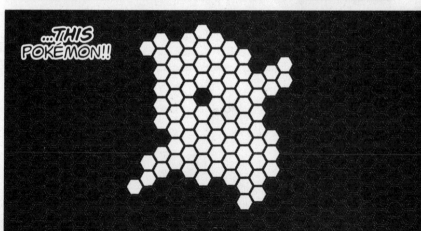

...THIS POKÉMON!!

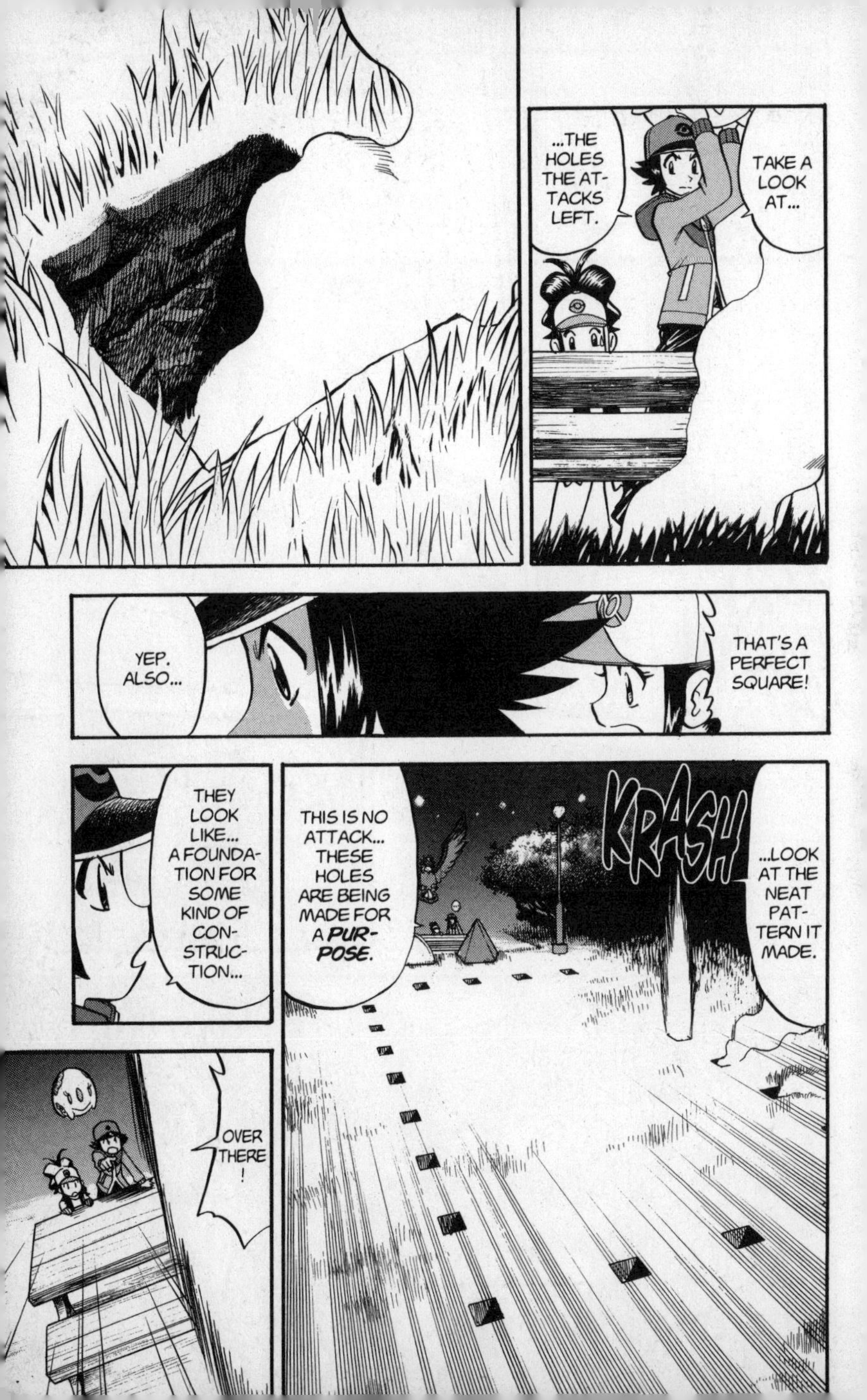
TAKE A LOOK AT...
...THE HOLES THE AT-TACKS LEFT.
THAT'S A PERFECT SQUARE!
YEP. ALSO...
KRASH
...LOOK AT THE NEAT PAT-TERN IT MADE.
THIS IS NO ATTACK... THESE HOLES ARE BEING MADE FOR A ***PUR-POSE***.
THEY LOOK LIKE... A FOUNDA-TION FOR SOME KIND OF CON-STRUC-TION...
OVER THERE!

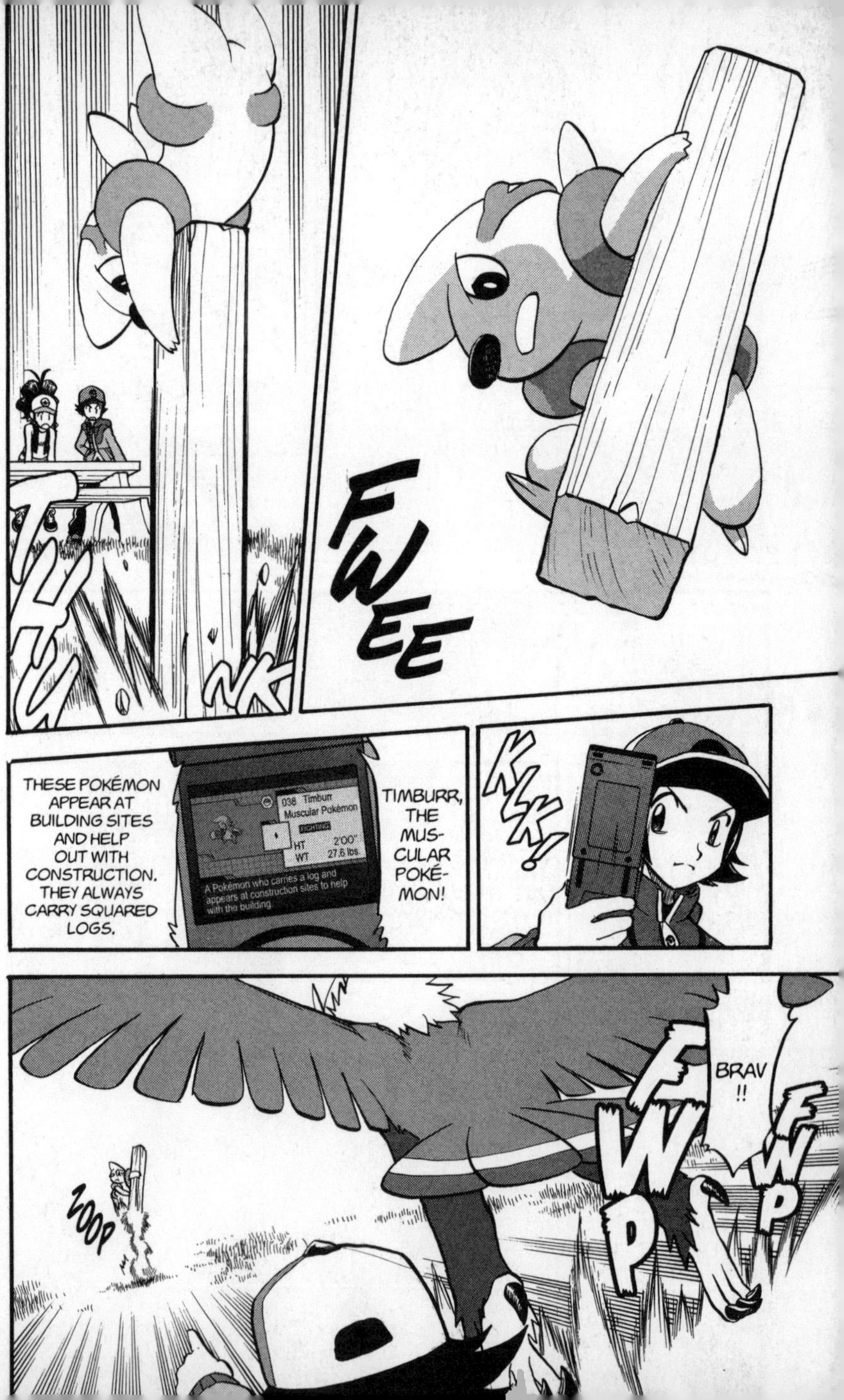
FWEE
THUNK
KLIK!
TIMBURR, THE MUSCULAR POKÉMON!
038 Timburr
Muscular Pokémon
FIGHTING
HT 2'00"
WT 27.6 lbs.
A Pokémon who carries a log and appears at construction sites to help with the building.
THESE POKÉMON APPEAR AT BUILDING SITES AND HELP OUT WITH CONSTRUCTION. THEY ALWAYS CARRY SQUARED LOGS.
BRAV!!
FWP
FWP
ZOOP

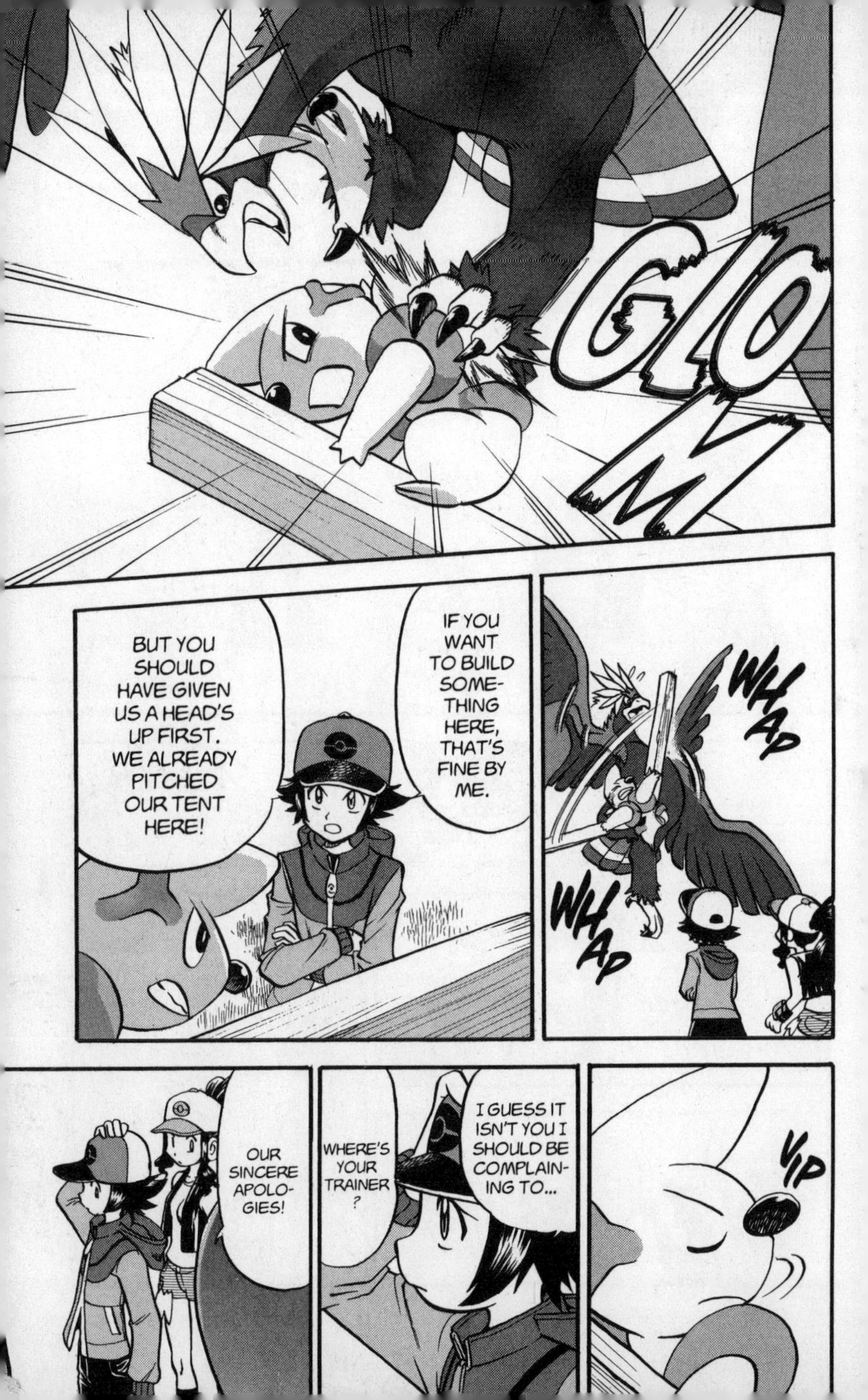
GLOM
WHAP
WHAP
IF YOU WANT TO BUILD SOMETHING HERE, THAT'S FINE BY ME.
BUT YOU SHOULD HAVE GIVEN US A HEAD'S UP FIRST. WE ALREADY PITCHED OUR TENT HERE!
VIP
I GUESS IT ISN'T YOU I SHOULD BE COMPLAINING TO...
WHERE'S YOUR TRAINER?
OUR SINCERE APOLOGIES!

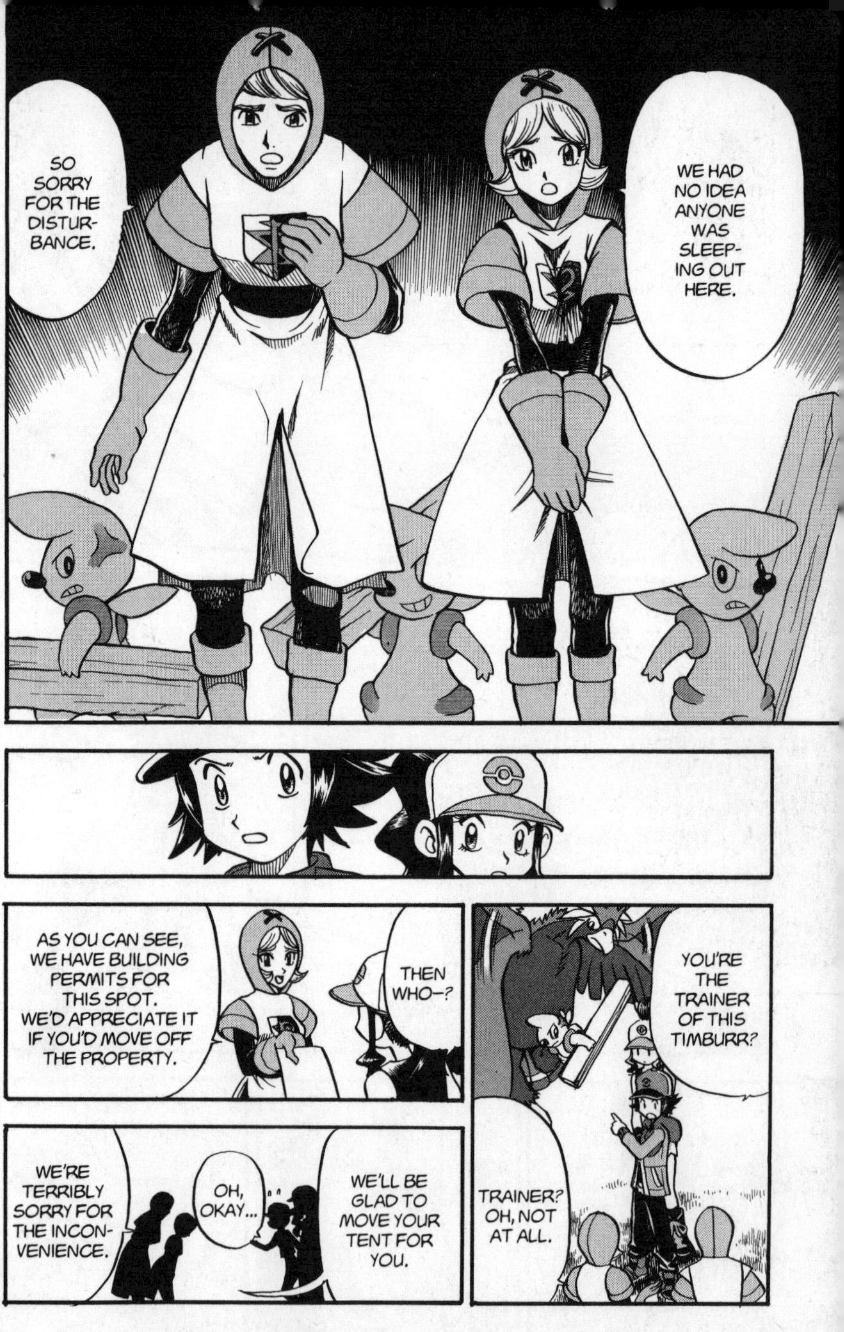
WE HAD NO IDEA ANYONE WAS SLEEPING OUT HERE.
SO SORRY FOR THE DISTURBANCE.
YOU'RE THE TRAINER OF THIS TIMBURR?
TRAINER? OH, NOT AT ALL.
THEN WHO-?
AS YOU CAN SEE, WE HAVE BUILDING PERMITS FOR THIS SPOT. WE'D APPRECIATE IT IF YOU'D MOVE OFF THE PROPERTY.
WE'LL BE GLAD TO MOVE YOUR TENT FOR YOU.
OH, OKAY...
WE'RE TERRIBLY SORRY FOR THE INCONVENIENCE.

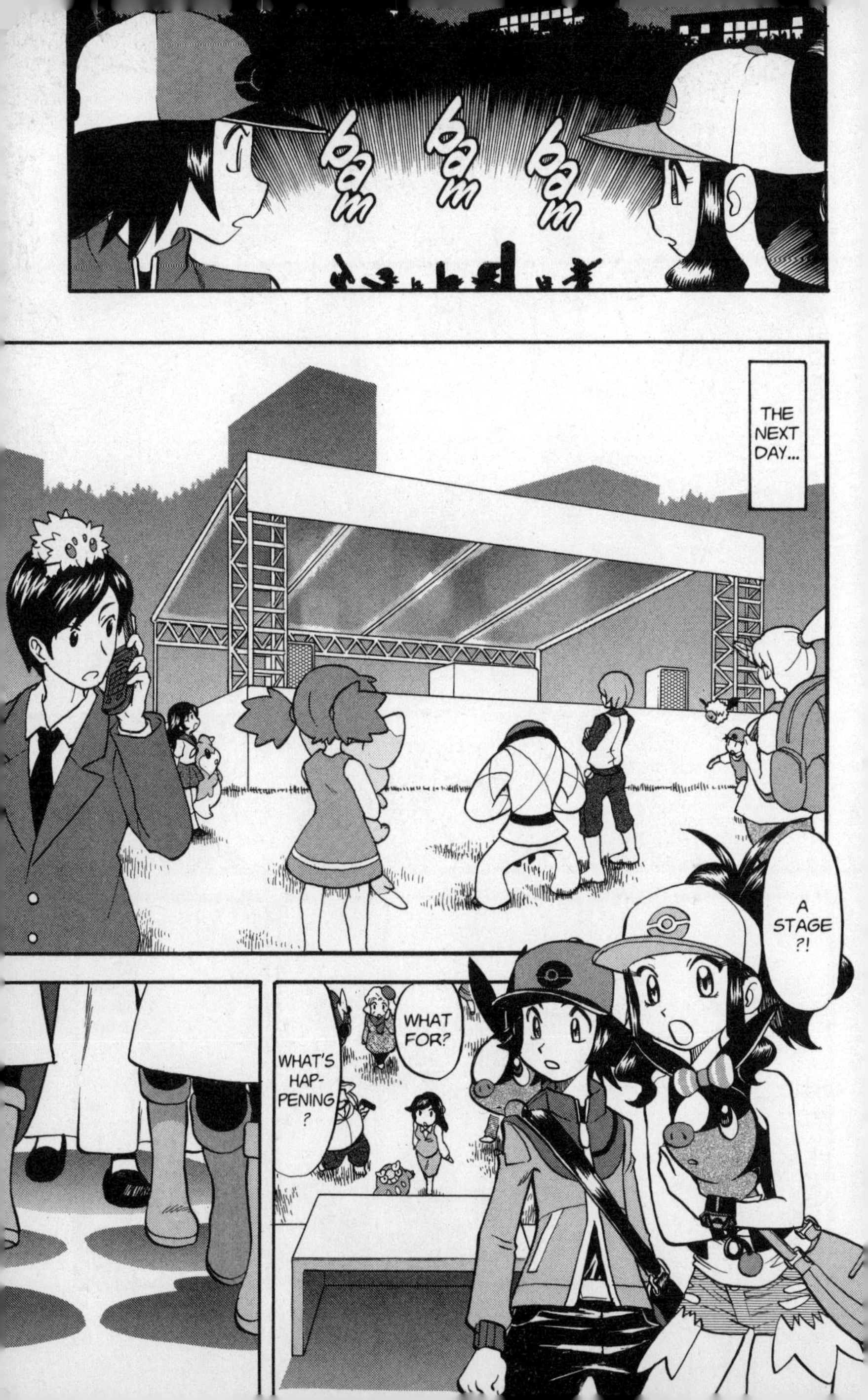
ba ba ba
bam bam bam
THE NEXT DAY...
A STAGE ?!
WHAT FOR?
WHAT'S HAP-PENING ?

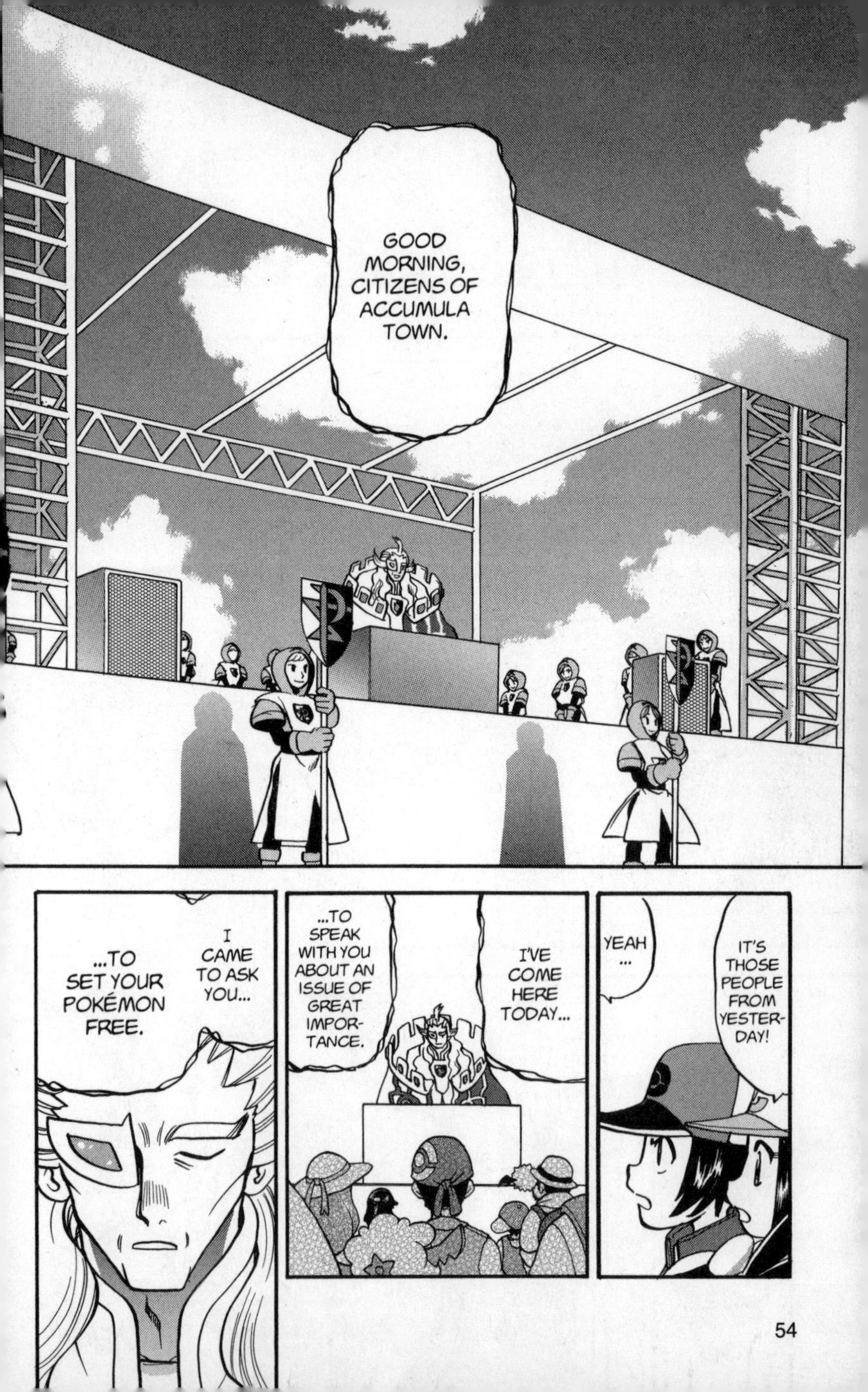
GOOD MORNING, CITIZENS OF ACCUMULA TOWN.
IT'S THOSE PEOPLE FROM YESTER-DAY!
YEAH ...
I'VE COME HERE TODAY...
...TO SPEAK WITH YOU ABOUT AN ISSUE OF GREAT IMPOR-TANCE.
I CAME TO ASK YOU...
...TO SET YOUR POKÉMON FREE.

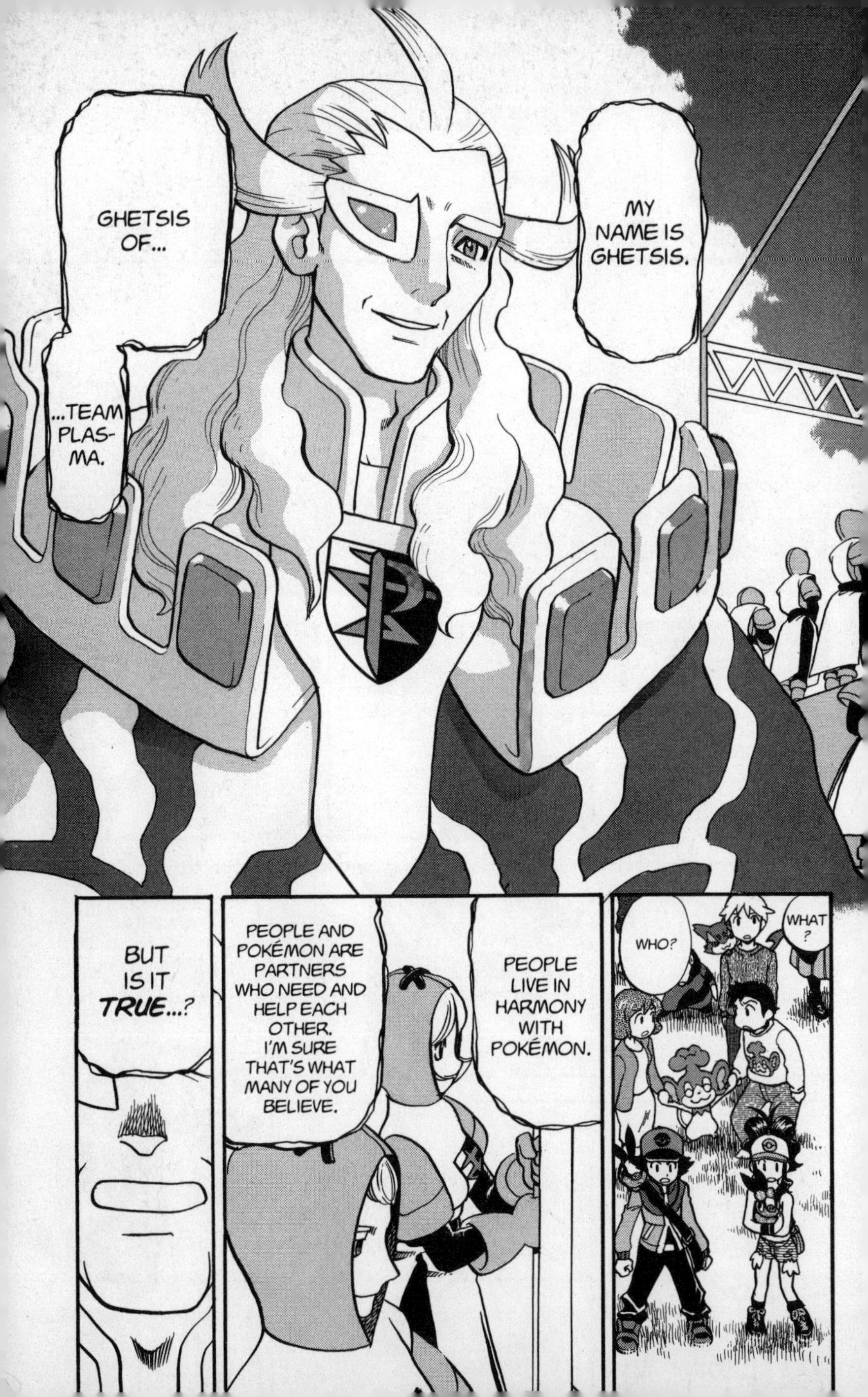
MY NAME IS GHETSIS.
GHETSIS OF...
...TEAM PLASMA.
WHAT?
WHO?
PEOPLE LIVE IN HARMONY WITH POKÉMON.
PEOPLE AND POKÉMON ARE PARTNERS WHO NEED AND HELP EACH OTHER. I'M SURE THAT'S WHAT MANY OF YOU BELIEVE.
BUT IS IT *TRUE*...?

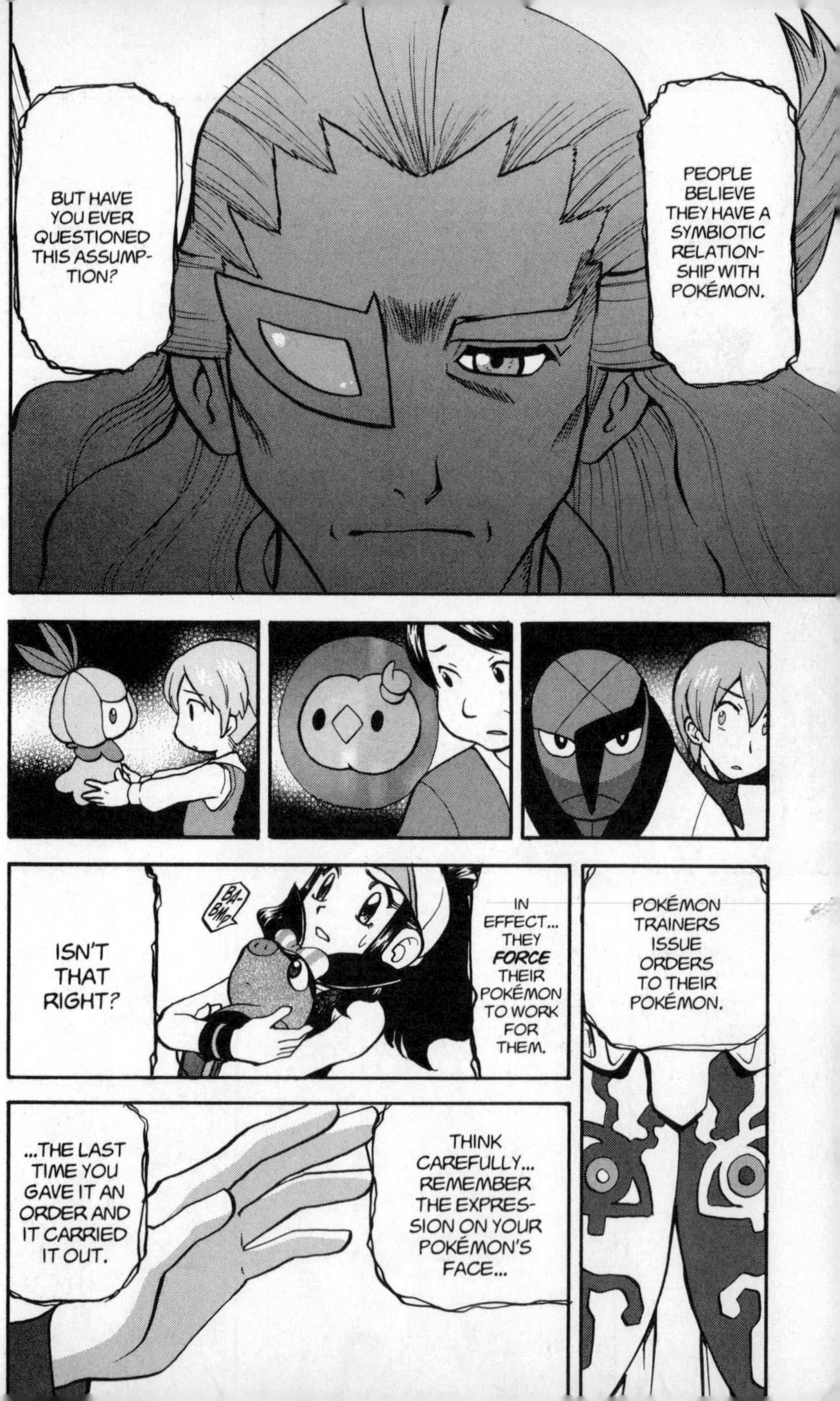
PEOPLE BELIEVE THEY HAVE A SYMBIOTIC RELATIONSHIP WITH POKÉMON.
BUT HAVE YOU EVER QUESTIONED THIS ASSUMPTION?
POKÉMON TRAINERS ISSUE ORDERS TO THEIR POKÉMON.
IN EFFECT... THEY *FORCE* THEIR POKÉMON TO WORK FOR THEM.
BA-BMP
ISN'T THAT RIGHT?
THINK CAREFULLY... REMEMBER THE EXPRESSION ON YOUR POKÉMON'S FACE...
...THE LAST TIME YOU GAVE IT AN ORDER AND IT CARRIED IT OUT.

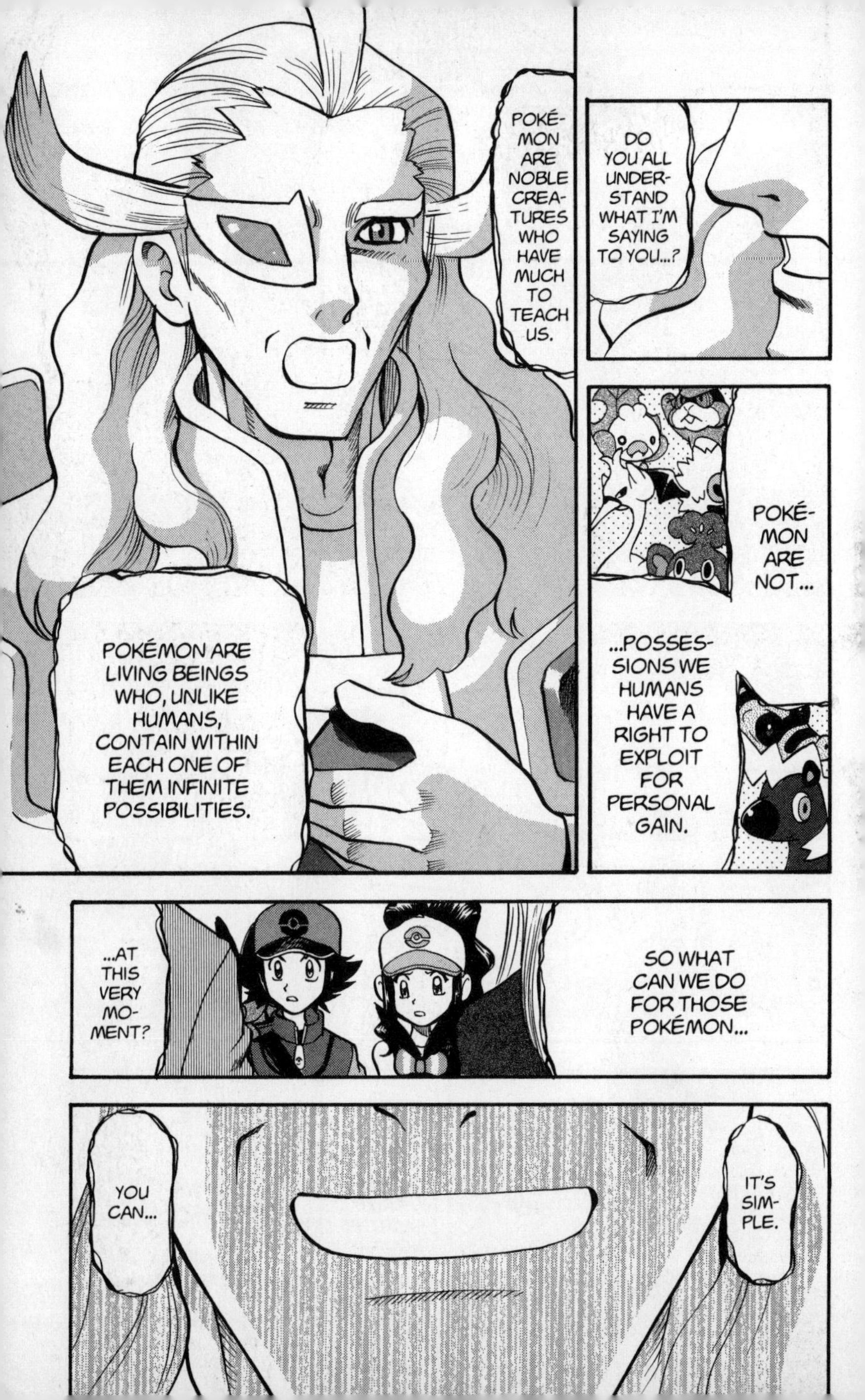
DO YOU ALL UNDERSTAND WHAT I'M SAYING TO YOU...?
POKÉMON ARE NOT...
...POSSESSIONS WE HUMANS HAVE A RIGHT TO EXPLOIT FOR PERSONAL GAIN.
POKÉMON ARE NOBLE CREATURES WHO HAVE MUCH TO TEACH US.
POKÉMON ARE LIVING BEINGS WHO, UNLIKE HUMANS, CONTAIN WITHIN EACH ONE OF THEM INFINITE POSSIBILITIES.
SO WHAT CAN WE DO FOR THOSE POKÉMON...
...AT THIS VERY MOMENT?
IT'S SIMPLE.
YOU CAN...

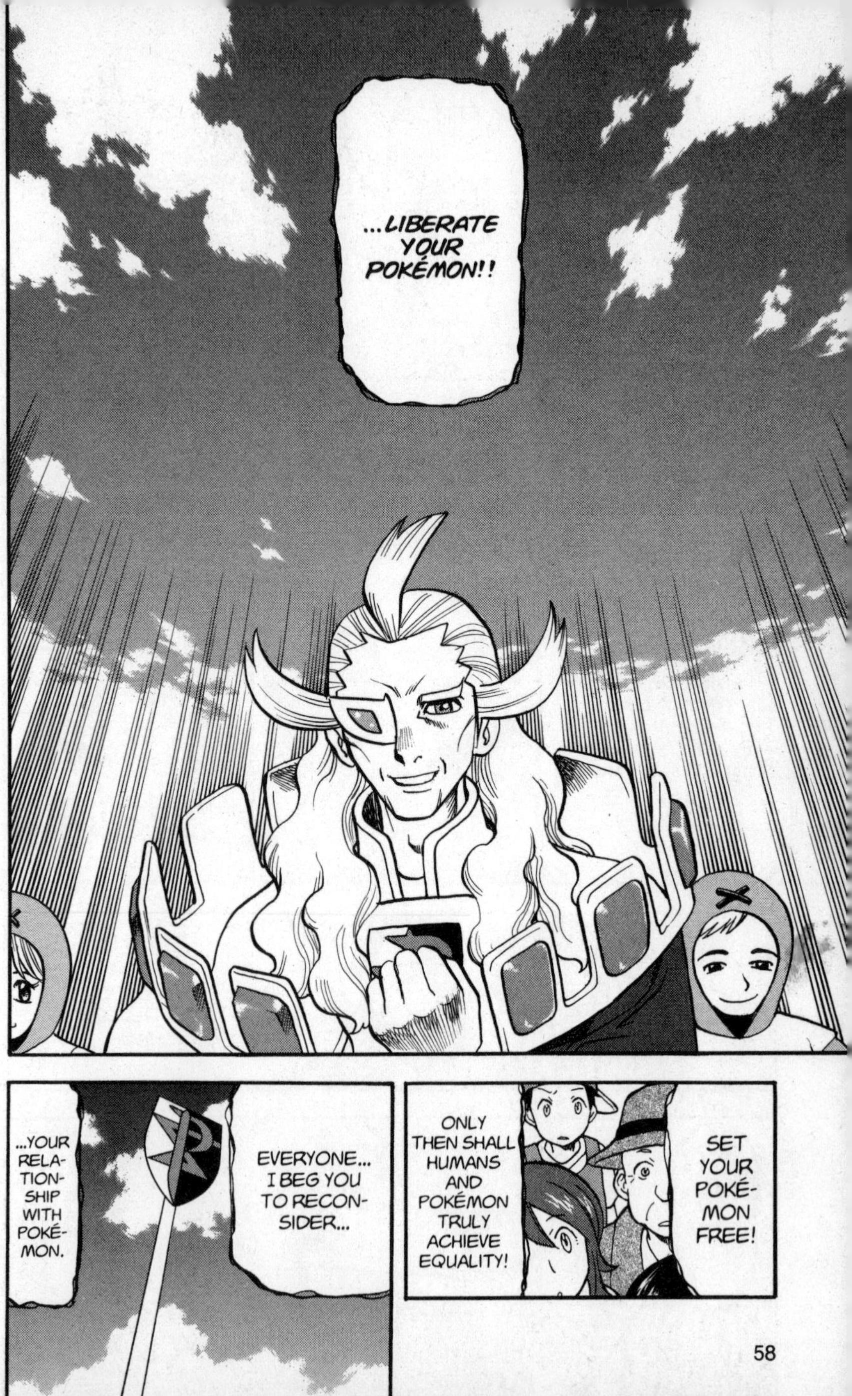
...LIBERATE YOUR POKÉMON!!
SET YOUR POKÉ-MON FREE!
ONLY THEN SHALL HUMANS AND POKÉMON TRULY ACHIEVE EQUALITY!
EVERYONE... I BEG YOU TO RECON-SIDER...
...YOUR RELA-TION-SHIP WITH POKÉ-MON.

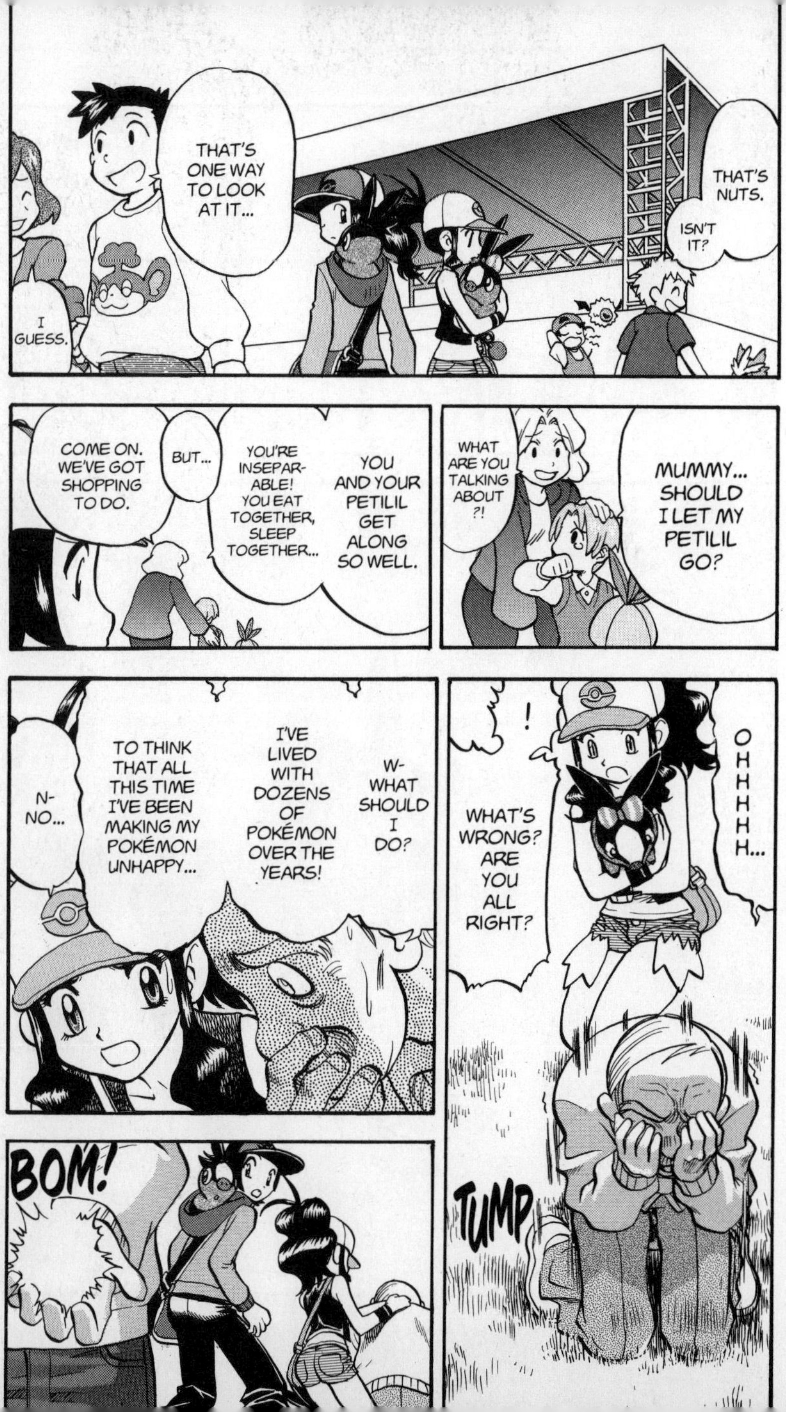
THAT'S NUTS.
ISN'T IT?
THAT'S ONE WAY TO LOOK AT IT...
I GUESS.
MUMMY... SHOULD I LET MY PETILIL GO?
WHAT ARE YOU TALKING ABOUT?!
YOU AND YOUR PETILIL GET ALONG SO WELL.
YOU'RE INSEPARABLE! YOU EAT TOGETHER, SLEEP TOGETHER...
BUT...
COME ON. WE'VE GOT SHOPPING TO DO.
OHHHHH...
!
WHAT'S WRONG? ARE YOU ALL RIGHT?
TUMP
W-WHAT SHOULD I DO?
I'VE LIVED WITH DOZENS OF POKÉMON OVER THE YEARS!
TO THINK THAT ALL THIS TIME I'VE BEEN MAKING MY POKÉMON UNHAPPY...
N-NO...
BOM!

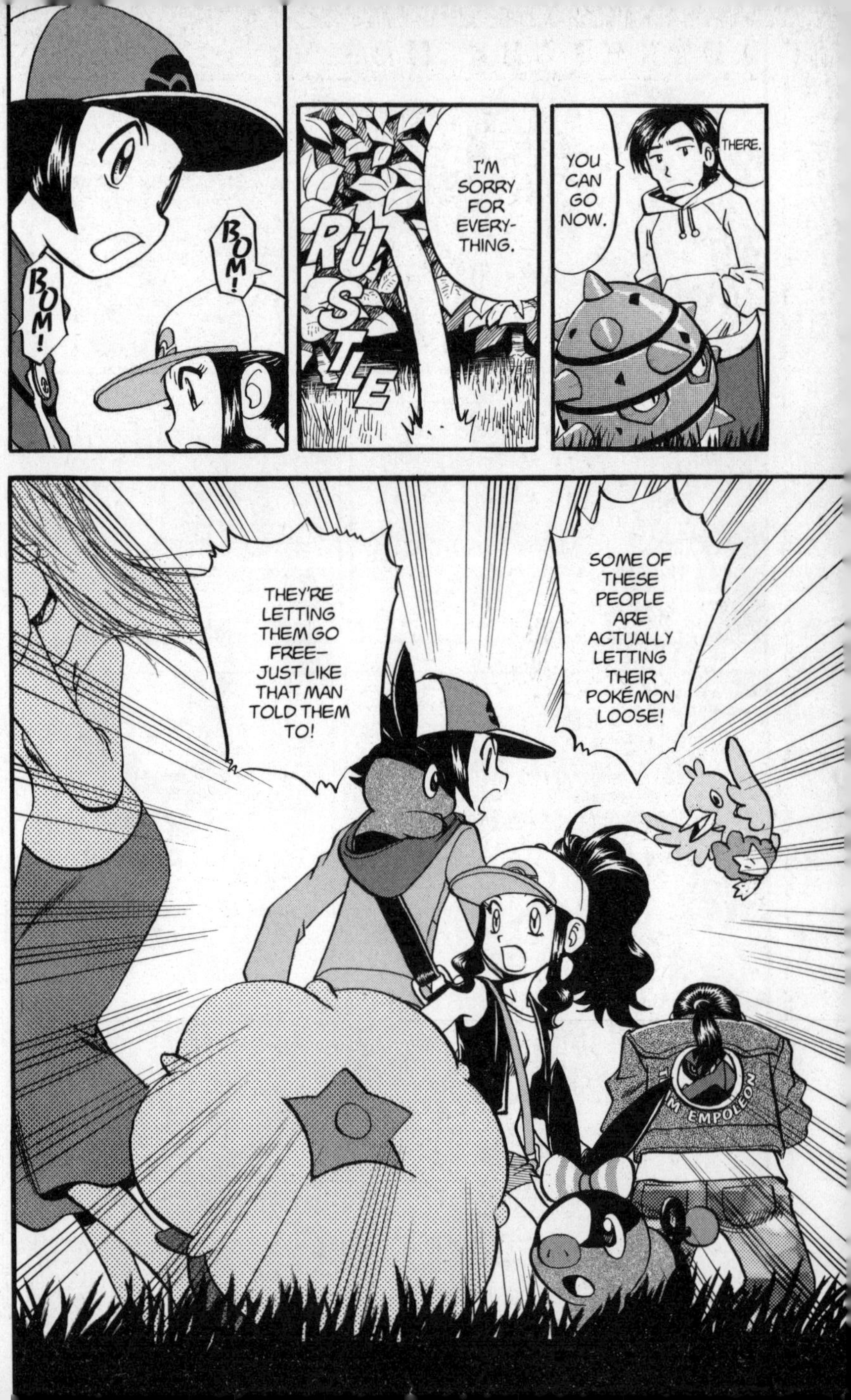
THERE.
YOU CAN GO NOW.
I'M SORRY FOR EVERY-THING.
RUSTLE
BOM!
BOM!
SOME OF THESE PEOPLE ARE ACTUALLY LETTING THEIR POKÉMON LOOSE!
THEY'RE LETTING THEM GO FREE— JUST LIKE THAT MAN TOLD THEM TO!

ADVENTURE MAP

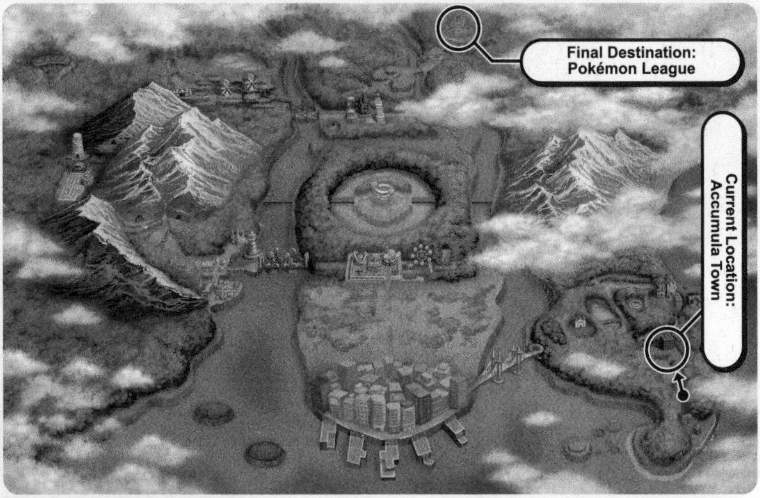
Final Destination:
Pokémon League
Current Location:
Accumula Town

Fire Pig Pokémon **Tep**
Tepig ♂ — Fire
Lv.15 Ability: Blaze

Dream Eater Pokémon **Musha**
Munna ♂ — Psychic
Lv.34 Ability: Forewarn

Valiant Pokémon **Brav**
Braviary ♂ — Normal Flying
Lv.54 Ability: Sheer Force

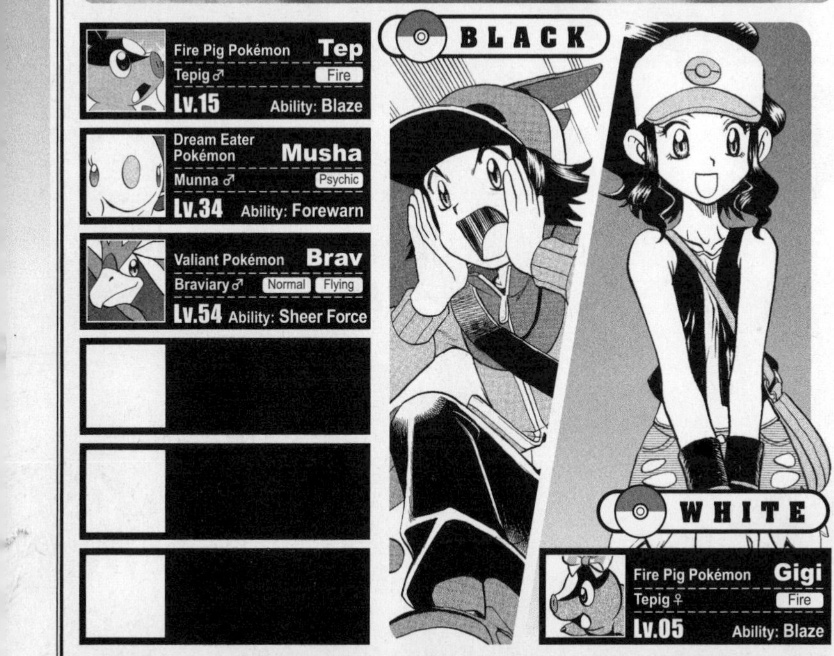
BLACK
WHITE

Fire Pig Pokémon **Gigi**
Tepig ♀ — Fire
Lv.05 Ability: Blaze

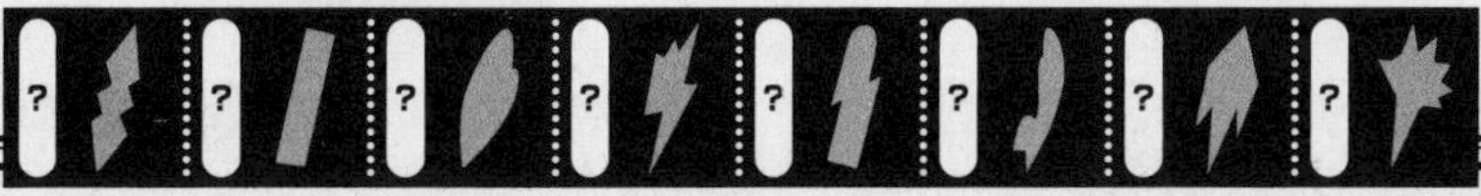
?
?
?
?
?
?
?
?

Pokémon Adventures Black & White

PURRLOIN

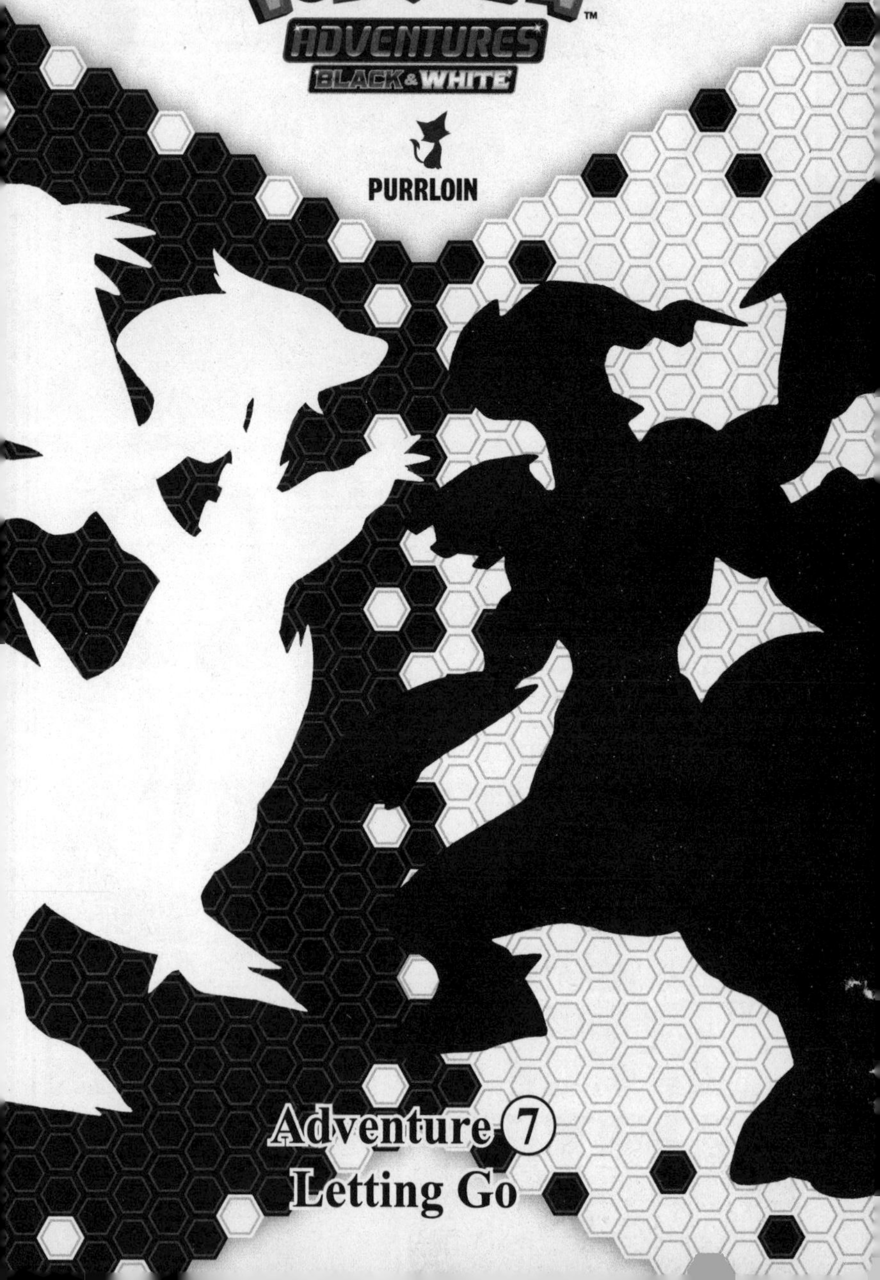

Adventure 7
Letting Go

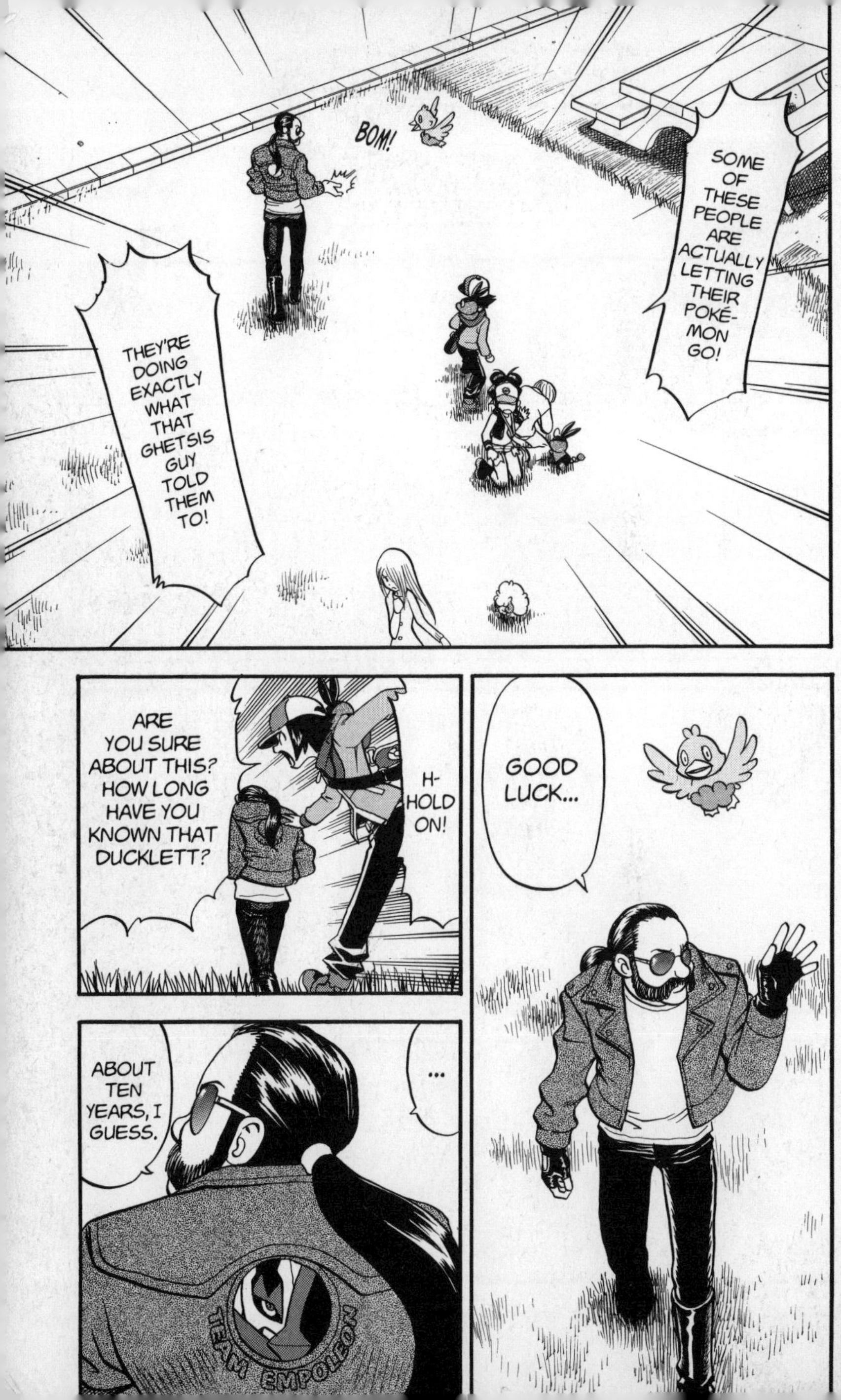
BOM!
SOME OF THESE PEOPLE ARE ACTUALLY LETTING THEIR POKÉMON GO!
THEY'RE DOING EXACTLY WHAT THAT GHETSIS GUY TOLD THEM TO!
GOOD LUCK...
H-HOLD ON!
ARE YOU SURE ABOUT THIS? HOW LONG HAVE YOU KNOWN THAT DUCKLETT?
...
ABOUT TEN YEARS, I GUESS.
TEAM EMPOLEON

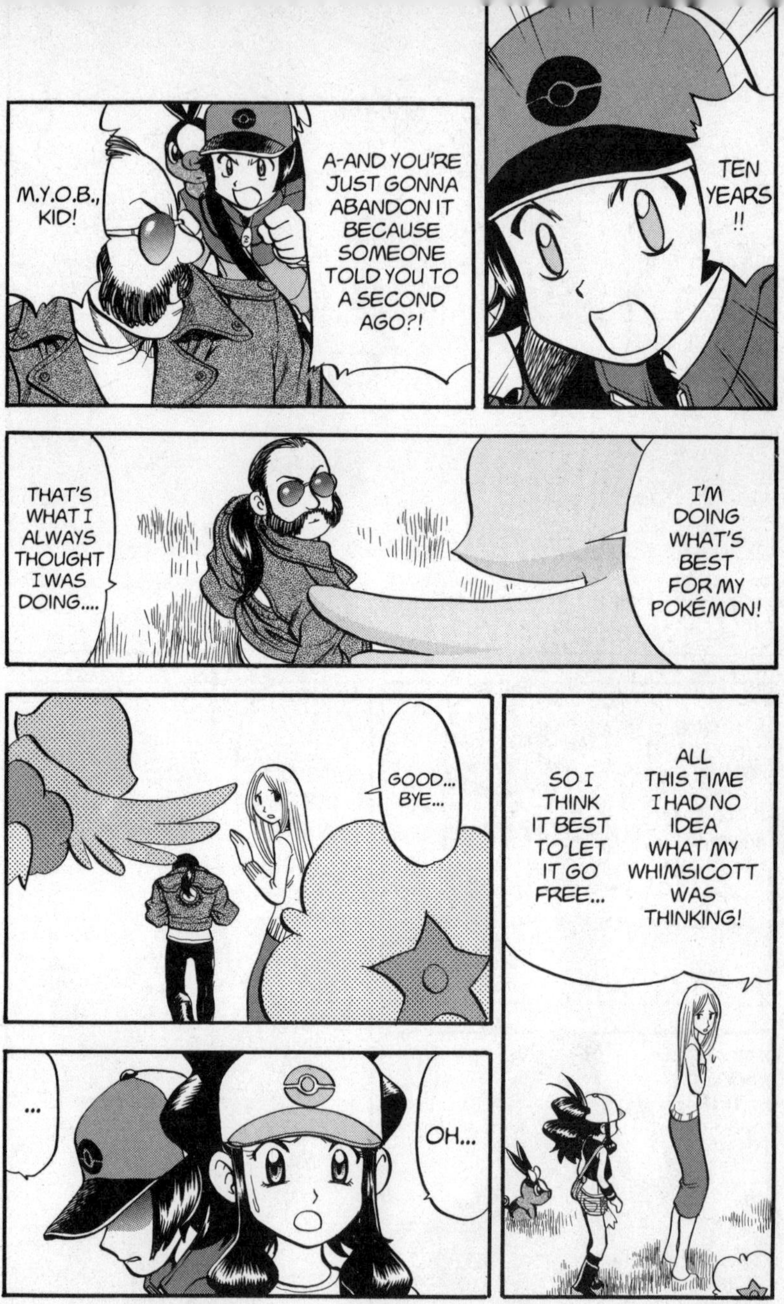
TEN YEARS !!
A-AND YOU'RE JUST GONNA ABANDON IT BECAUSE SOMEONE TOLD YOU TO A SECOND AGO?!
M.Y.O.B., KID!
I'M DOING WHAT'S BEST FOR MY POKÉMON!
THAT'S WHAT I ALWAYS THOUGHT I WAS DOING....
ALL THIS TIME I HAD NO IDEA WHAT MY WHIMSICOTT WAS THINKING!
SO I THINK IT BEST TO LET IT GO FREE...
GOOD... BYE...
OH...
...

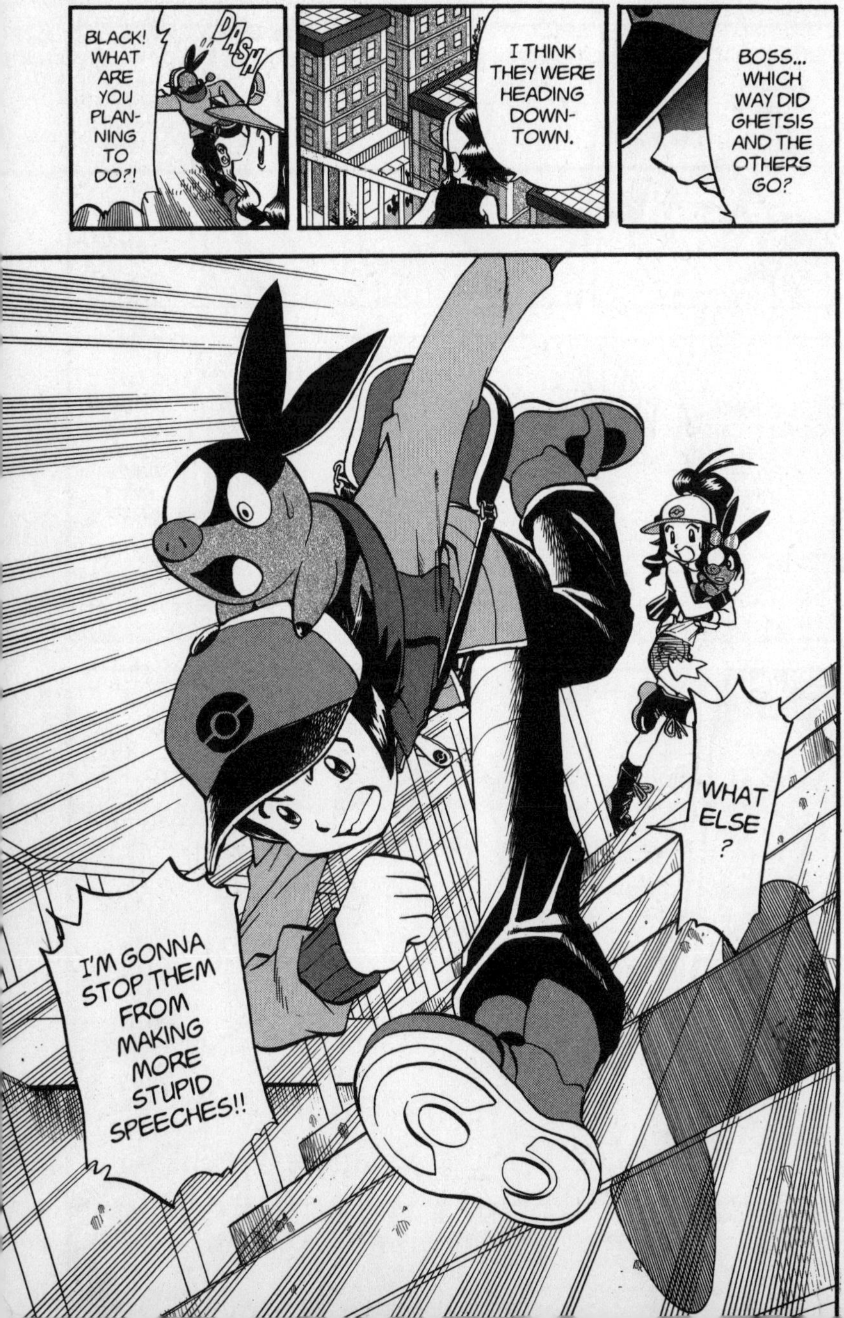
BOSS... WHICH WAY DID GHETSIS AND THE OTHERS GO?
I THINK THEY WERE HEADING DOWN-TOWN.
DASH
BLACK! WHAT ARE YOU PLAN-NING TO DO?!
WHAT ELSE ?
I'M GONNA STOP THEM FROM MAKING MORE STUPID SPEECHES!!

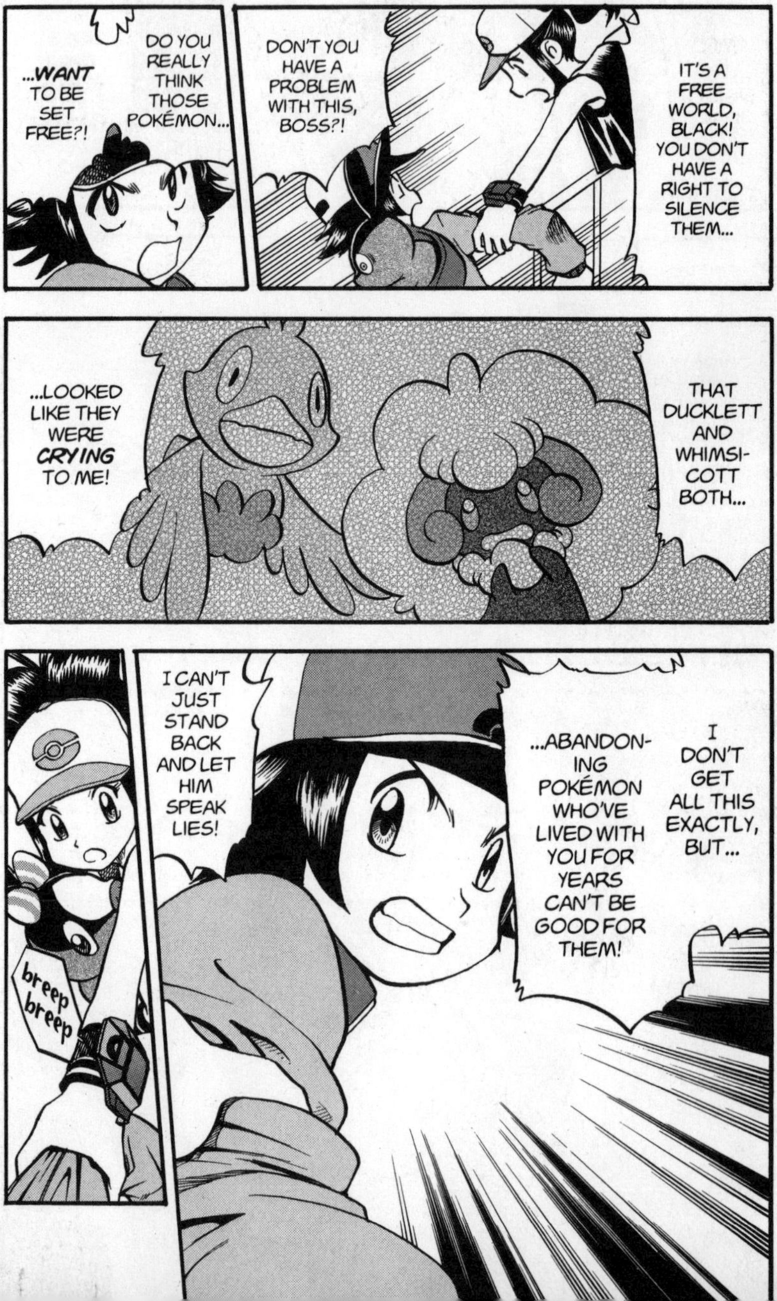
IT'S A FREE WORLD, BLACK! YOU DON'T HAVE A RIGHT TO SILENCE THEM...
DON'T YOU HAVE A PROBLEM WITH THIS, BOSS?!
DO YOU REALLY THINK THOSE POKÉMON...
...*WANT* TO BE SET FREE?!
THAT DUCKLETT AND WHIMSI-COTT BOTH...
...LOOKED LIKE THEY WERE *CRYING* TO ME!
I DON'T GET ALL THIS EXACTLY, BUT...
...ABANDON-ING POKÉMON WHO'VE LIVED WITH YOU FOR YEARS CAN'T BE GOOD FOR THEM!
I CAN'T JUST STAND BACK AND LET HIM SPEAK LIES!
breep breep

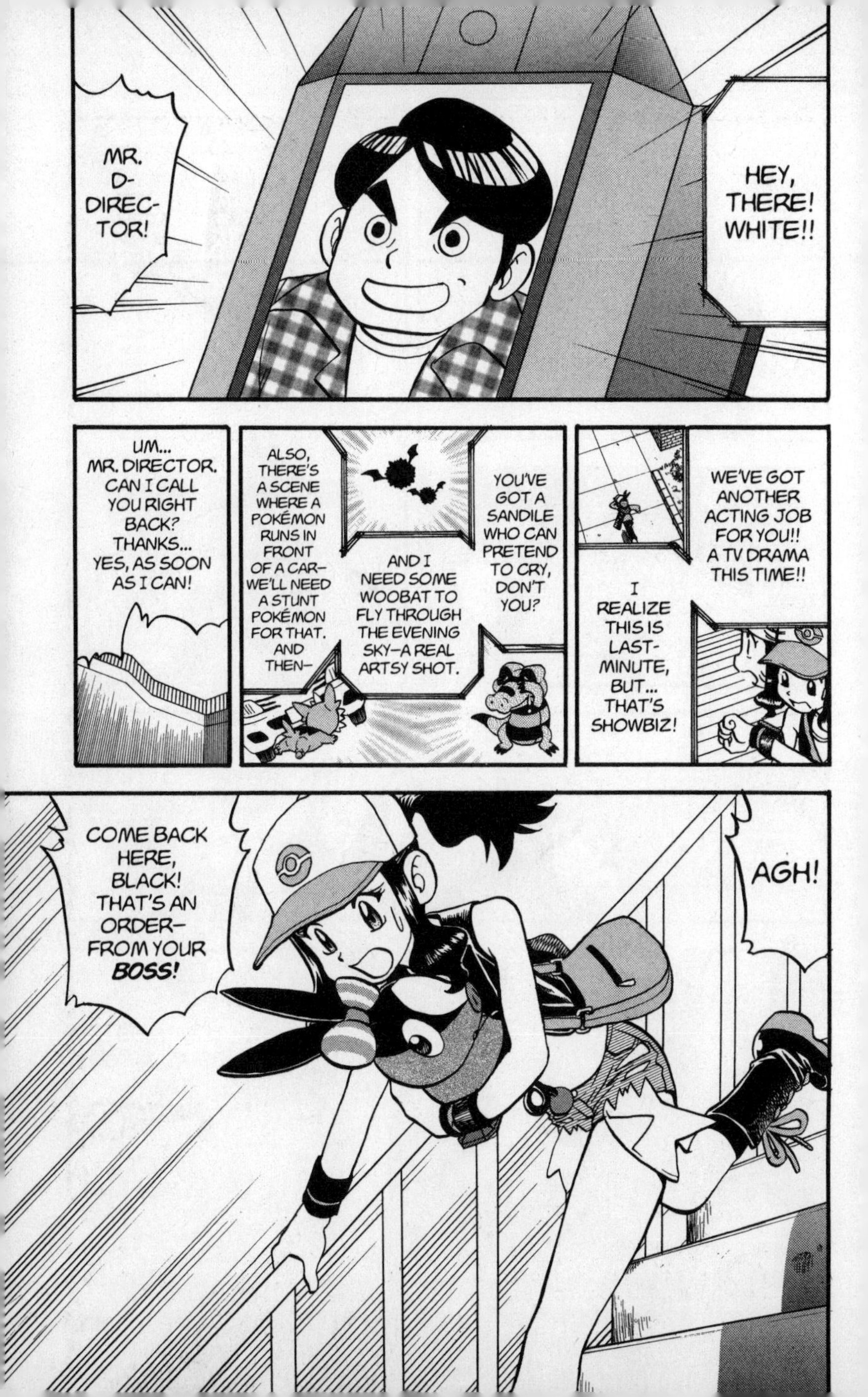
HEY, THERE! WHITE!!
MR. D-DIRECTOR!
WE'VE GOT ANOTHER ACTING JOB FOR YOU!! A TV DRAMA THIS TIME!!
I REALIZE THIS IS LAST-MINUTE, BUT... THAT'S SHOWBIZ!
YOU'VE GOT A SANDILE WHO CAN PRETEND TO CRY, DON'T YOU?
AND I NEED SOME WOOBAT TO FLY THROUGH THE EVENING SKY—A REAL ARTSY SHOT.
ALSO, THERE'S A SCENE WHERE A POKÉMON RUNS IN FRONT OF A CAR—WE'LL NEED A STUNT POKÉMON FOR THAT. AND THEN—
UM... MR. DIRECTOR. CAN I CALL YOU RIGHT BACK? THANKS... YES, AS SOON AS I CAN!
AGH!
COME BACK HERE, BLACK! THAT'S AN ORDER—FROM YOUR ***BOSS!***

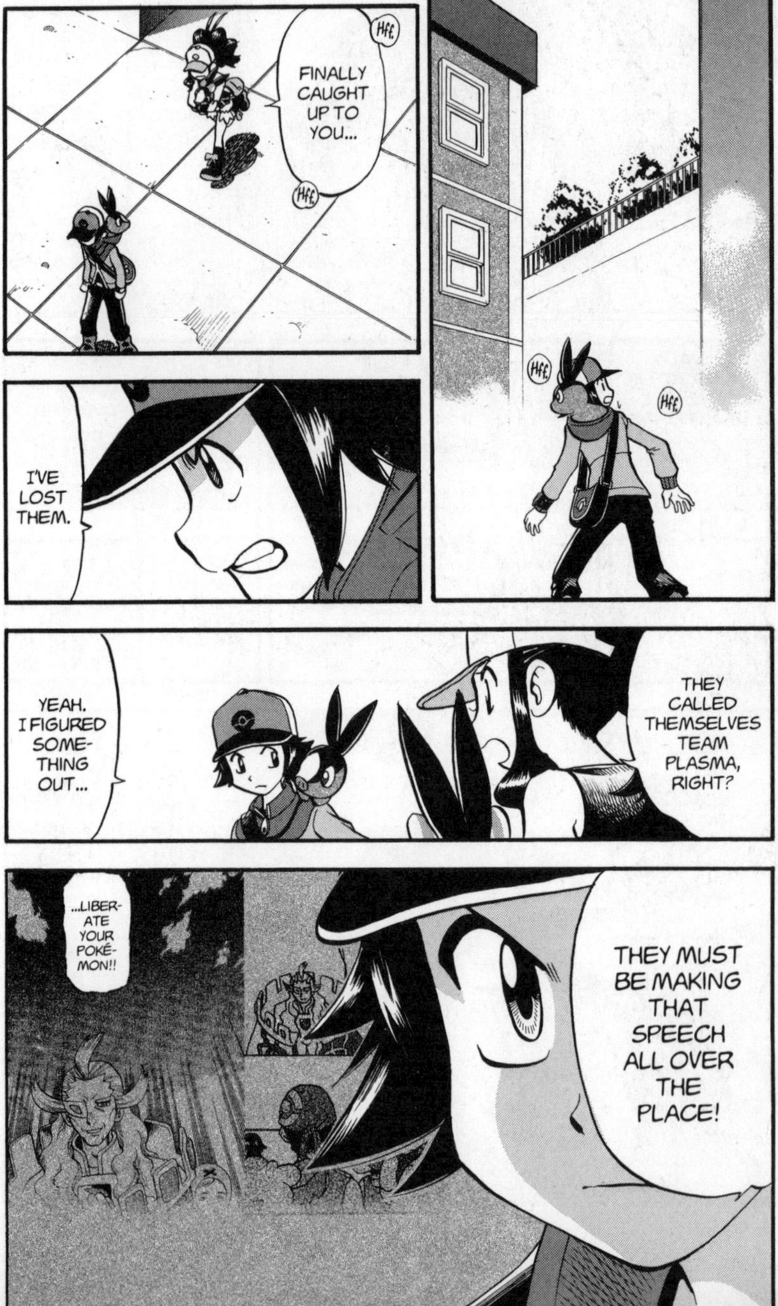
Hff.
Hff.
Hff.
FINALLY CAUGHT UP TO YOU...
Hff.
I'VE LOST THEM.
THEY CALLED THEMSELVES TEAM PLASMA, RIGHT?
YEAH. I FIGURED SOME-THING OUT...
THEY MUST BE MAKING THAT SPEECH ALL OVER THE PLACE!
...LIBER-ATE YOUR POKÉ-MON!!

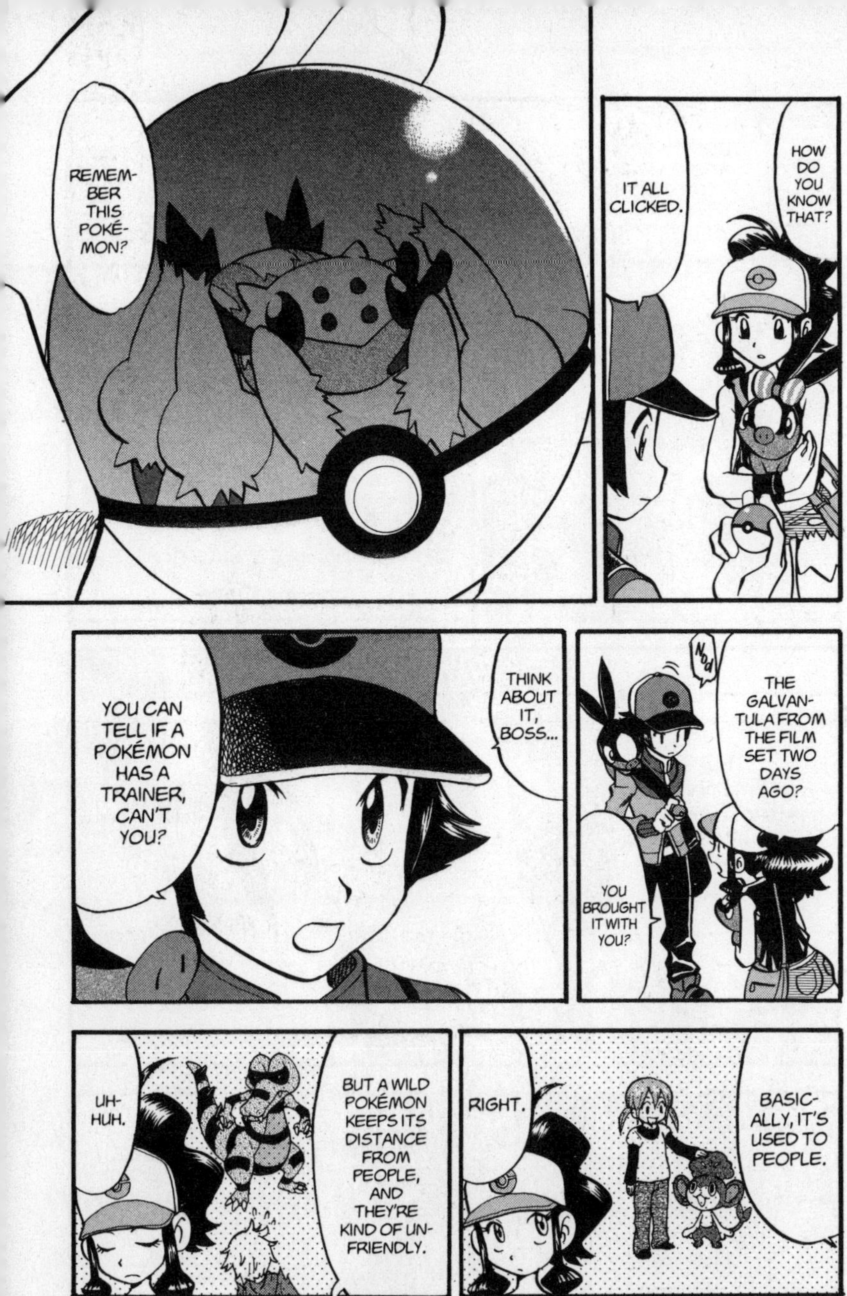
HOW DO YOU KNOW THAT?
IT ALL CLICKED.
REMEMBER THIS POKÉMON?
Nod
THE GALVANTULA FROM THE FILM SET TWO DAYS AGO?
YOU BROUGHT IT WITH YOU?
THINK ABOUT IT, BOSS...
YOU CAN TELL IF A POKÉMON HAS A TRAINER, CAN'T YOU?
BASICALLY, IT'S USED TO PEOPLE.
RIGHT.
BUT A WILD POKÉMON KEEPS ITS DISTANCE FROM PEOPLE, AND THEY'RE KIND OF UNFRIENDLY.
UH-HUH.

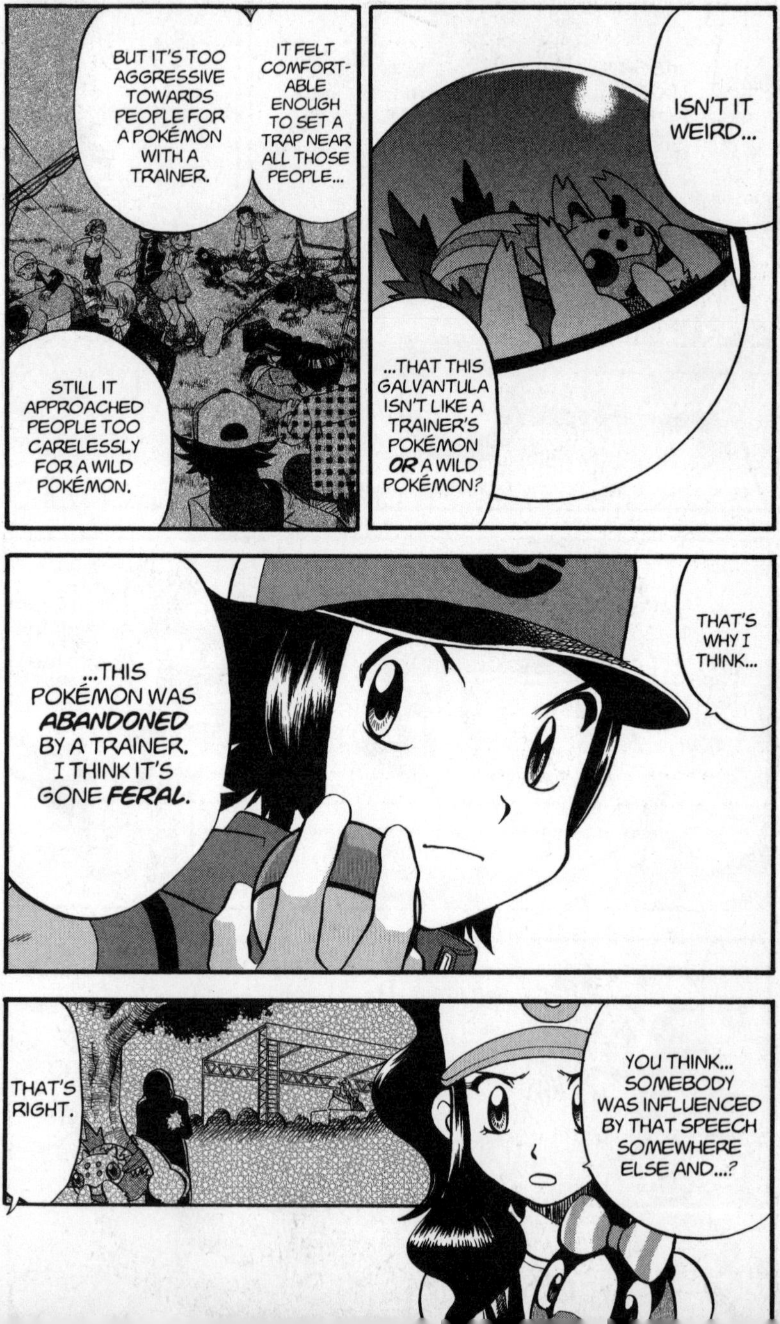
ISN'T IT WEIRD...
...THAT THIS GALVANTULA ISN'T LIKE A TRAINER'S POKÉMON **OR** A WILD POKÉMON?
IT FELT COMFORTABLE ENOUGH TO SET A TRAP NEAR ALL THOSE PEOPLE...
BUT IT'S TOO AGGRESSIVE TOWARDS PEOPLE FOR A POKÉMON WITH A TRAINER.
STILL IT APPROACHED PEOPLE TOO CARELESSLY FOR A WILD POKÉMON.
THAT'S WHY I THINK...
...THIS POKÉMON WAS **ABANDONED** BY A TRAINER. I THINK IT'S GONE **FERAL**.
YOU THINK... SOMEBODY WAS INFLUENCED BY THAT SPEECH SOMEWHERE ELSE AND...?
THAT'S RIGHT.

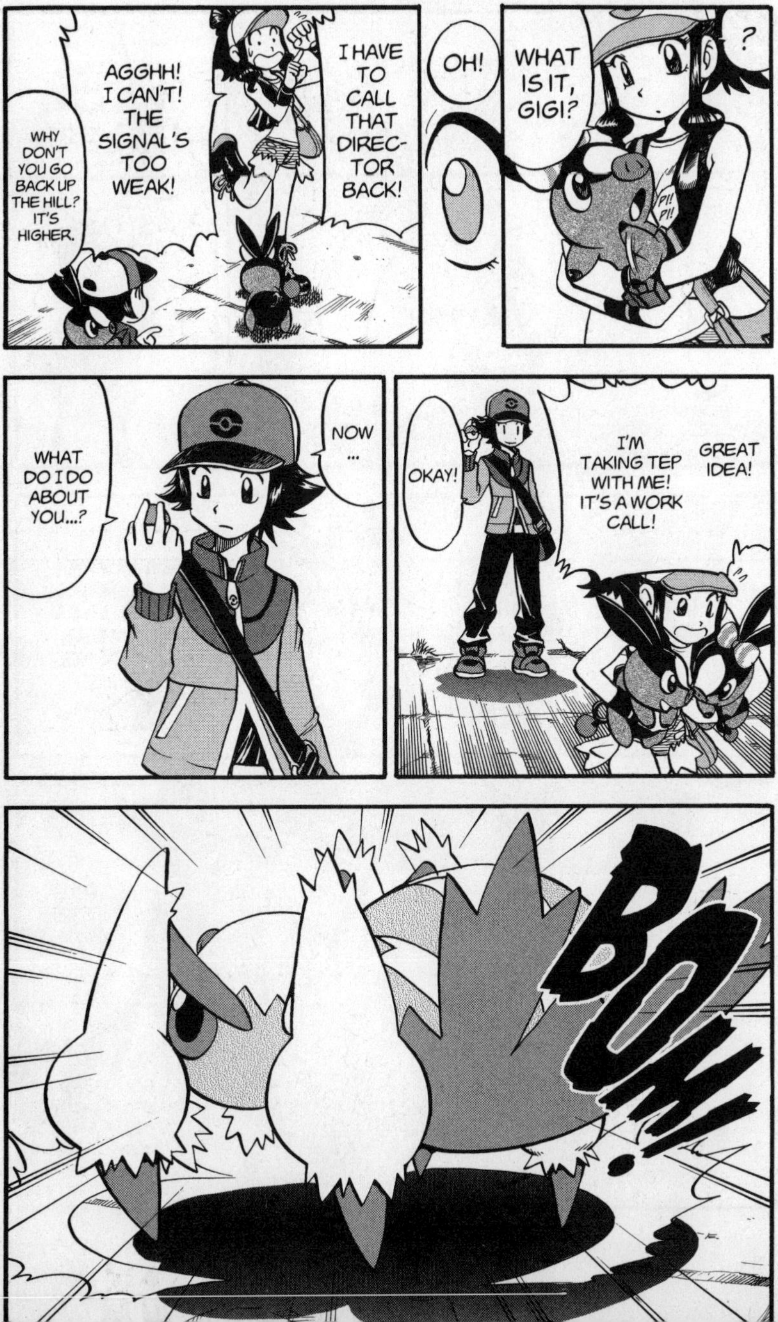
?
WHAT IS IT, GIGI?
OH!
PI! PI!
I HAVE TO CALL THAT DIREC-TOR BACK!
AGGHH! I CAN'T! THE SIGNAL'S TOO WEAK!
WHY DON'T YOU GO BACK UP THE HILL? IT'S HIGHER.
GREAT IDEA!
I'M TAKING TEP WITH ME! IT'S A WORK CALL!
OKAY!
NOW ...
WHAT DO I DO ABOUT YOU...?
BOM!!

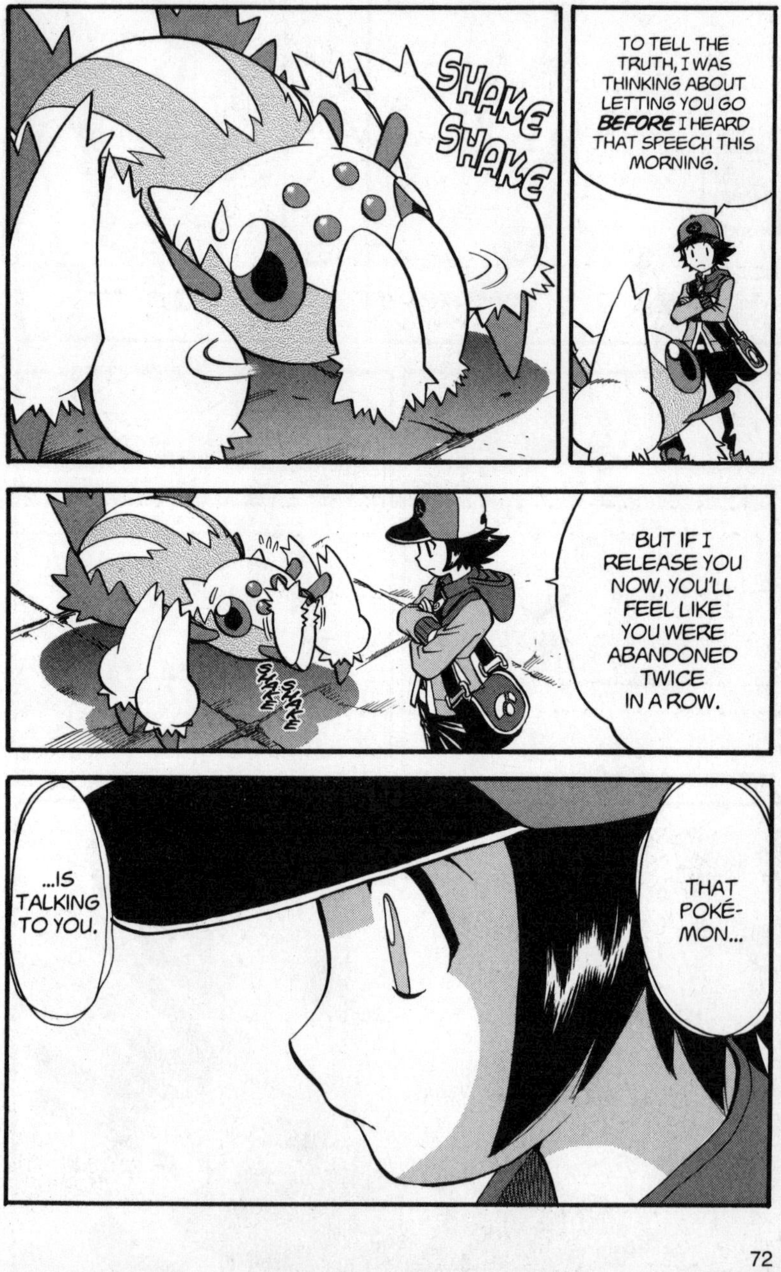
TO TELL THE TRUTH, I WAS THINKING ABOUT LETTING YOU GO **BEFORE** I HEARD THAT SPEECH THIS MORNING.
SHAKE SHAKE
BUT IF I RELEASE YOU NOW, YOU'LL FEEL LIKE YOU WERE ABANDONED TWICE IN A ROW.
SHAKE SHAKE
THAT POKÉ-MON...
...IS TALKING TO YOU.

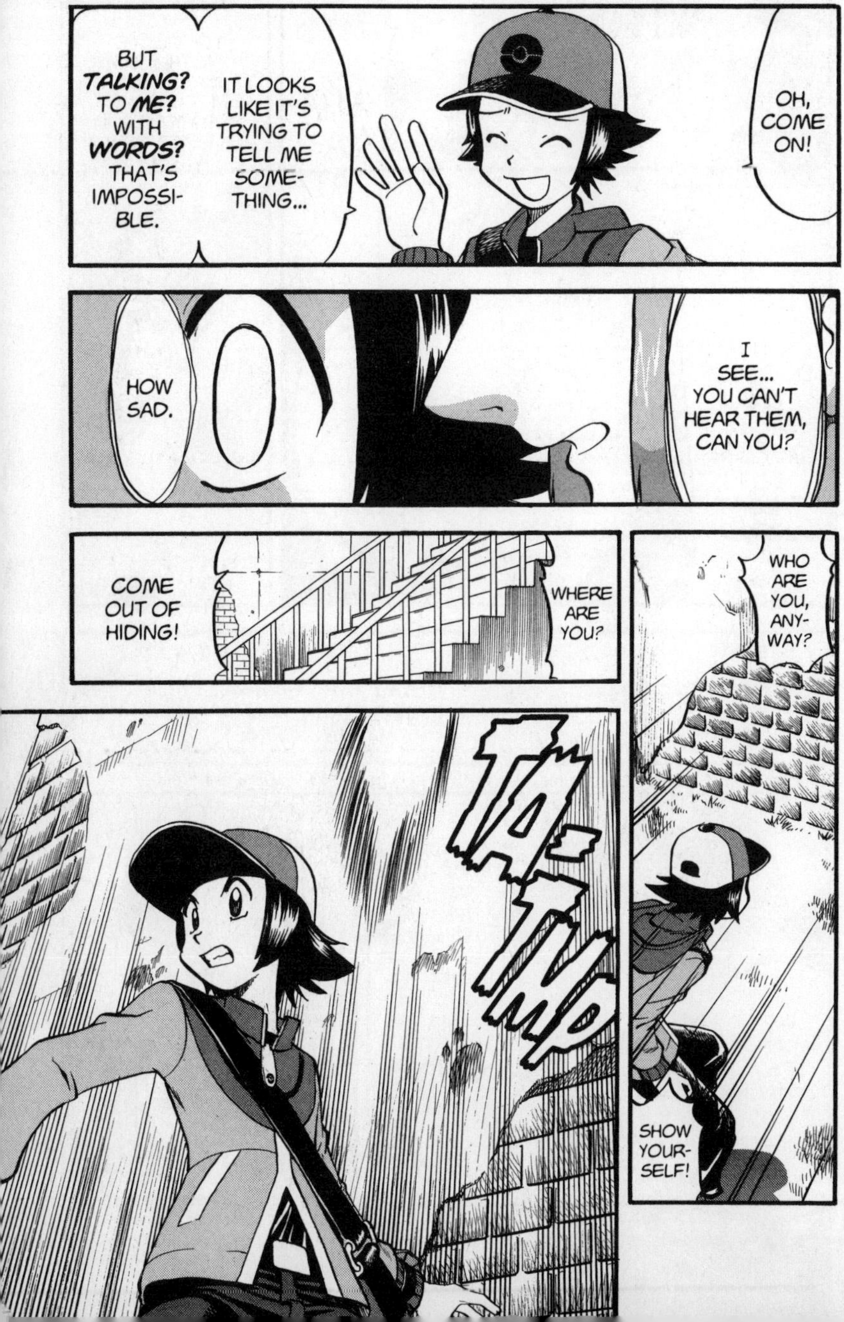
OH, COME ON!
IT LOOKS LIKE IT'S TRYING TO TELL ME SOME-THING...
BUT TALKING? TO ME? WITH WORDS? THAT'S IMPOSSI-BLE.
I SEE... YOU CAN'T HEAR THEM, CAN YOU?
HOW SAD.
WHO ARE YOU, ANY-WAY?
SHOW YOUR-SELF!
WHERE ARE YOU?
COME OUT OF HIDING!
TA-TMP

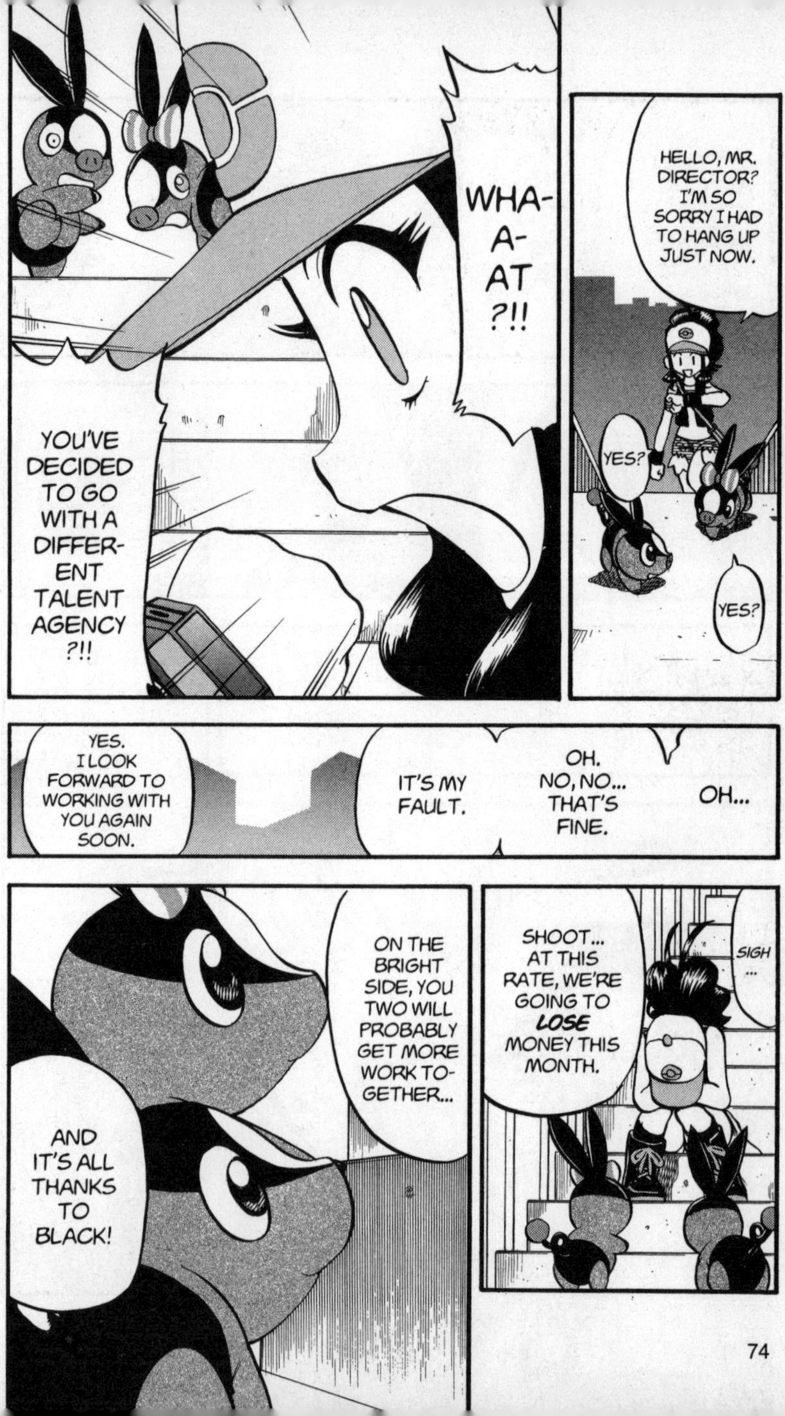
HELLO, MR. DIRECTOR? I'M SO SORRY I HAD TO HANG UP JUST NOW.
YES?
YES?
WHA-A-AT?!!
YOU'VE DECIDED TO GO WITH A DIFFERENT TALENT AGENCY?!!
OH...
OH. NO, NO... THAT'S FINE.
IT'S MY FAULT.
YES. I LOOK FORWARD TO WORKING WITH YOU AGAIN SOON.
SIGH...
SHOOT... AT THIS RATE, WE'RE GOING TO LOSE MONEY THIS MONTH.
ON THE BRIGHT SIDE, YOU TWO WILL PROBABLY GET MORE WORK TOGETHER...
AND IT'S ALL THANKS TO BLACK!

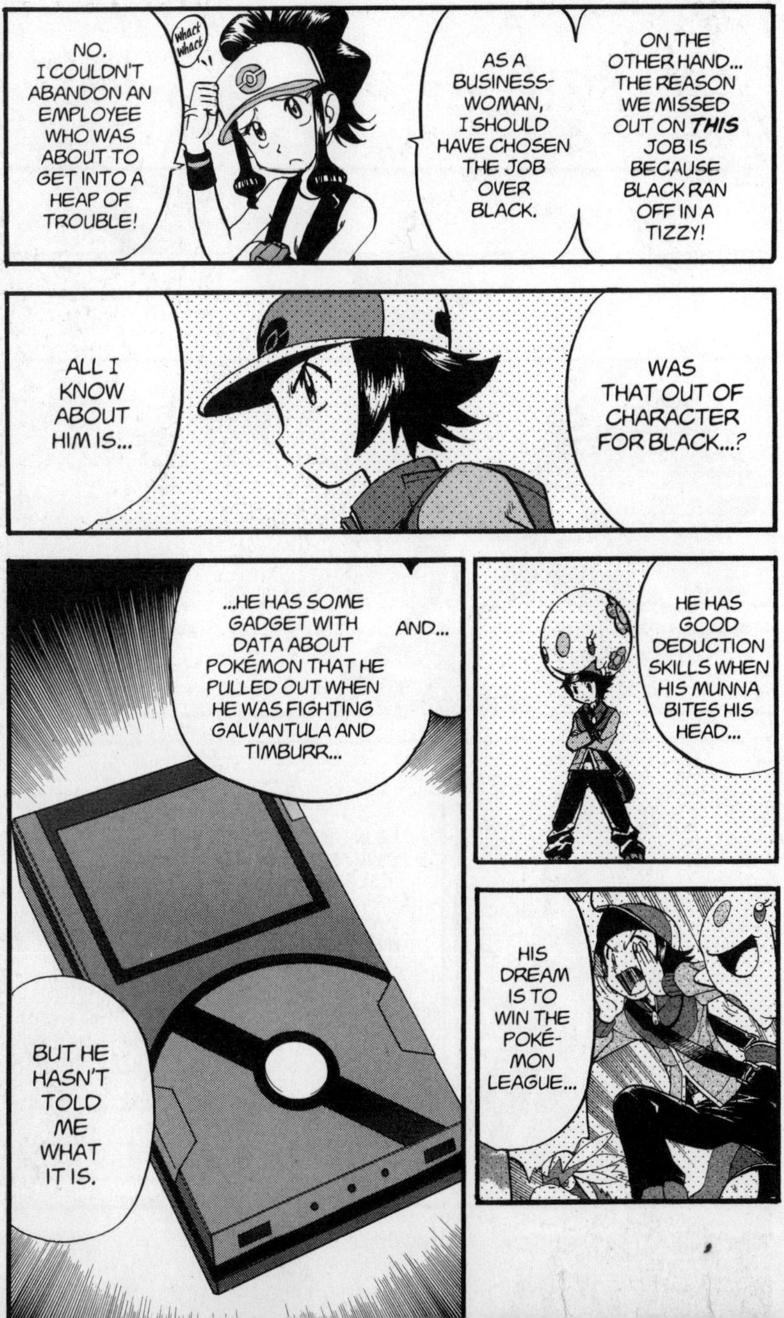
ON THE OTHER HAND... THE REASON WE MISSED OUT ON **THIS** JOB IS BECAUSE BLACK RAN OFF IN A TIZZY!
AS A BUSINESS-WOMAN, I SHOULD HAVE CHOSEN THE JOB OVER BLACK.
Whack whack
NO. I COULDN'T ABANDON AN EMPLOYEE WHO WAS ABOUT TO GET INTO A HEAP OF TROUBLE!
WAS THAT OUT OF CHARACTER FOR BLACK...?
ALL I KNOW ABOUT HIM IS...
HE HAS GOOD DEDUCTION SKILLS WHEN HIS MUNNA BITES HIS HEAD...
HIS DREAM IS TO WIN THE POKÉ-MON LEAGUE...
AND...
...HE HAS SOME GADGET WITH DATA ABOUT POKÉMON THAT HE PULLED OUT WHEN HE WAS FIGHTING GALVANTULA AND TIMBURR...
BUT HE HASN'T TOLD ME WHAT IT IS.

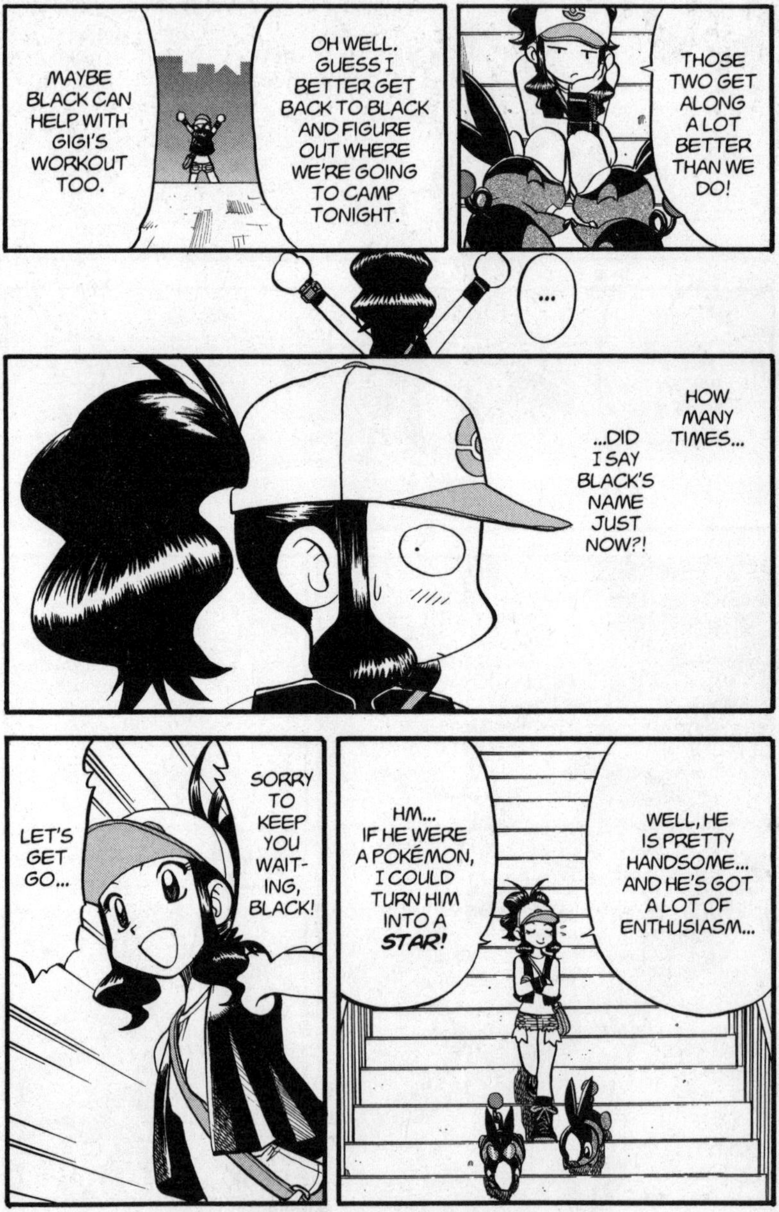
THOSE TWO GET ALONG A LOT BETTER THAN WE DO!
OH WELL. GUESS I BETTER GET BACK TO BLACK AND FIGURE OUT WHERE WE'RE GOING TO CAMP TONIGHT.
MAYBE BLACK CAN HELP WITH GIGI'S WORKOUT TOO.
...
HOW MANY TIMES...
...DID I SAY BLACK'S NAME JUST NOW?!
WELL, HE IS PRETTY HANDSOME... AND HE'S GOT A LOT OF ENTHUSIASM...
HM... IF HE WERE A POKÉMON, I COULD TURN HIM INTO A *STAR!*
SORRY TO KEEP YOU WAIT-ING, BLACK!
LET'S GET GO...

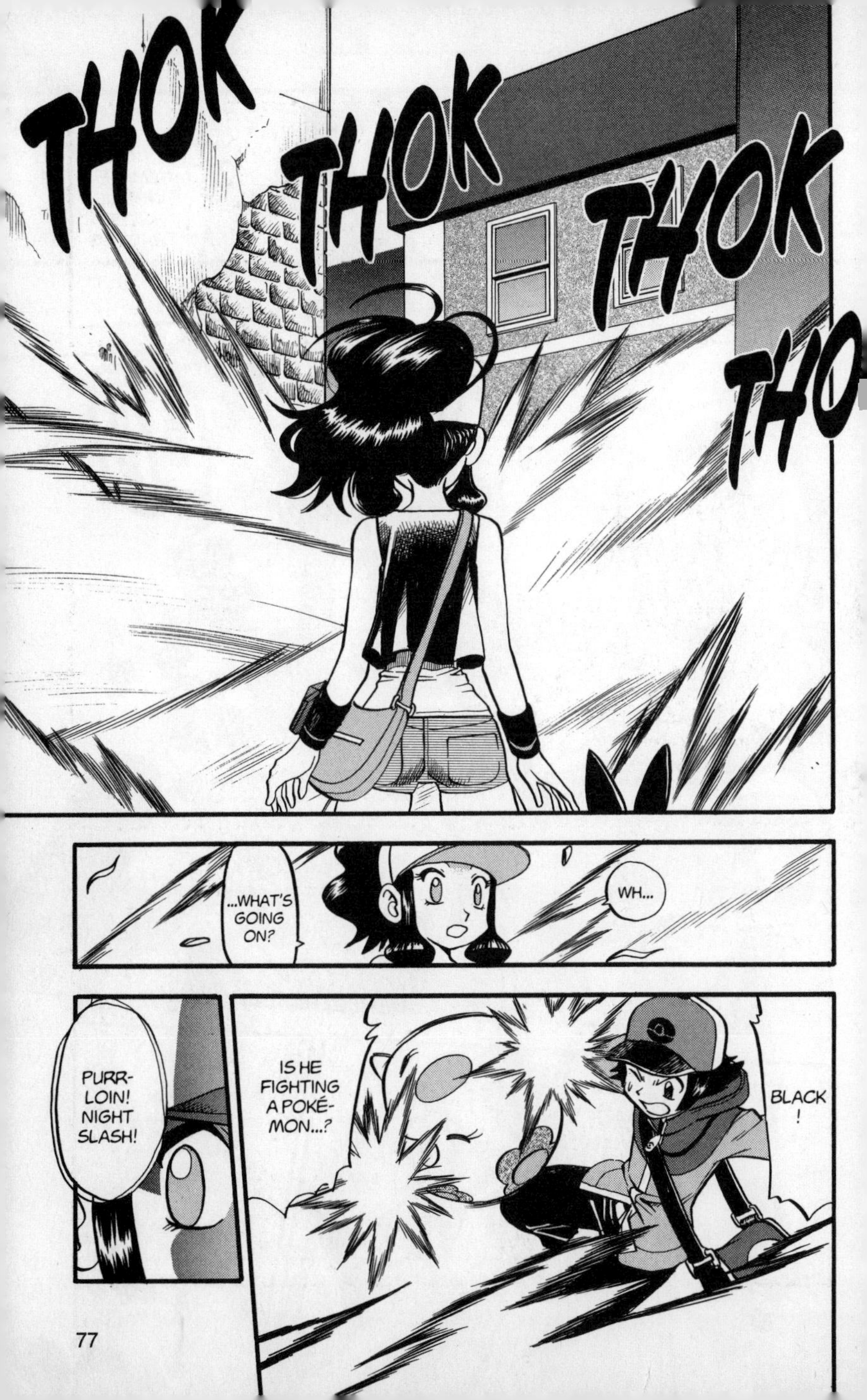
THOK
THOK
THOK
THO
WH...
...WHAT'S GOING ON?
BLACK!
IS HE FIGHTING A POKÉMON...?
PURR-LOIN! NIGHT SLASH!

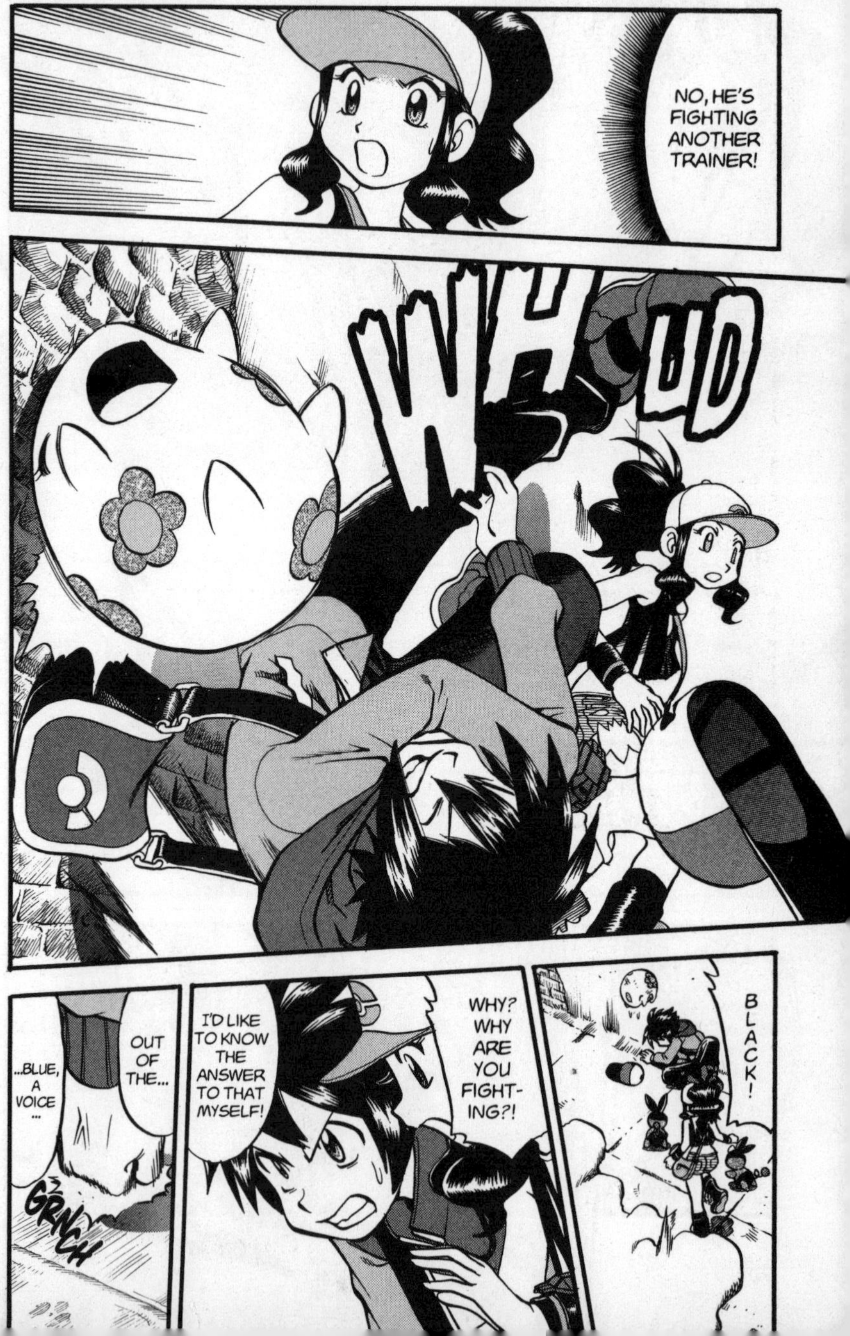
NO, HE'S FIGHTING ANOTHER TRAINER!
WHUD
BLACK!
WHY? WHY ARE YOU FIGHT-ING?!
I'D LIKE TO KNOW THE ANSWER TO THAT MYSELF!
OUT OF THE...
...BLUE, A VOICE ...
GRNCH

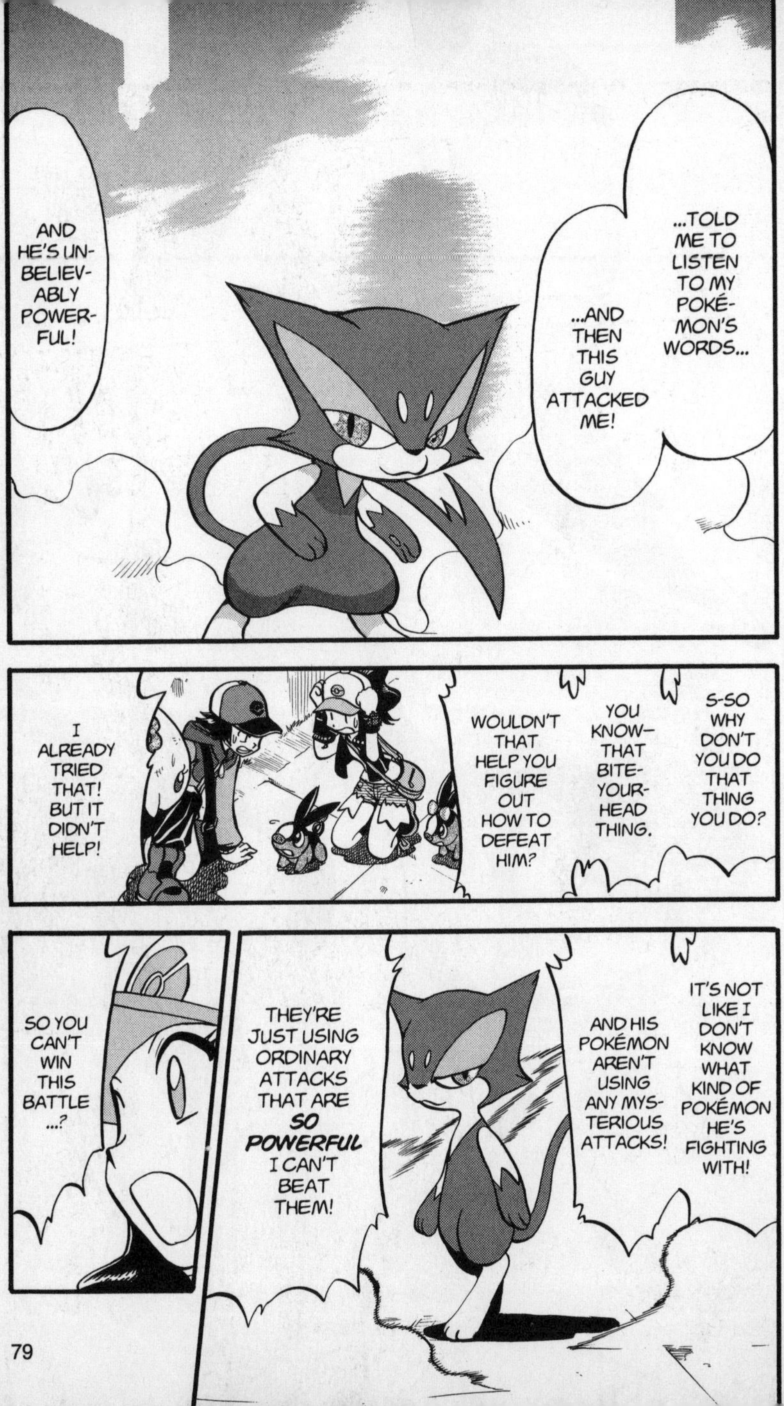
...TOLD ME TO LISTEN TO MY POKÉMON'S WORDS...
...AND THEN THIS GUY ATTACKED ME!
AND HE'S UN-BELIEV-ABLY POWER-FUL!
S-SO WHY DON'T YOU DO THAT THING YOU DO?
YOU KNOW—THAT BITE-YOUR-HEAD THING.
WOULDN'T THAT HELP YOU FIGURE OUT HOW TO DEFEAT HIM?
I ALREADY TRIED THAT! BUT IT DIDN'T HELP!
IT'S NOT LIKE I DON'T KNOW WHAT KIND OF POKÉMON HE'S FIGHTING WITH!
AND HIS POKÉMON AREN'T USING ANY MYS-TERIOUS ATTACKS!
THEY'RE JUST USING ORDINARY ATTACKS THAT ARE ***SO POWERFUL*** I CAN'T BEAT THEM!
SO YOU CAN'T WIN THIS BATTLE ...?

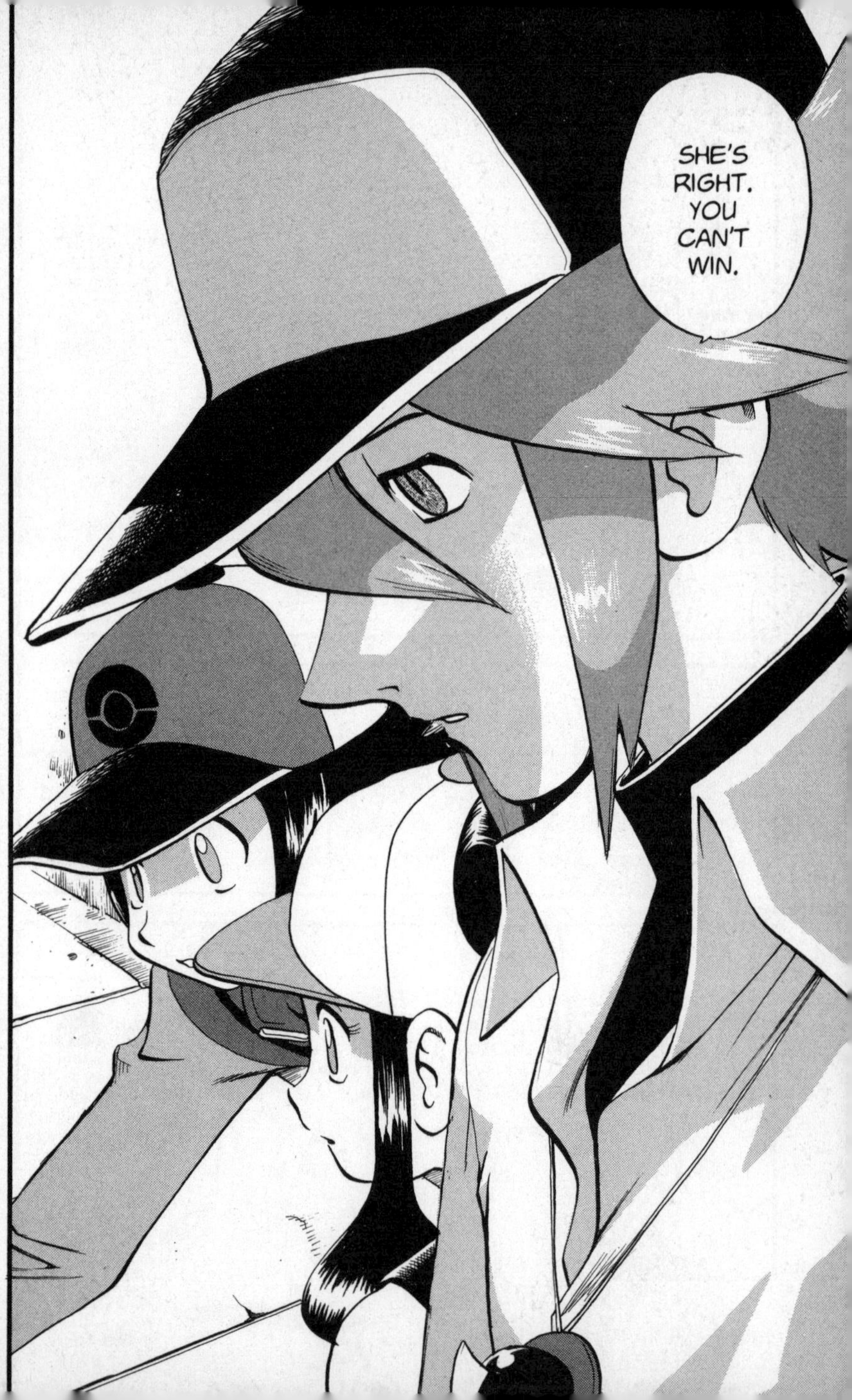
SHE'S RIGHT. YOU CAN'T WIN.

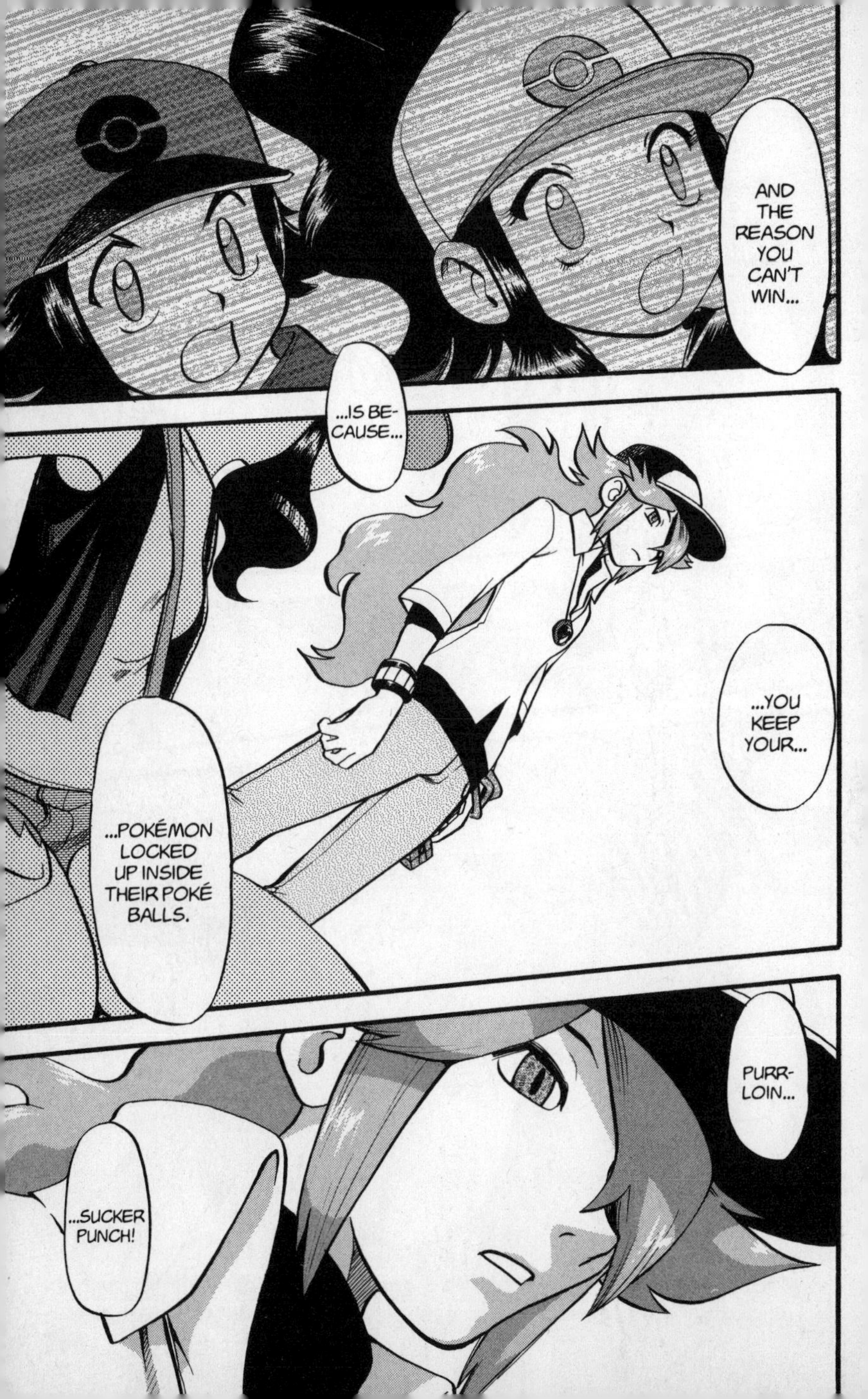
AND THE REASON YOU CAN'T WIN...
...IS BE-CAUSE...
...YOU KEEP YOUR...
...POKÉMON LOCKED UP INSIDE THEIR POKÉ BALLS.
PURR-LOIN...
...SUCKER PUNCH!

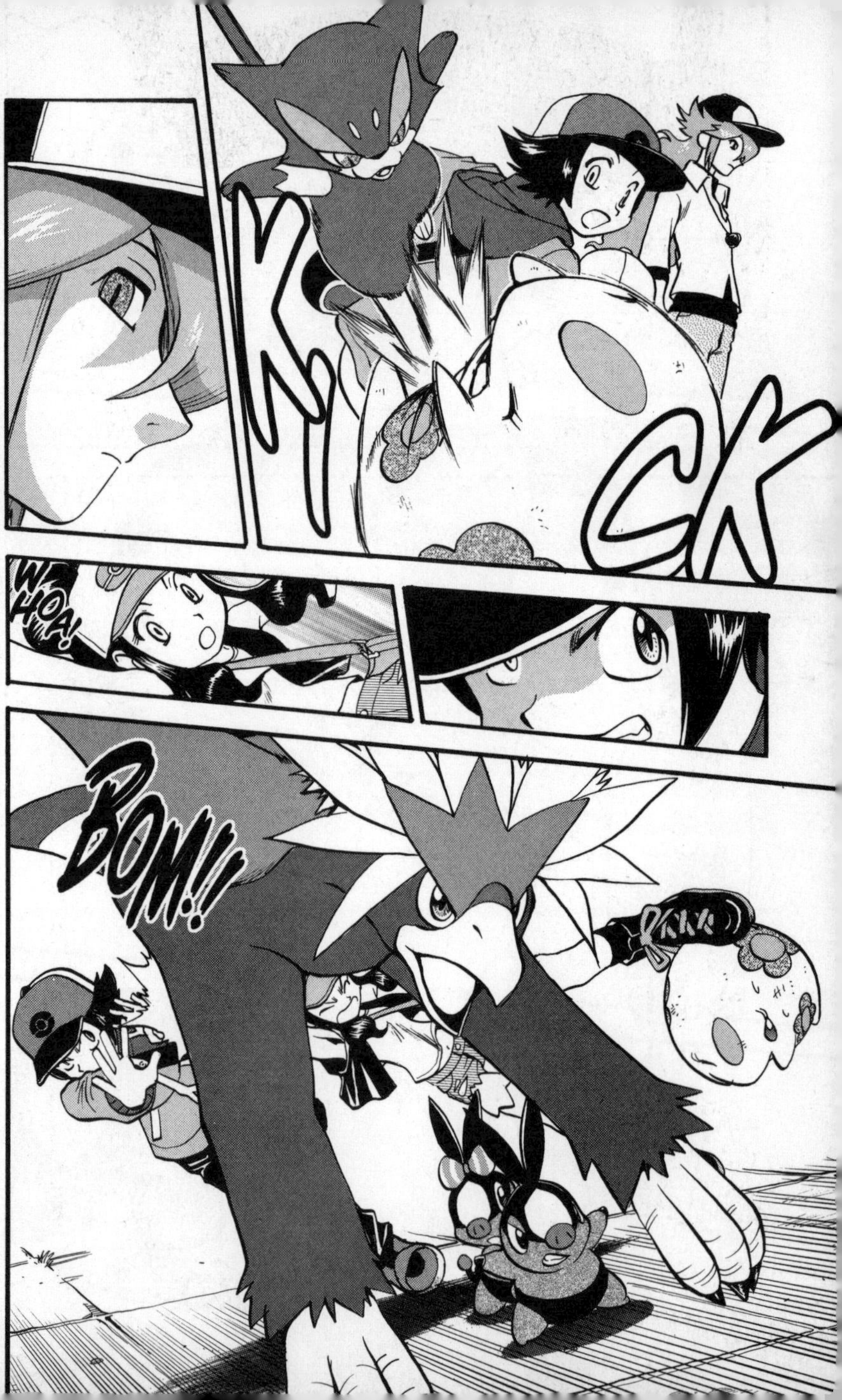
KICK
WHOA!
BOM!!

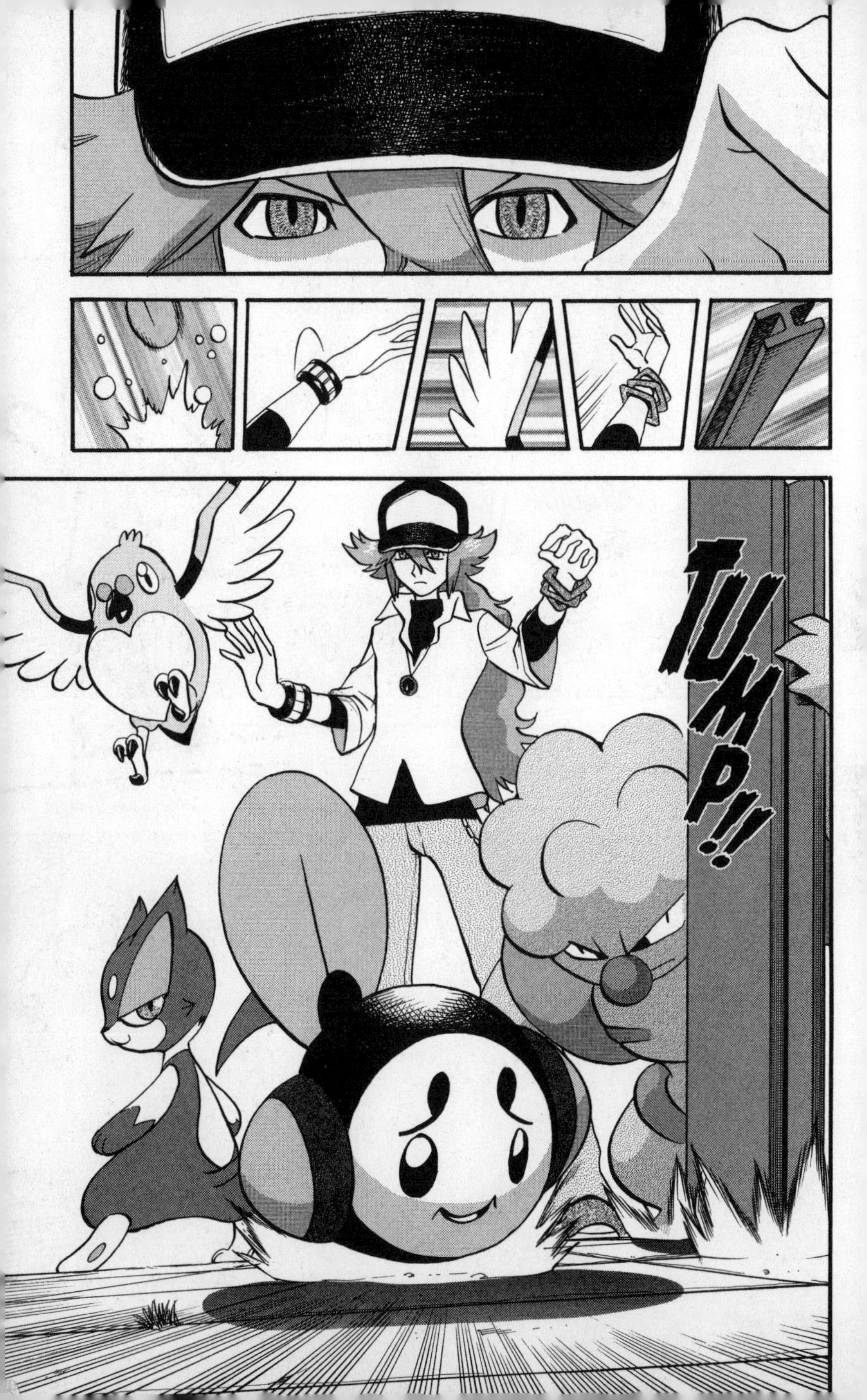
TUMP!!

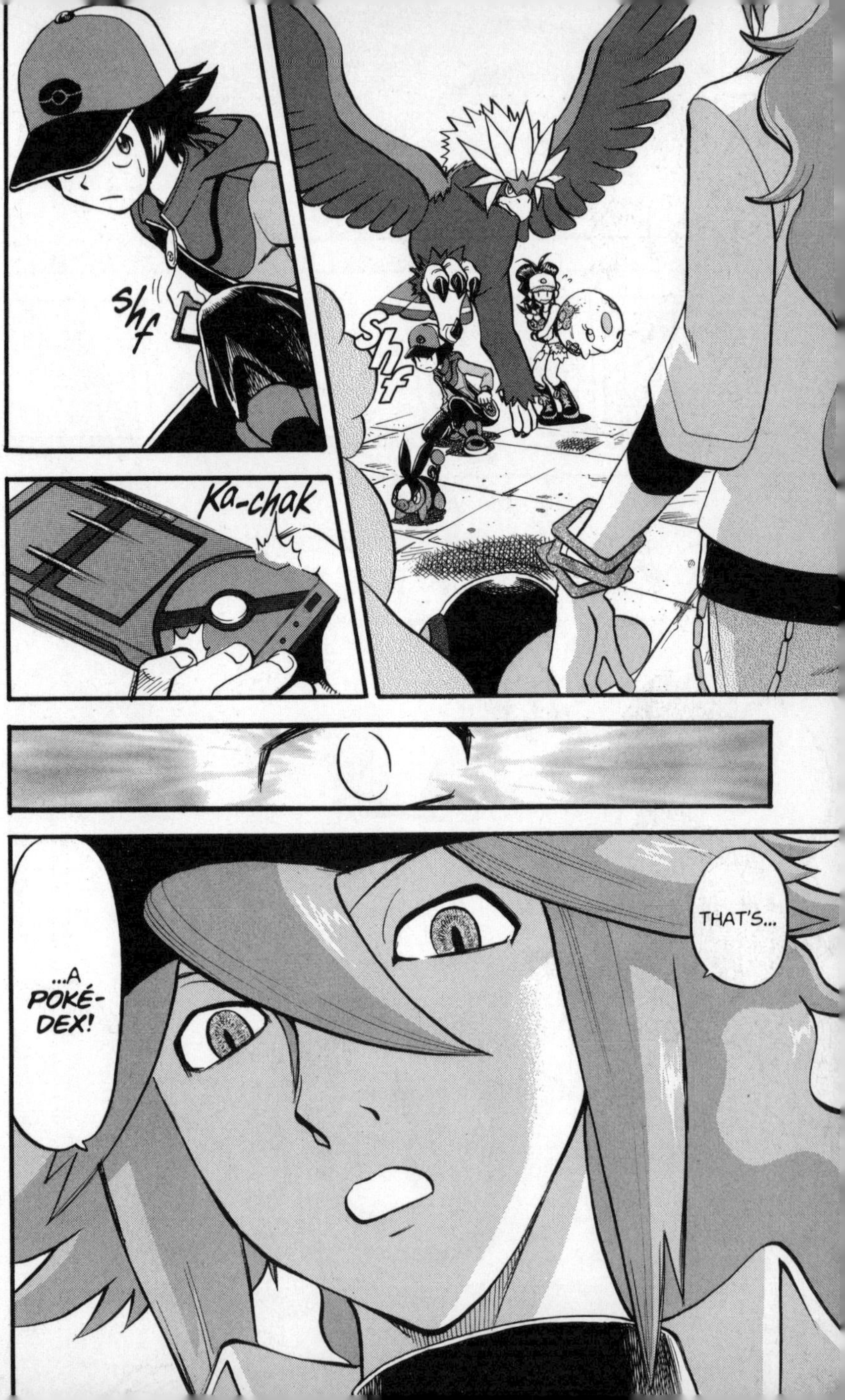
shf
shf
Ka-chak
THAT'S...
...A POKÉ-DEX!

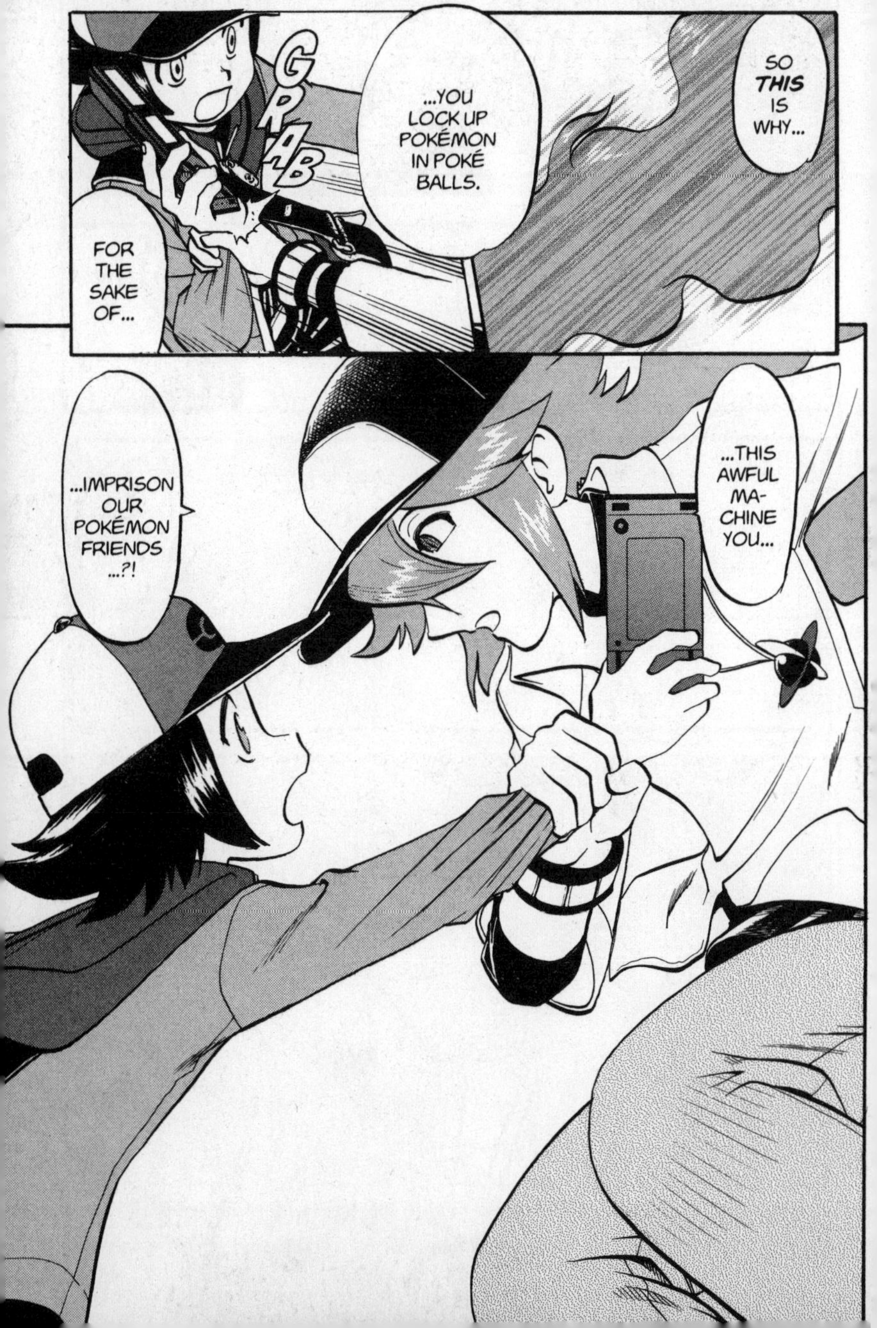
SO THIS IS WHY...
...YOU LOCK UP POKÉMON IN POKÉ BALLS.
GRAB
FOR THE SAKE OF...
...THIS AWFUL MA-CHINE YOU...
...IMPRISON OUR POKÉMON FRIENDS ...?!

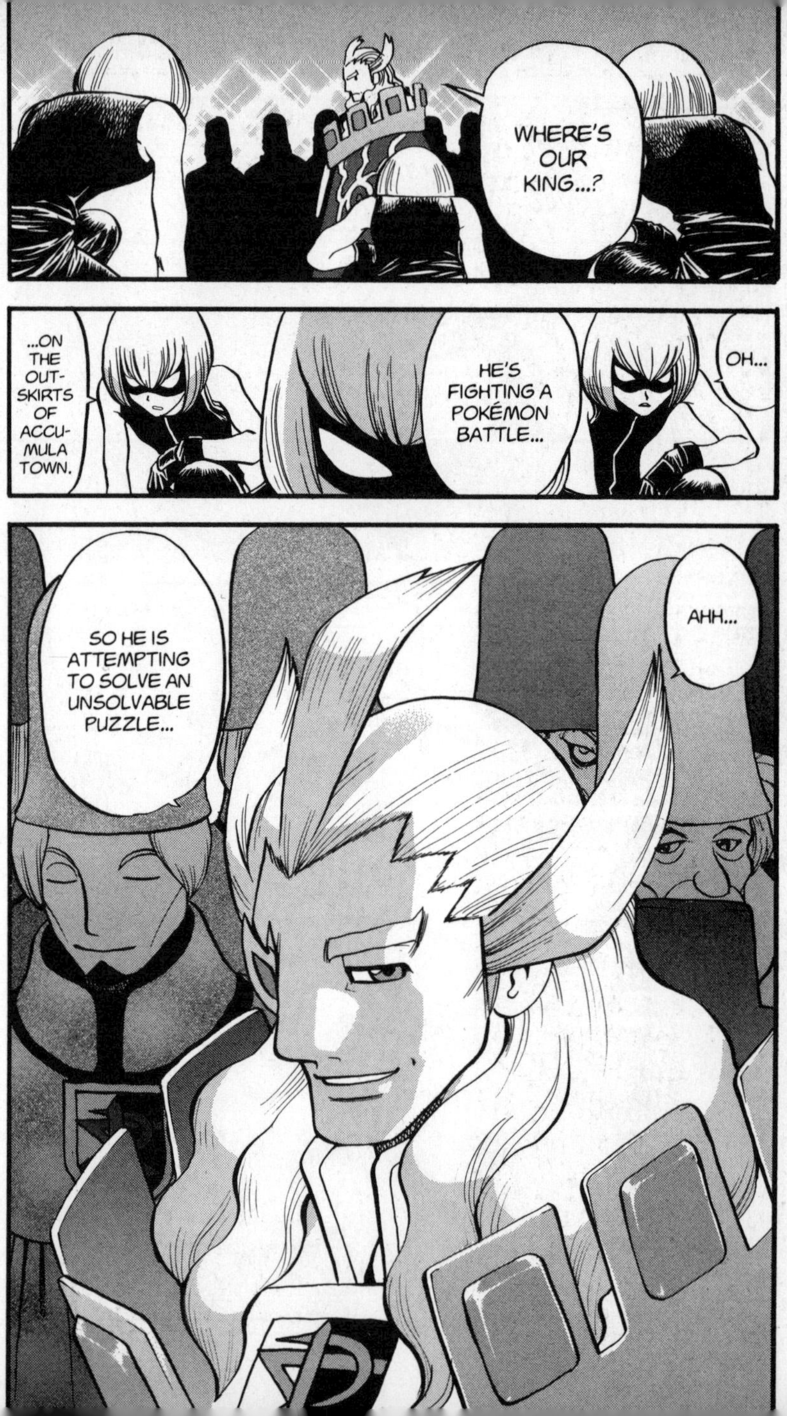
WHERE'S OUR KING...?
OH...
HE'S FIGHTING A POKÉMON BATTLE...
...ON THE OUTSKIRTS OF ACCUMULA TOWN.
AHH...
SO HE IS ATTEMPTING TO SOLVE AN UNSOLVABLE PUZZLE...

ADVENTURE MAP

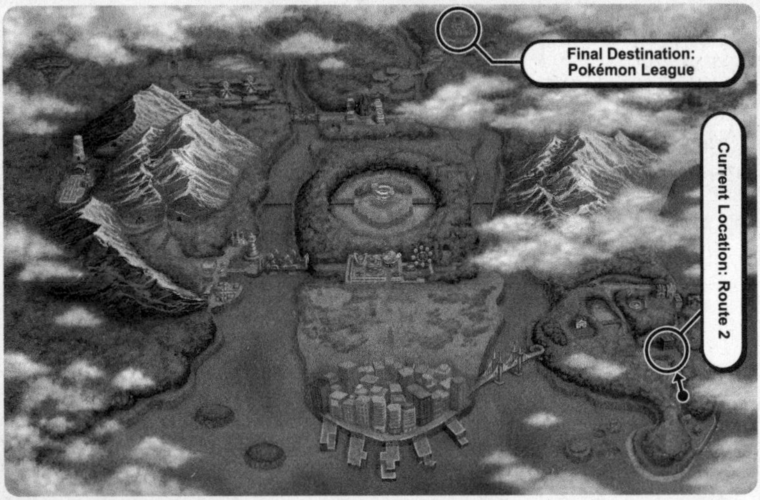
Final Destination: Pokémon League
Current Location: Route 2

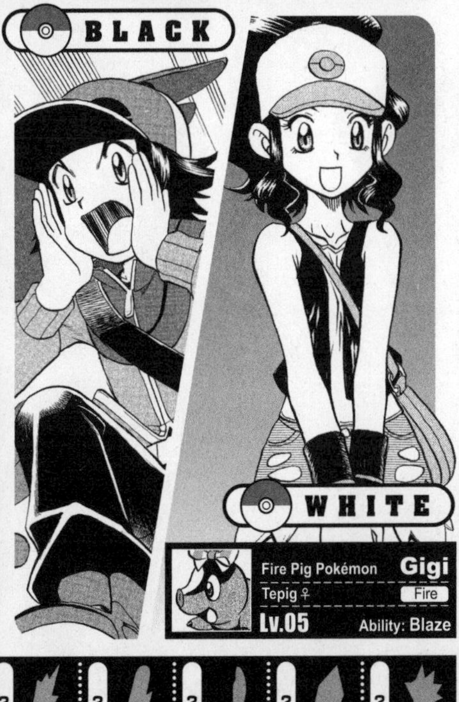
BLACK
WHITE

Tep
Fire Pig Pokémon
Tepig ♂ — Fire
Lv.15 — Ability: Blaze

Musha
Dream Eater Pokémon
Munna ♂ — Psychic
Lv.34 — Ability: Forewarn

Brav
Valiant Pokémon
Braviary ♂ — Normal / Flying
Lv.54 — Ability: Sheer Force

Tula
EleSpider Pokémon
Galvantula ♂ — Bug / Electric
Lv.36 — Ability: Unnerve

Gigi
Fire Pig Pokémon
Tepig ♀ — Fire
Lv.05 — Ability: Blaze

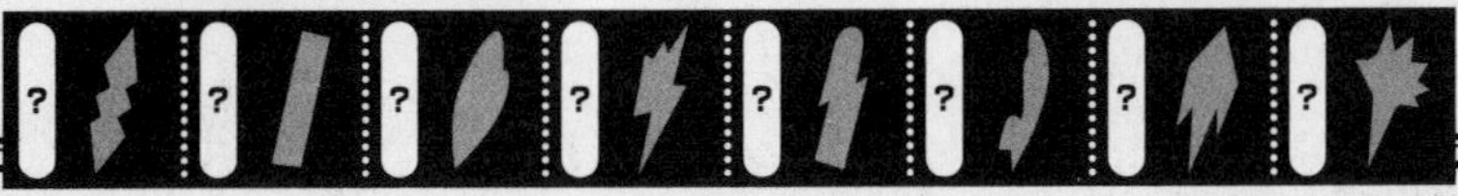
?
?
?
?
?
?
?
?

Pokémon™ Adventures Black & White

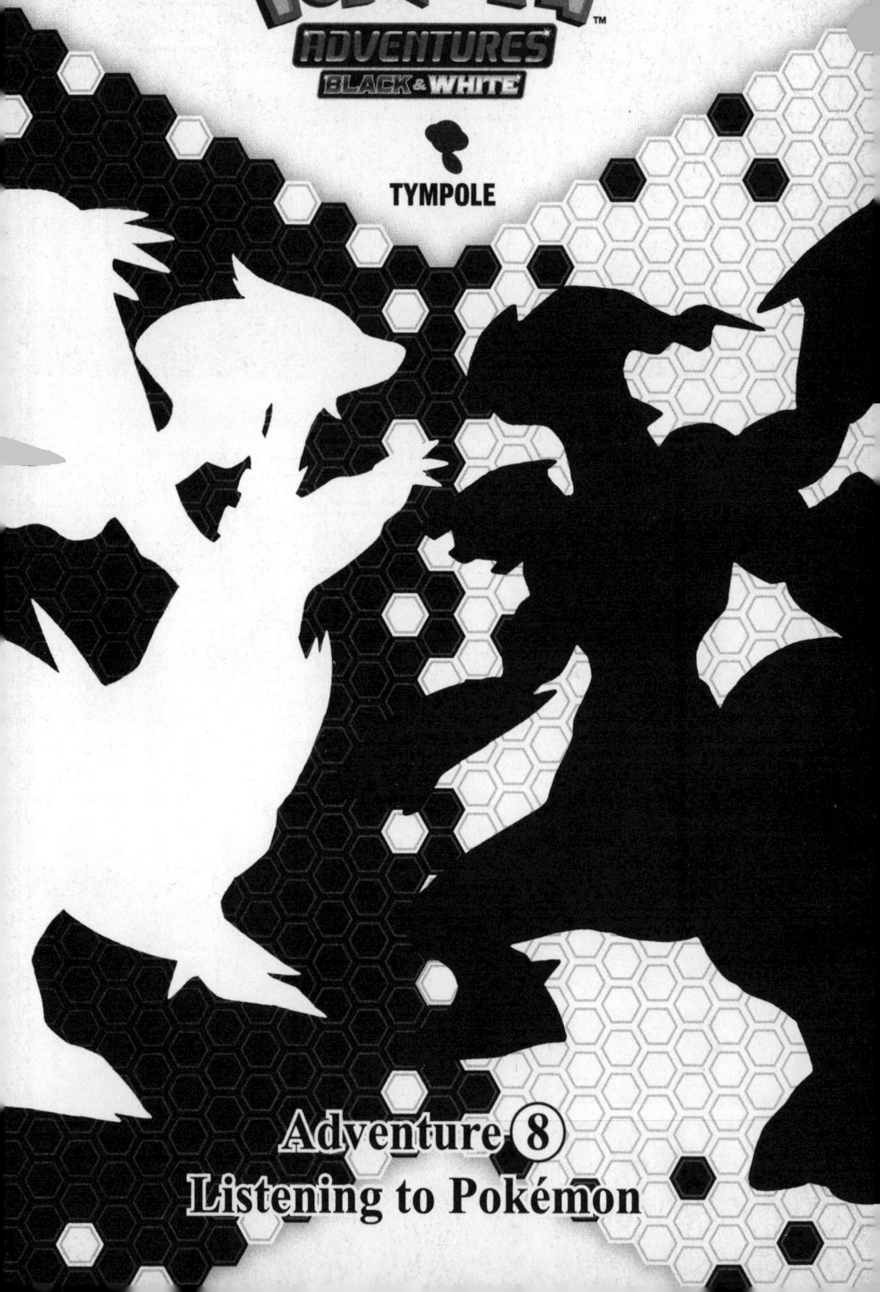
TYMPOLE

Adventure 8
Listening to Pokémon

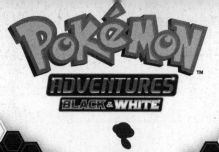

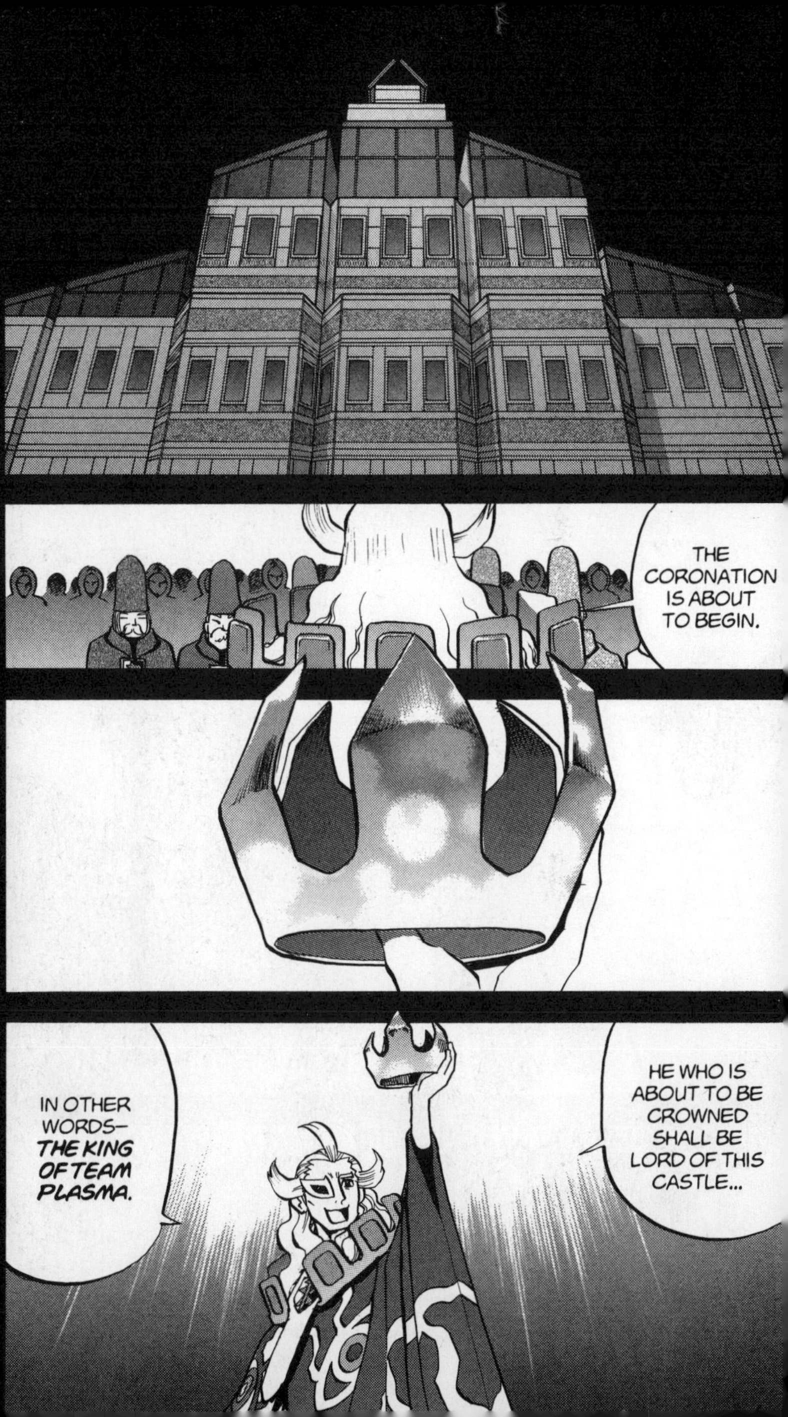
THE CORONATION IS ABOUT TO BEGIN.
HE WHO IS ABOUT TO BE CROWNED SHALL BE LORD OF THIS CASTLE...
IN OTHER WORDS— ***THE KING OF TEAM PLASMA.***

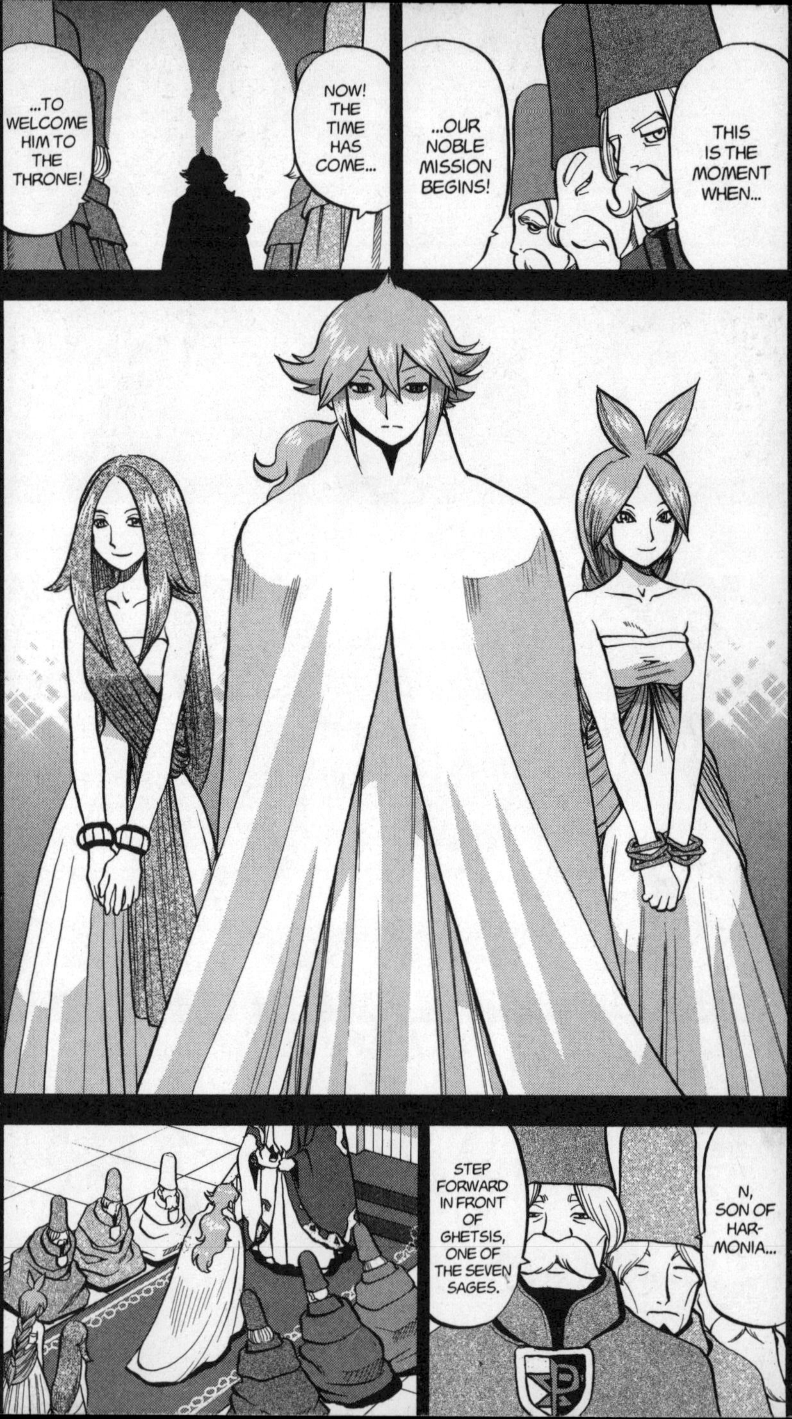
THIS IS THE MOMENT WHEN...
...OUR NOBLE MISSION BEGINS!
NOW! THE TIME HAS COME...
...TO WELCOME HIM TO THE THRONE!
N, SON OF HAR-MONIA...
STEP FORWARD IN FRONT OF GHETSIS, ONE OF THE SEVEN SAGES.

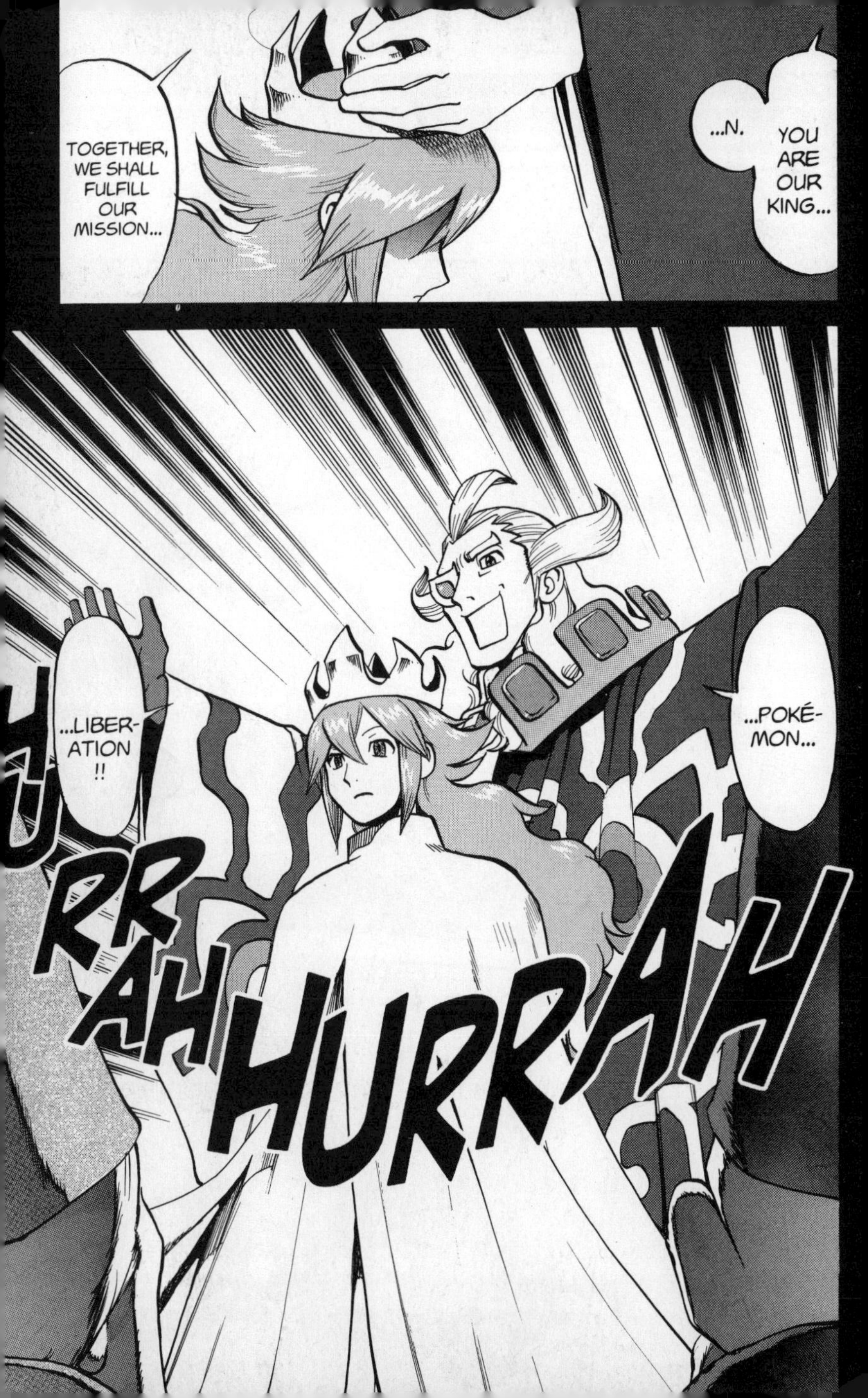
...N.
YOU ARE OUR KING...
TOGETHER, WE SHALL FULFILL OUR MISSION...
...POKÉMON...
...LIBERATION!!
HURRAH
HURRAH

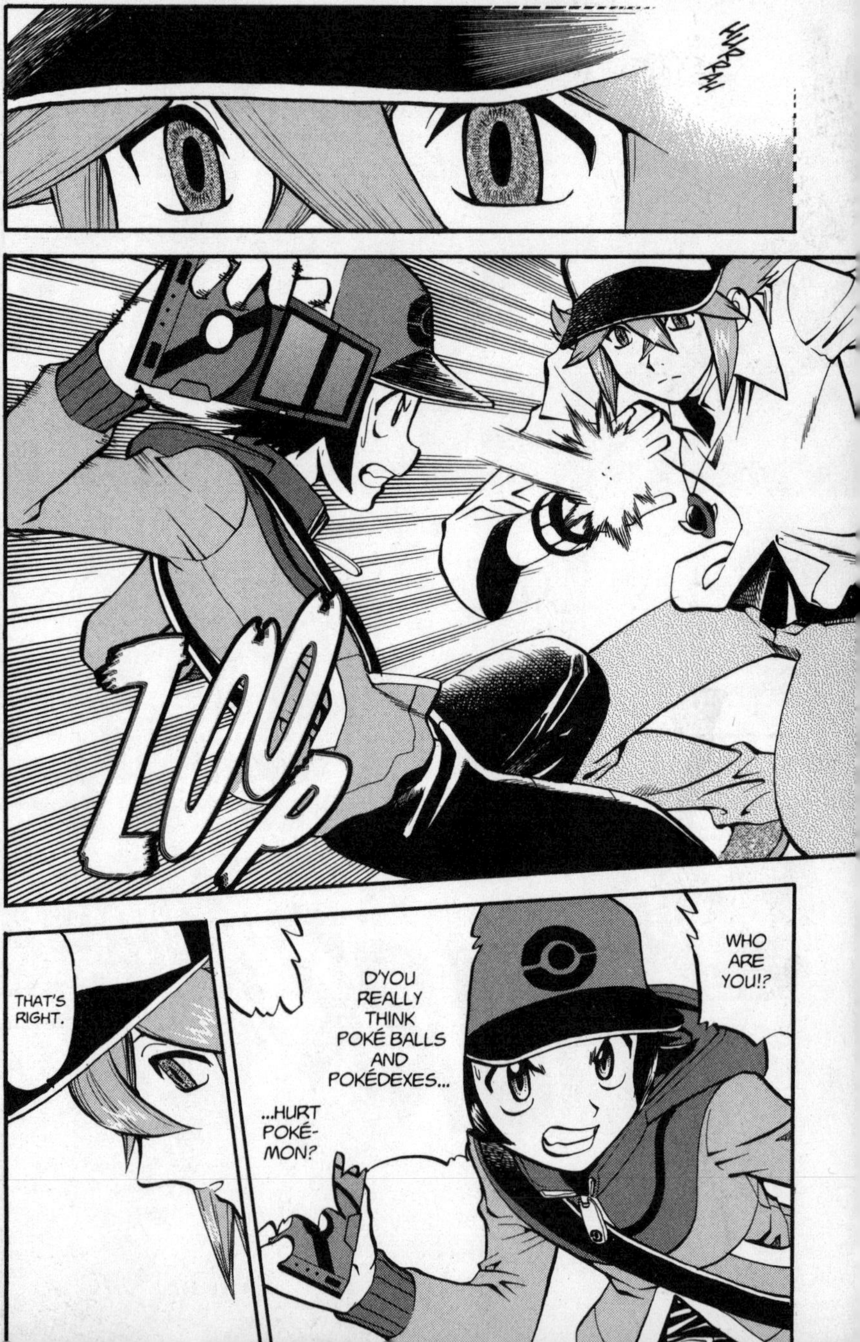
HWRRAH
ZOOP
WHO ARE YOU!?
D'YOU REALLY THINK POKÉ BALLS AND POKÉDEXES...
...HURT POKÉMON?
THAT'S RIGHT.

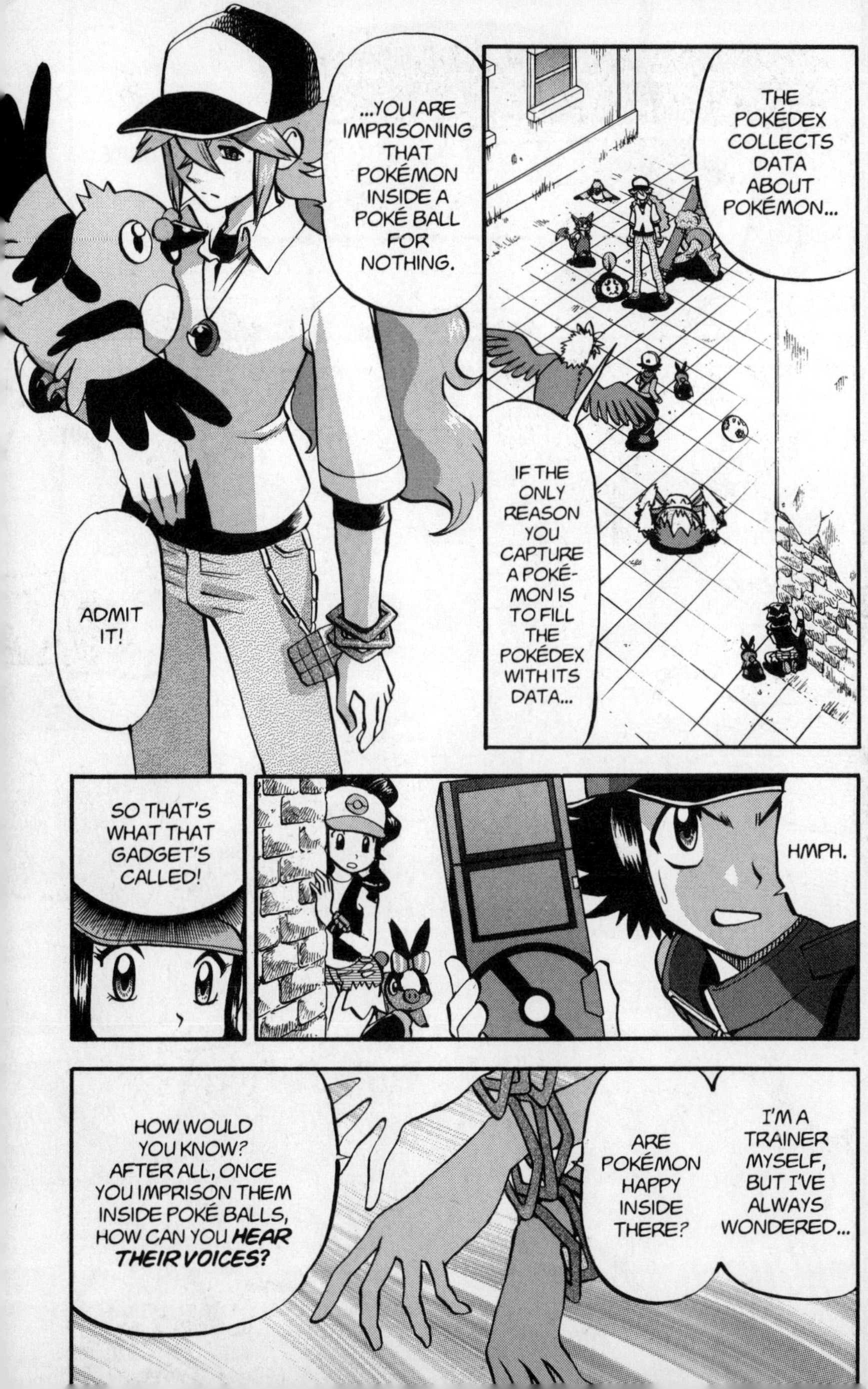
THE POKÉDEX COLLECTS DATA ABOUT POKÉMON...
IF THE ONLY REASON YOU CAPTURE A POKÉ-MON IS TO FILL THE POKÉDEX WITH ITS DATA...
...YOU ARE IMPRISONING THAT POKÉMON INSIDE A POKÉ BALL FOR NOTHING.
ADMIT IT!
HMPH.
SO THAT'S WHAT THAT GADGET'S CALLED!
I'M A TRAINER MYSELF, BUT I'VE ALWAYS WONDERED...
ARE POKÉMON HAPPY INSIDE THERE?
HOW WOULD YOU KNOW? AFTER ALL, ONCE YOU IMPRISON THEM INSIDE POKÉ BALLS, HOW CAN YOU ***HEAR THEIR VOICES?***

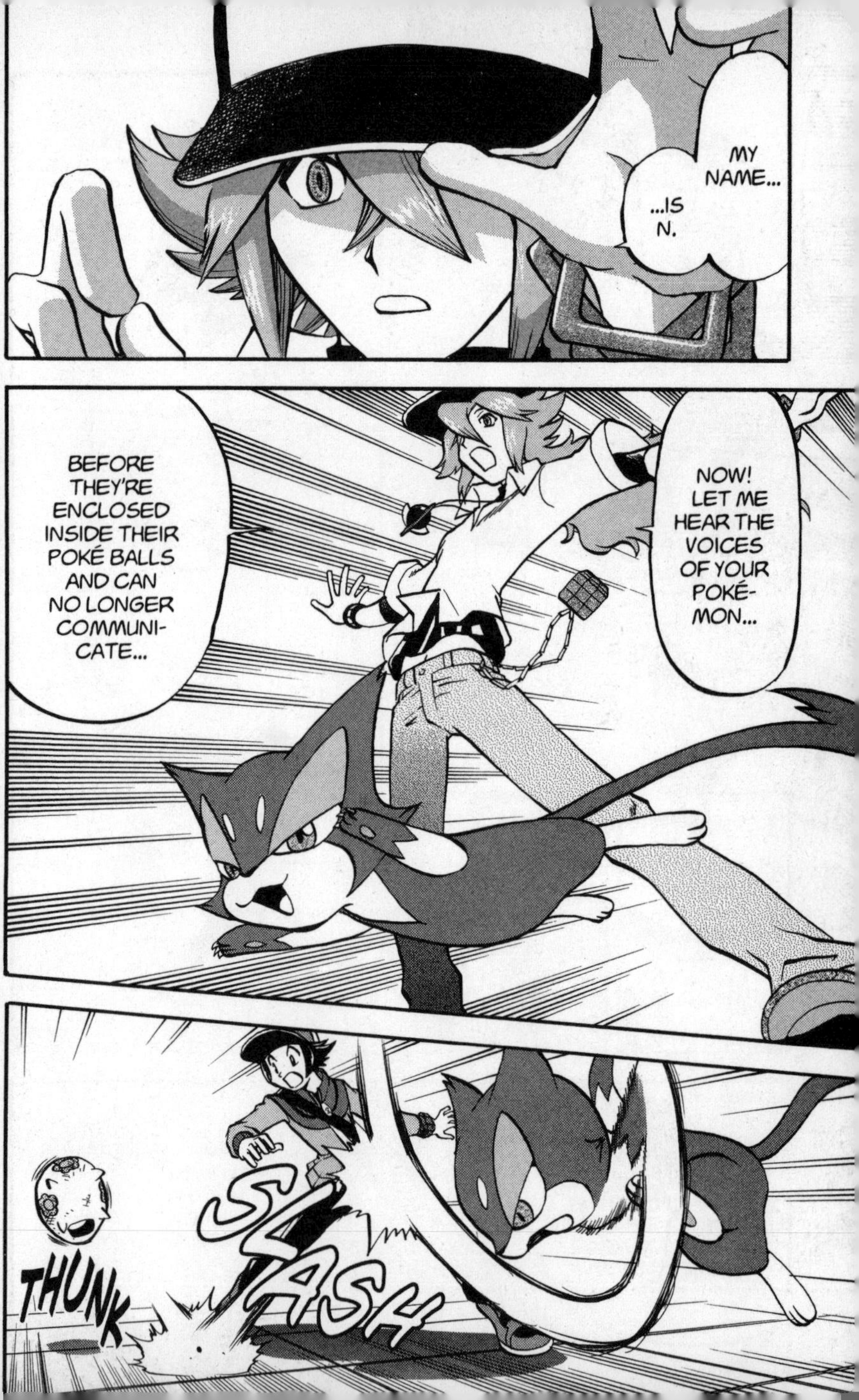
MY NAME...
...IS N.
NOW! LET ME HEAR THE VOICES OF YOUR POKÉ-MON...
BEFORE THEY'RE ENCLOSED INSIDE THEIR POKÉ BALLS AND CAN NO LONGER COMMUNI-CATE...
SLASH
THUNK

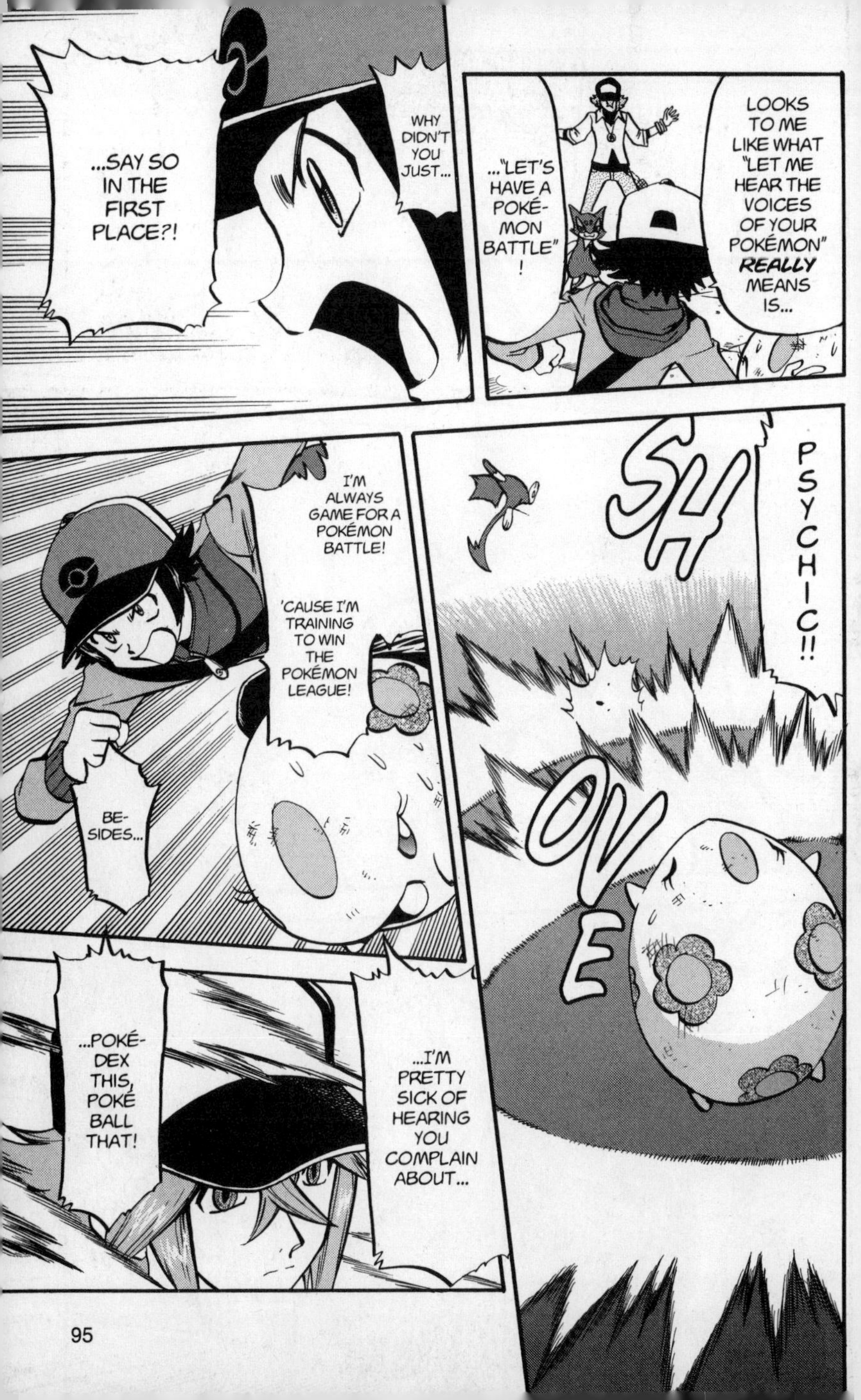

LOOKS TO ME LIKE WHAT "LET ME HEAR THE VOICES OF YOUR POKÉMON" ***REALLY*** MEANS IS...
..."LET'S HAVE A POKÉ-MON BATTLE"!
WHY DIDN'T YOU JUST...
...SAY SO IN THE FIRST PLACE?!
PSYCHIC!!
SHOVE
I'M ALWAYS GAME FOR A POKÉMON BATTLE!
'CAUSE I'M TRAINING TO WIN THE POKÉMON LEAGUE!
BE-SIDES...
...I'M PRETTY SICK OF HEARING YOU COMPLAIN ABOUT...
...POKÉ-DEX THIS, POKÉ BALL THAT!

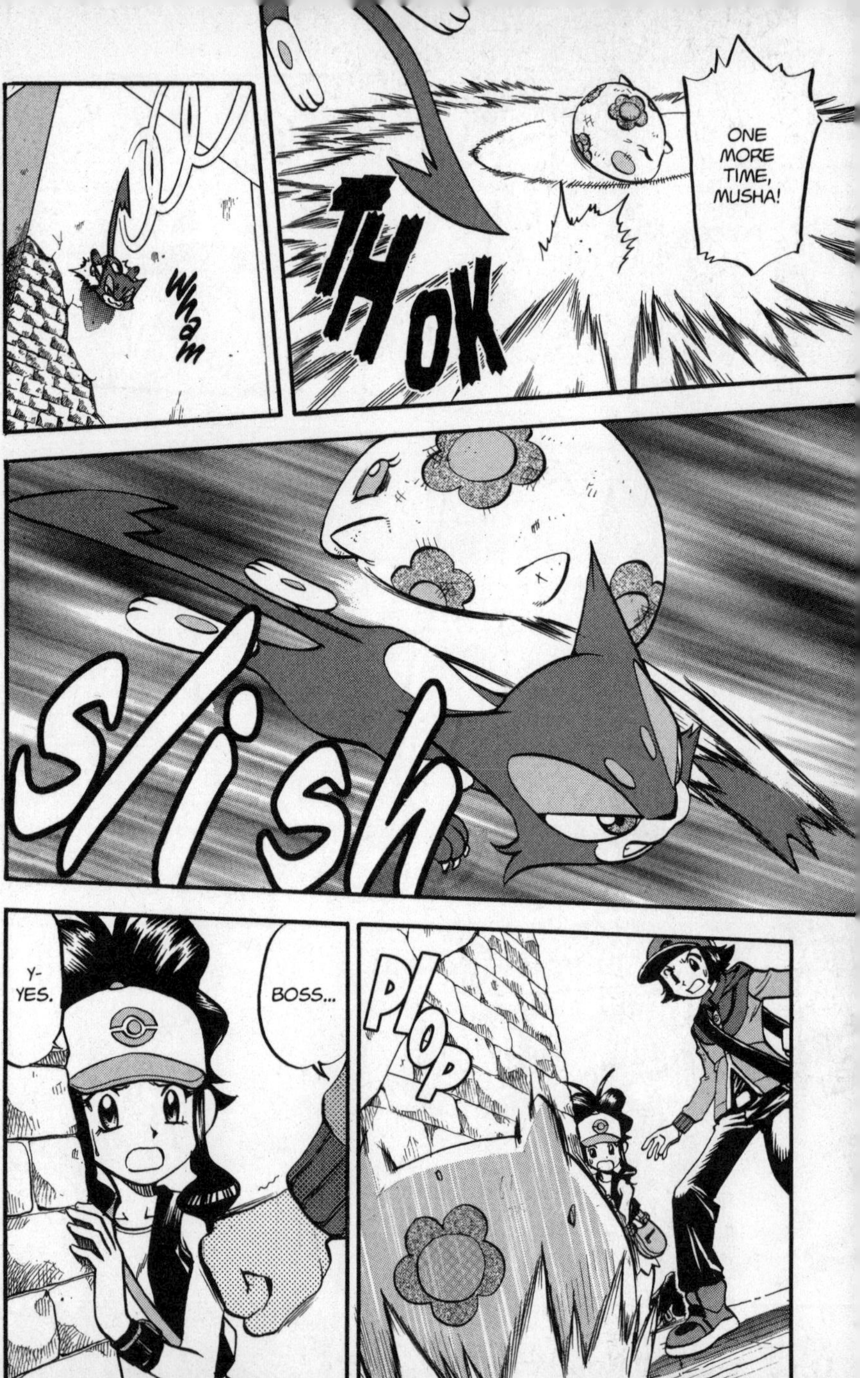
ONE MORE TIME, MUSHA!
THOK
wham
slish
PLOP
BOSS...
Y-YES.

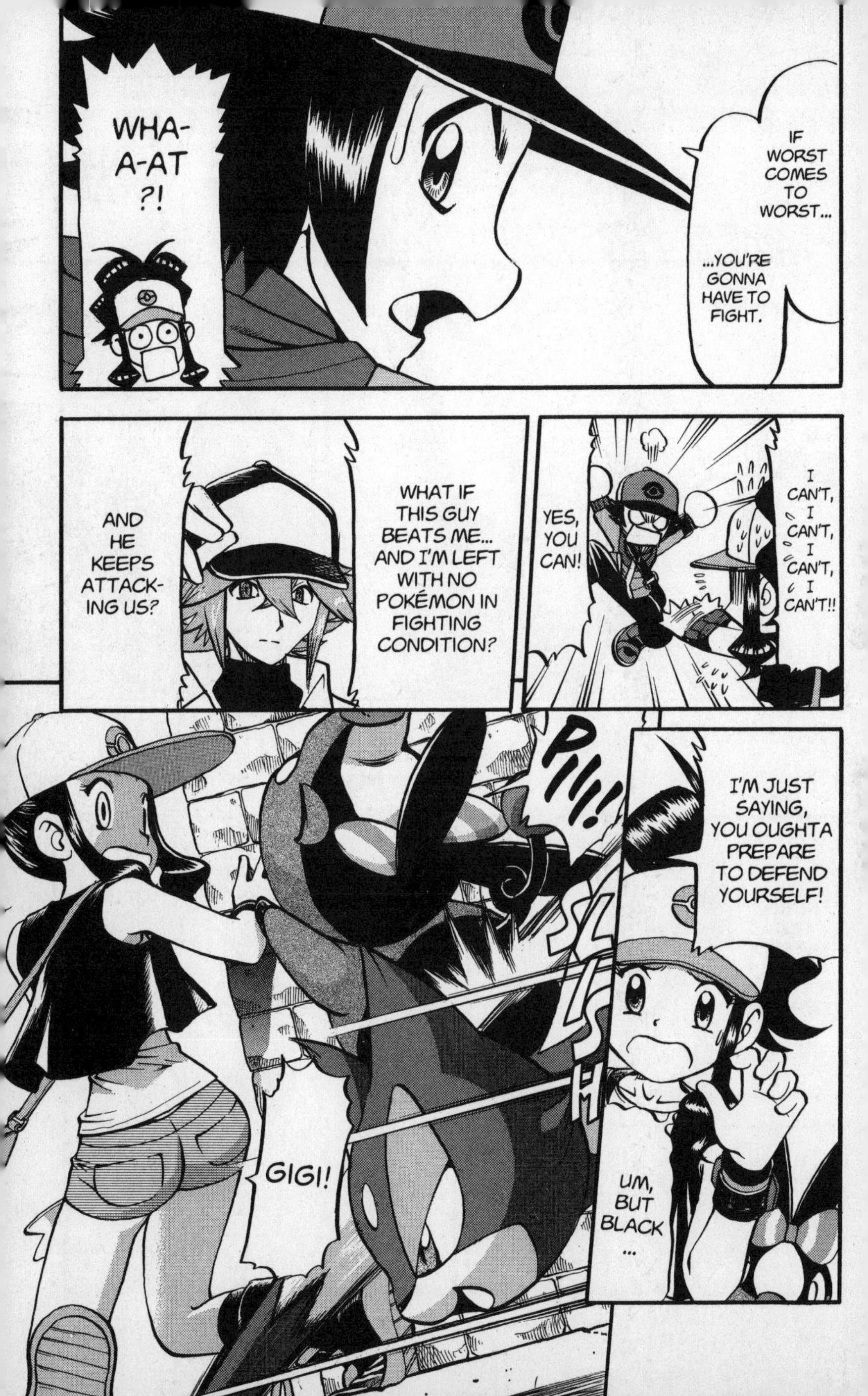
IF WORST COMES TO WORST...
...YOU'RE GONNA HAVE TO FIGHT.
WHA-A-AT?!
I CAN'T, I CAN'T, I CAN'T, I CAN'T!!
YES, YOU CAN!
WHAT IF THIS GUY BEATS ME... AND I'M LEFT WITH NO POKÉMON IN FIGHTING CONDITION?
AND HE KEEPS ATTACK-ING US?
I'M JUST SAYING, YOU OUGHTA PREPARE TO DEFEND YOURSELF!
UM, BUT BLACK ...
PI!!
GIGI!

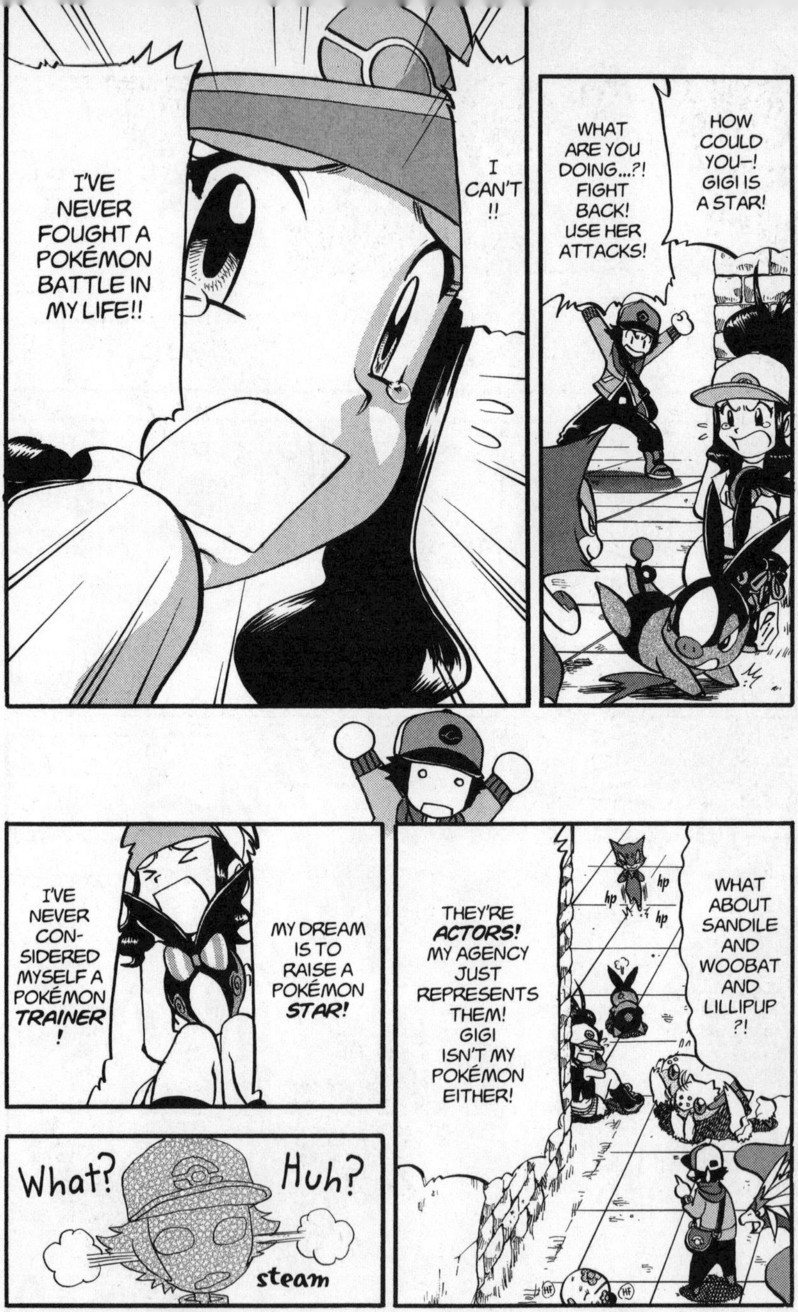
HOW COULD YOU–! GIGI IS A STAR!
WHAT ARE YOU DOING...?! FIGHT BACK! USE HER ATTACKS!
I CAN'T !!
I'VE NEVER FOUGHT A POKÉMON BATTLE IN MY LIFE!!
WHAT ABOUT SANDILE AND WOOBAT AND LILLIPUP ?!
hp
hp
hp
THEY'RE **ACTORS!** MY AGENCY JUST REPRESENTS THEM! GIGI ISN'T MY POKÉMON EITHER!
MY DREAM IS TO RAISE A POKÉMON **STAR!**
I'VE NEVER CONSIDERED MYSELF A POKÉMON **TRAINER** !
Huh?
What?
steam

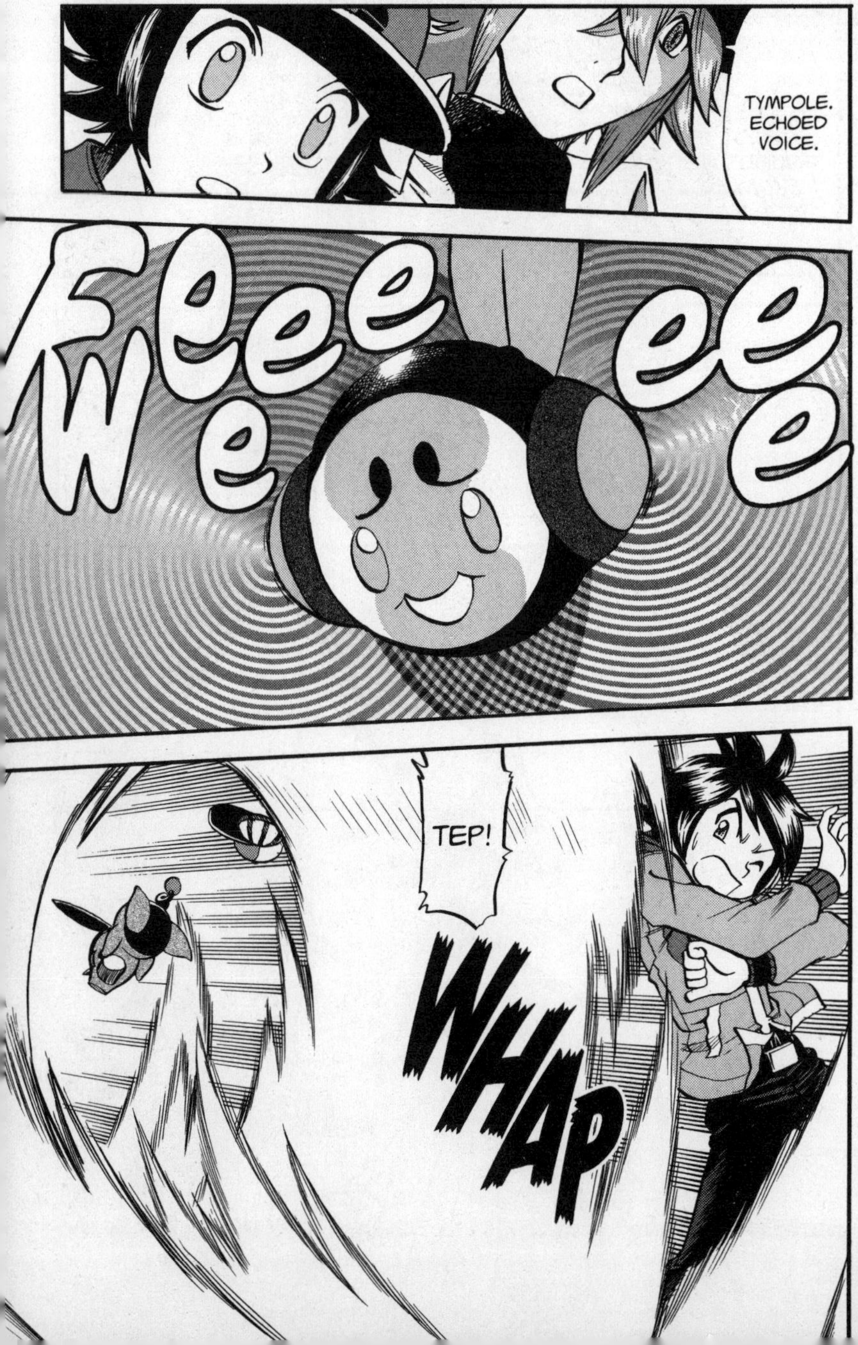
TYMPOLE. ECHOED VOICE.
FWEEEEEEEE
TEP!
WHAP

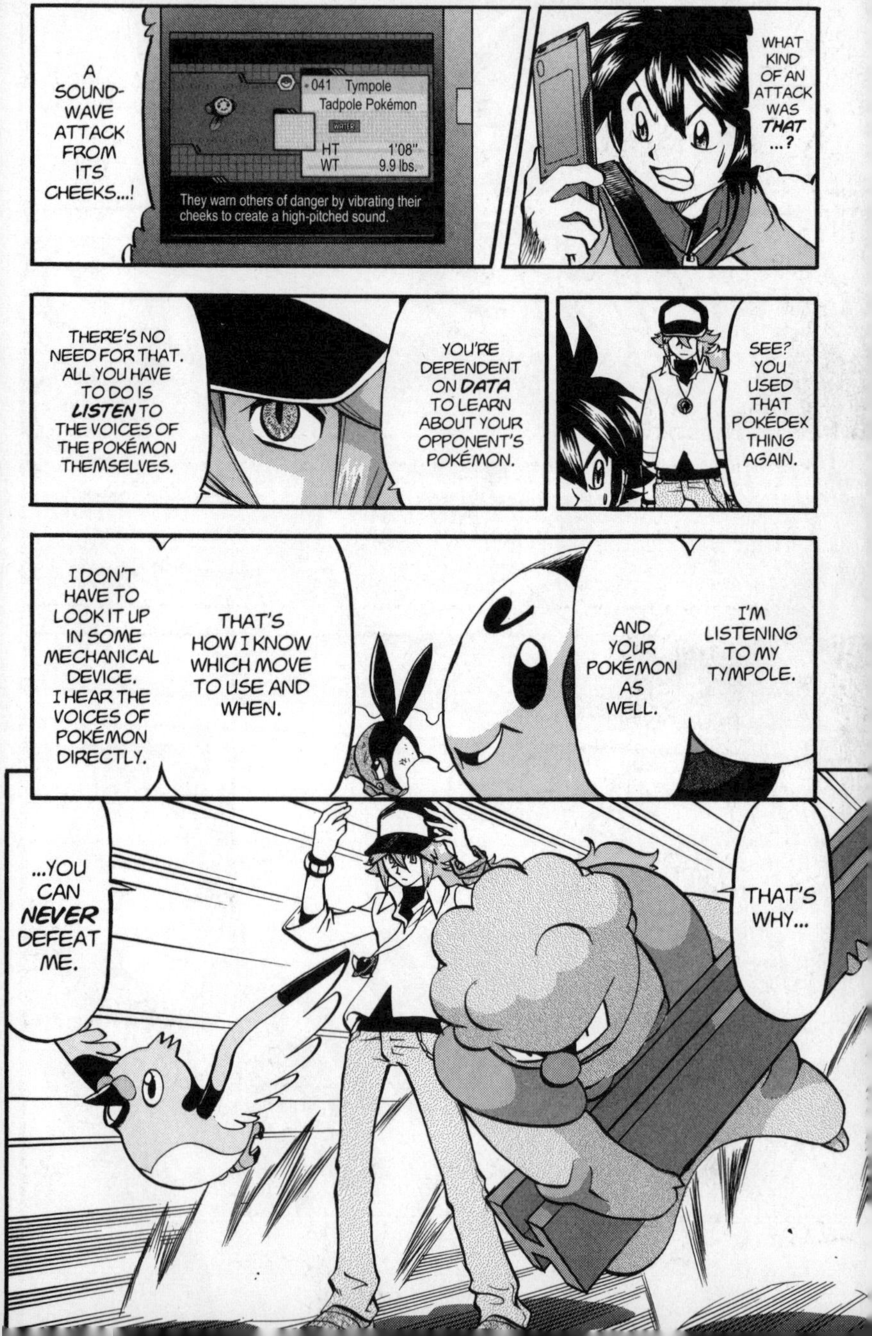
WHAT KIND OF AN ATTACK WAS THAT...?
041 Tympole
Tadpole Pokémon
WATER
HT 1'08"
WT 9.9 lbs.
They warn others of danger by vibrating their cheeks to create a high-pitched sound.
A SOUND-WAVE ATTACK FROM ITS CHEEKS...!
SEE? YOU USED THAT POKÉDEX THING AGAIN.
YOU'RE DEPENDENT ON DATA TO LEARN ABOUT YOUR OPPONENT'S POKÉMON.
THERE'S NO NEED FOR THAT. ALL YOU HAVE TO DO IS LISTEN TO THE VOICES OF THE POKÉMON THEMSELVES.
I'M LISTENING TO MY TYMPOLE.
AND YOUR POKÉMON AS WELL.
THAT'S HOW I KNOW WHICH MOVE TO USE AND WHEN.
I DON'T HAVE TO LOOK IT UP IN SOME MECHANICAL DEVICE. I HEAR THE VOICES OF POKÉMON DIRECTLY.
THAT'S WHY...
...YOU CAN NEVER DEFEAT ME.

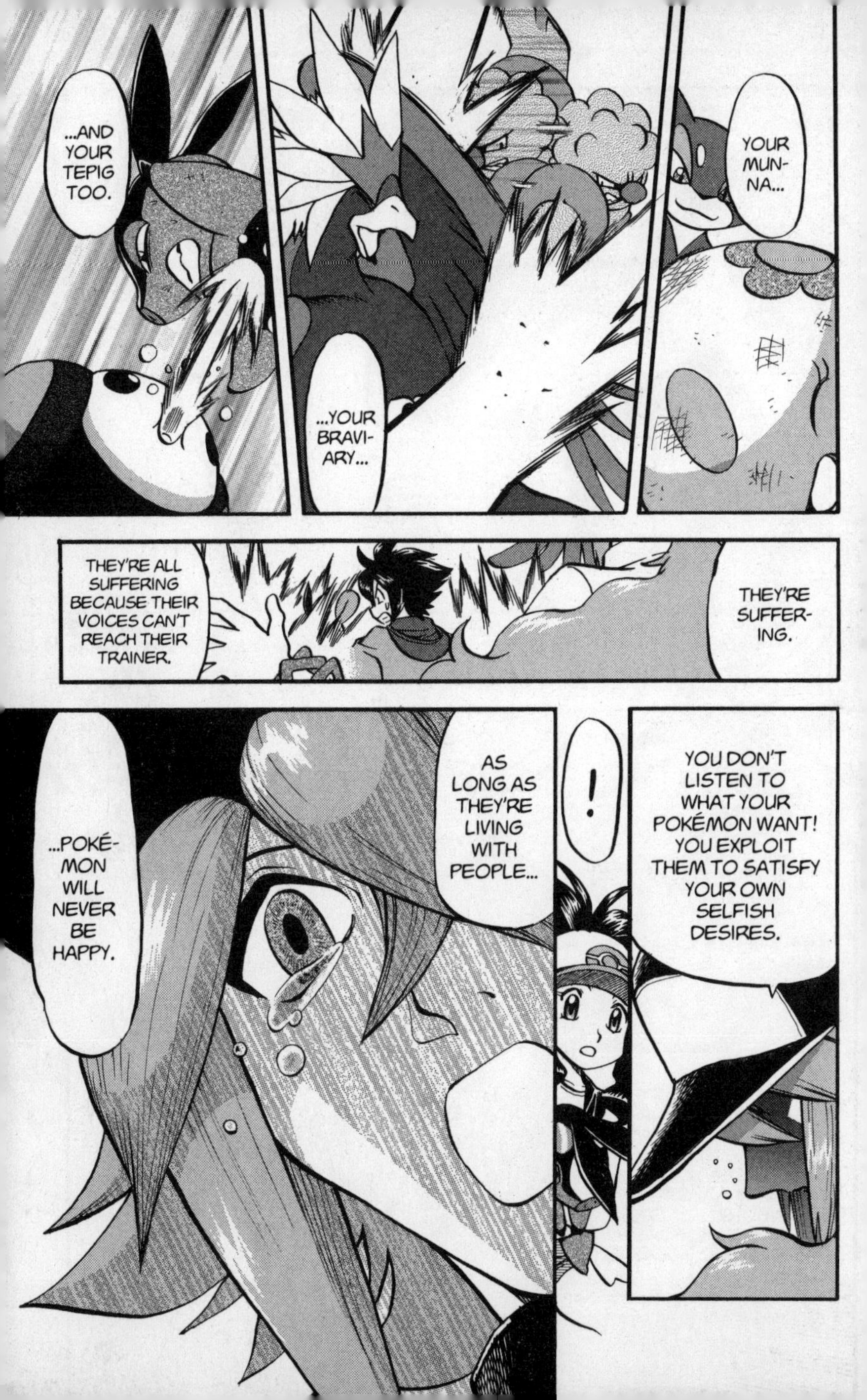
YOUR MUNNA...
...YOUR BRAVIARY...
...AND YOUR TEPIG TOO.
THEY'RE SUFFERING.
THEY'RE ALL SUFFERING BECAUSE THEIR VOICES CAN'T REACH THEIR TRAINER.
YOU DON'T LISTEN TO WHAT YOUR POKÉMON WANT! YOU EXPLOIT THEM TO SATISFY YOUR OWN SELFISH DESIRES.
!
AS LONG AS THEY'RE LIVING WITH PEOPLE...
...POKÉMON WILL NEVER BE HAPPY.

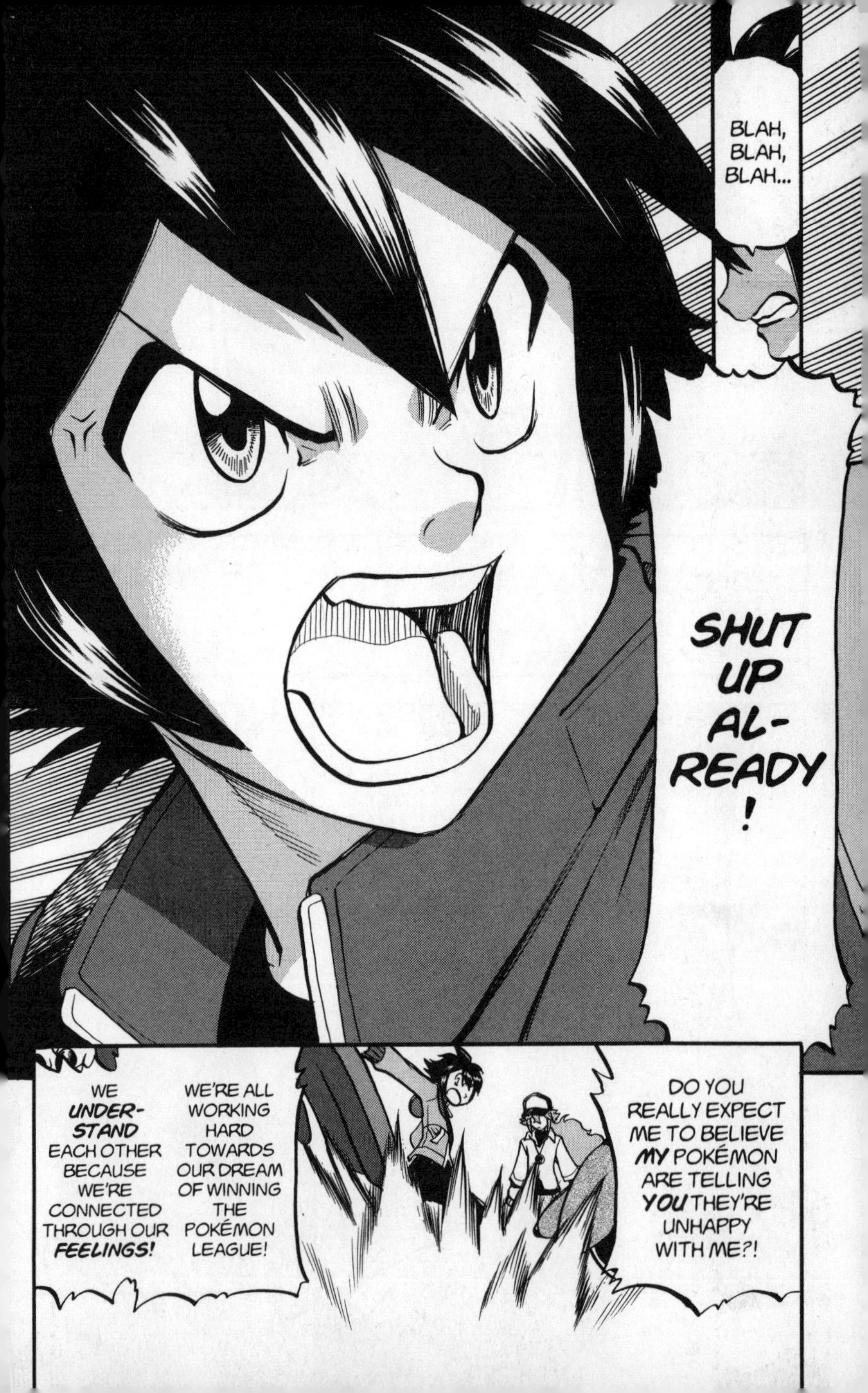

BLAH, BLAH, BLAH...
SHUT UP AL-READY!
DO YOU REALLY EXPECT ME TO BELIEVE *MY* POKÉMON ARE TELLING *YOU* THEY'RE UNHAPPY WITH ME?!
WE'RE ALL WORKING HARD TOWARDS OUR DREAM OF WINNING THE POKÉMON LEAGUE!
WE *UNDERSTAND* EACH OTHER BECAUSE WE'RE CONNECTED THROUGH OUR *FEELINGS!*

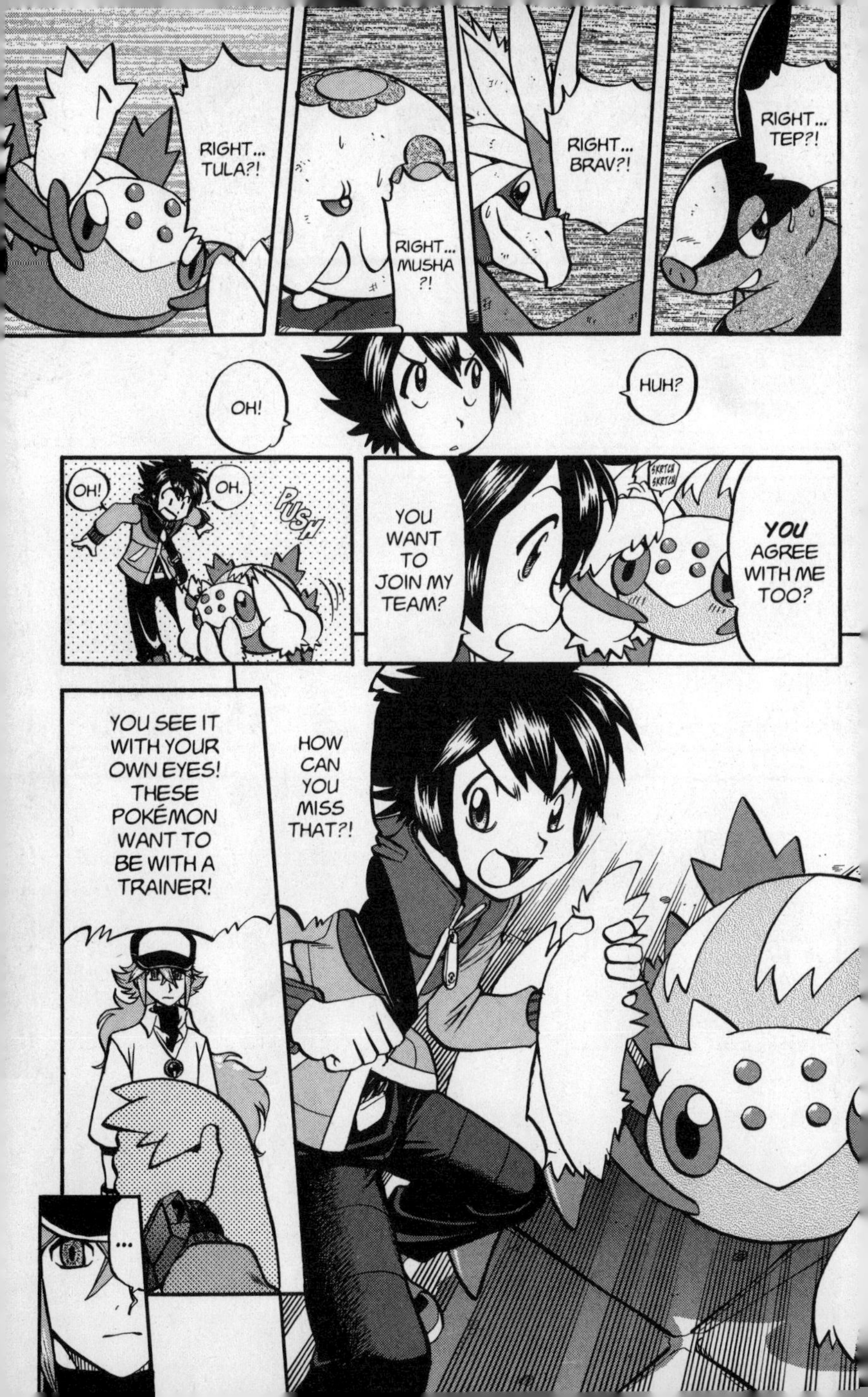
RIGHT... TEP?!
RIGHT... BRAV?!
RIGHT... MUSHA ?!
RIGHT... TULA?!
HUH?
OH!
YOU AGREE WITH ME TOO?
SKRTCH SKRTCH
YOU WANT TO JOIN MY TEAM?
OH.
OH!
PUSH
HOW CAN YOU MISS THAT?!
YOU SEE IT WITH YOUR OWN EYES! THESE POKÉMON WANT TO BE WITH A TRAINER!
...

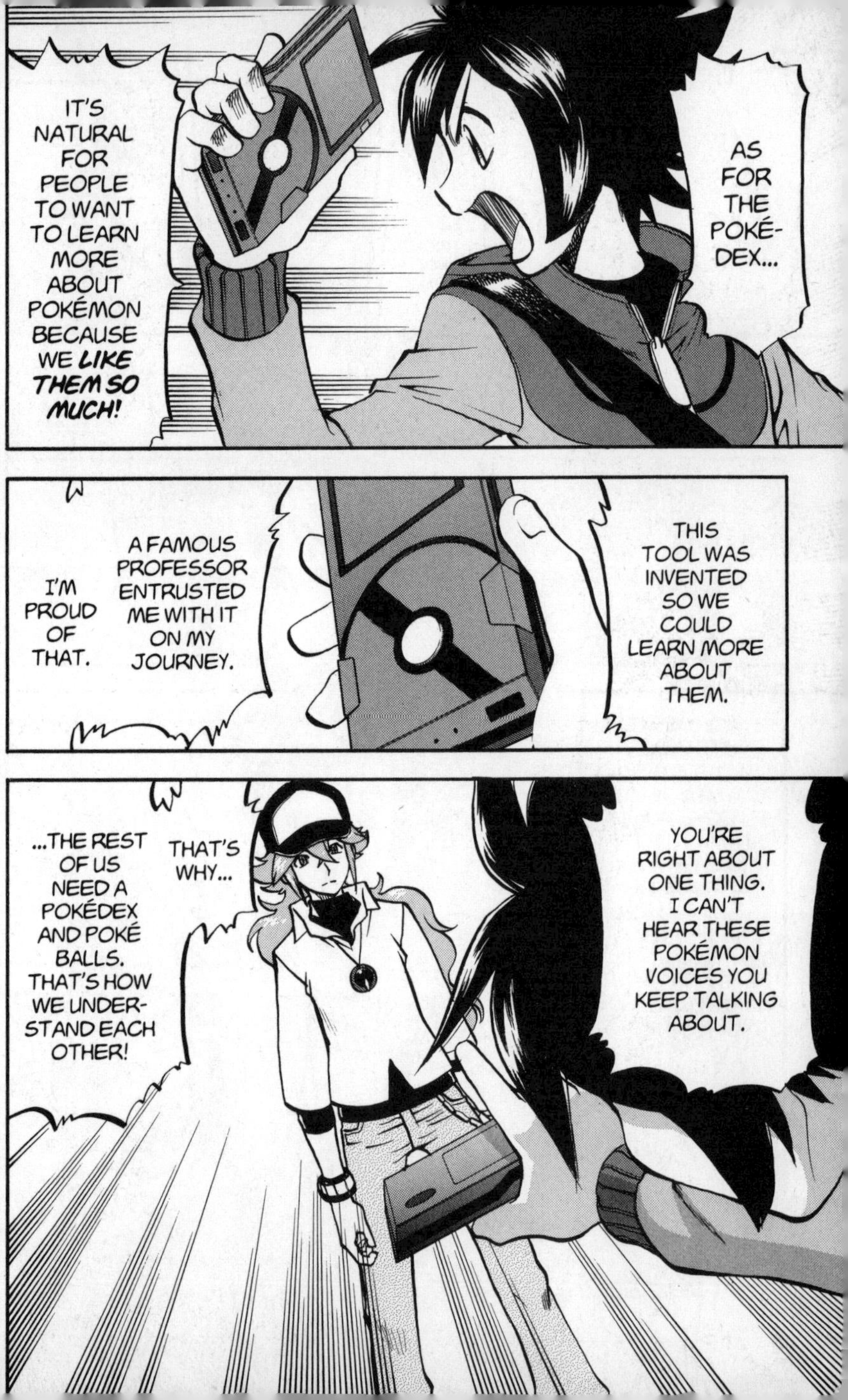
AS FOR THE POKÉDEX...
IT'S NATURAL FOR PEOPLE TO WANT TO LEARN MORE ABOUT POKÉMON BECAUSE WE ***LIKE THEM SO MUCH!***
THIS TOOL WAS INVENTED SO WE COULD LEARN MORE ABOUT THEM.
A FAMOUS PROFESSOR ENTRUSTED ME WITH IT ON MY JOURNEY.
I'M PROUD OF THAT.
YOU'RE RIGHT ABOUT ONE THING. I CAN'T HEAR THESE POKÉMON VOICES YOU KEEP TALKING ABOUT.
THAT'S WHY...
...THE REST OF US NEED A POKÉDEX AND POKÉ BALLS. THAT'S HOW WE UNDER-STAND EACH OTHER!

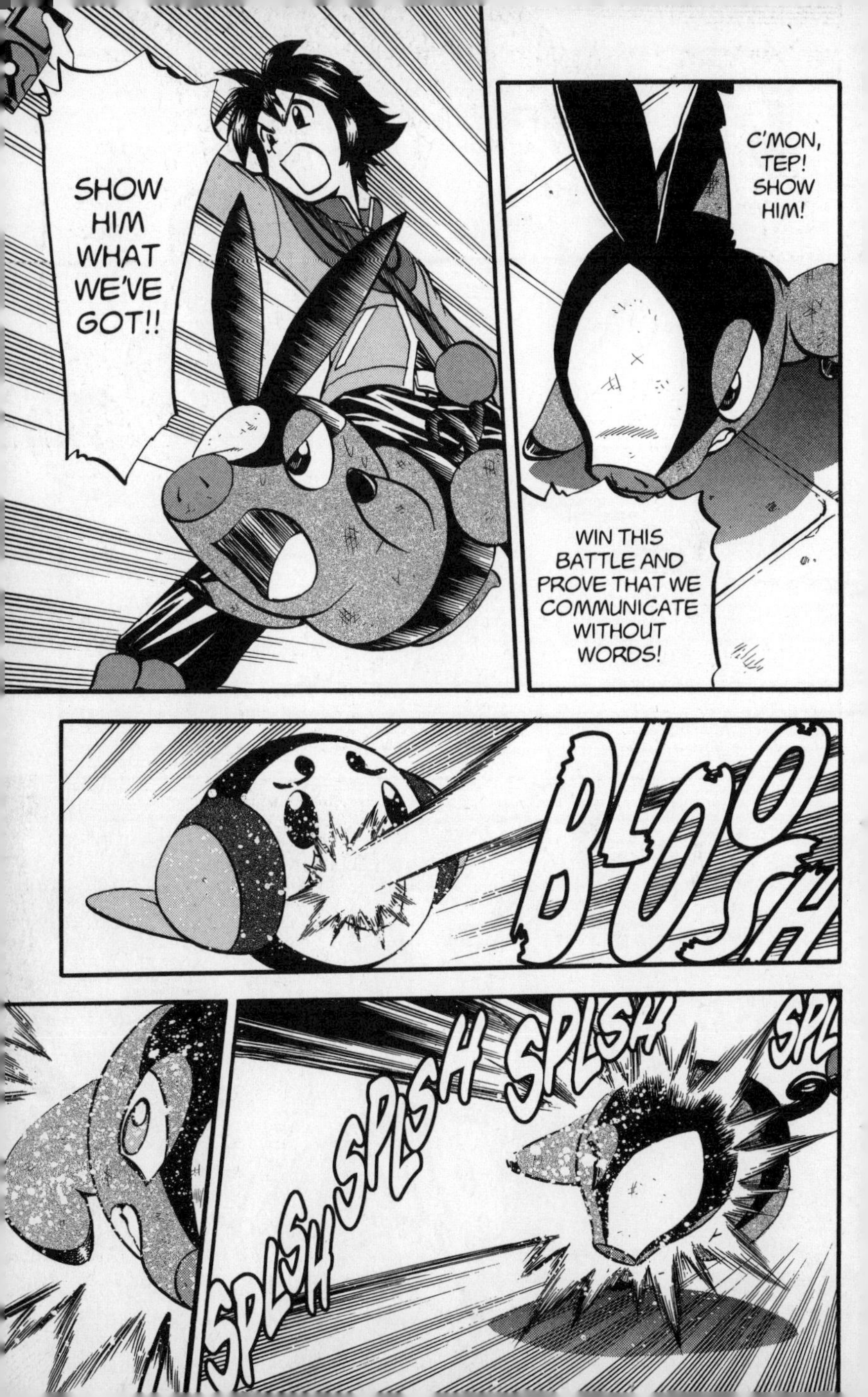
C'MON, TEP! SHOW HIM!
WIN THIS BATTLE AND PROVE THAT WE COMMUNICATE WITHOUT WORDS!
SHOW HIM WHAT WE'VE GOT!!
BLOOSH
SPLSH SPLSH SPLSH SPLSH SPL

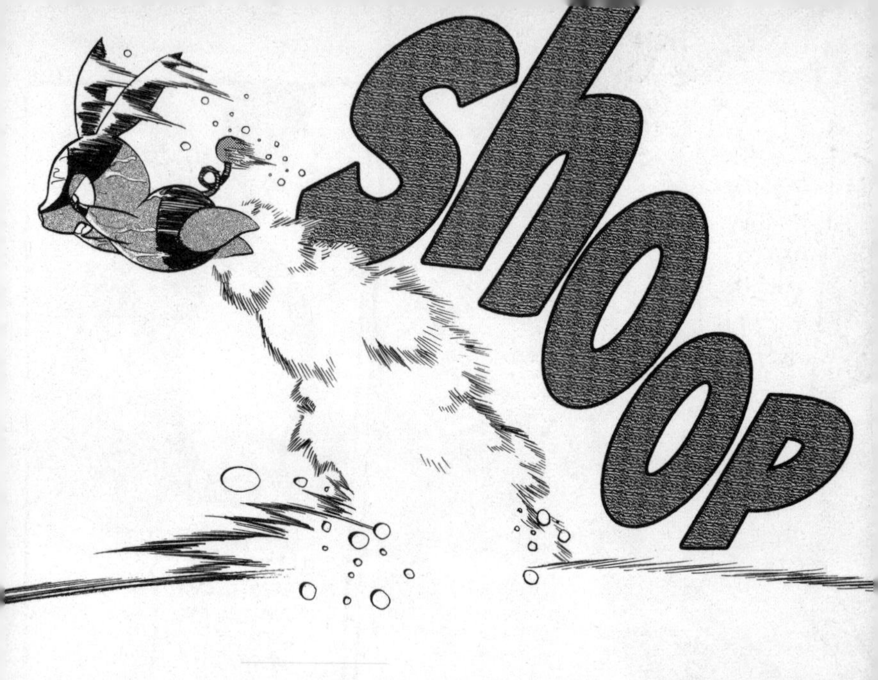
SHOOOP

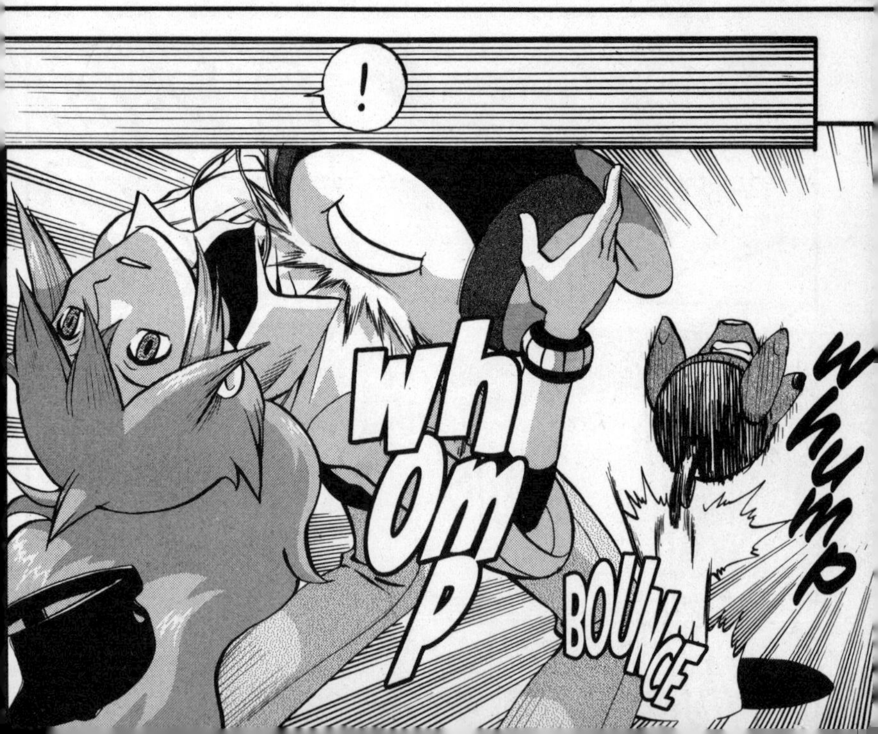
!
WHUMP
WHOMP
BOUNCE

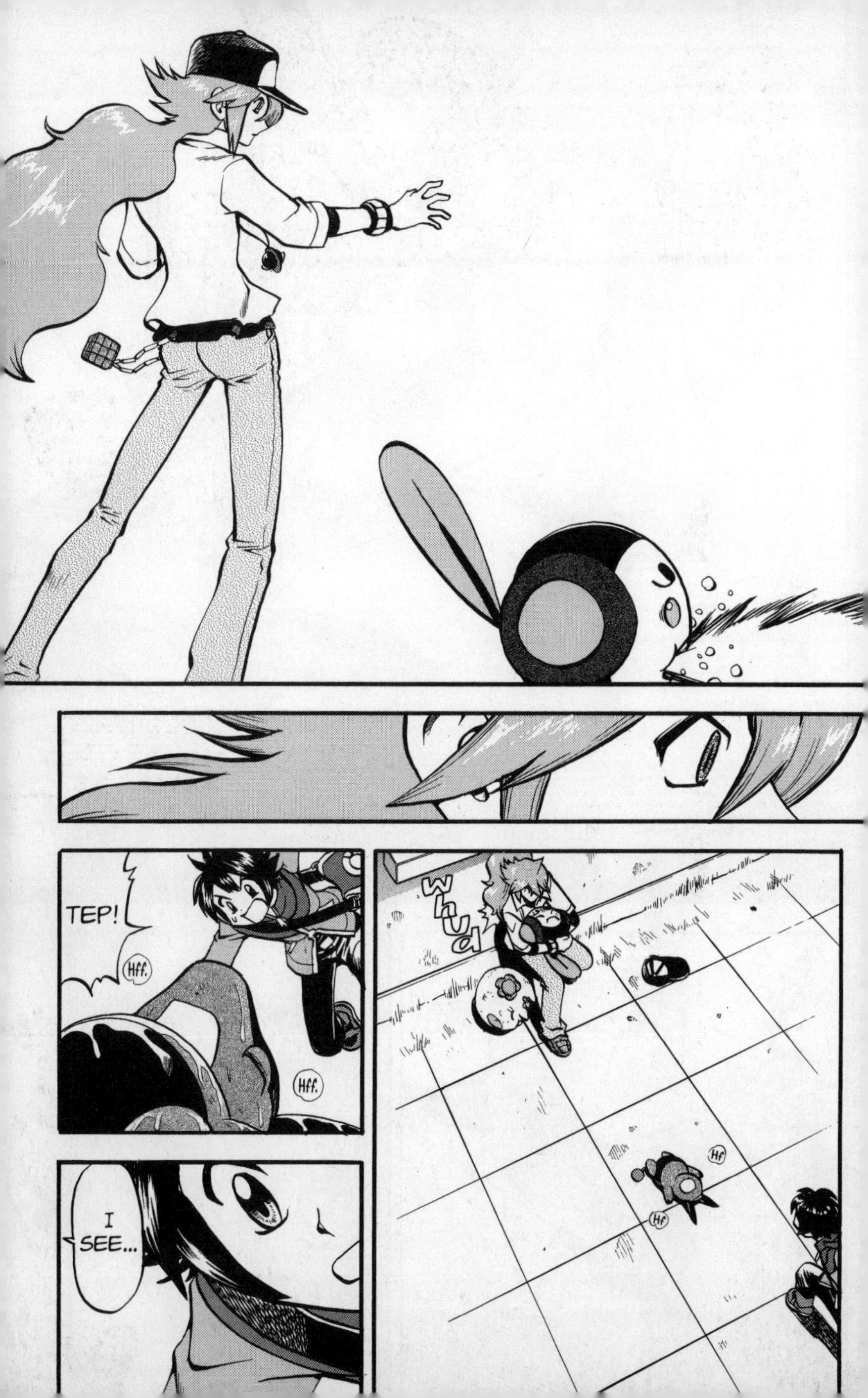
whud
Hf
Hf
TEP!
Hff.
Hff.
I SEE...

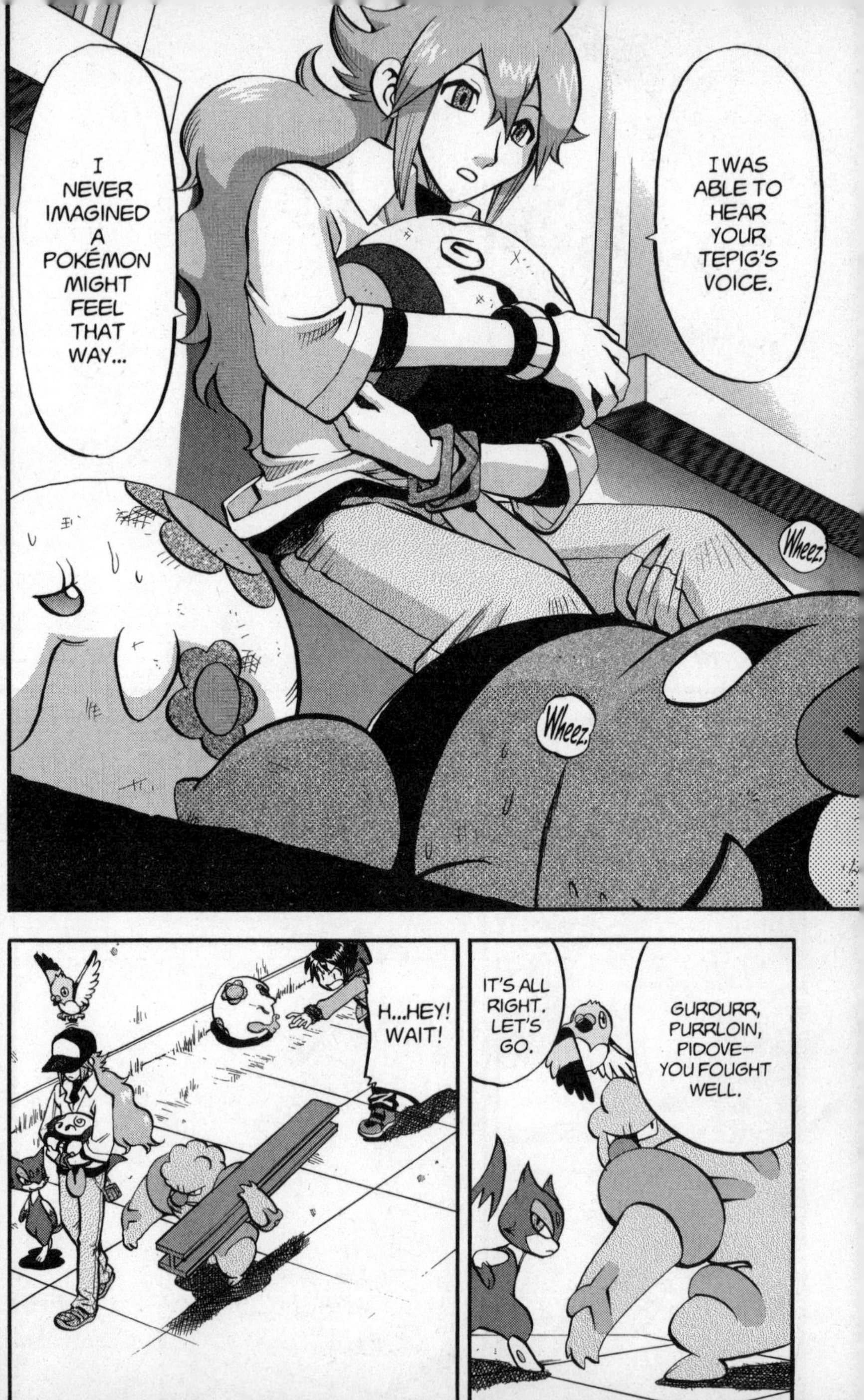

I WAS ABLE TO HEAR YOUR TEPIG'S VOICE.
I NEVER IMAGINED A POKÉMON MIGHT FEEL THAT WAY...
Wheez.
Wheez.
GURDURR, PURRLOIN, PIDOVE— YOU FOUGHT WELL.
IT'S ALL RIGHT. LET'S GO.
H...HEY! WAIT!

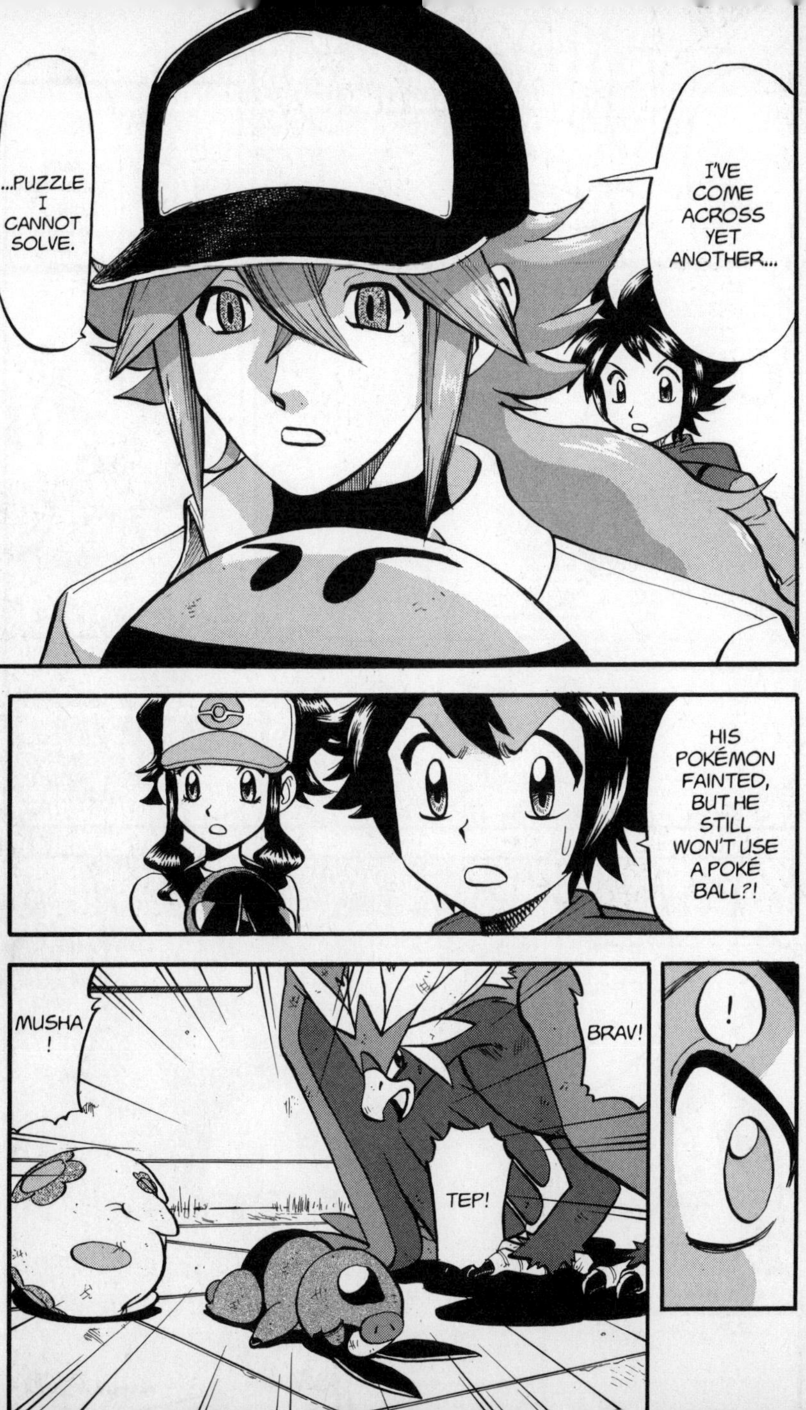
I'VE COME ACROSS YET ANOTHER...
...PUZZLE I CANNOT SOLVE.
HIS POKÉMON FAINTED, BUT HE STILL WON'T USE A POKÉ BALL?!
!
BRAV!
MUSHA!
TEP!

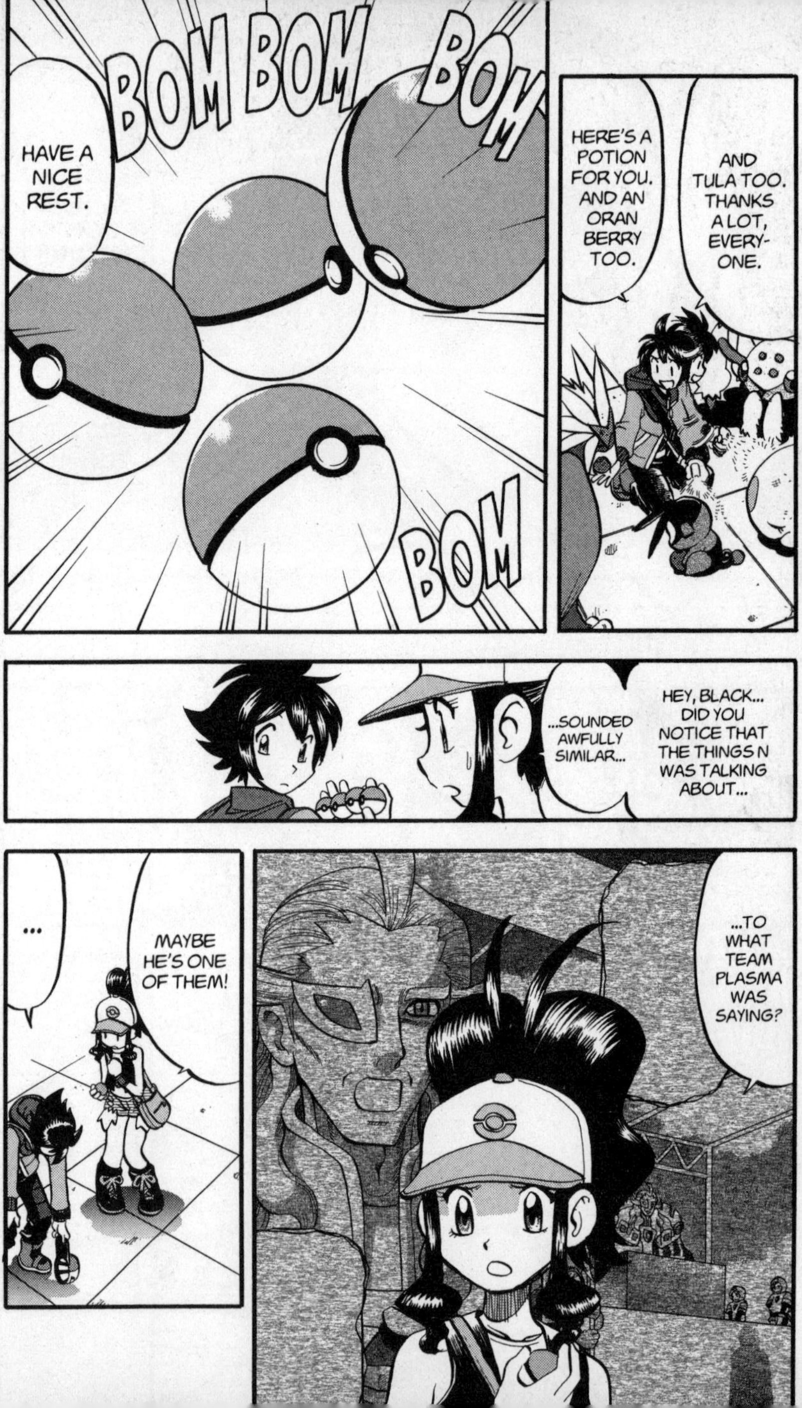
HERE'S A POTION FOR YOU. AND AN ORAN BERRY TOO.
AND TULA TOO. THANKS A LOT, EVERY-ONE.
BOM BOM BOM
BOM
HAVE A NICE REST.
HEY, BLACK... DID YOU NOTICE THAT THE THINGS N WAS TALKING ABOUT...
...SOUNDED AWFULLY SIMILAR...
...TO WHAT TEAM PLASMA WAS SAYING?
MAYBE HE'S ONE OF THEM!
...

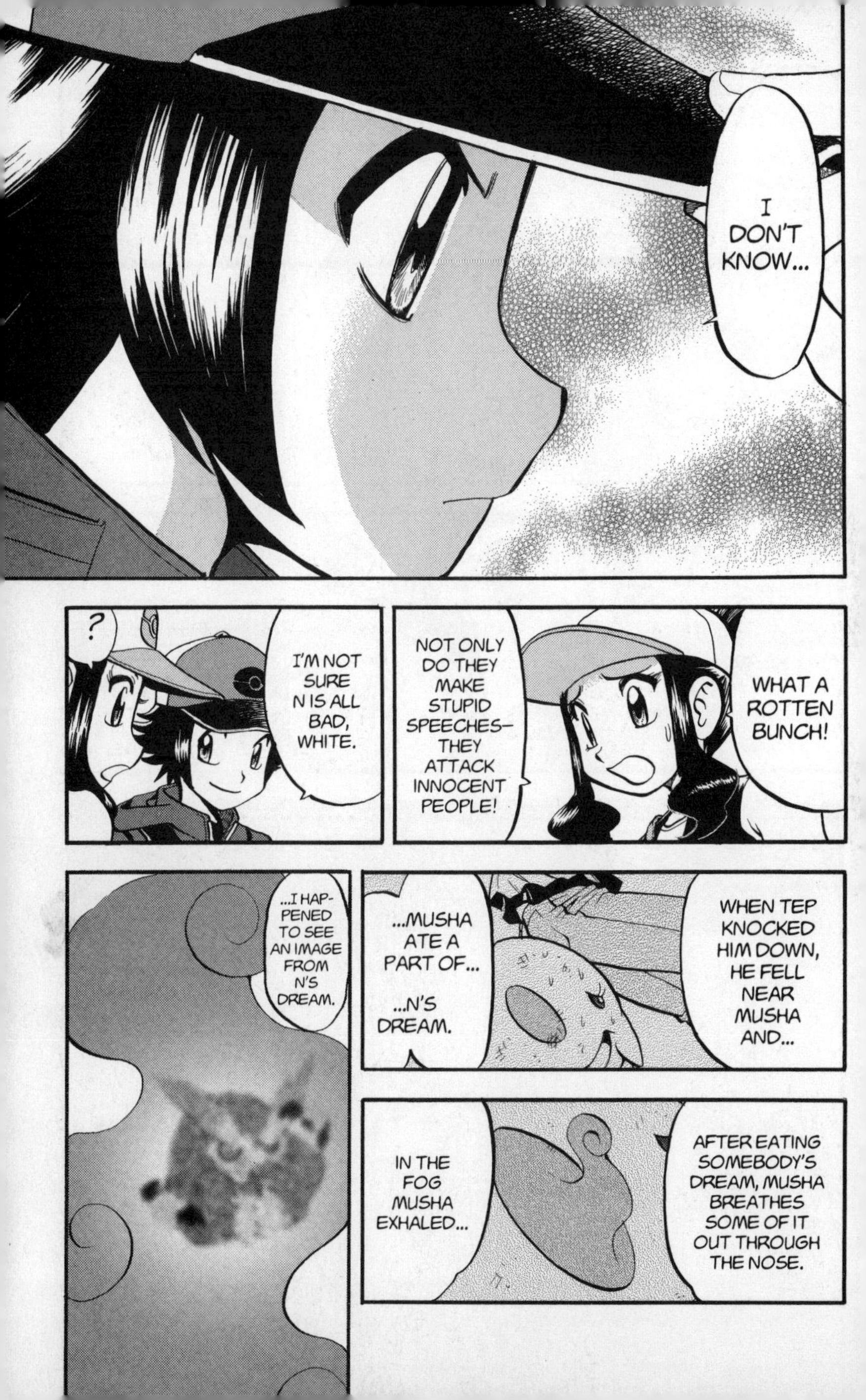
I DON'T KNOW...
WHAT A ROTTEN BUNCH!
NOT ONLY DO THEY MAKE STUPID SPEECHES— THEY ATTACK INNOCENT PEOPLE!
?
I'M NOT SURE N IS ALL BAD, WHITE.
WHEN TEP KNOCKED HIM DOWN, HE FELL NEAR MUSHA AND...
...MUSHA ATE A PART OF...
...N'S DREAM.
AFTER EATING SOMEBODY'S DREAM, MUSHA BREATHES SOME OF IT OUT THROUGH THE NOSE.
IN THE FOG MUSHA EXHALED...
...I HAPPENED TO SEE AN IMAGE FROM N'S DREAM.

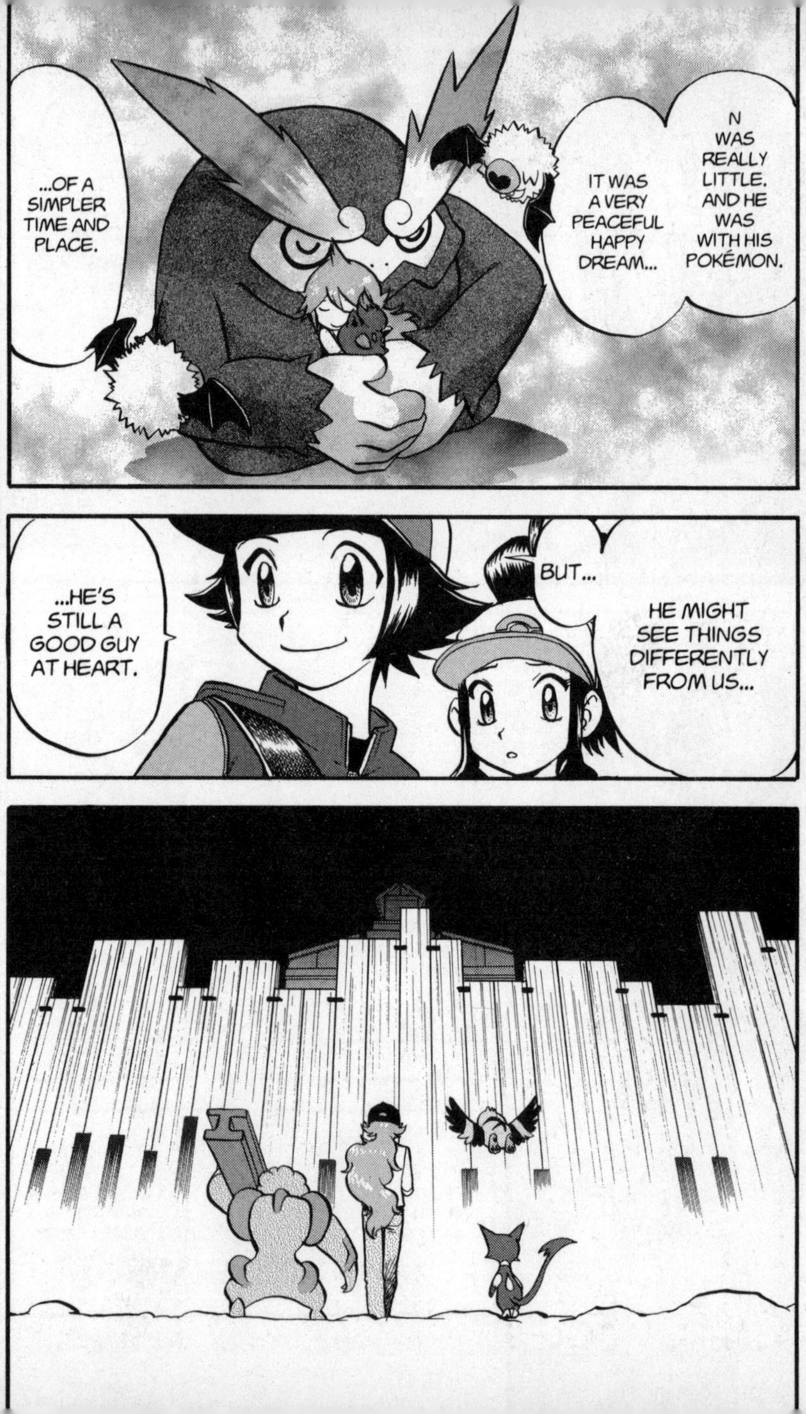
N WAS REALLY LITTLE. AND HE WAS WITH HIS POKÉMON.
IT WAS A VERY PEACEFUL HAPPY DREAM...
...OF A SIMPLER TIME AND PLACE.
BUT...
HE MIGHT SEE THINGS DIFFERENTLY FROM US...
...HE'S STILL A GOOD GUY AT HEART.

Final Destination:
Pokémon League

Current Location:
Striaton City

Fire Pig Pokémon **Tep**
Tepig ♂ | Fire
Lv.15 | Ability: Blaze

Dream Eater Pokémon **Musha**
Munna ♂ | Psychic
Lv.35 | Ability: Forewarn

Valiant Pokémon **Brav**
Braviary ♂ | Normal | Flying
Lv.54 | Ability: Sheer Force

EleSpider Pokémon **Tula**
Galvantula ♂ | Bug | Electric
Lv.37 | Ability: Unnerve

BLACK

WHITE

Fire Pig Pokémon **Gigi**
Tepig ♀ | Fire
Lv.05 | Ability: Blaze

Pokémon™ Adventures Black & White

AUDINO

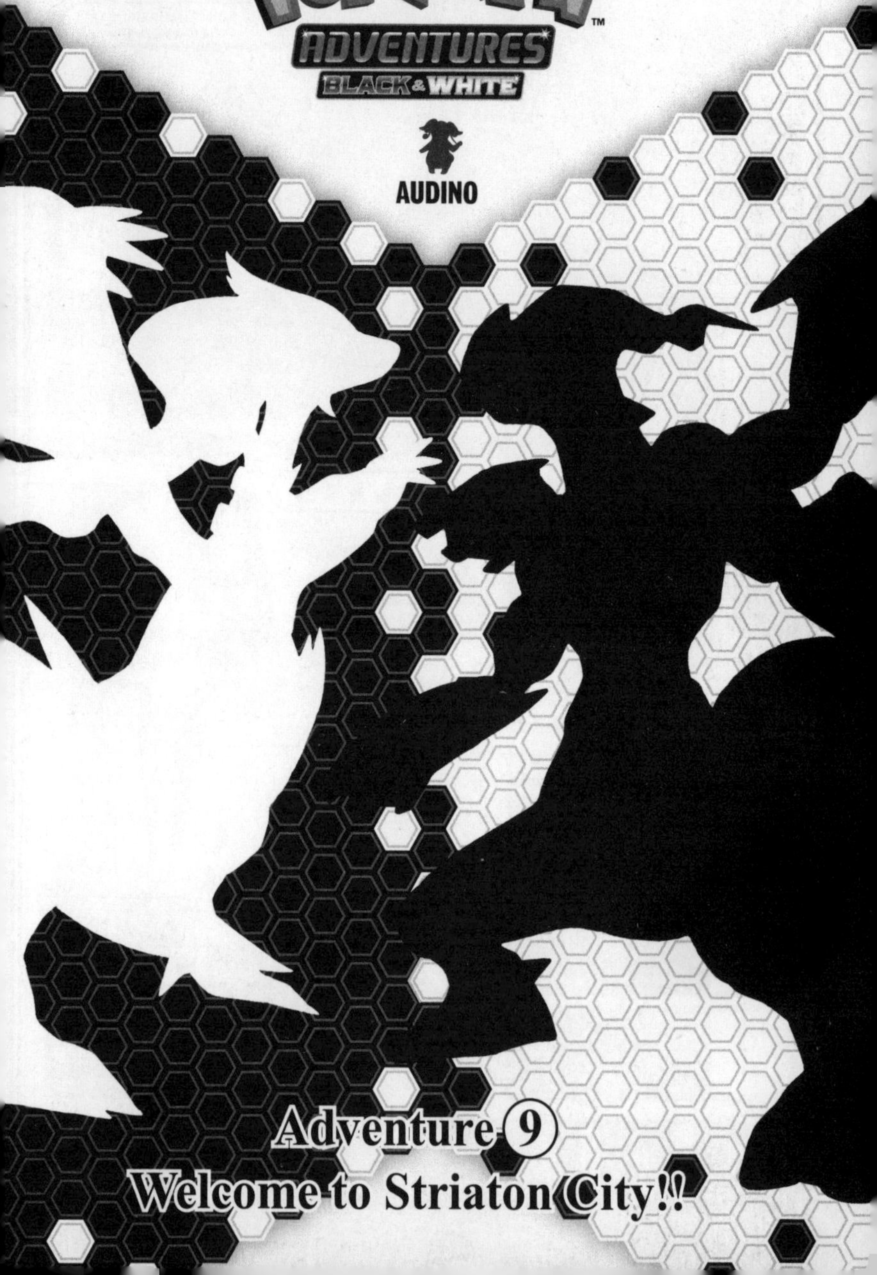

Adventure 9
Welcome to Striaton City!!

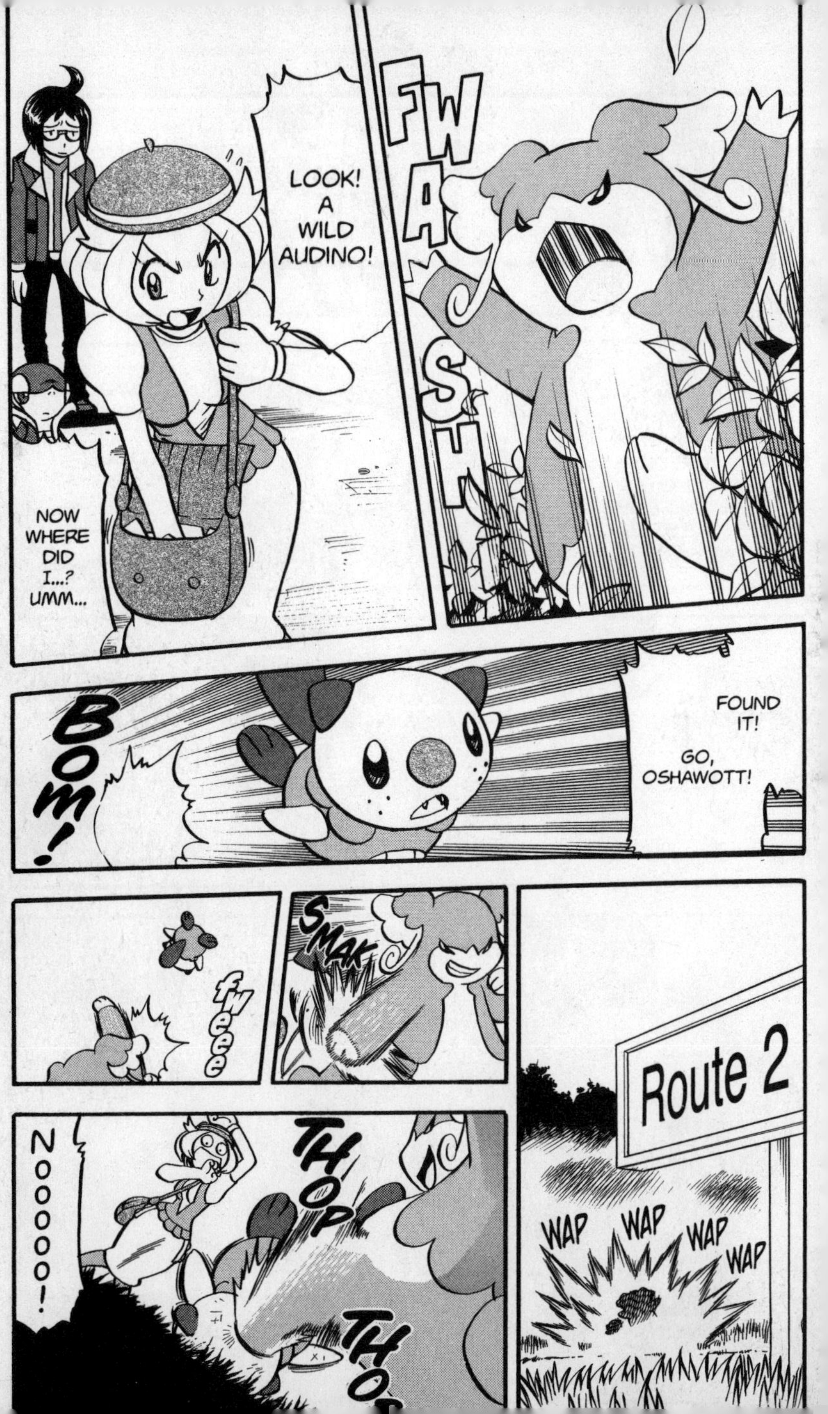
FWASH
LOOK! A WILD AUDINO!
NOW WHERE DID I...? UMM...
FOUND IT!
GO, OSHAWOTT!
BOOM!
Route 2
WAP WAP WAP WAP
SMAK
fweee
THOOP
THOO
NOOOOOO!

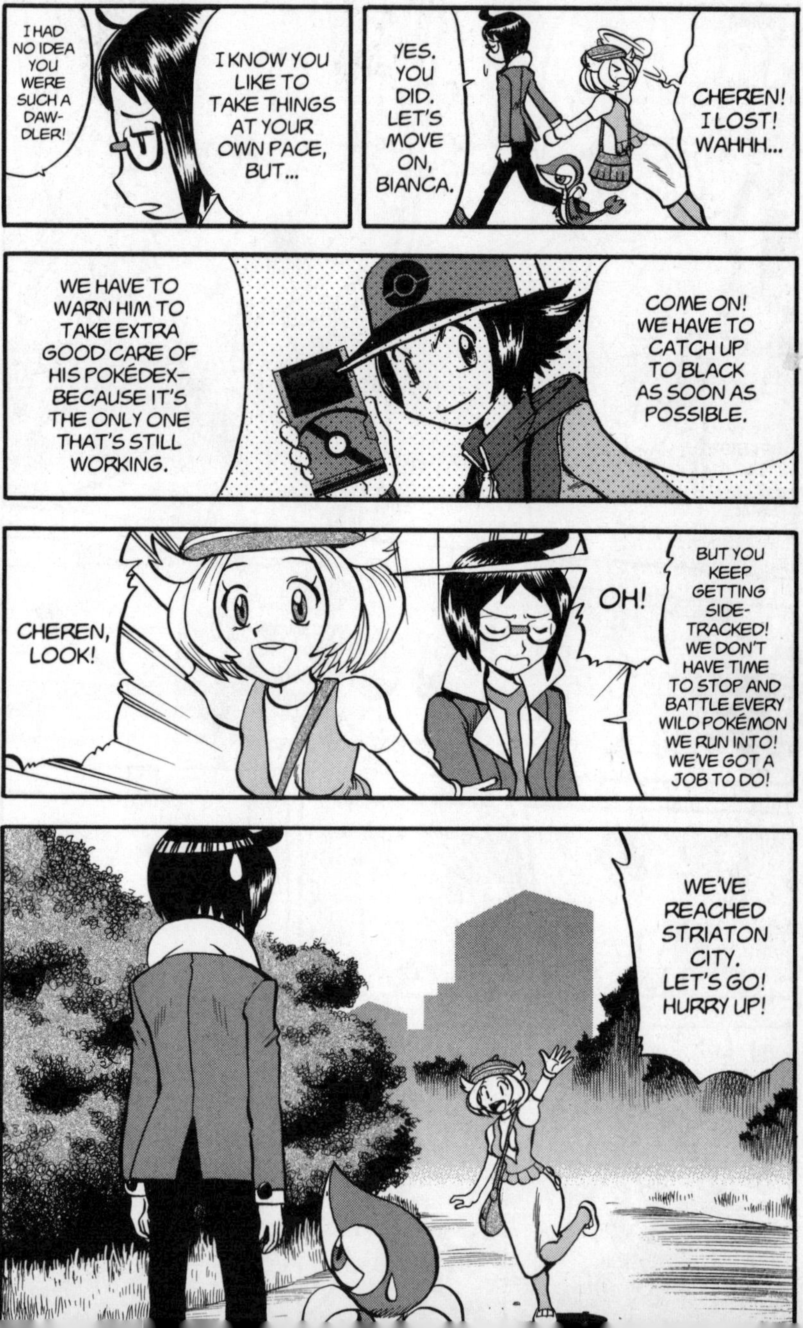
CHEREN! I LOST! WAHHH...
YES. YOU DID. LET'S MOVE ON, BIANCA.
I KNOW YOU LIKE TO TAKE THINGS AT YOUR OWN PACE, BUT...
I HAD NO IDEA YOU WERE SUCH A DAW-DLER!
COME ON! WE HAVE TO CATCH UP TO BLACK AS SOON AS POSSIBLE.
WE HAVE TO WARN HIM TO TAKE EXTRA GOOD CARE OF HIS POKÉDEX— BECAUSE IT'S THE ONLY ONE THAT'S STILL WORKING.
BUT YOU KEEP GETTING SIDE-TRACKED! WE DON'T HAVE TIME TO STOP AND BATTLE EVERY WILD POKÉMON WE RUN INTO! WE'VE GOT A JOB TO DO!
OH!
CHEREN, LOOK!
WE'VE REACHED STRIATON CITY. LET'S GO! HURRY UP!

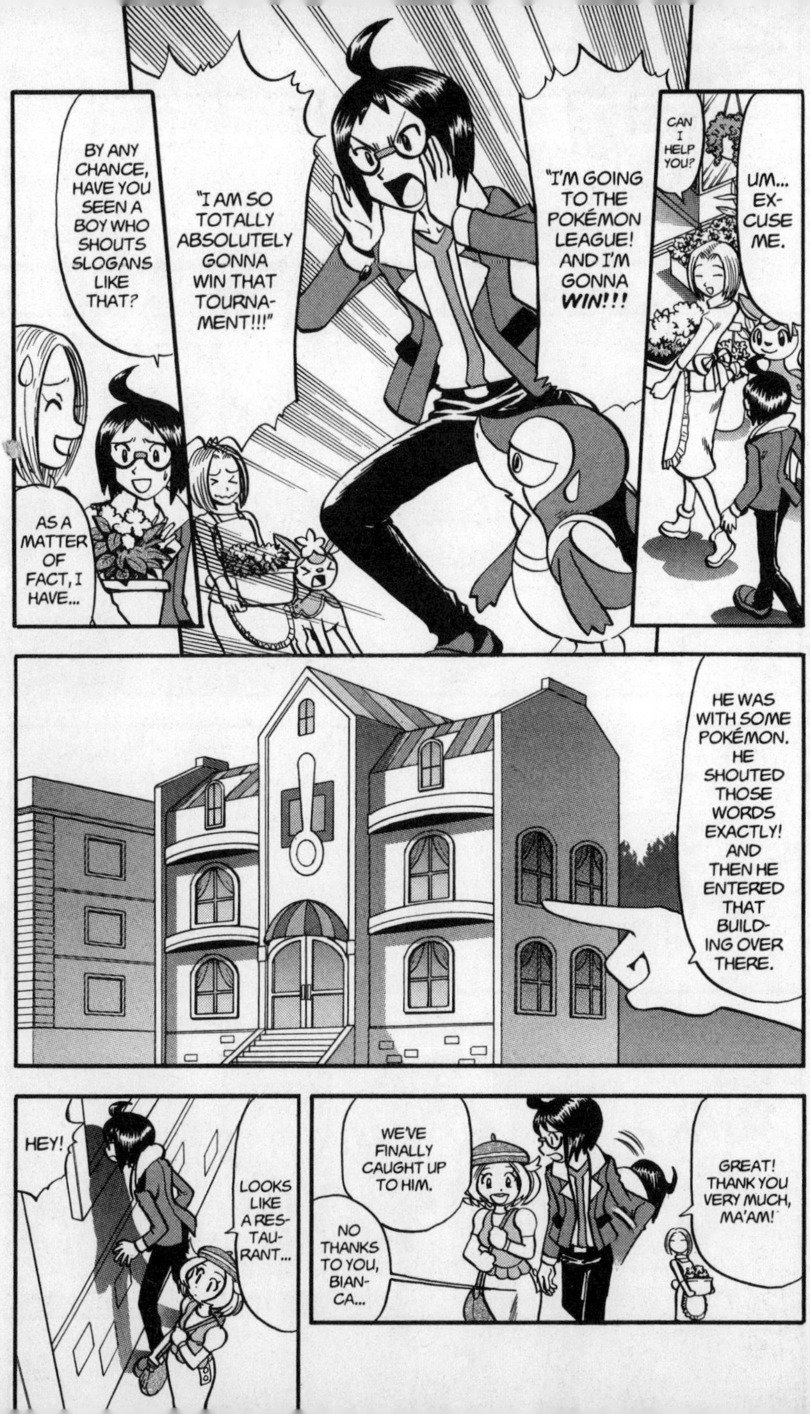
UM... EX-CUSE ME.
CAN I HELP YOU?
"I'M GOING TO THE POKÉMON LEAGUE! AND I'M GONNA **WIN!!!**
"I AM SO TOTALLY ABSOLUTELY GONNA WIN THAT TOURNA-MENT!!!"
BY ANY CHANCE, HAVE YOU SEEN A BOY WHO SHOUTS SLOGANS LIKE THAT?
AS A MATTER OF FACT, I HAVE...
HE WAS WITH SOME POKÉMON. HE SHOUTED THOSE WORDS EXACTLY! AND THEN HE ENTERED THAT BUILD-ING OVER THERE.
GREAT! THANK YOU VERY MUCH, MA'AM!
WE'VE FINALLY CAUGHT UP TO HIM.
NO THANKS TO YOU, BIAN-CA...
LOOKS LIKE A RES-TAU-RANT...
HEY!

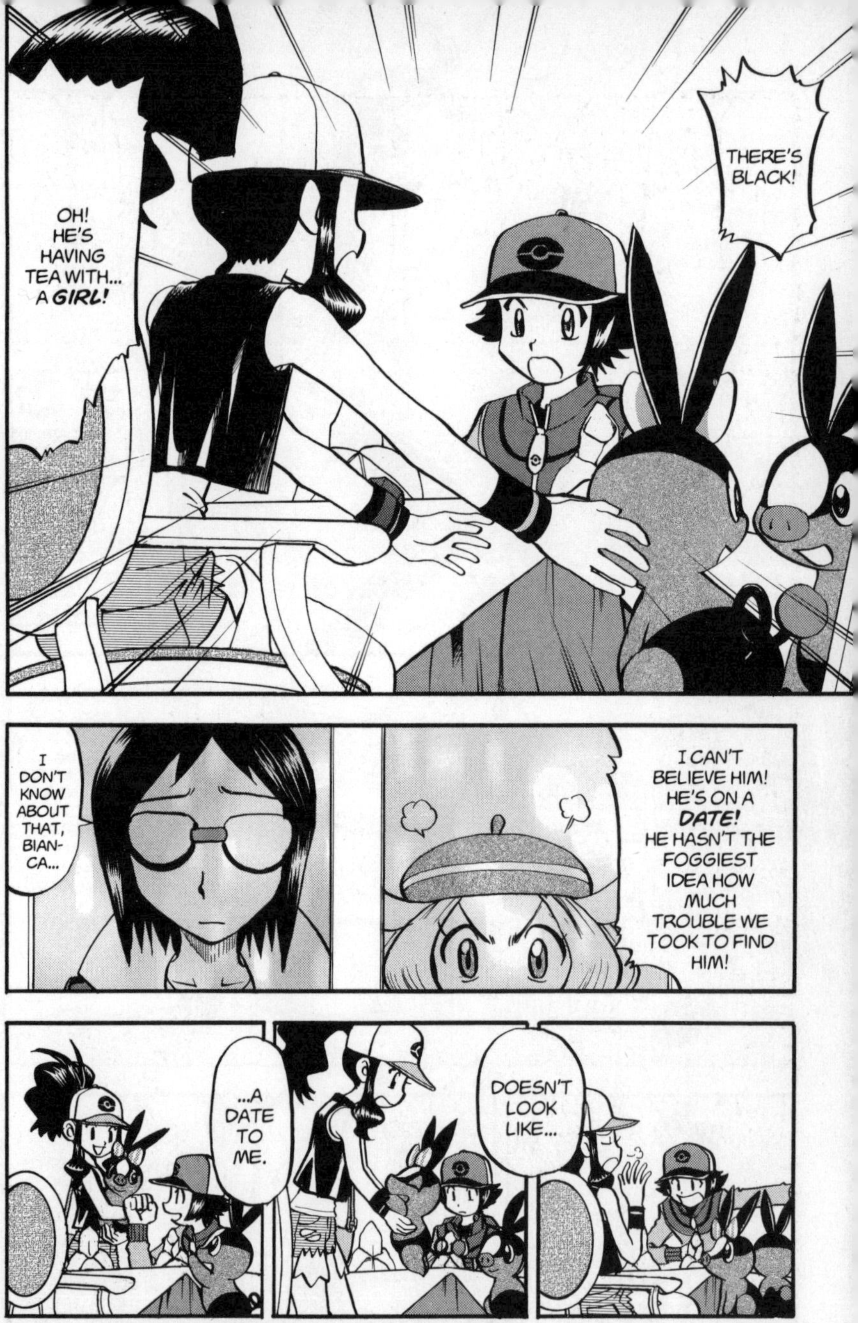
THERE'S BLACK!
OH! HE'S HAVING TEA WITH... A GIRL!
I CAN'T BELIEVE HIM! HE'S ON A DATE! HE HASN'T THE FOGGIEST IDEA HOW MUCH TROUBLE WE TOOK TO FIND HIM!
I DON'T KNOW ABOUT THAT, BIANCA...
DOESN'T LOOK LIKE...
...A DATE TO ME.

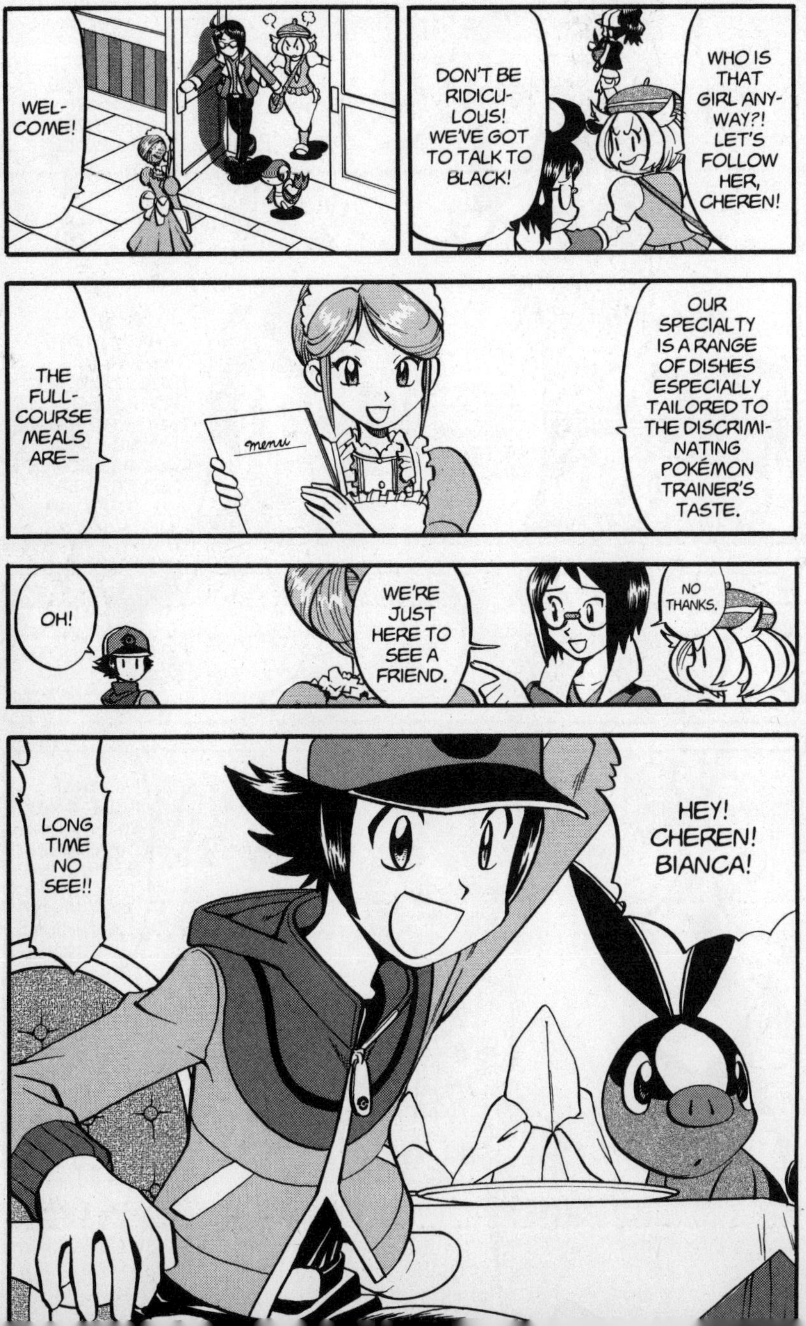
WHO IS THAT GIRL ANYWAY?! LET'S FOLLOW HER, CHEREN!
DON'T BE RIDICULOUS! WE'VE GOT TO TALK TO BLACK!
WELCOME!
OUR SPECIALTY IS A RANGE OF DISHES ESPECIALLY TAILORED TO THE DISCRIMINATING POKÉMON TRAINER'S TASTE.
menu
THE FULL-COURSE MEALS ARE–
NO THANKS.
WE'RE JUST HERE TO SEE A FRIEND.
OH!
HEY! CHEREN! BIANCA!
LONG TIME NO SEE!!

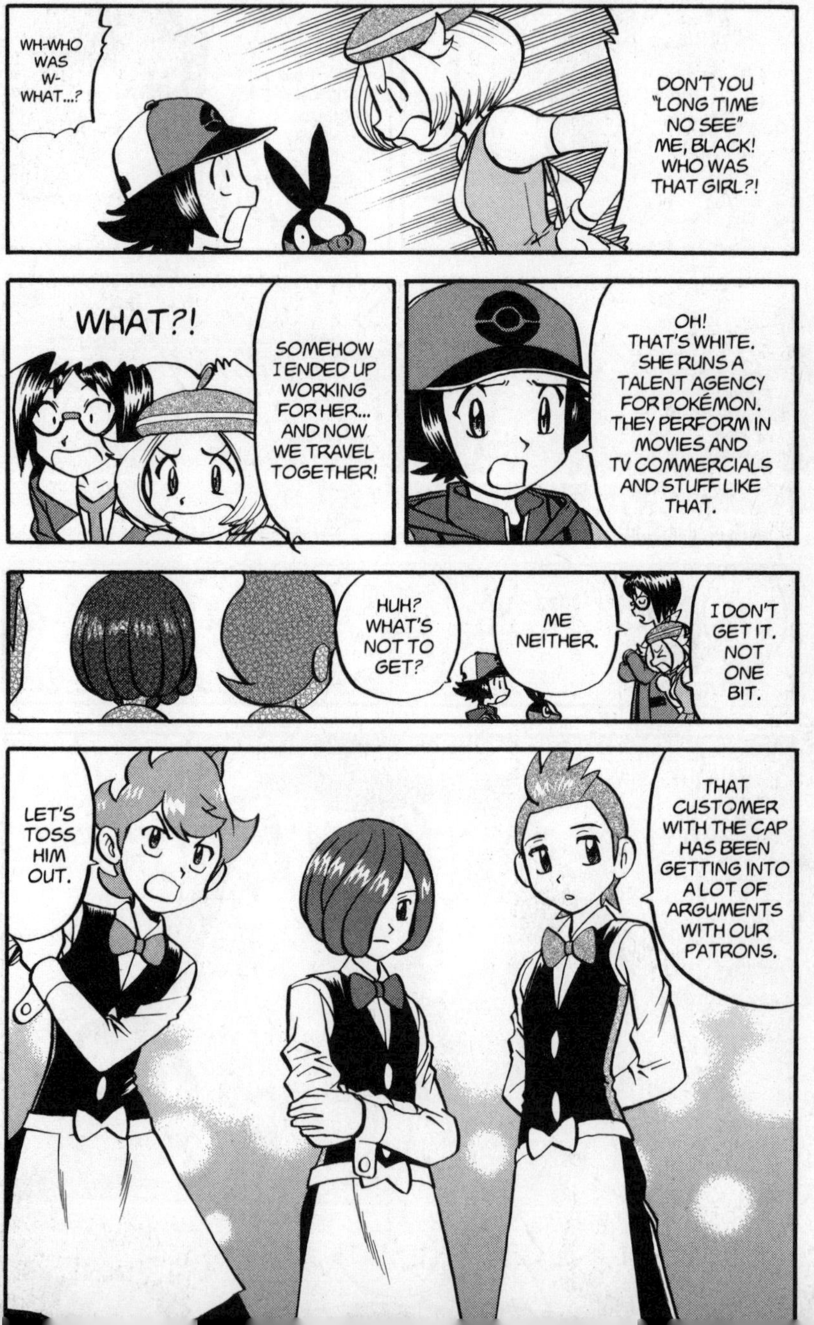
DON'T YOU "LONG TIME NO SEE" ME, BLACK! WHO WAS THAT GIRL?!
WH-WHO WAS W-WHAT...?
OH! THAT'S WHITE. SHE RUNS A TALENT AGENCY FOR POKÉMON. THEY PERFORM IN MOVIES AND TV COMMERCIALS AND STUFF LIKE THAT.
SOMEHOW I ENDED UP WORKING FOR HER... AND NOW WE TRAVEL TOGETHER!
WHAT?!
I DON'T GET IT. NOT ONE BIT.
ME NEITHER.
HUH? WHAT'S NOT TO GET?
THAT CUSTOMER WITH THE CAP HAS BEEN GETTING INTO A LOT OF ARGUMENTS WITH OUR PATRONS.
LET'S TOSS HIM OUT.

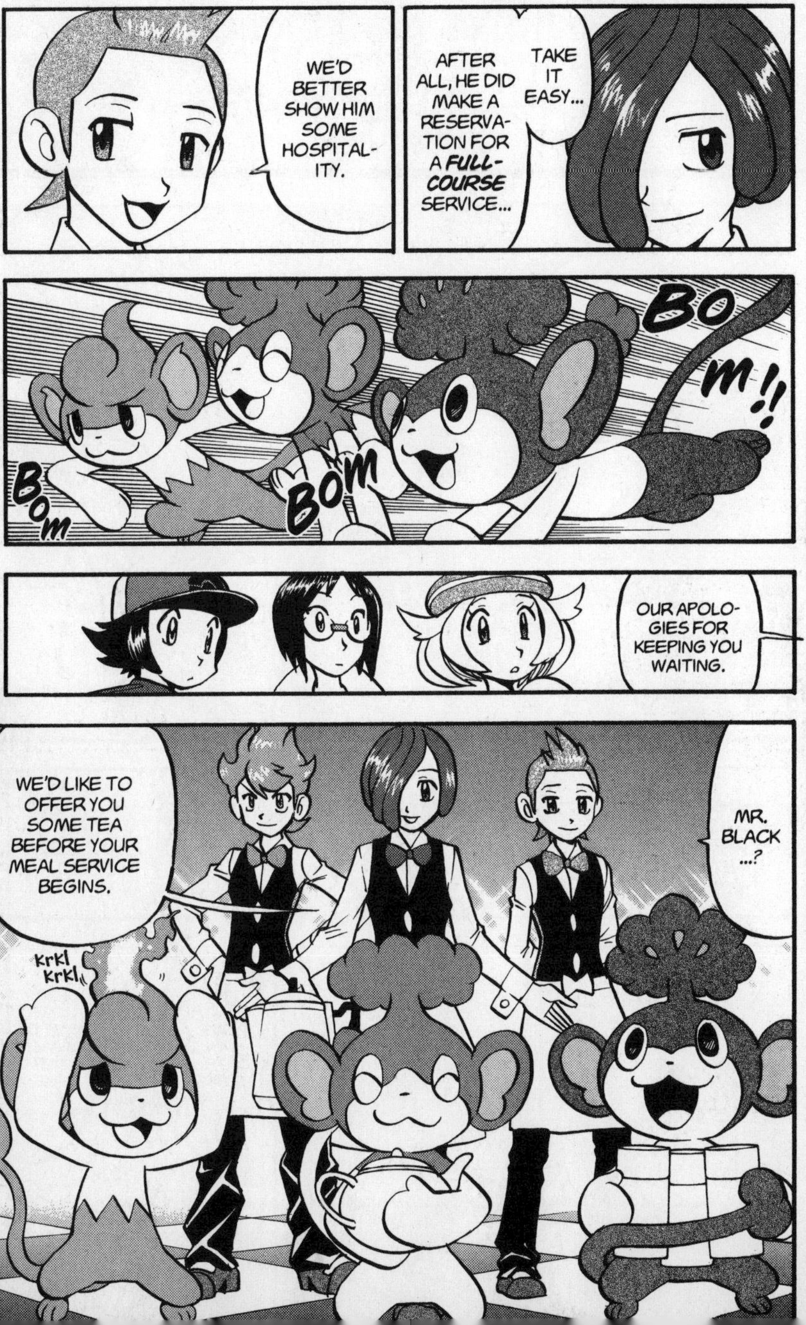
TAKE IT EASY...
AFTER ALL, HE DID MAKE A RESERVATION FOR A **FULL-COURSE** SERVICE...
WE'D BETTER SHOW HIM SOME HOSPITALITY.
BOm!!
BOM
Bom
OUR APOLOGIES FOR KEEPING YOU WAITING.
MR. BLACK ...?
WE'D LIKE TO OFFER YOU SOME TEA BEFORE YOUR MEAL SERVICE BEGINS.
krkl krkl

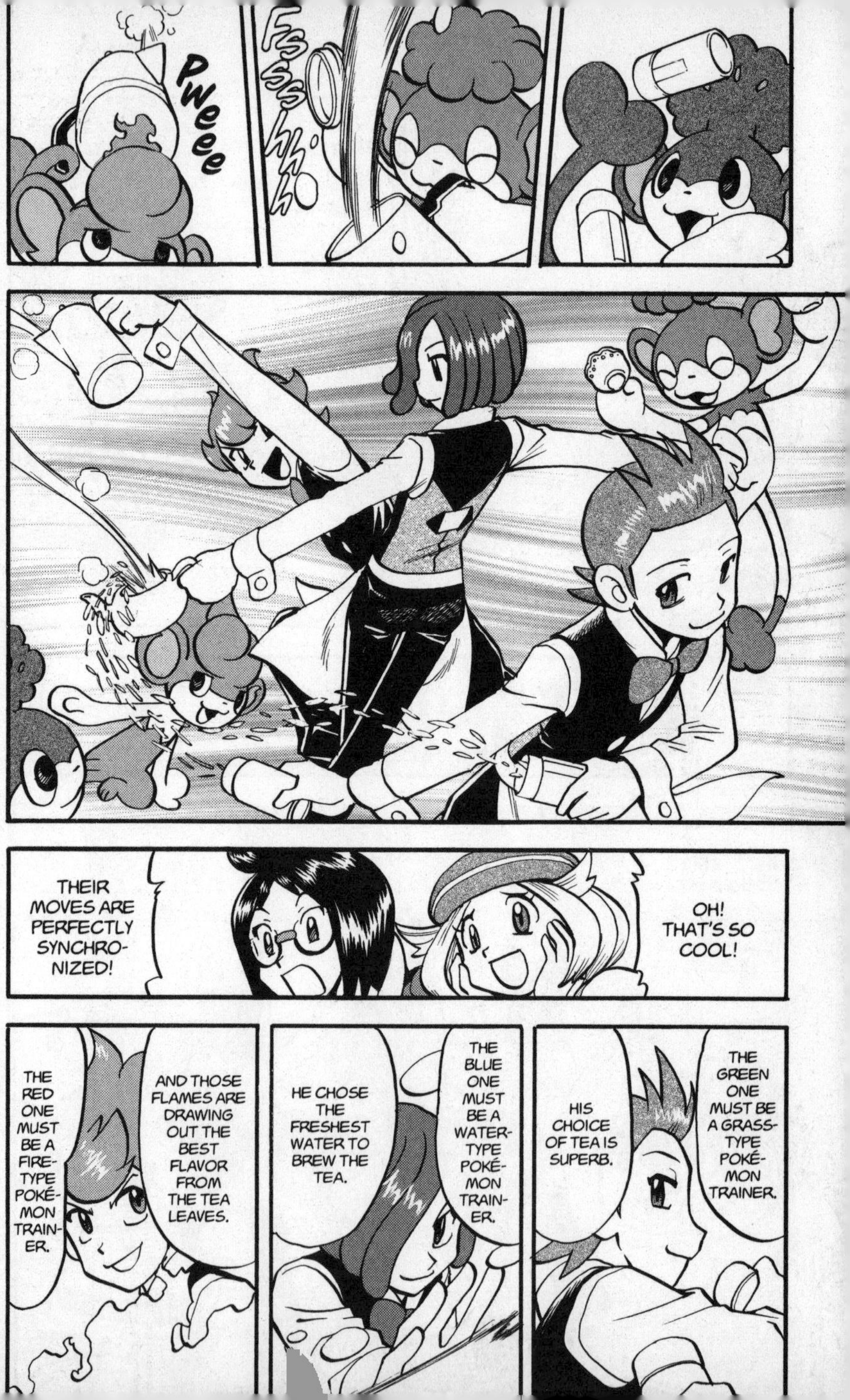
Fssshhhh
Pweeee
OH! THAT'S SO COOL!
THEIR MOVES ARE PERFECTLY SYNCHRO-NIZED!
THE GREEN ONE MUST BE A GRASS-TYPE POKÉ-MON TRAINER.
HIS CHOICE OF TEA IS SUPERB.
THE BLUE ONE MUST BE A WATER-TYPE POKÉ-MON TRAIN-ER.
HE CHOSE THE FRESHEST WATER TO BREW THE TEA.
THE RED ONE MUST BE A FIRE-TYPE POKÉ-MON TRAIN-ER.
AND THOSE FLAMES ARE DRAWING OUT THE BEST FLAVOR FROM THE TEA LEAVES.

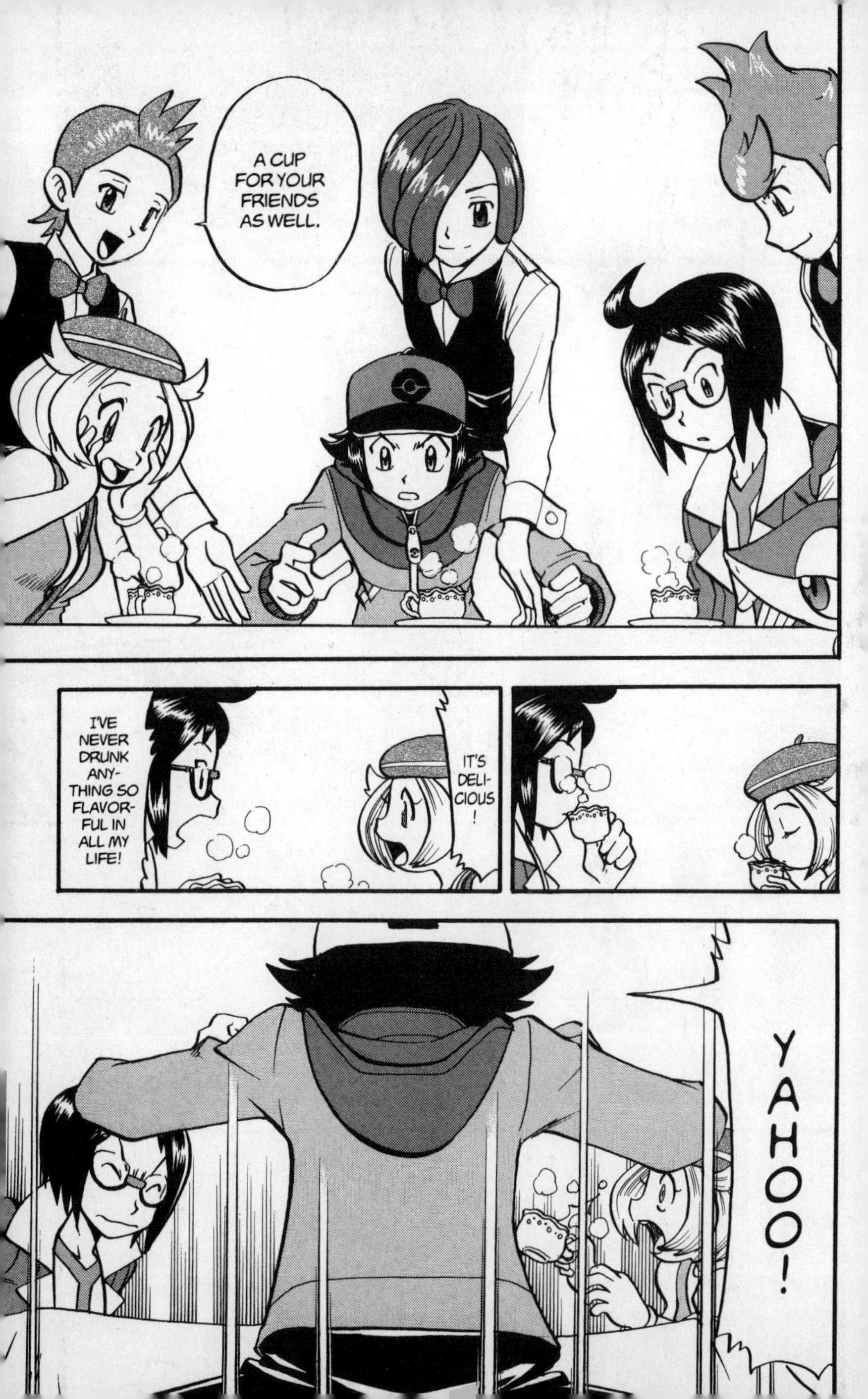
A CUP FOR YOUR FRIENDS AS WELL.
IT'S DELICIOUS!
I'VE NEVER DRUNK ANYTHING SO FLAVORFUL IN ALL MY LIFE!
YAHOO!

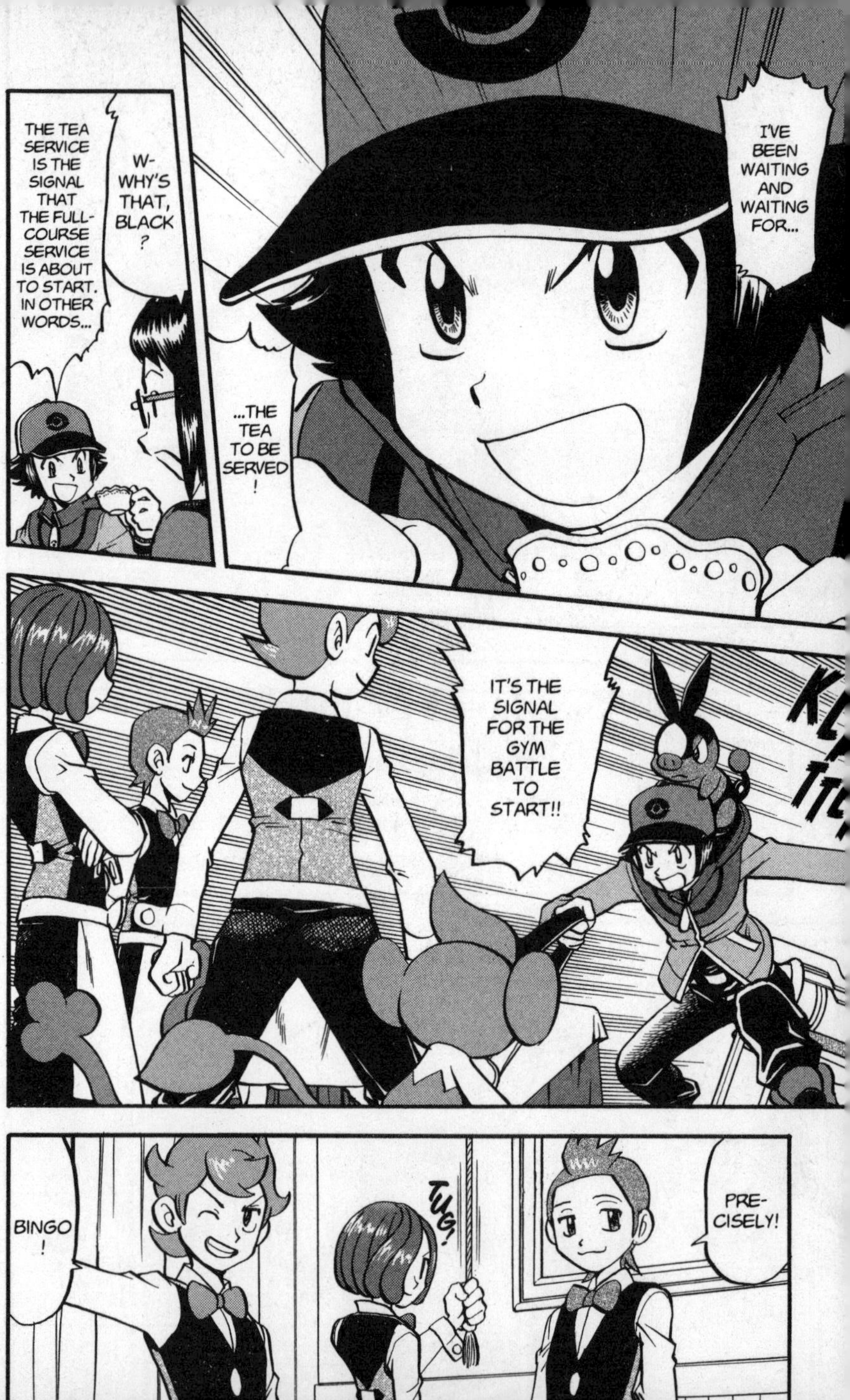
I'VE BEEN WAITING AND WAITING FOR...
...THE TEA TO BE SERVED!
W-WHY'S THAT, BLACK?
THE TEA SERVICE IS THE SIGNAL THAT THE FULL-COURSE SERVICE IS ABOUT TO START. IN OTHER WORDS...
IT'S THE SIGNAL FOR THE GYM BATTLE TO START!!
PRE-CISELY!
TUG!
BINGO!

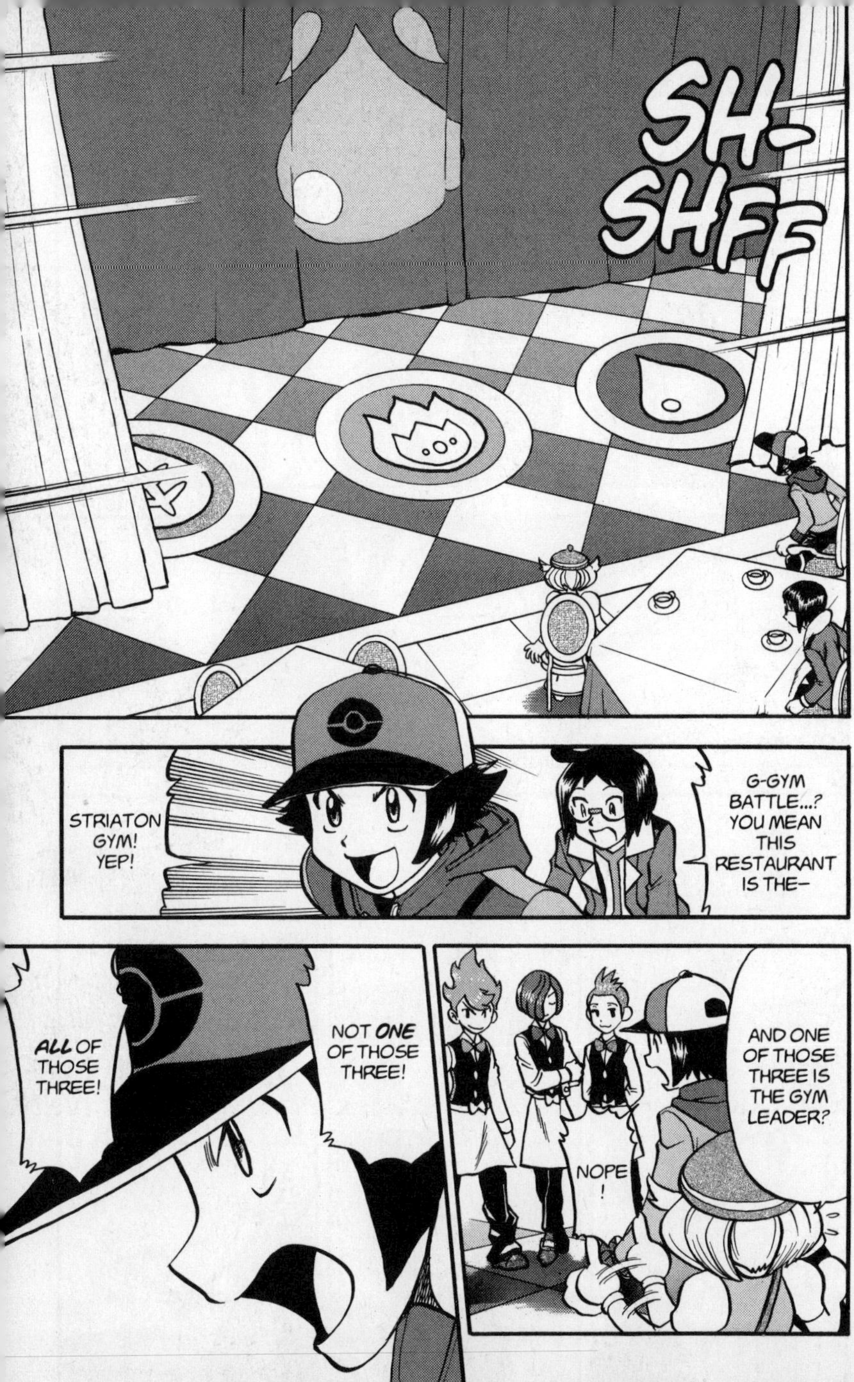
SH-SHFF
G-GYM BATTLE...? YOU MEAN THIS RESTAURANT IS THE–
STRIATON GYM! YEP!
AND ONE OF THOSE THREE IS THE GYM LEADER?
NOPE!
NOT **ONE** OF THOSE THREE!
ALL OF THOSE THREE!

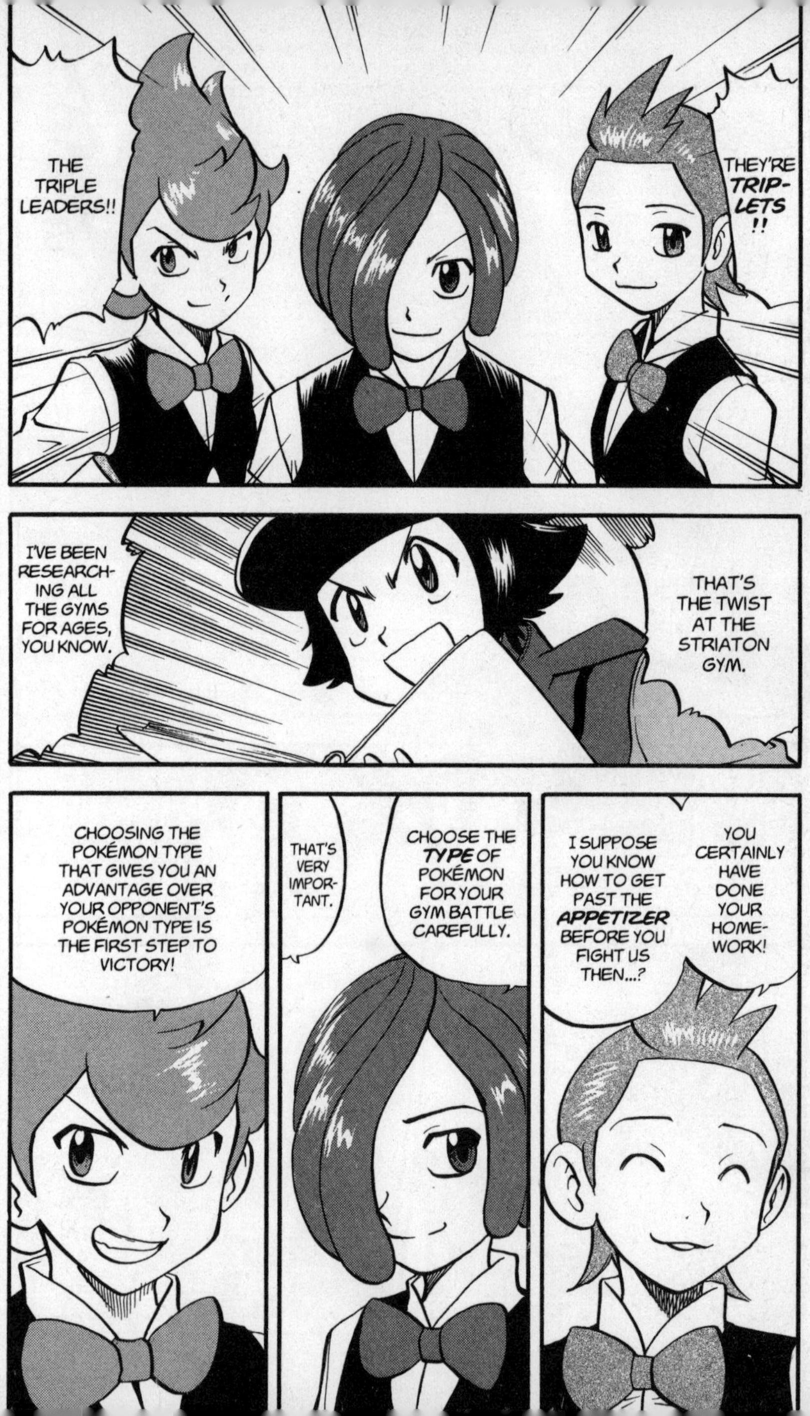
THEY'RE TRIPLETS!!
THE TRIPLE LEADERS!!
THAT'S THE TWIST AT THE STRIATON GYM.
I'VE BEEN RESEARCHING ALL THE GYMS FOR AGES, YOU KNOW.
YOU CERTAINLY HAVE DONE YOUR HOMEWORK!
I SUPPOSE YOU KNOW HOW TO GET PAST THE APPETIZER BEFORE YOU FIGHT US THEN...?
CHOOSE THE TYPE OF POKÉMON FOR YOUR GYM BATTLE CAREFULLY.
THAT'S VERY IMPORTANT.
CHOOSING THE POKÉMON TYPE THAT GIVES YOU AN ADVANTAGE OVER YOUR OPPONENT'S POKÉMON TYPE IS THE FIRST STEP TO VICTORY!

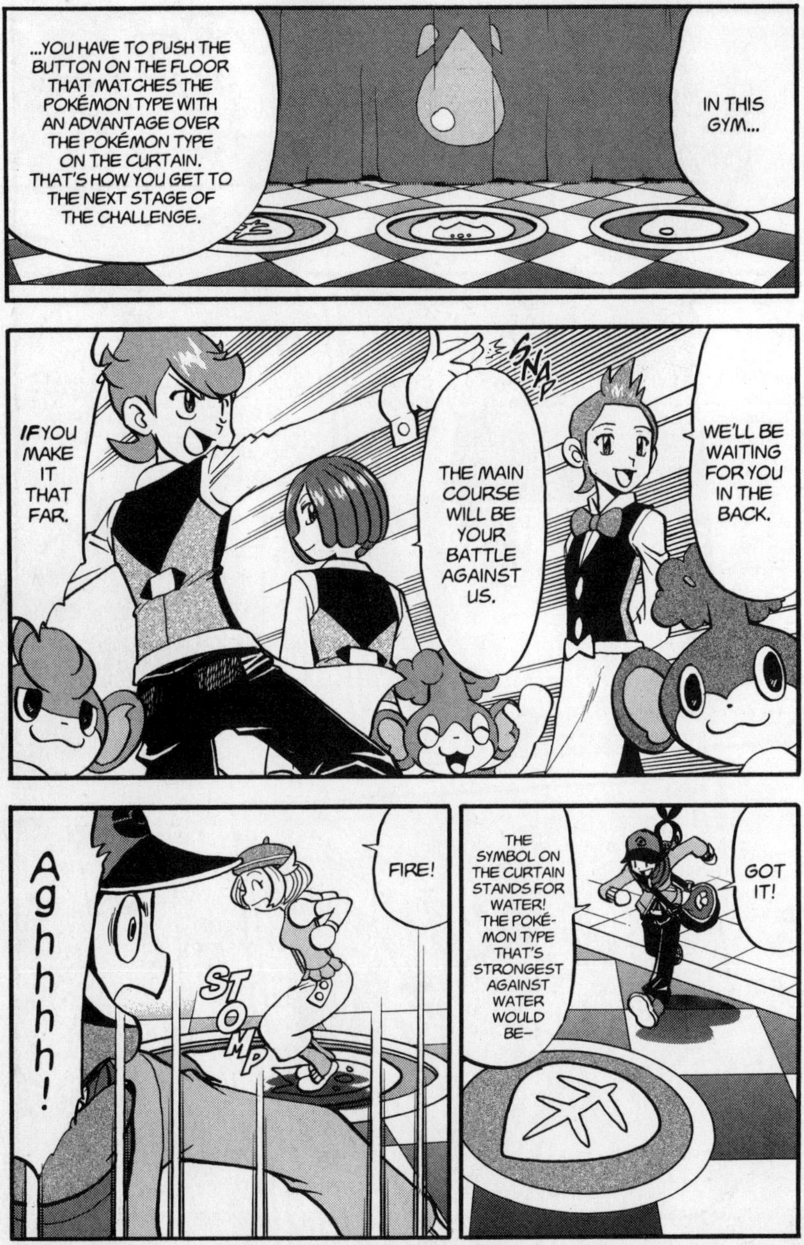
IN THIS GYM...
...YOU HAVE TO PUSH THE BUTTON ON THE FLOOR THAT MATCHES THE POKÉMON TYPE WITH AN ADVANTAGE OVER THE POKÉMON TYPE ON THE CURTAIN. THAT'S HOW YOU GET TO THE NEXT STAGE OF THE CHALLENGE.
WE'LL BE WAITING FOR YOU IN THE BACK.
SNAP
THE MAIN COURSE WILL BE YOUR BATTLE AGAINST US.
IF YOU MAKE IT THAT FAR.
GOT IT!
THE SYMBOL ON THE CURTAIN STANDS FOR WATER! THE POKÉ-MON TYPE THAT'S STRONGEST AGAINST WATER WOULD BE–
FIRE!
STOMP
Aghhhhh!

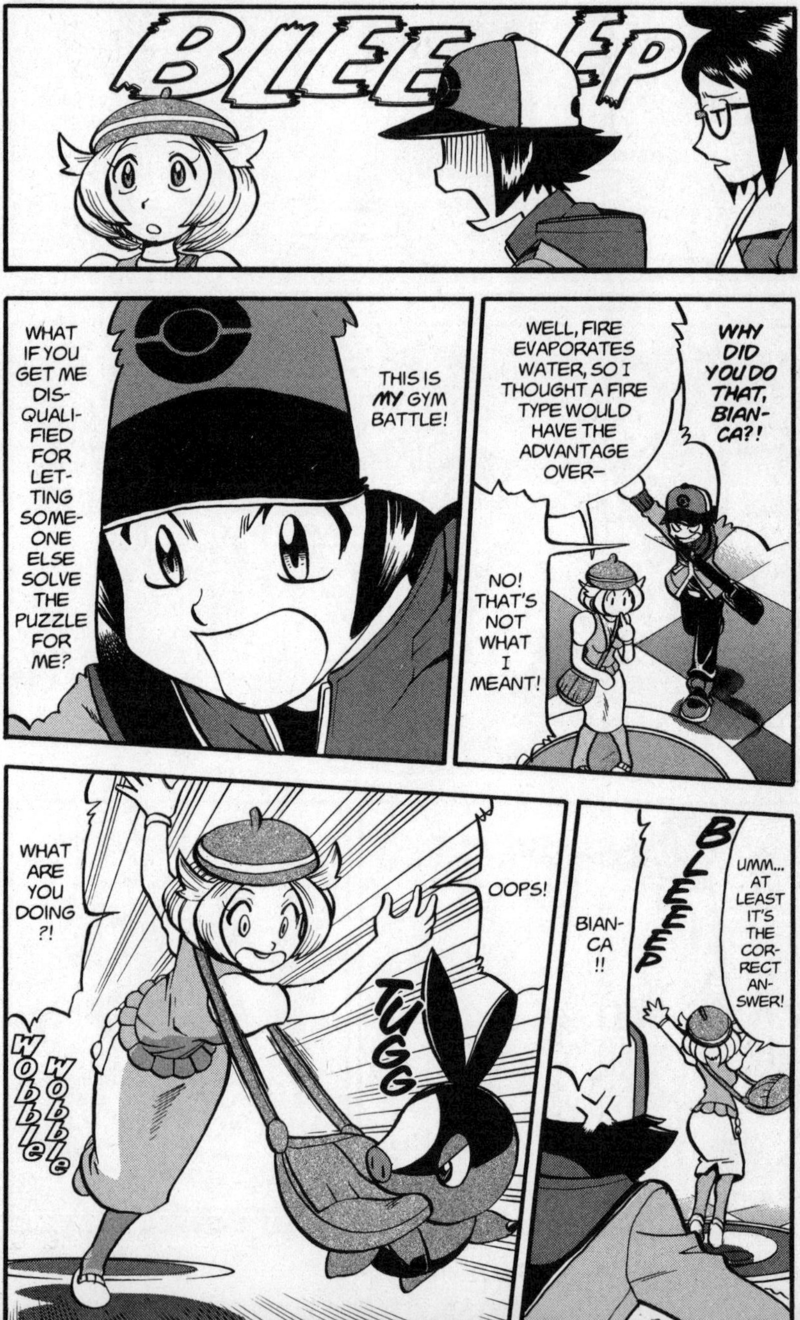
BLIEEEP
WHY DID YOU DO THAT, BIANCA?!
WELL, FIRE EVAPORATES WATER, SO I THOUGHT A FIRE TYPE WOULD HAVE THE ADVANTAGE OVER–
NO! THAT'S NOT WHAT I MEANT!
THIS IS MY GYM BATTLE!
WHAT IF YOU GET ME DISQUALIFIED FOR LETTING SOMEONE ELSE SOLVE THE PUZZLE FOR ME?
UMM... AT LEAST IT'S THE CORRECT ANSWER!
BLEEEP
BIANCA!!
OOPS!
WHAT ARE YOU DOING?!
TUGG
wobble wobble

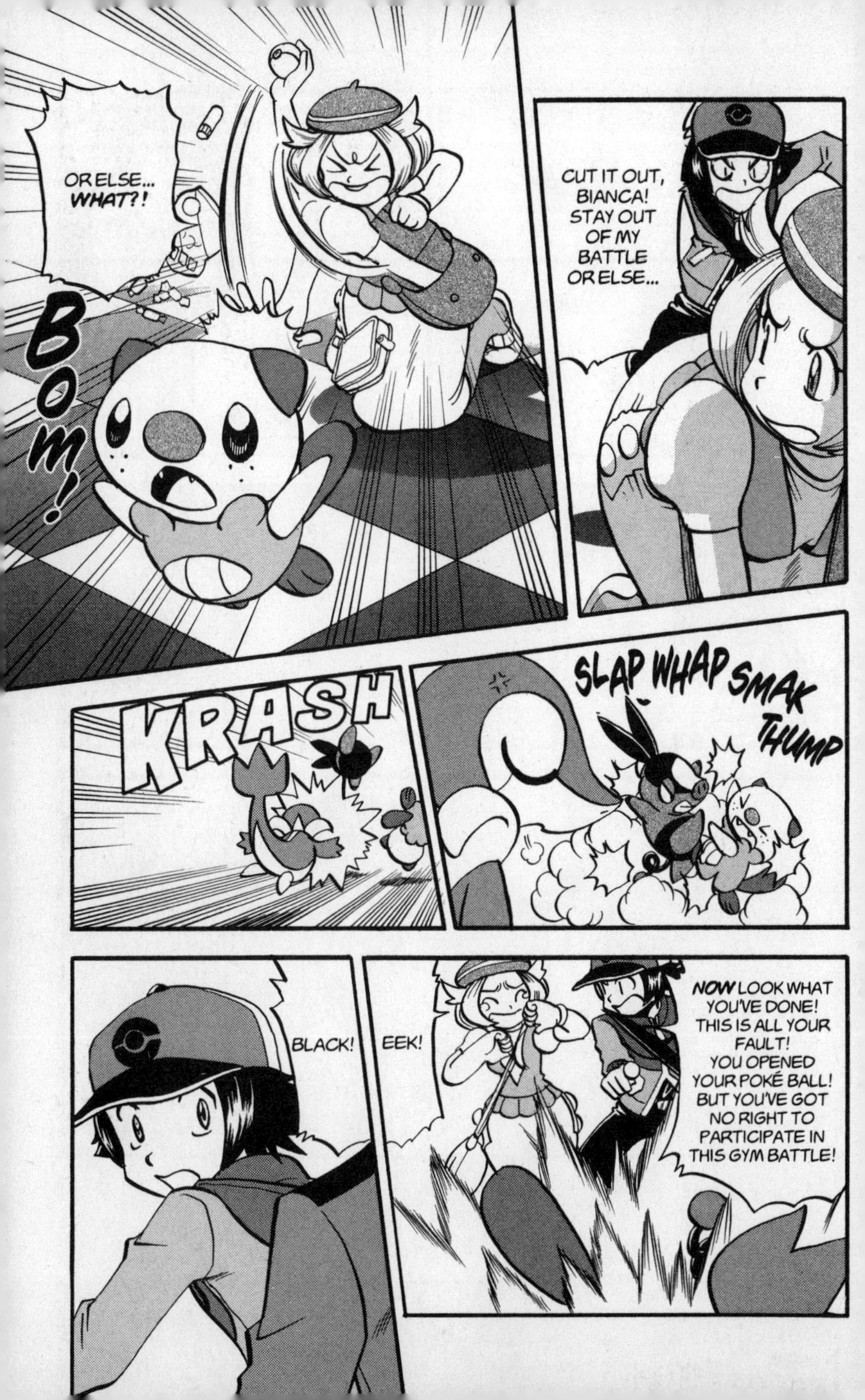
CUT IT OUT, BIANCA! STAY OUT OF MY BATTLE OR ELSE...
OR ELSE... WHAT?!
Bom!
SLAP WHAP SMAK THUMP
KRASH
NOW LOOK WHAT YOU'VE DONE! THIS IS ALL YOUR FAULT! YOU OPENED YOUR POKÉ BALL! BUT YOU'VE GOT NO RIGHT TO PARTICIPATE IN THIS GYM BATTLE!
EEK!
BLACK!

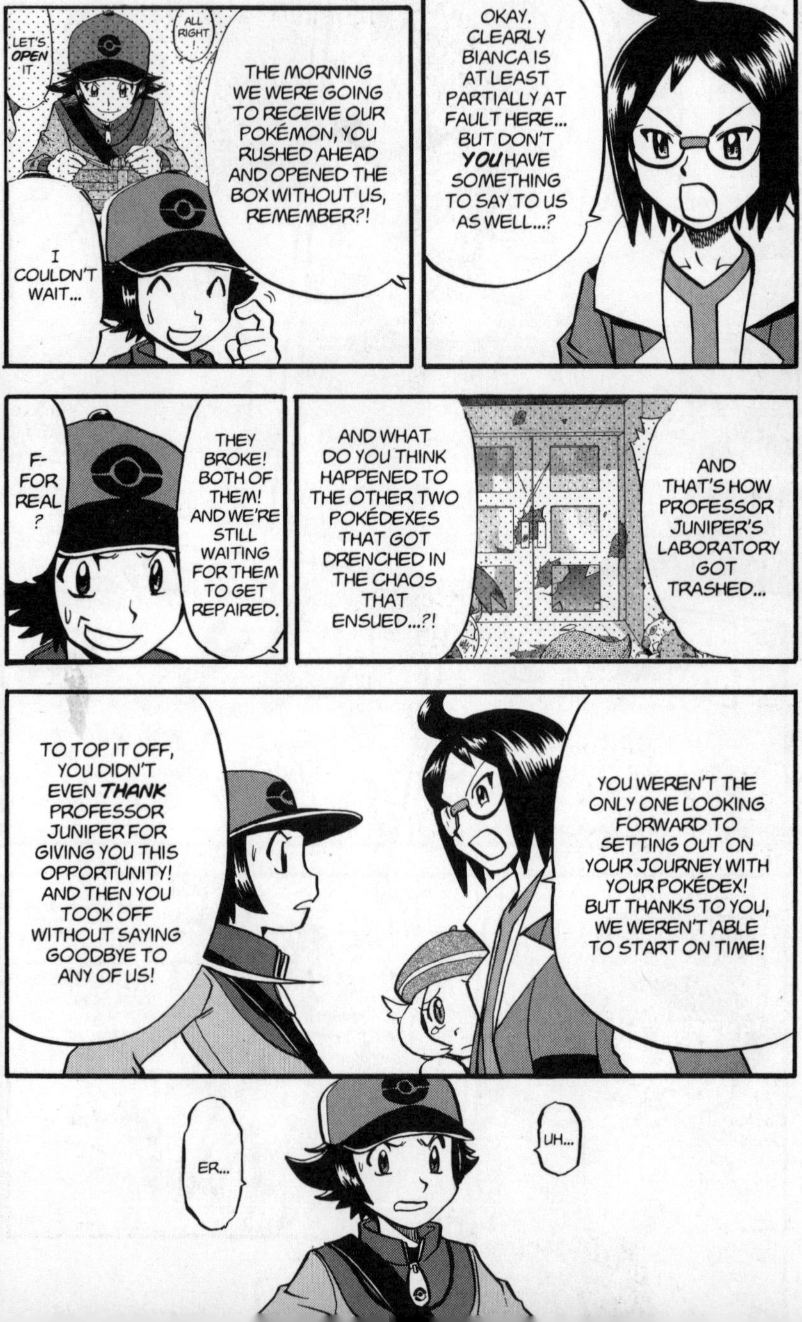
OKAY. CLEARLY BIANCA IS AT LEAST PARTIALLY AT FAULT HERE... BUT DON'T **YOU** HAVE SOMETHING TO SAY TO US AS WELL...?
THE MORNING WE WERE GOING TO RECEIVE OUR POKÉMON, YOU RUSHED AHEAD AND OPENED THE BOX WITHOUT US, REMEMBER?!
ALL RIGHT!
LET'S **OPEN** IT.
I COULDN'T WAIT...
AND THAT'S HOW PROFESSOR JUNIPER'S LABORATORY GOT TRASHED...
AND WHAT DO YOU THINK HAPPENED TO THE OTHER TWO POKÉDEXES THAT GOT DRENCHED IN THE CHAOS THAT ENSUED...?!
THEY BROKE! BOTH OF THEM! AND WE'RE STILL WAITING FOR THEM TO GET REPAIRED.
F-FOR REAL?
YOU WEREN'T THE ONLY ONE LOOKING FORWARD TO SETTING OUT ON YOUR JOURNEY WITH YOUR POKÉDEX! BUT THANKS TO YOU, WE WEREN'T ABLE TO START ON TIME!
TO TOP IT OFF, YOU DIDN'T EVEN **THANK** PROFESSOR JUNIPER FOR GIVING YOU THIS OPPORTUNITY! AND THEN YOU TOOK OFF WITHOUT SAYING GOODBYE TO ANY OF US!
UH...
ER...

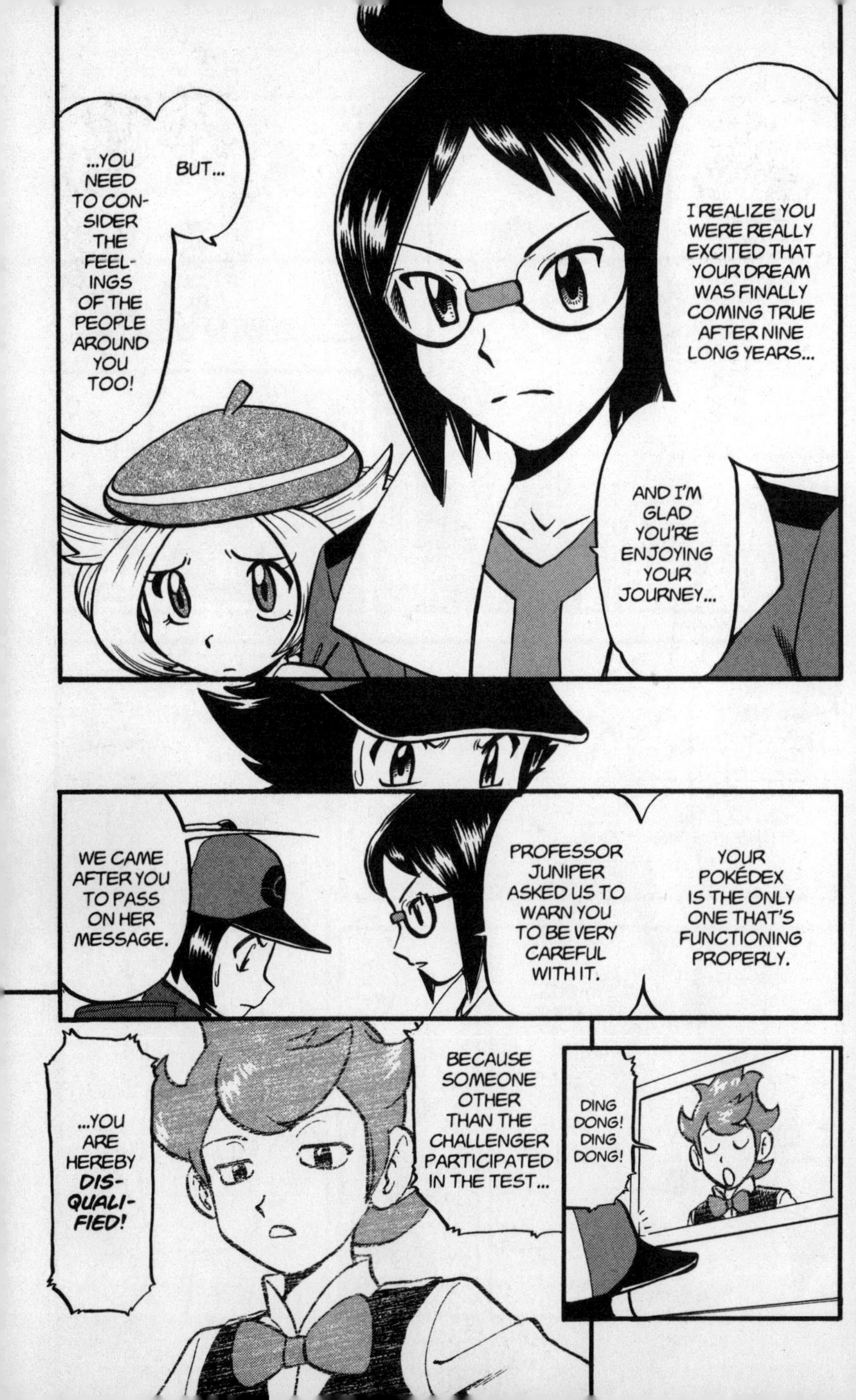
I REALIZE YOU WERE REALLY EXCITED THAT YOUR DREAM WAS FINALLY COMING TRUE AFTER NINE LONG YEARS...
AND I'M GLAD YOU'RE ENJOYING YOUR JOURNEY...
BUT...
...YOU NEED TO CON-SIDER THE FEEL-INGS OF THE PEOPLE AROUND YOU TOO!
YOUR POKÉDEX IS THE ONLY ONE THAT'S FUNCTIONING PROPERLY.
PROFESSOR JUNIPER ASKED US TO WARN YOU TO BE VERY CAREFUL WITH IT.
WE CAME AFTER YOU TO PASS ON HER MESSAGE.
DING DONG! DING DONG!
BECAUSE SOMEONE OTHER THAN THE CHALLENGER PARTICIPATED IN THE TEST...
...YOU ARE HEREBY DIS-QUALI-FIED!

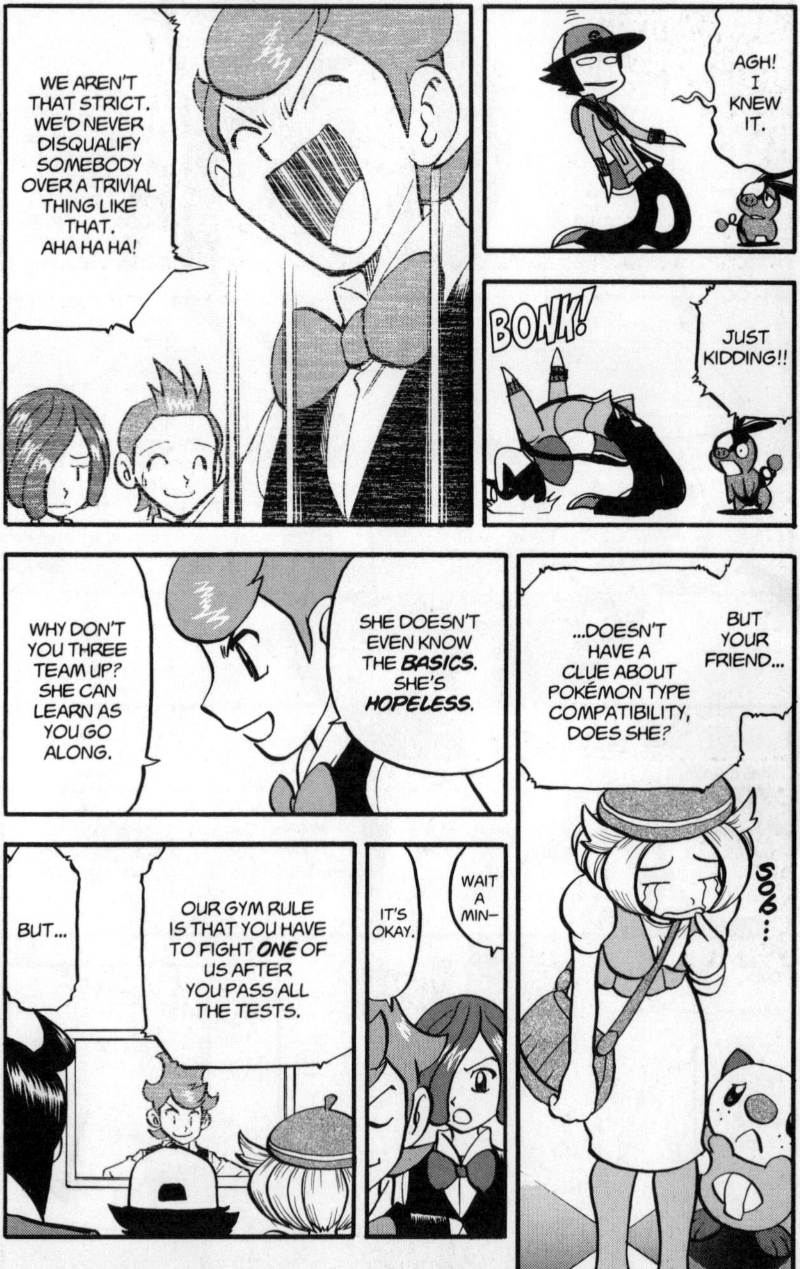
AGH! I KNEW IT.
BONK!
JUST KIDDING!!
WE AREN'T THAT STRICT. WE'D NEVER DISQUALIFY SOMEBODY OVER A TRIVIAL THING LIKE THAT. AHA HA HA!
BUT YOUR FRIEND...
...DOESN'T HAVE A CLUE ABOUT POKÉMON TYPE COMPATIBILITY, DOES SHE?
SOB...
SHE DOESN'T EVEN KNOW THE **BASICS**. SHE'S ***HOPELESS***.
WHY DON'T YOU THREE TEAM UP? SHE CAN LEARN AS YOU GO ALONG.
WAIT A MIN—
IT'S OKAY.
OUR GYM RULE IS THAT YOU HAVE TO FIGHT ***ONE*** OF US AFTER YOU PASS ALL THE TESTS.
BUT...

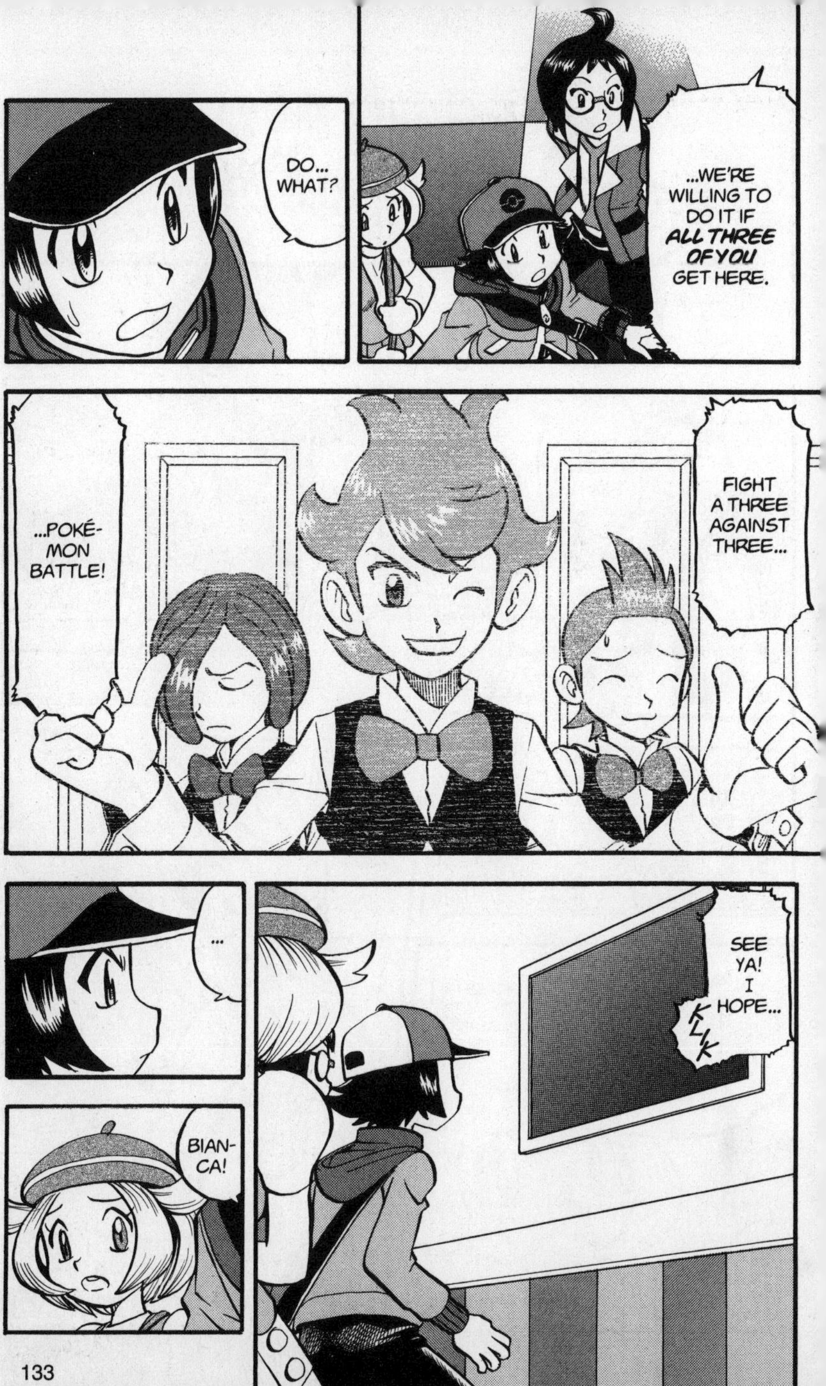
...WE'RE WILLING TO DO IT IF ALL THREE OF YOU GET HERE.
DO... WHAT?
FIGHT A THREE AGAINST THREE...
...POKÉ-MON BATTLE!
SEE YA! I HOPE...
KLIK
...
BIAN-CA!

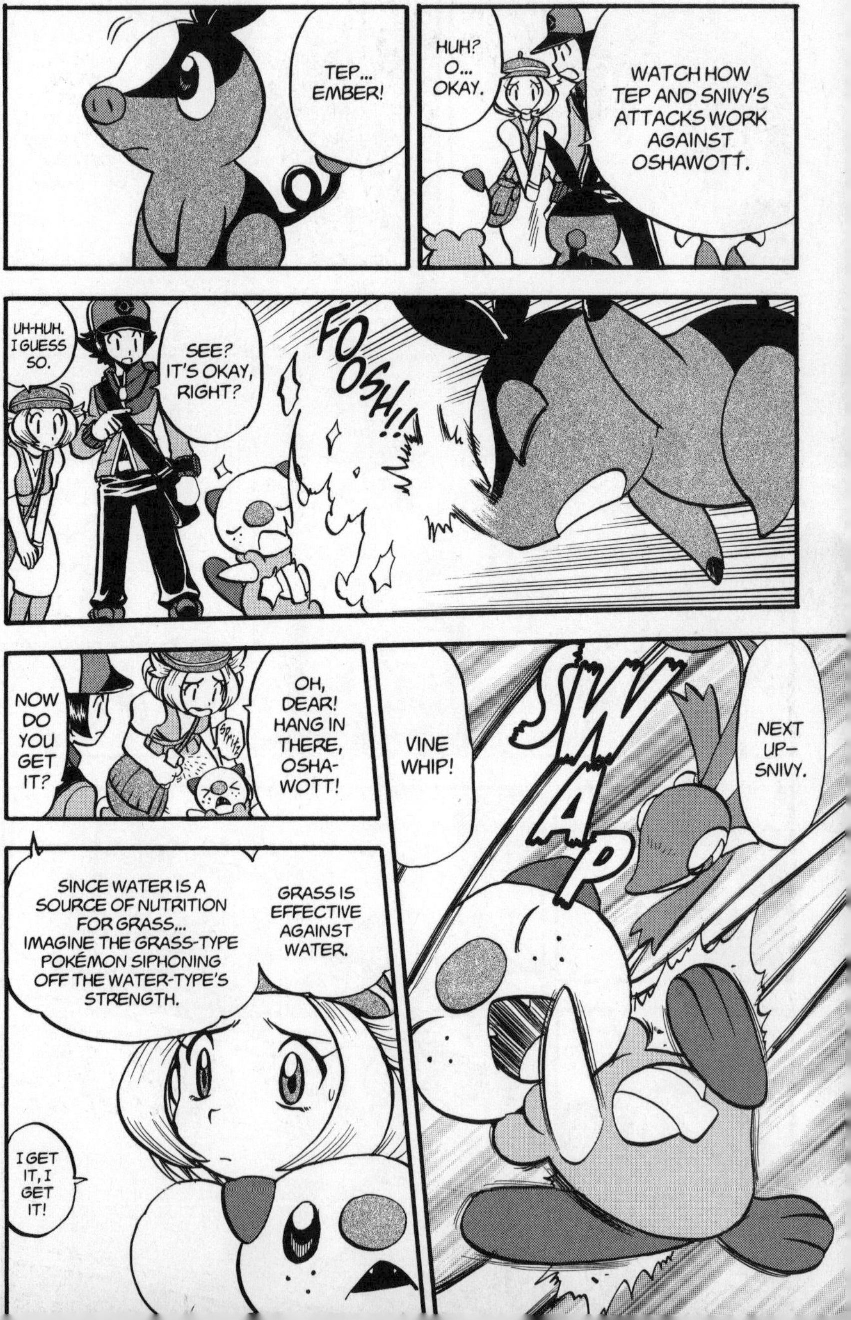
WATCH HOW TEP AND SNIVY'S ATTACKS WORK AGAINST OSHAWOTT.
HUH? O... OKAY.
TEP... EMBER!
FOOSH!!
SEE? IT'S OKAY, RIGHT?
UH-HUH. I GUESS SO.
NEXT UP— SNIVY.
VINE WHIP!
SWAP
OH, DEAR! HANG IN THERE, OSHA-WOTT!
Spritz
NOW DO YOU GET IT?
GRASS IS EFFECTIVE AGAINST WATER.
SINCE WATER IS A SOURCE OF NUTRITION FOR GRASS... IMAGINE THE GRASS-TYPE POKÉMON SIPHONING OFF THE WATER-TYPE'S STRENGTH.
I GET IT, I GET IT!

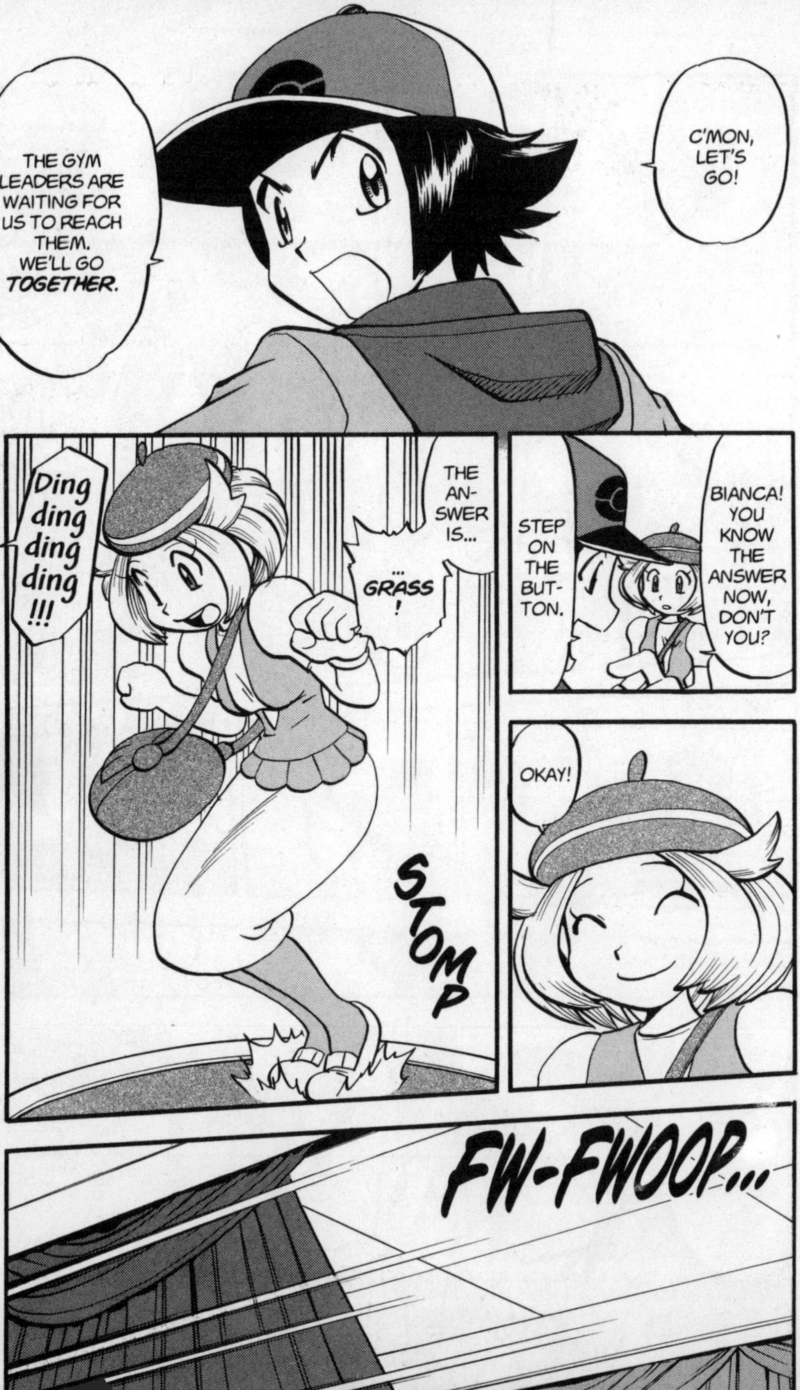
C'MON, LET'S GO!
THE GYM LEADERS ARE WAITING FOR US TO REACH THEM. WE'LL GO *TOGETHER*.
BIANCA! YOU KNOW THE ANSWER NOW, DON'T YOU?
STEP ON THE BUT-TON.
OKAY!
THE AN-SWER IS...
... *GRASS*!
Ding ding ding ding !!!
STOMP
FW-FWOOP...

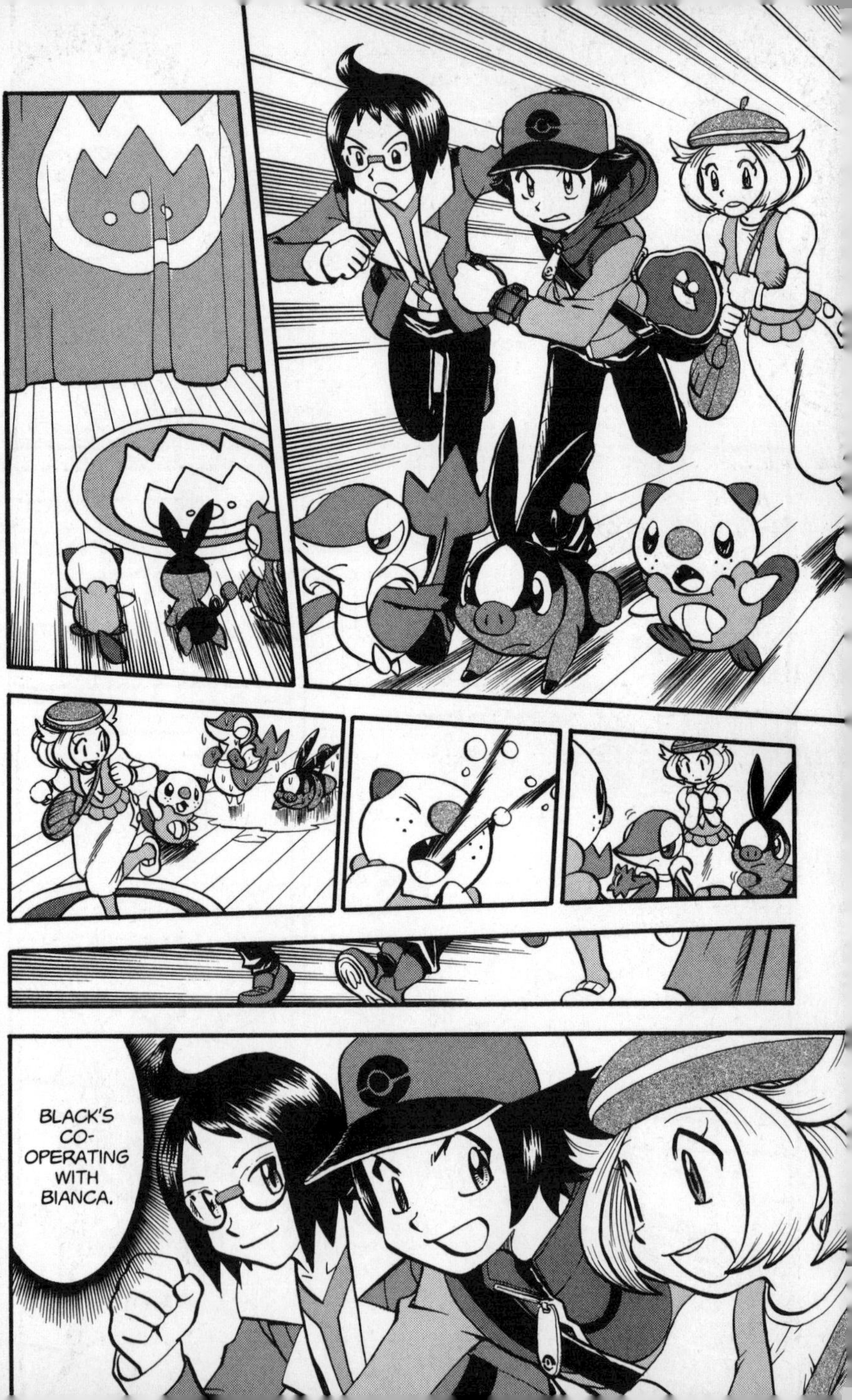
BLACK'S CO-OPERATING WITH BIANCA.

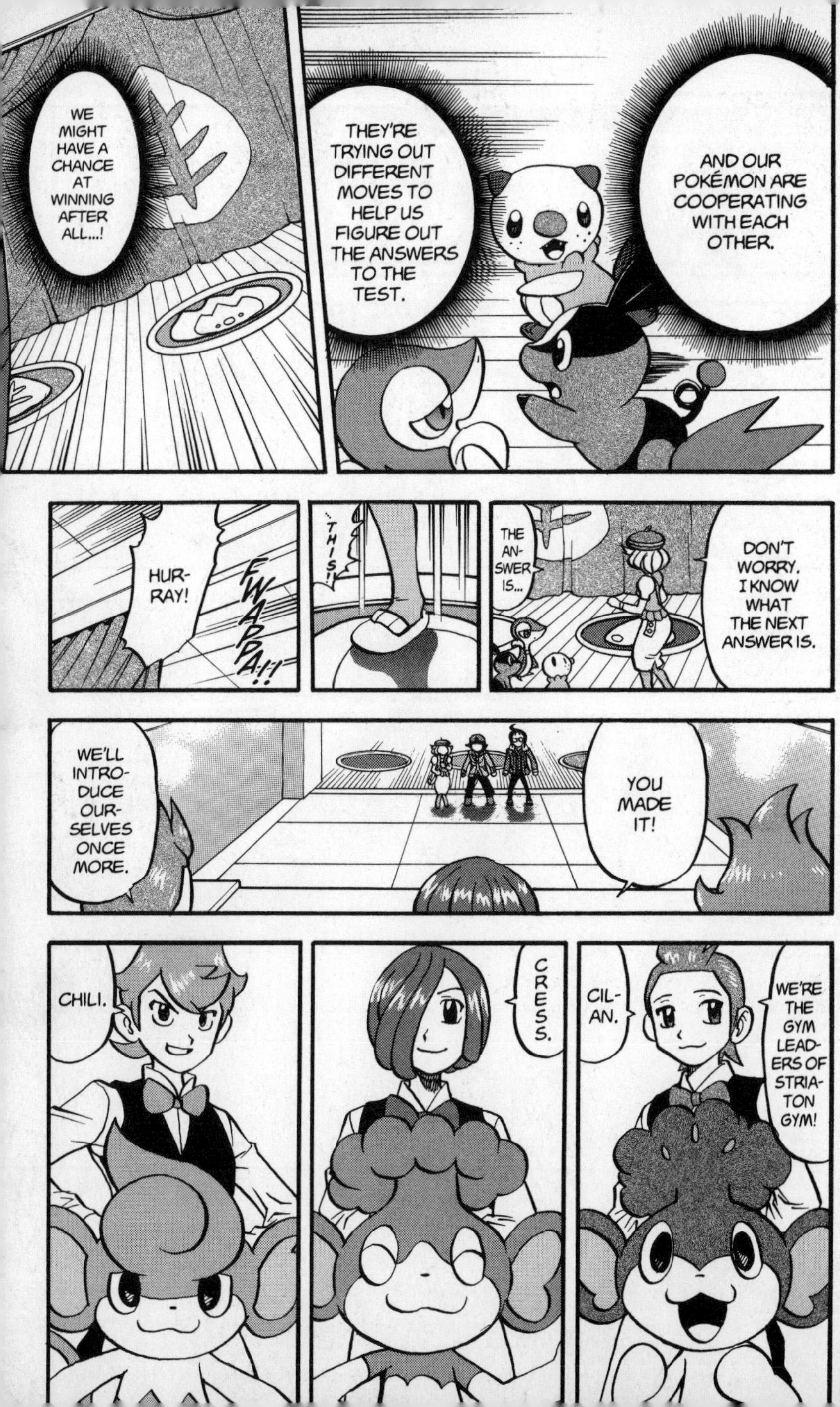

AND OUR POKÉMON ARE COOPERATING WITH EACH OTHER.
THEY'RE TRYING OUT DIFFERENT MOVES TO HELP US FIGURE OUT THE ANSWERS TO THE TEST.
WE MIGHT HAVE A CHANCE AT WINNING AFTER ALL...!
DON'T WORRY. I KNOW WHAT THE NEXT ANSWER IS.
THE ANSWER IS...
...THIS!
FWAPPA!!
HURRAY!
YOU MADE IT!
WE'LL INTRODUCE OURSELVES ONCE MORE.
WE'RE THE GYM LEADERS OF STRIATON GYM!
CILAN.
CRESS.
CHILI.

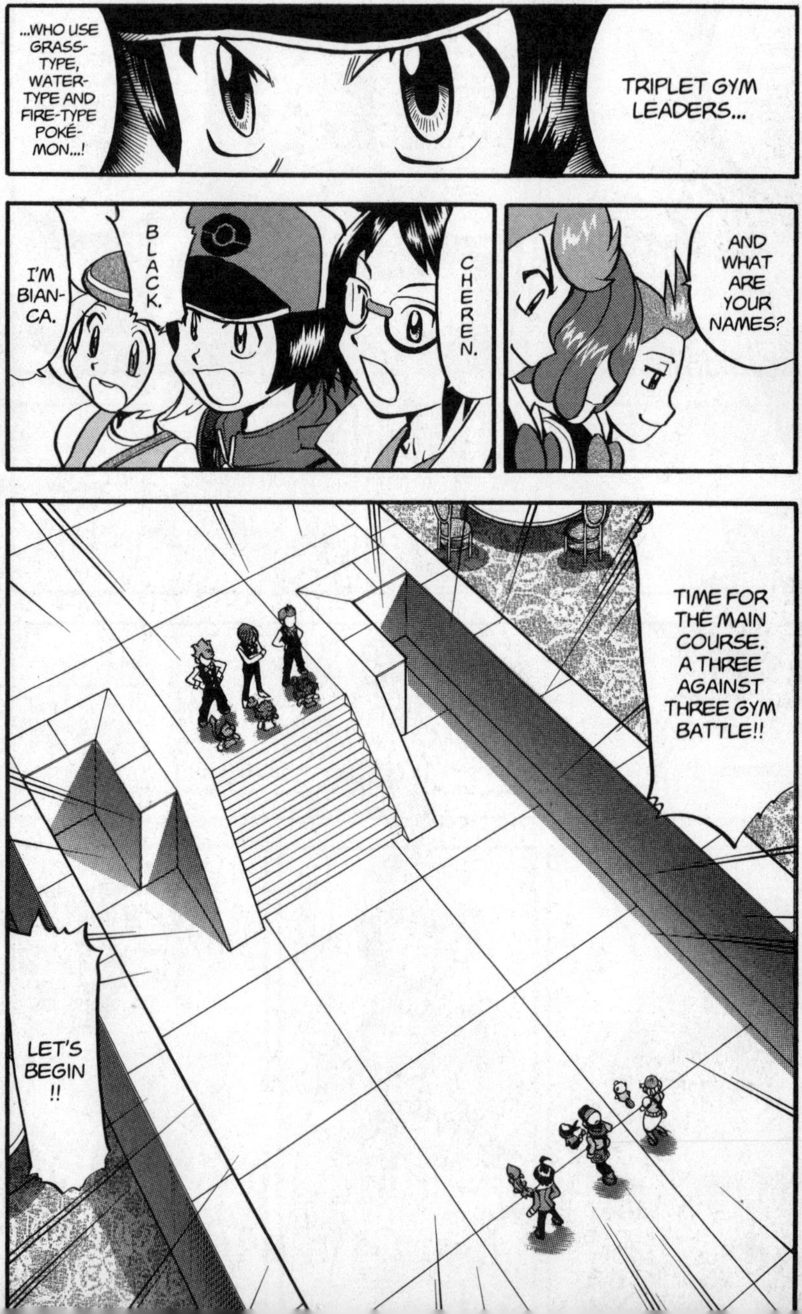
TRIPLET GYM LEADERS...
...WHO USE GRASS-TYPE, WATER-TYPE AND FIRE-TYPE POKÉMON...!
AND WHAT ARE YOUR NAMES?
CHEREN.
BLACK.
I'M BIANCA.
TIME FOR THE MAIN COURSE. A THREE AGAINST THREE GYM BATTLE!!
LET'S BEGIN!!

Pokémon Adventures Black & White

PANSAGE•PANSEAR•
PANPOUR

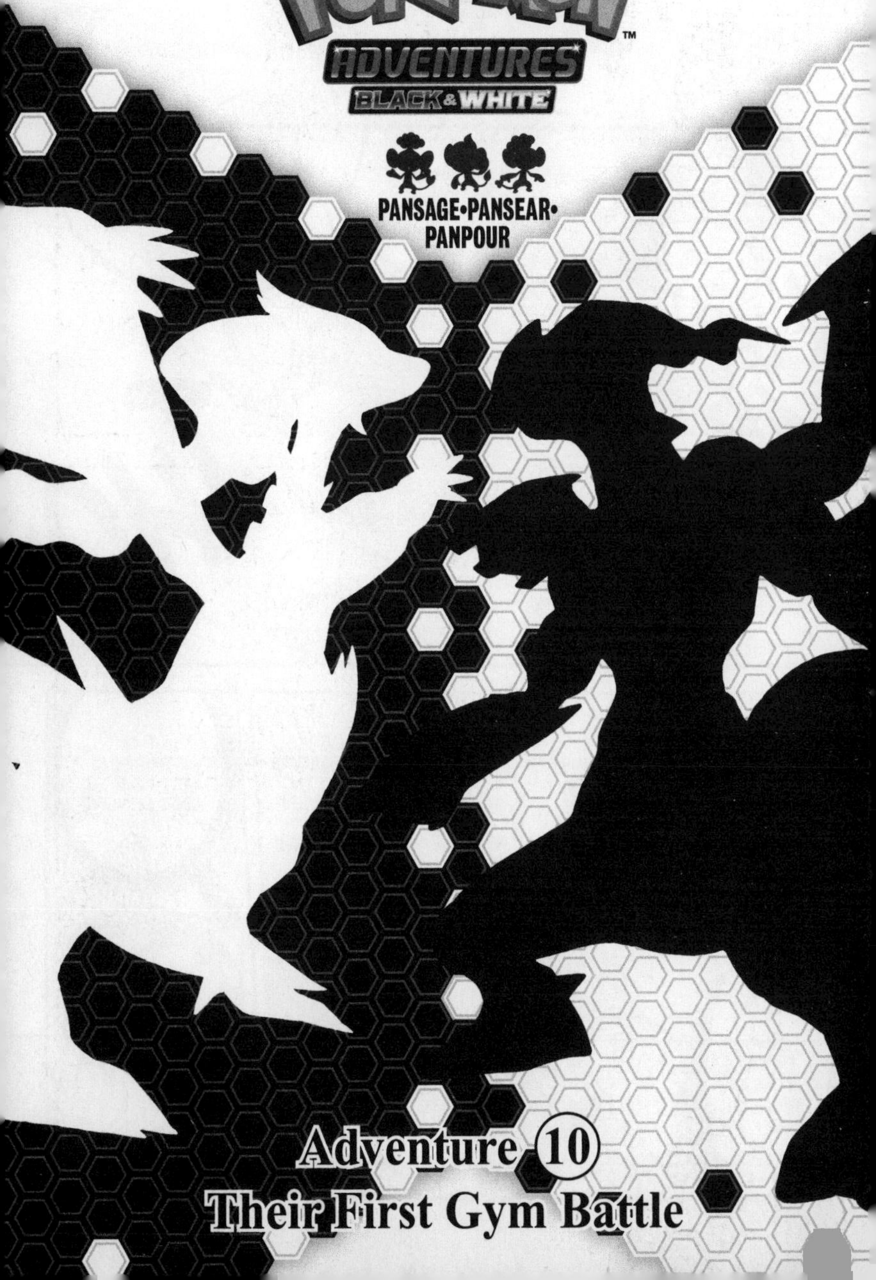

Adventure 10
Their First Gym Battle

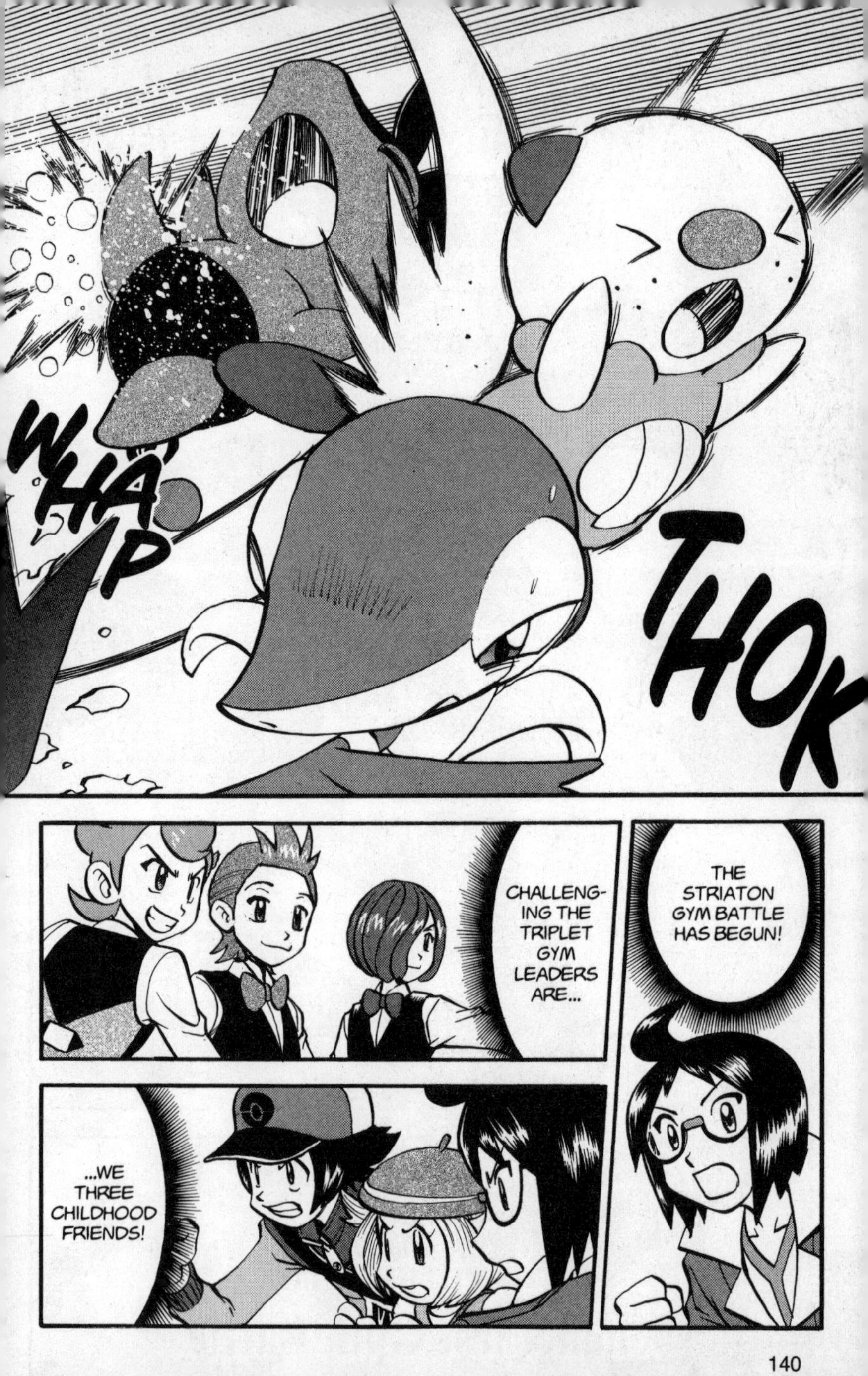
THOK
WHAP
THE STRIATON GYM BATTLE HAS BEGUN!
CHALLENG-ING THE TRIPLET GYM LEADERS ARE...
...WE THREE CHILDHOOD FRIENDS!

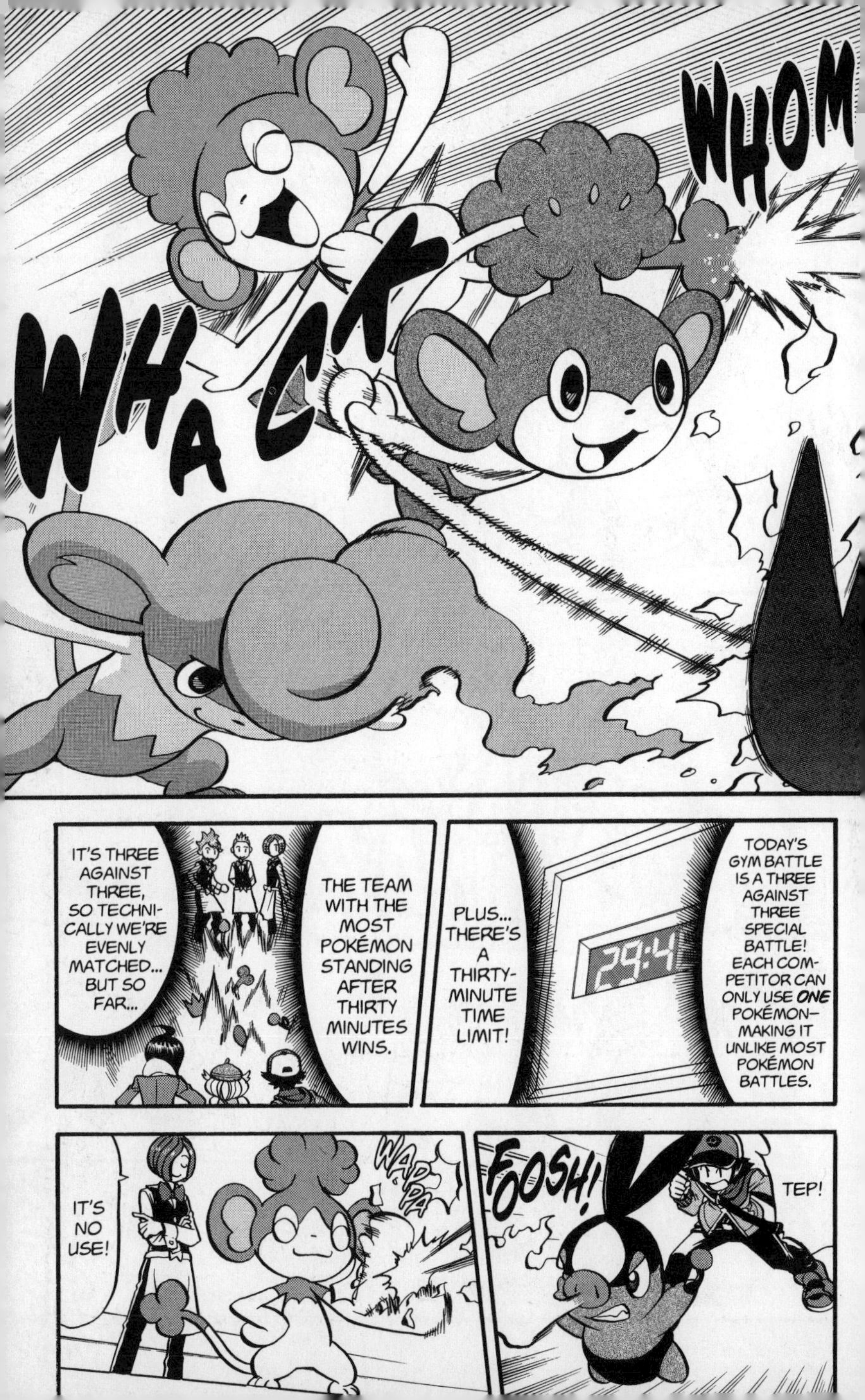
WHOM
WHACK
TODAY'S GYM BATTLE IS A THREE AGAINST THREE SPECIAL BATTLE! EACH COMPETITOR CAN ONLY USE ONE POKÉMON—MAKING IT UNLIKE MOST POKÉMON BATTLES.
29:4
PLUS... THERE'S A THIRTY-MINUTE TIME LIMIT!
THE TEAM WITH THE MOST POKÉMON STANDING AFTER THIRTY MINUTES WINS.
IT'S THREE AGAINST THREE, SO TECHNICALLY WE'RE EVENLY MATCHED... BUT SO FAR...
TEP!
FOOSH!
WAPA
IT'S NO USE!

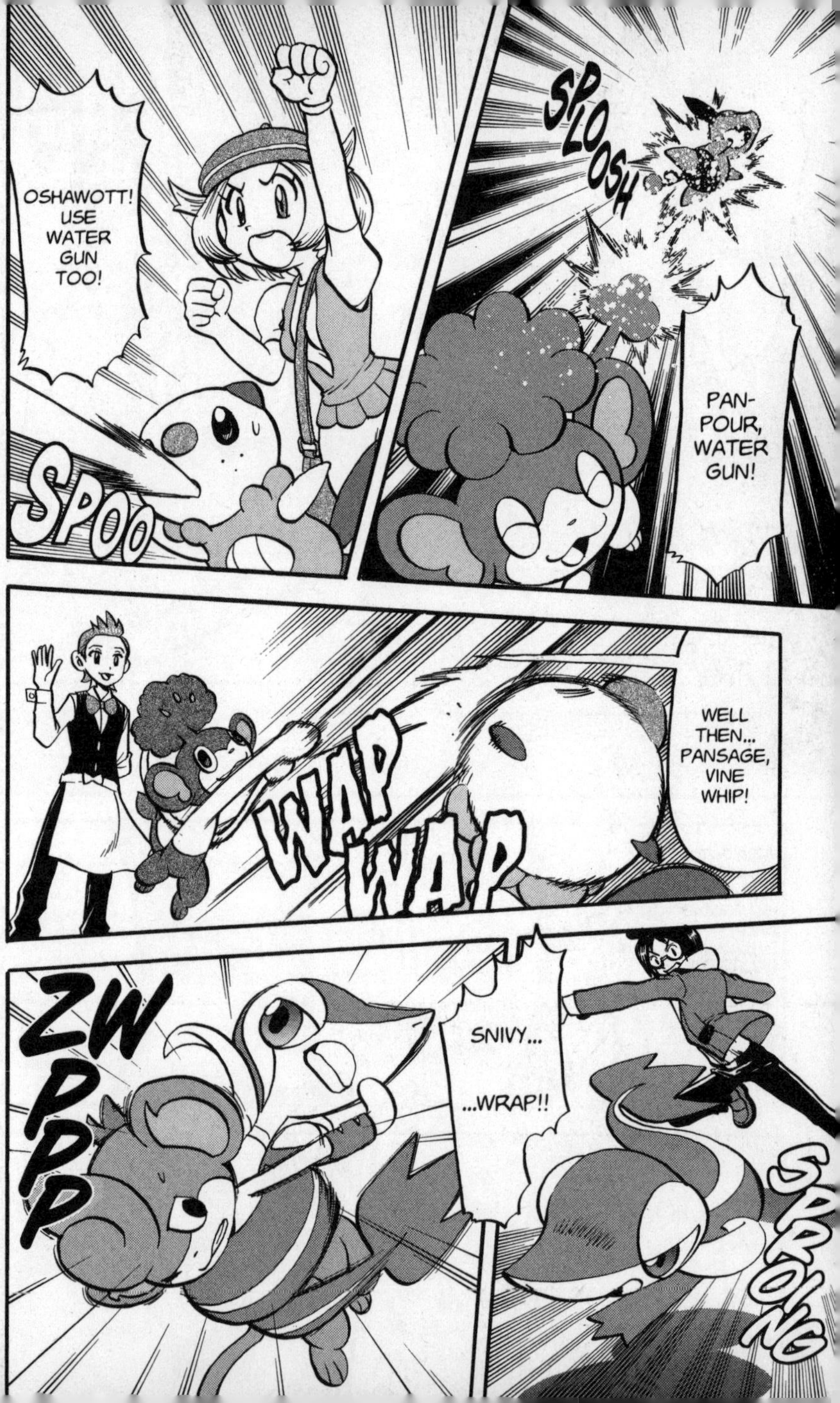
PAN-POUR, WATER GUN!
SPLOOSH
OSHAWOTT! USE WATER GUN TOO!
SPOO
WELL THEN... PANSAGE, VINE WHIP!
WAP WAP
SNIVY...
...WRAP!!
SPROING
ZWPPP

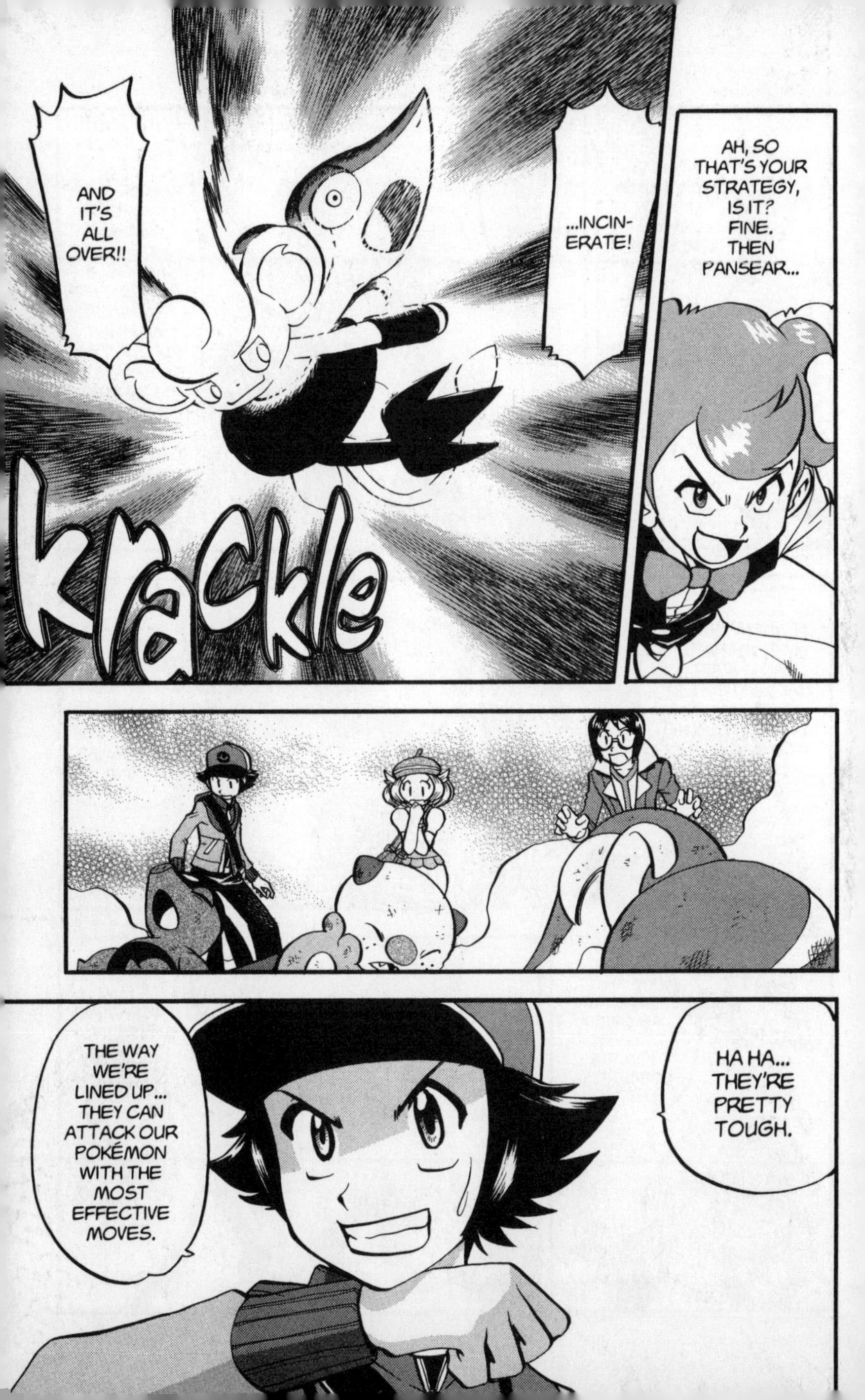
AH, SO THAT'S YOUR STRATEGY, IS IT? FINE. THEN PANSEAR...
...INCIN-ERATE!
AND IT'S ALL OVER!!
krackle
HA HA... THEY'RE PRETTY TOUGH.
THE WAY WE'RE LINED UP... THEY CAN ATTACK OUR POKÉMON WITH THE MOST EFFECTIVE MOVES.

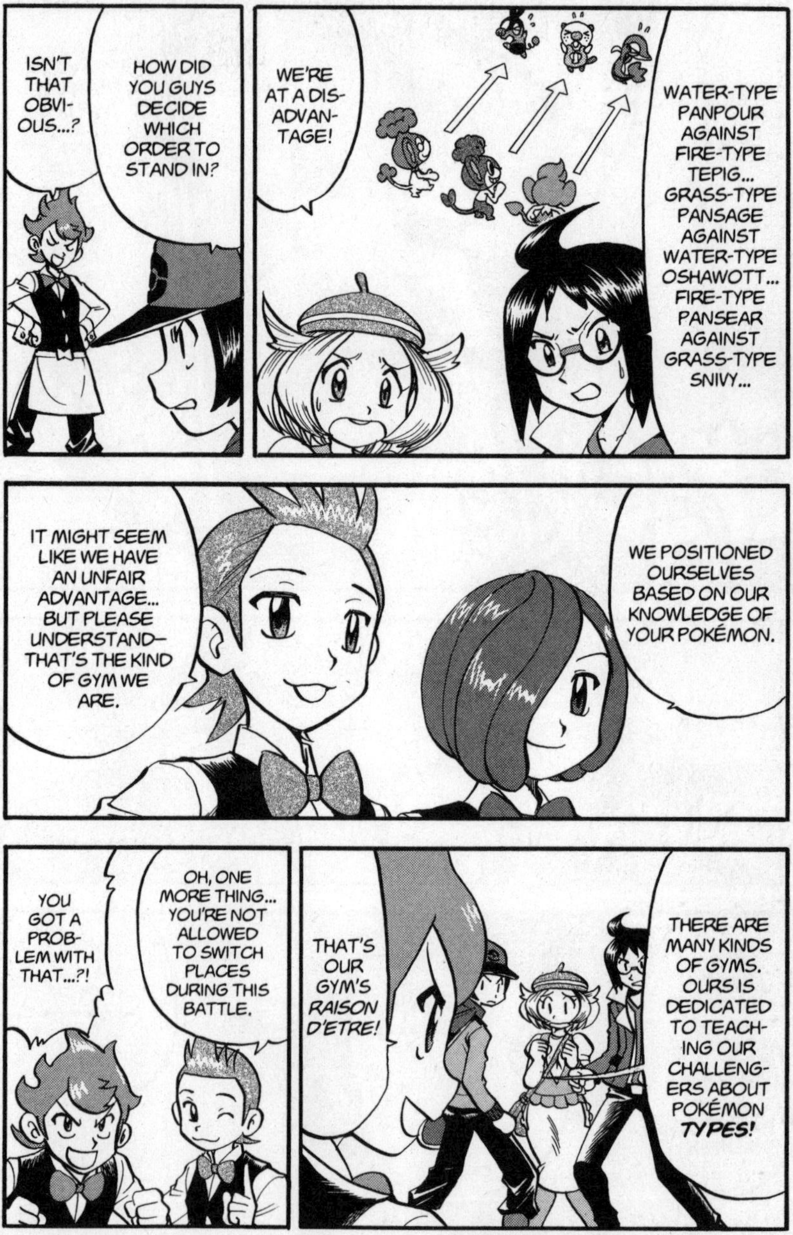
WATER-TYPE PANPOUR AGAINST FIRE-TYPE TEPIG... GRASS-TYPE PANSAGE AGAINST WATER-TYPE OSHAWOTT... FIRE-TYPE PANSEAR AGAINST GRASS-TYPE SNIVY...
WE'RE AT A DIS-ADVANTAGE!
HOW DID YOU GUYS DECIDE WHICH ORDER TO STAND IN?
ISN'T THAT OBVIOUS...?
WE POSITIONED OURSELVES BASED ON OUR KNOWLEDGE OF YOUR POKÉMON.
IT MIGHT SEEM LIKE WE HAVE AN UNFAIR ADVANTAGE... BUT PLEASE UNDERSTAND— THAT'S THE KIND OF GYM WE ARE.
THERE ARE MANY KINDS OF GYMS. OURS IS DEDICATED TO TEACHING OUR CHALLENGERS ABOUT POKÉMON ***TYPES!***
THAT'S OUR GYM'S *RAISON D'ETRE!*
OH, ONE MORE THING... YOU'RE NOT ALLOWED TO SWITCH PLACES DURING THIS BATTLE.
YOU GOT A PROBLEM WITH THAT...?!

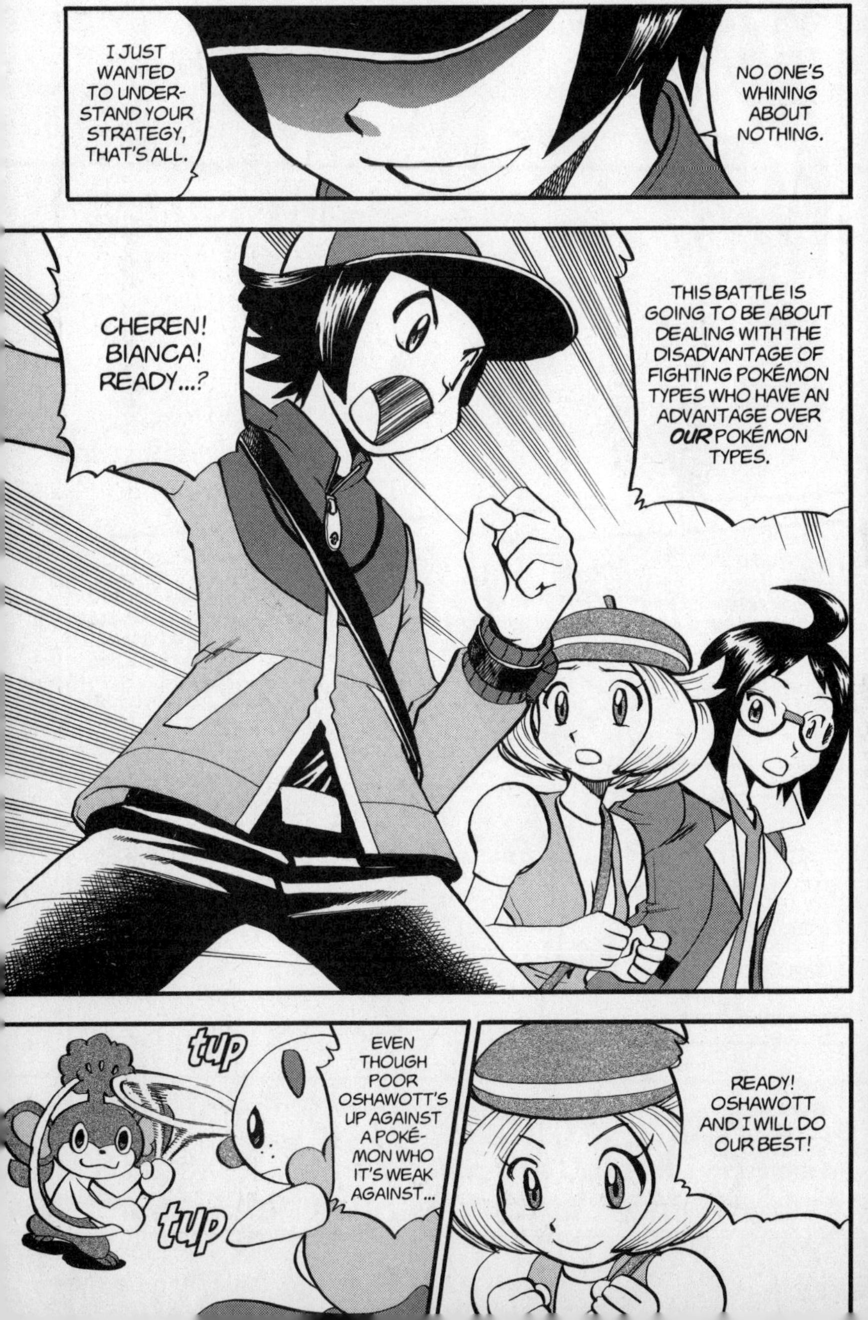
NO ONE'S WHINING ABOUT NOTHING.
I JUST WANTED TO UNDER-STAND YOUR STRATEGY, THAT'S ALL.
THIS BATTLE IS GOING TO BE ABOUT DEALING WITH THE DISADVANTAGE OF FIGHTING POKÉMON TYPES WHO HAVE AN ADVANTAGE OVER *OUR* POKÉMON TYPES.
CHEREN! BIANCA! READY...?
READY! OSHAWOTT AND I WILL DO OUR BEST!
EVEN THOUGH POOR OSHAWOTT'S UP AGAINST A POKÉ-MON WHO IT'S WEAK AGAINST...
tup
tup

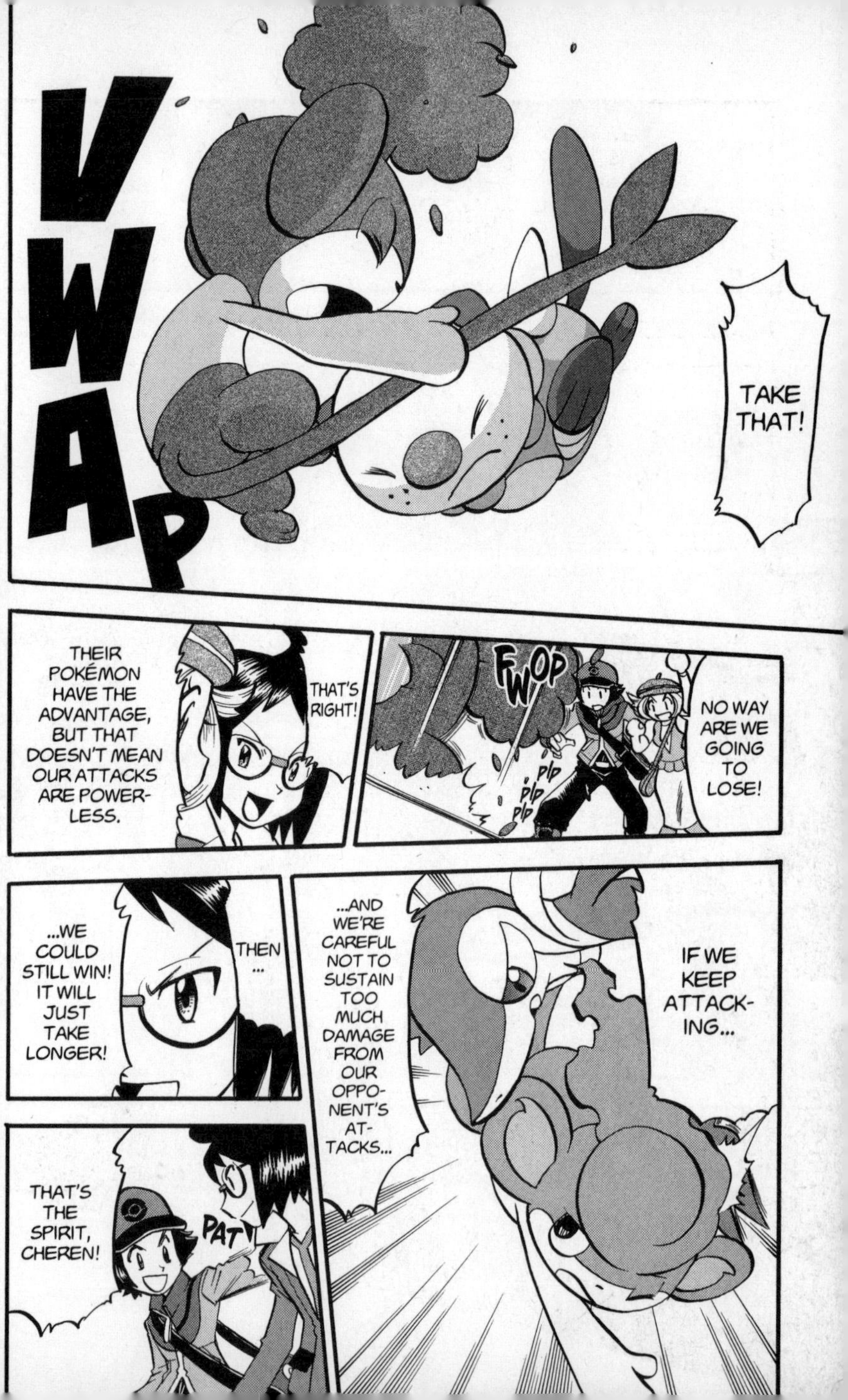
TAKE THAT!
VWAP
NO WAY ARE WE GOING TO LOSE!
FWOP
PIP PIP PIP
THAT'S RIGHT!
THEIR POKÉMON HAVE THE ADVANTAGE, BUT THAT DOESN'T MEAN OUR ATTACKS ARE POWER-LESS.
IF WE KEEP ATTACK-ING...
...AND WE'RE CAREFUL NOT TO SUSTAIN TOO MUCH DAMAGE FROM OUR OPPO-NENT'S AT-TACKS...
THEN...
...WE COULD STILL WIN! IT WILL JUST TAKE LONGER!
PAT
THAT'S THE SPIRIT, CHEREN!

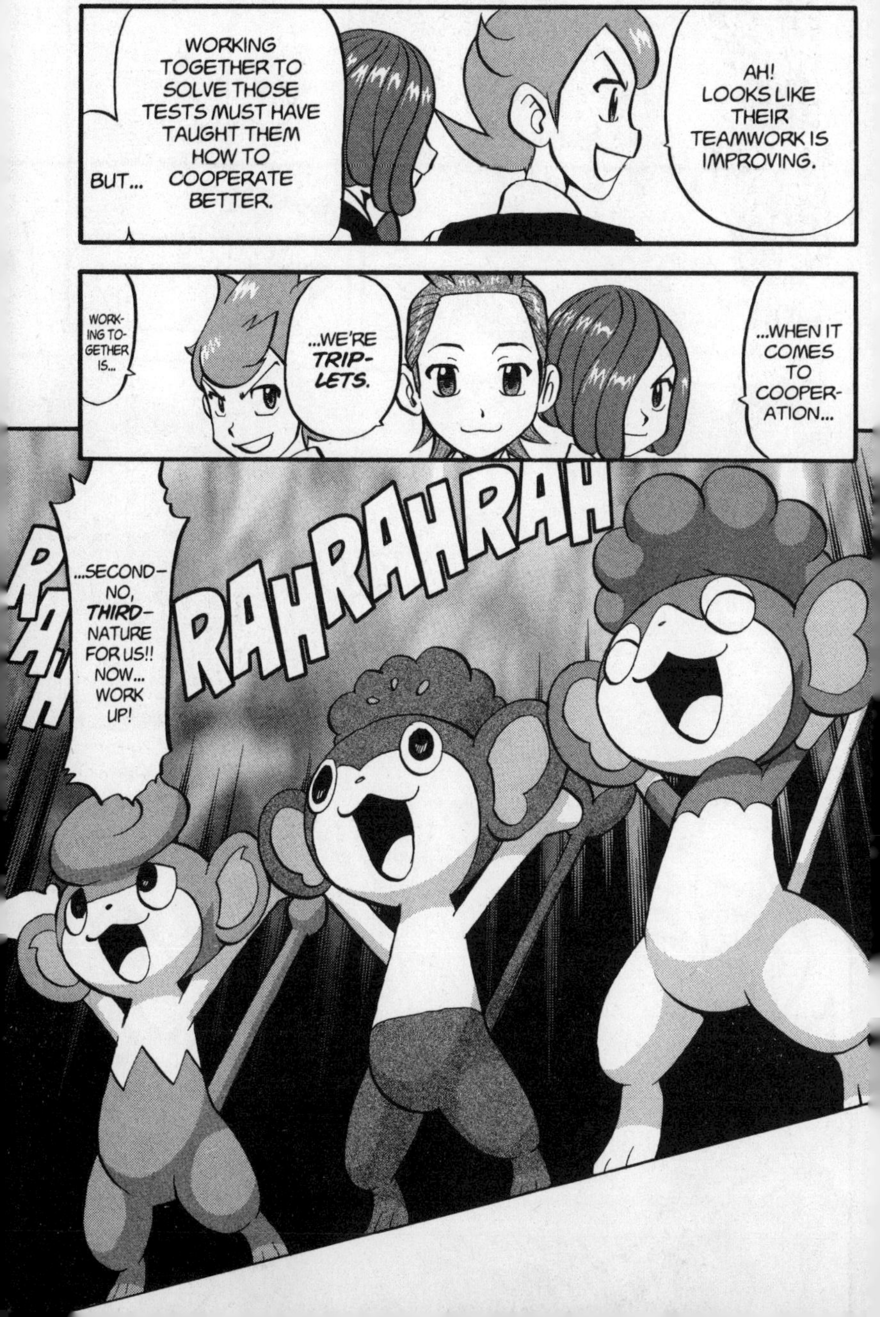

AH! LOOKS LIKE THEIR TEAMWORK IS IMPROVING.
WORKING TOGETHER TO SOLVE THOSE TESTS MUST HAVE TAUGHT THEM HOW TO COOPERATE BETTER.
BUT...
...WHEN IT COMES TO COOPER-ATION...
...WE'RE *TRIP-LETS.*
WORK-ING TO-GETHER IS...
...SECOND—NO, ***THIRD***—NATURE FOR US!! NOW... WORK UP!
RAHRAHRAHRAH

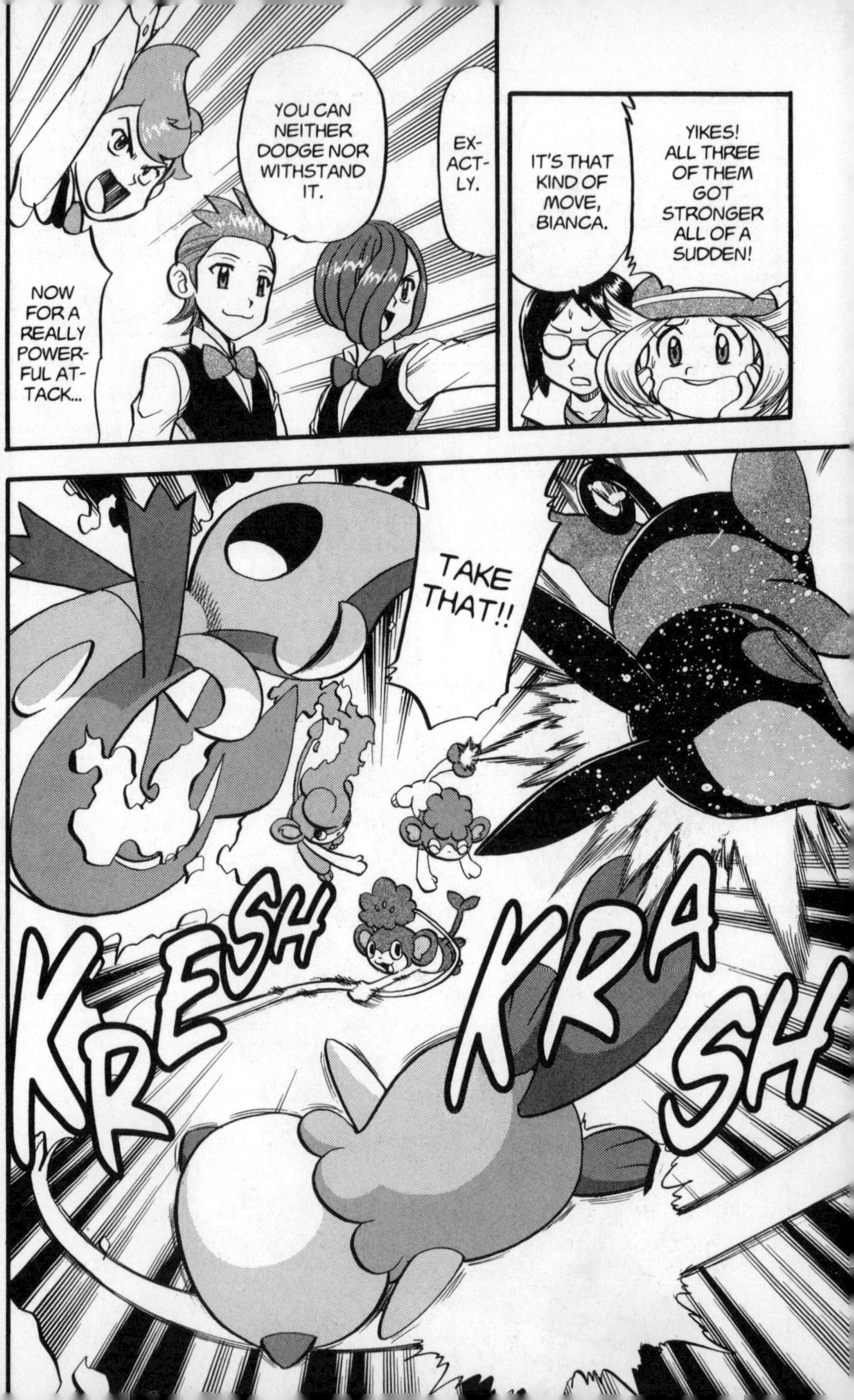
YIKES! ALL THREE OF THEM GOT STRONGER ALL OF A SUDDEN!
IT'S THAT KIND OF MOVE, BIANCA.
EX-ACT-LY.
YOU CAN NEITHER DODGE NOR WITHSTAND IT.
NOW FOR A REALLY POWER-FUL AT-TACK...
TAKE THAT!!
KRASH
KRESH

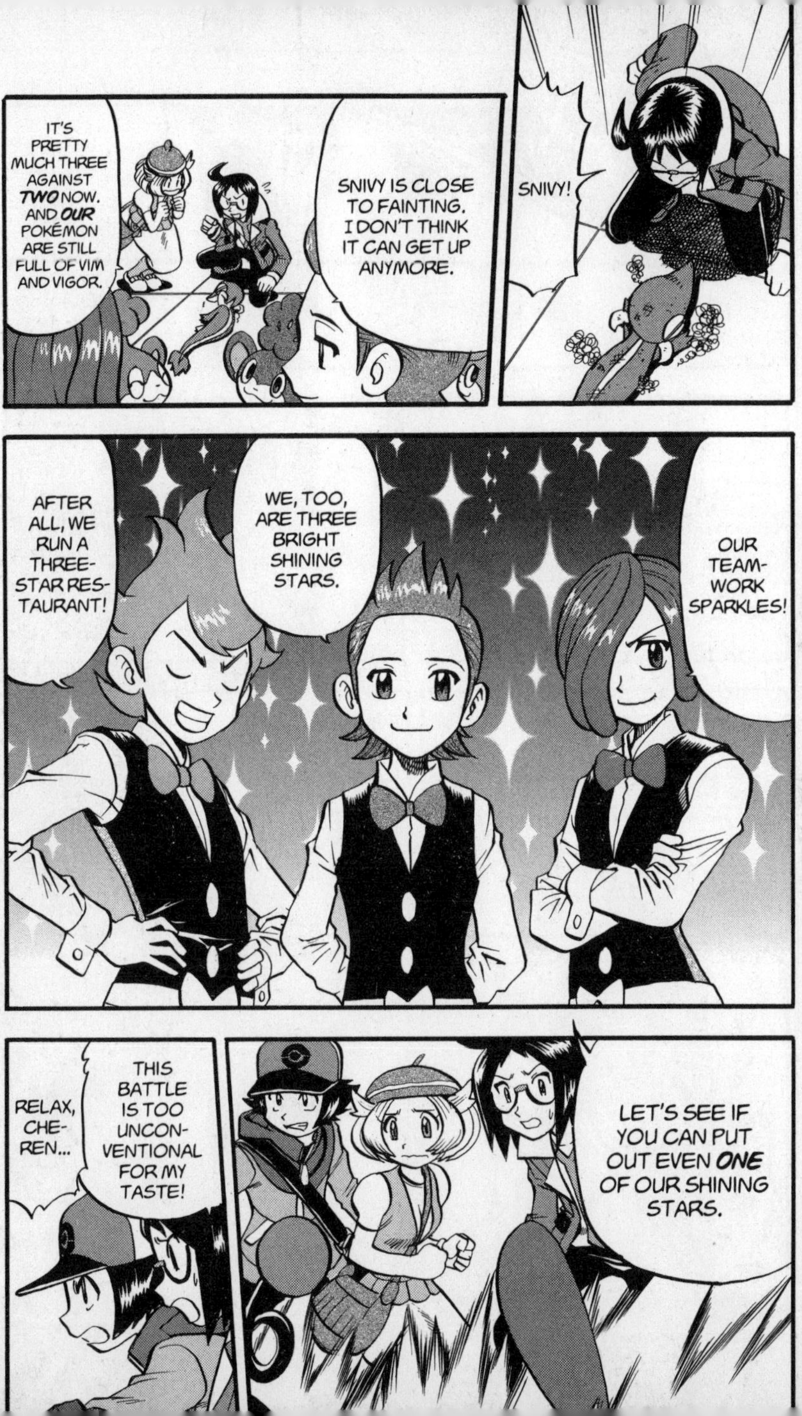
SNIVY!
SNIVY IS CLOSE TO FAINTING. I DON'T THINK IT CAN GET UP ANYMORE.
IT'S PRETTY MUCH THREE AGAINST **TWO** NOW. AND **OUR** POKÉMON ARE STILL FULL OF VIM AND VIGOR.
OUR TEAM-WORK SPARKLES!
WE, TOO, ARE THREE BRIGHT SHINING STARS.
AFTER ALL, WE RUN A THREE-STAR RES-TAURANT!
LET'S SEE IF YOU CAN PUT OUT EVEN **ONE** OF OUR SHINING STARS.
THIS BATTLE IS TOO UNCON-VENTIONAL FOR MY TASTE!
RELAX, CHE-REN...

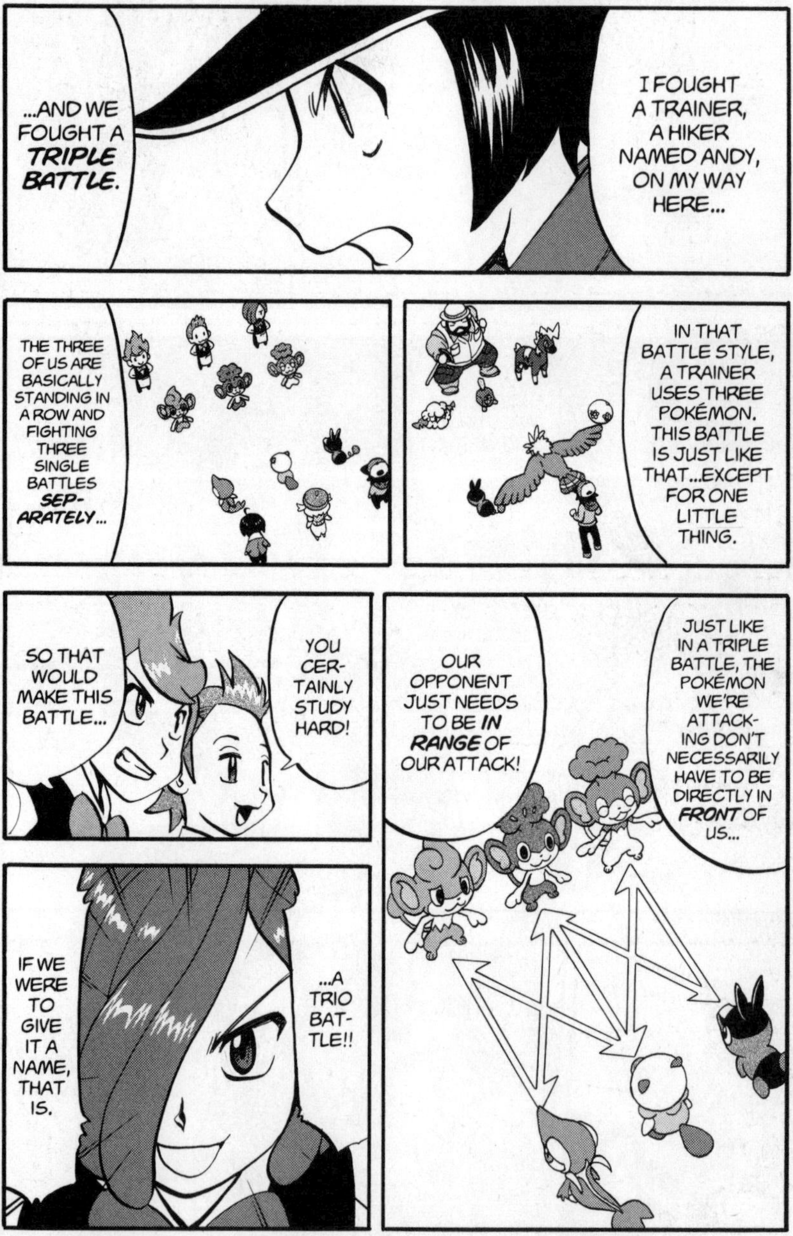
I FOUGHT A TRAINER, A HIKER NAMED ANDY, ON MY WAY HERE...
...AND WE FOUGHT A TRIPLE BATTLE.
IN THAT BATTLE STYLE, A TRAINER USES THREE POKéMON. THIS BATTLE IS JUST LIKE THAT...EXCEPT FOR ONE LITTLE THING.
THE THREE OF US ARE BASICALLY STANDING IN A ROW AND FIGHTING THREE SINGLE BATTLES SEPARATELY...
JUST LIKE IN A TRIPLE BATTLE, THE POKéMON WE'RE ATTACKING DON'T NECESSARILY HAVE TO BE DIRECTLY IN FRONT OF US...
OUR OPPONENT JUST NEEDS TO BE IN RANGE OF OUR ATTACK!
YOU CERTAINLY STUDY HARD!
SO THAT WOULD MAKE THIS BATTLE...
...A TRIO BATTLE!!
IF WE WERE TO GIVE IT A NAME, THAT IS.

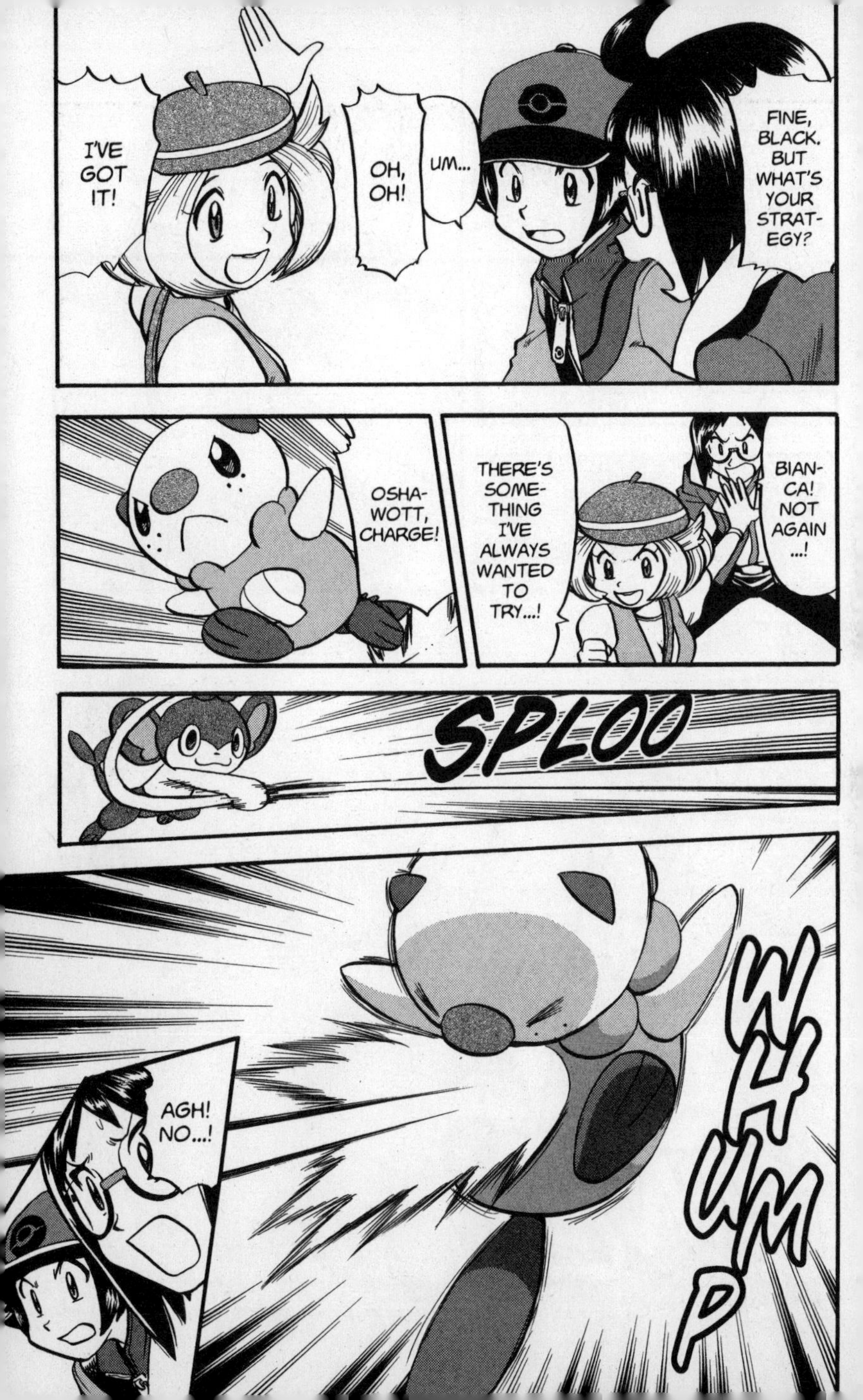
FINE, BLACK. BUT WHAT'S YOUR STRAT-EGY?
UM...
OH, OH!
I'VE GOT IT!
BIAN-CA! NOT AGAIN ...!
THERE'S SOME-THING I'VE ALWAYS WANTED TO TRY...!
OSHA-WOTT, CHARGE!
SPLOO
WHUMP
AGH! NO...!

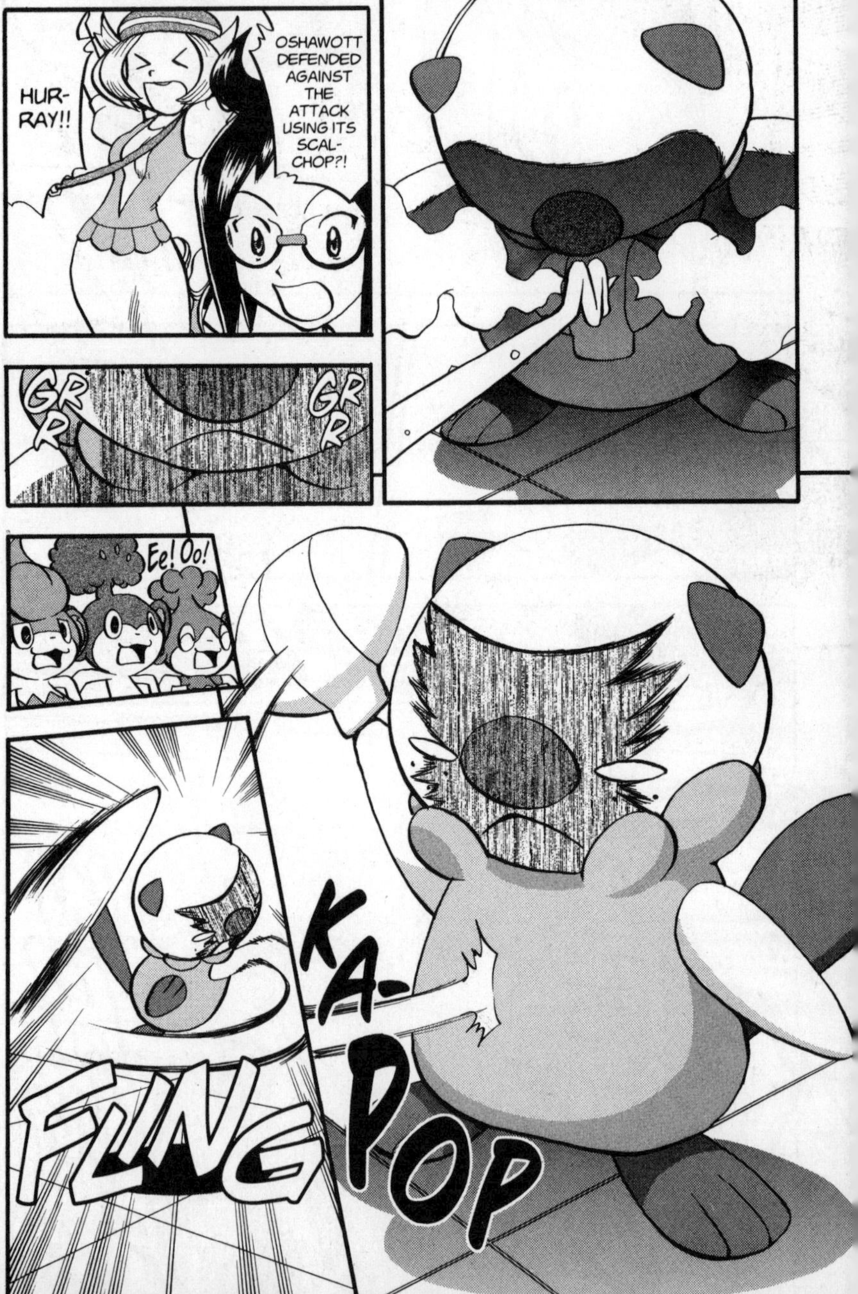
OSHAWOTT DEFENDED AGAINST THE ATTACK USING ITS SCAL-CHOP?!
HUR-RAY!!
GRR
GRR
Ee! Oo!
KA-POP
FLING

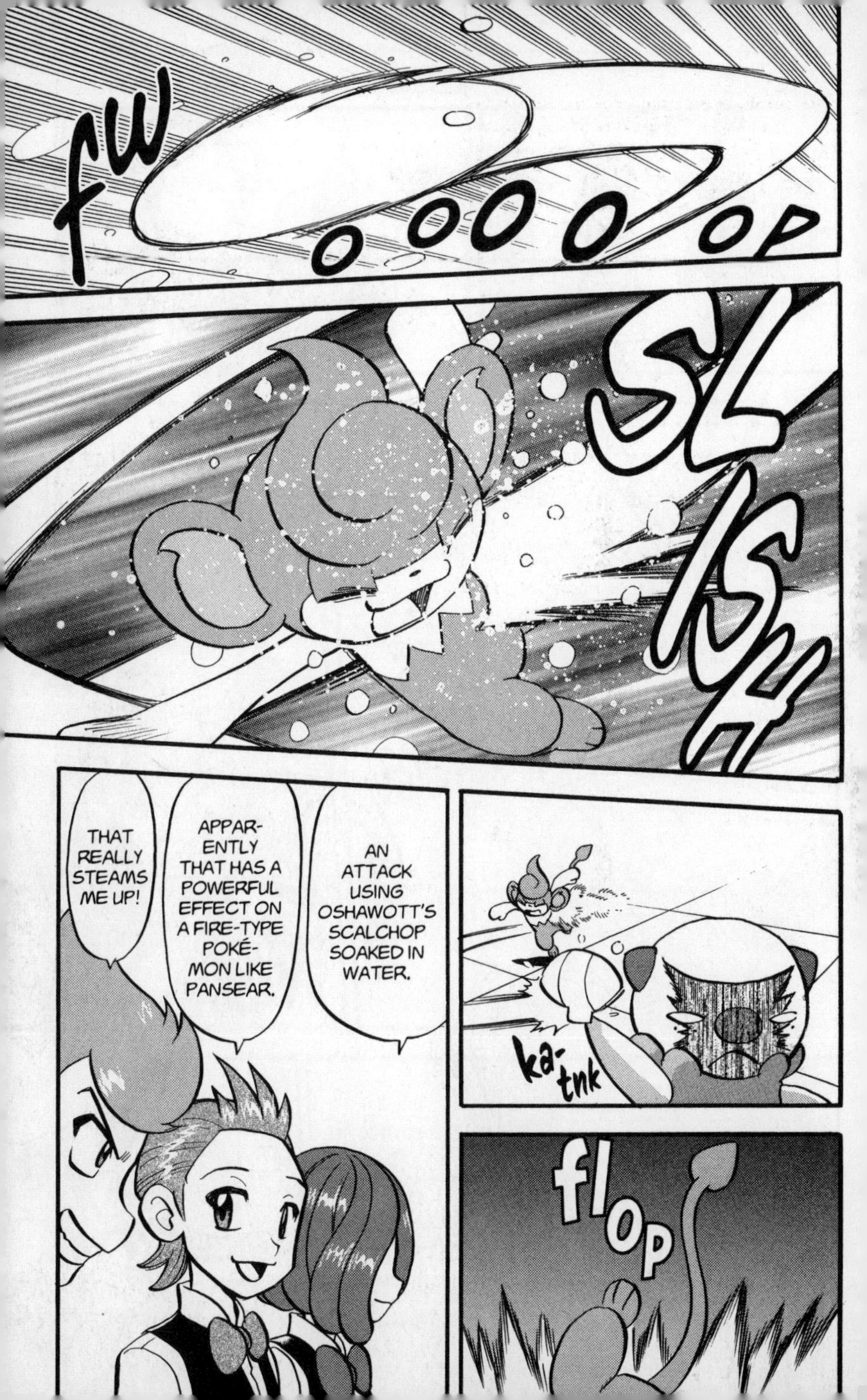
fwooooop
SLOSH
ka-tnk
flop
AN ATTACK USING OSHAWOTT'S SCALCHOP SOAKED IN WATER.
APPARENTLY THAT HAS A POWERFUL EFFECT ON A FIRE-TYPE POKÉMON LIKE PANSEAR.
THAT REALLY STEAMS ME UP!

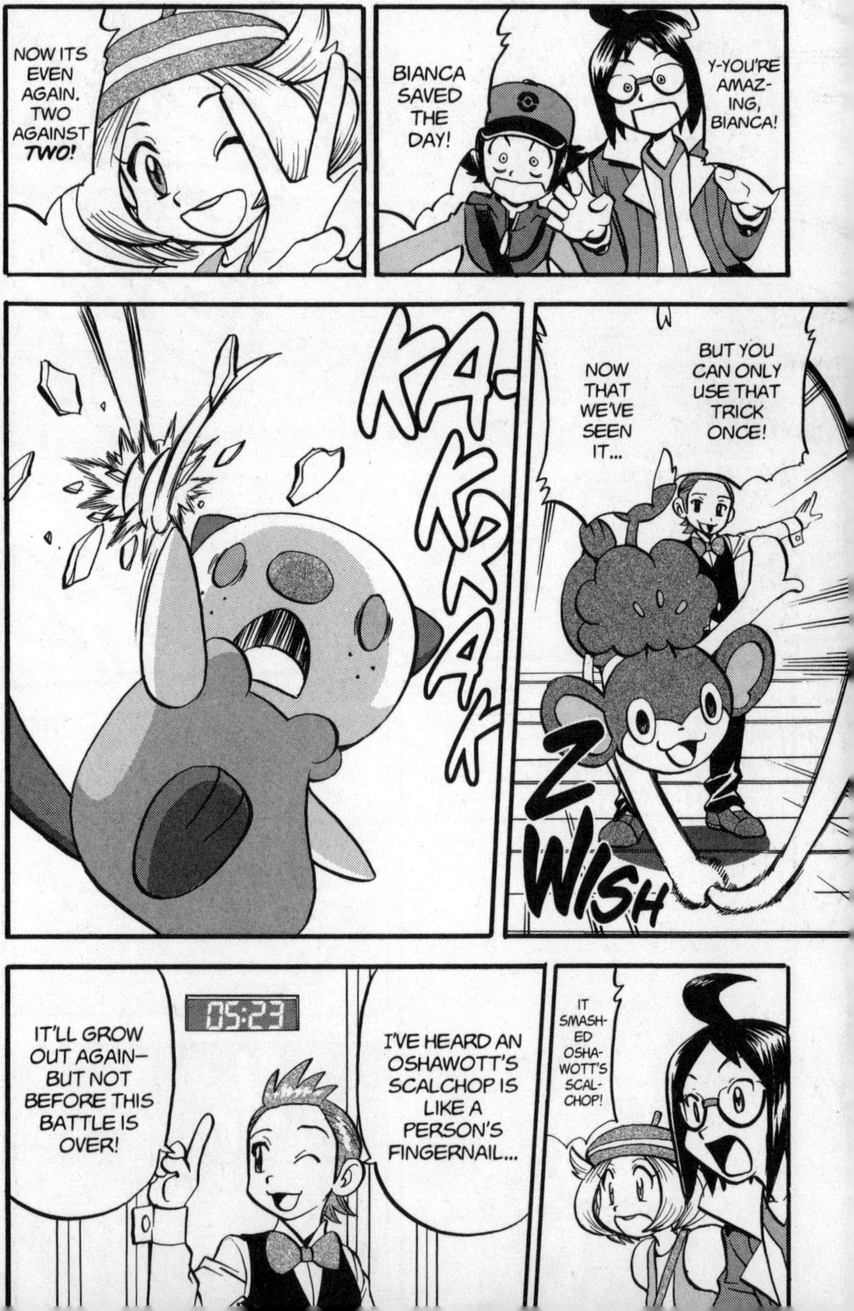
Y-YOU'RE AMAZ-ING, BIANCA!
BIANCA SAVED THE DAY!
NOW ITS EVEN AGAIN. TWO AGAINST **TWO!**
BUT YOU CAN ONLY USE THAT TRICK ONCE!
NOW THAT WE'VE SEEN IT...
ZWISH
KA-KRAK
IT SMASH-ED OSHA-WOTT'S SCAL-CHOP!
I'VE HEARD AN OSHAWOTT'S SCALCHOP IS LIKE A PERSON'S FINGERNAIL...
05:23
IT'LL GROW OUT AGAIN— BUT NOT BEFORE THIS BATTLE IS OVER!

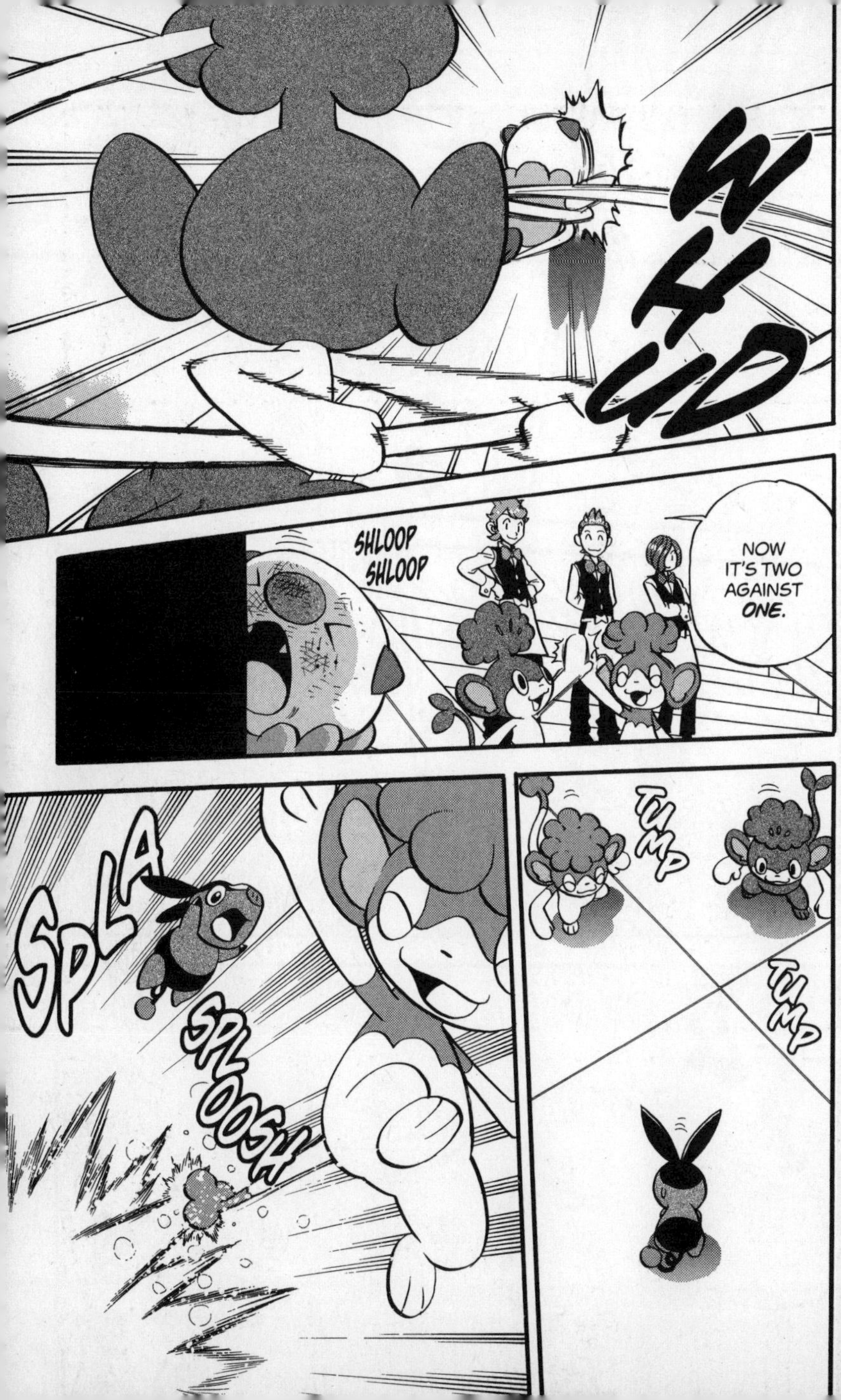
WHUD
NOW IT'S TWO AGAINST ONE.
SHLOOP SHLOOP
TUMP
TUMP
SPLA
SPLOOSH

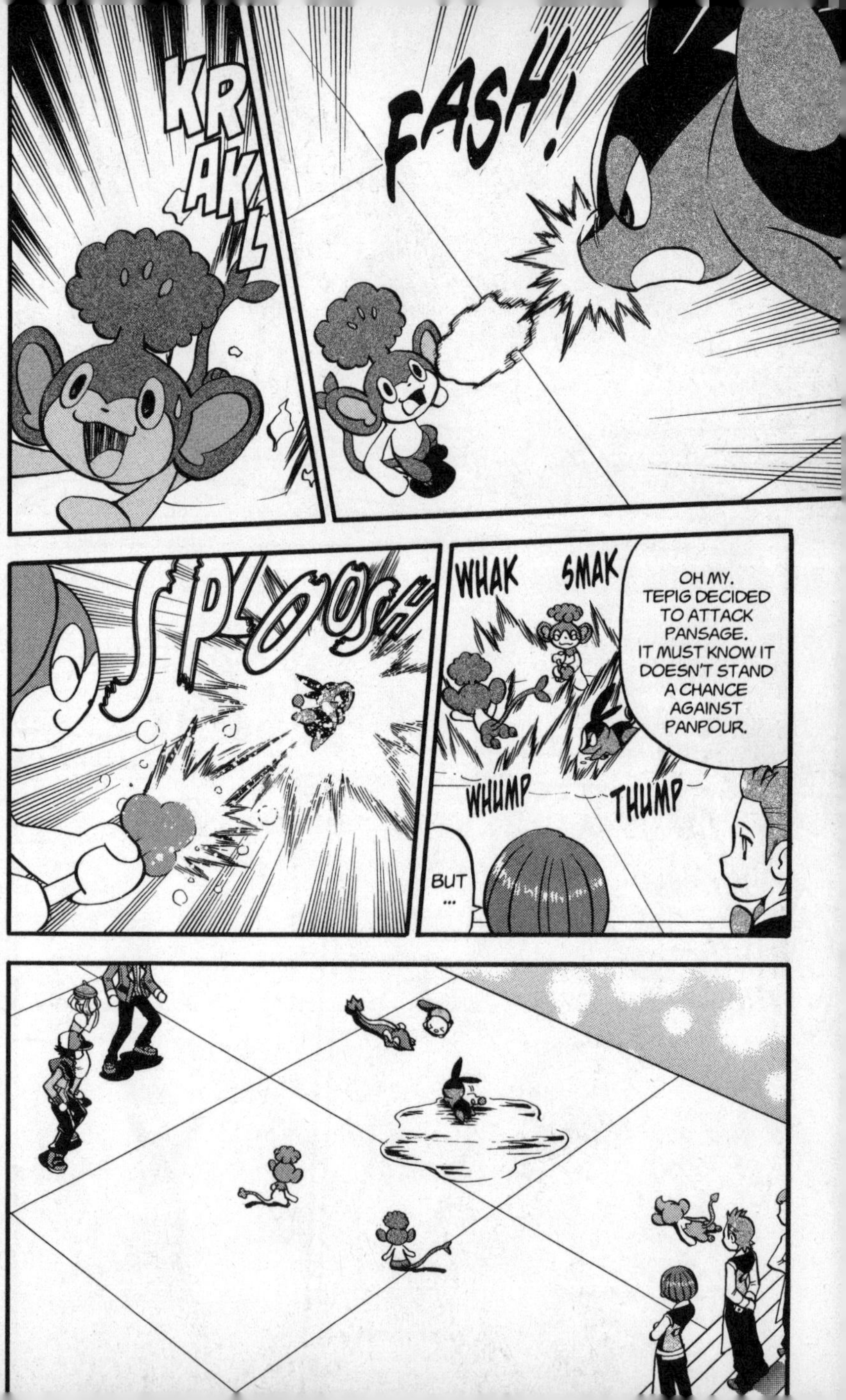
FASH!
KRAKL
OH MY. TEPIG DECIDED TO ATTACK PANSAGE. IT MUST KNOW IT DOESN'T STAND A CHANCE AGAINST PANPOUR.
SMAK
WHAK
THUMP
WHUMP
BUT ...
SPLOOSH

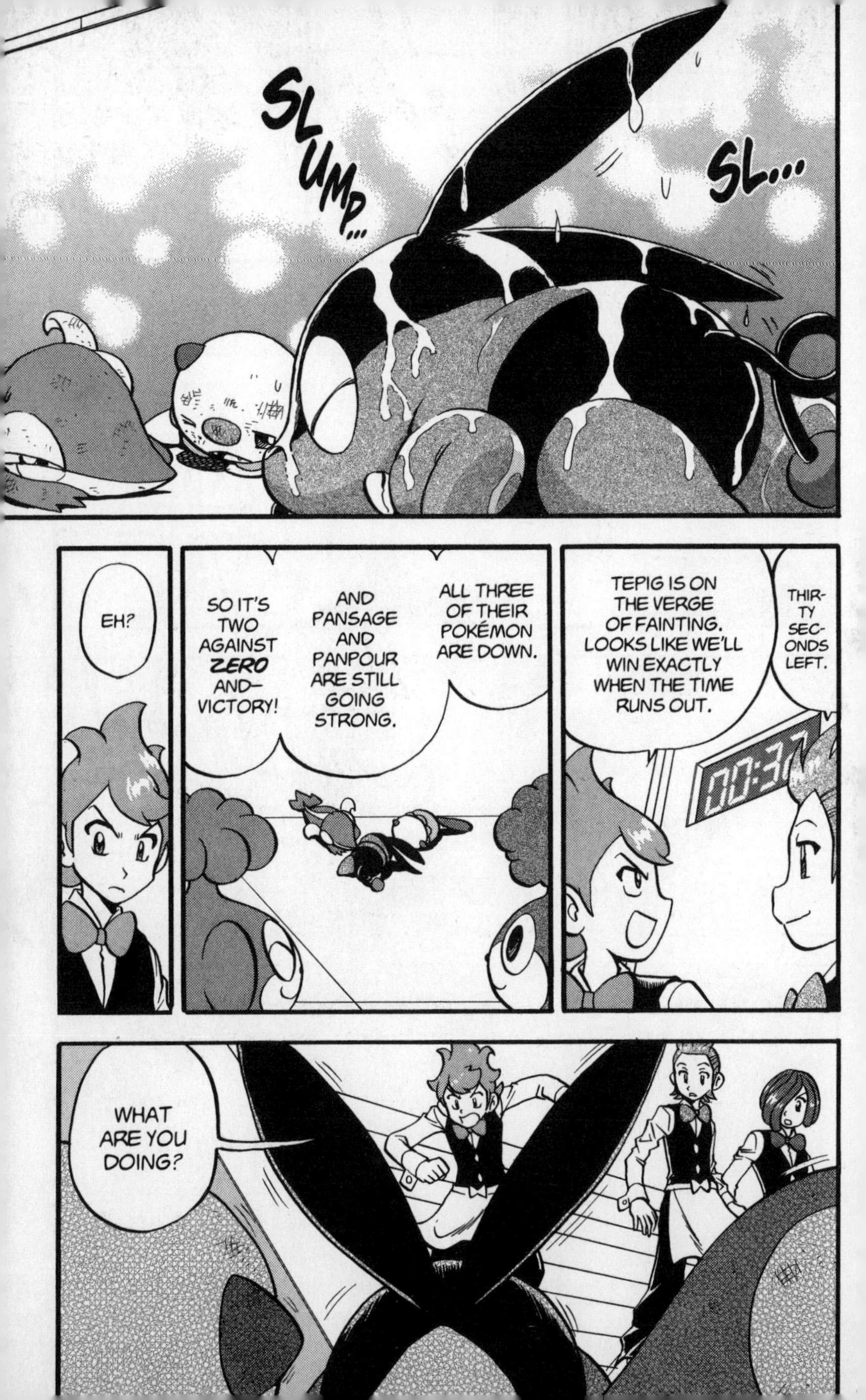
SL...
SLUMP...
THIRTY SECONDS LEFT.
TEPIG IS ON THE VERGE OF FAINTING. LOOKS LIKE WE'LL WIN EXACTLY WHEN THE TIME RUNS OUT.
ALL THREE OF THEIR POKÉMON ARE DOWN.
AND PANSAGE AND PANPOUR ARE STILL GOING STRONG.
SO IT'S TWO AGAINST **ZERO** AND— VICTORY!
EH?
WHAT ARE YOU DOING?

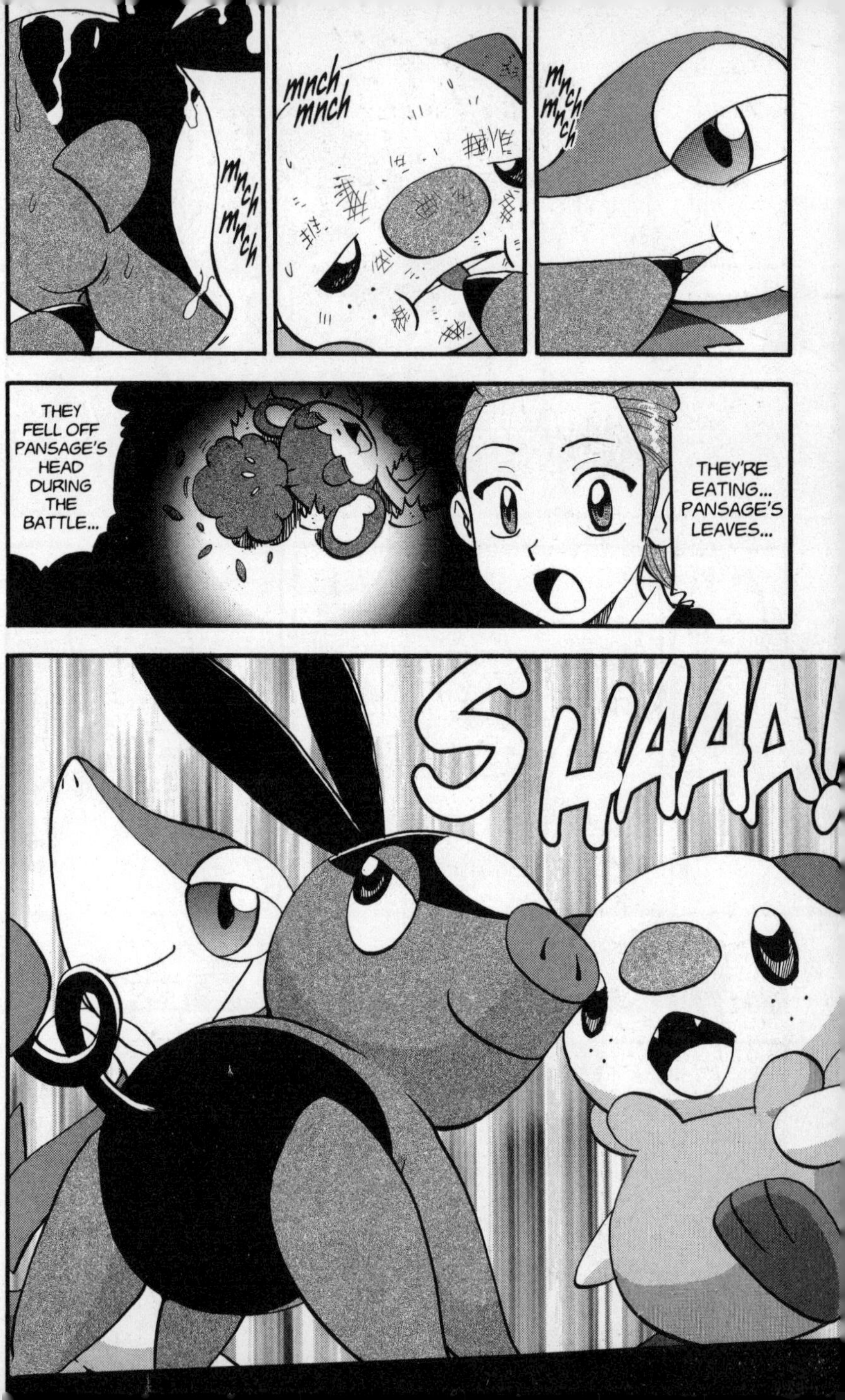
mnch mnch
mnch mnch
mnch mnch
THEY'RE EATING... PANSAGE'S LEAVES...
THEY FELL OFF PANSAGE'S HEAD DURING THE BATTLE...
SHAAA!

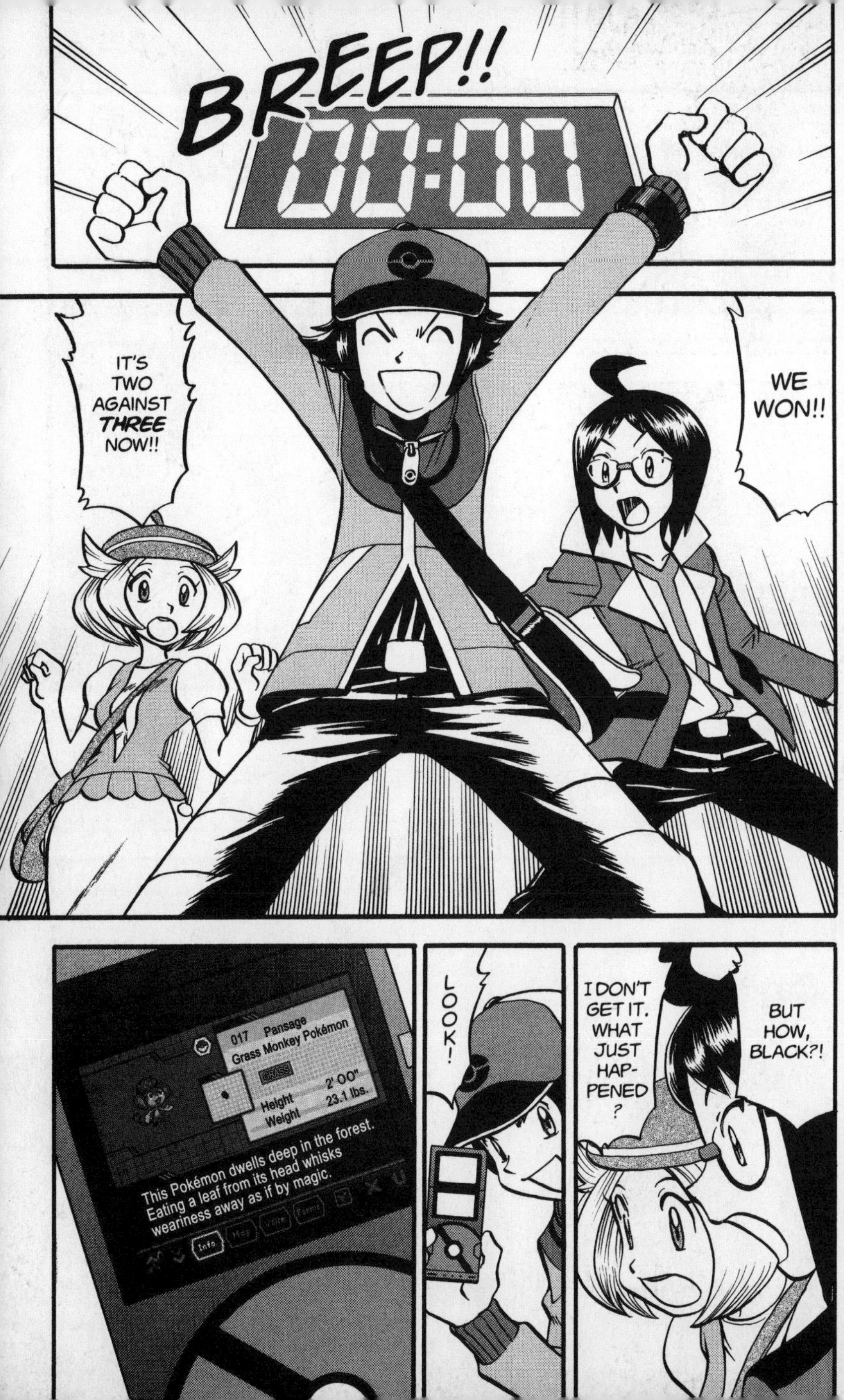
BREEP!!
00:00
WE WON!!
IT'S TWO AGAINST THREE NOW!!
BUT HOW, BLACK?!
I DON'T GET IT. WHAT JUST HAP-PENED?
LOOK!
017 Pansage
Grass Monkey Pokémon
GRASS
Height 2' 00"
Weight 23.1 lbs.
This Pokémon dwells deep in the forest. Eating a leaf from its head whisks weariness away as if by magic.
Info
Map

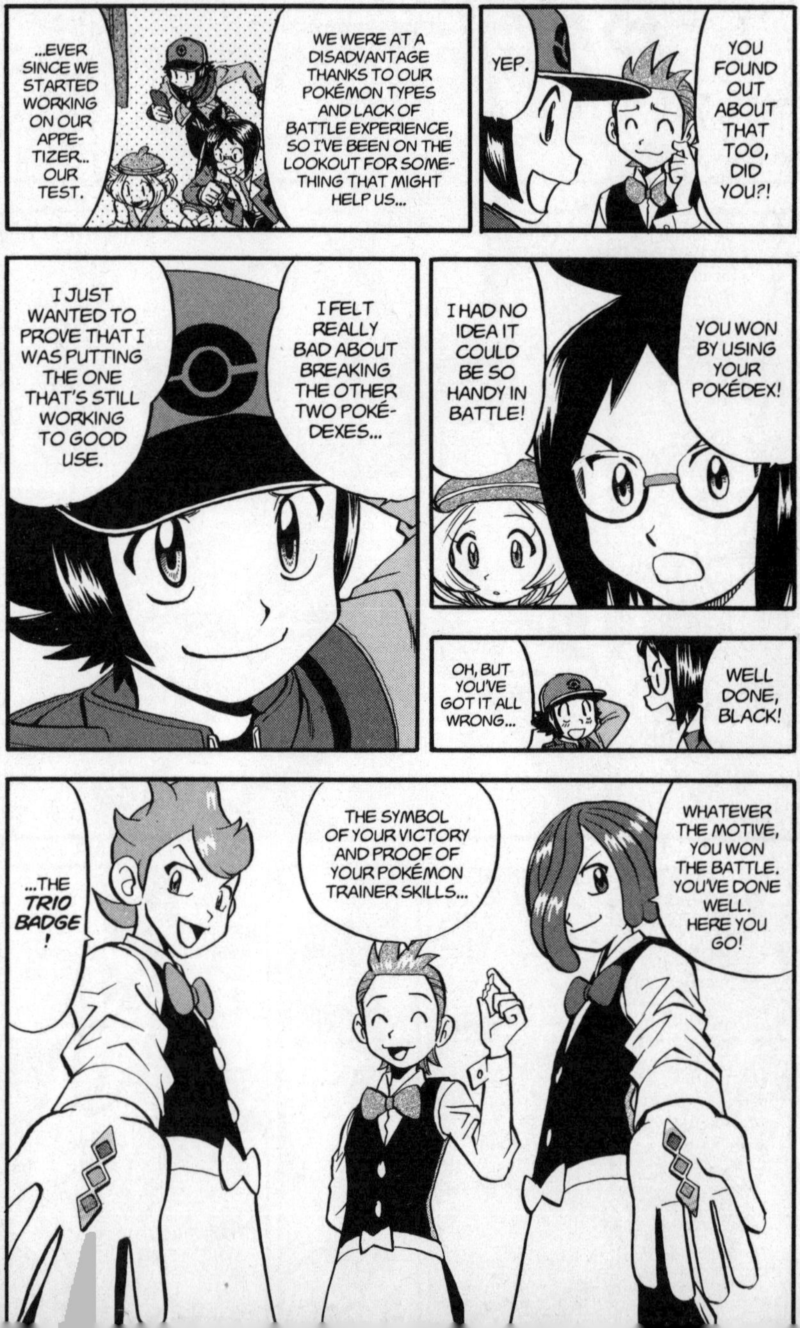
YOU FOUND OUT ABOUT THAT TOO, DID YOU?!
YEP.
WE WERE AT A DISADVANTAGE THANKS TO OUR POKÉMON TYPES AND LACK OF BATTLE EXPERIENCE, SO I'VE BEEN ON THE LOOKOUT FOR SOME-THING THAT MIGHT HELP US...
...EVER SINCE WE STARTED WORKING ON OUR APPE-TIZER.. OUR TEST.
YOU WON BY USING YOUR POKÉDEX!
I HAD NO IDEA IT COULD BE SO HANDY IN BATTLE!
WELL DONE, BLACK!
OH, BUT YOU'VE GOT IT ALL WRONG...
I FELT REALLY BAD ABOUT BREAKING THE OTHER TWO POKÉ-DEXES...
I JUST WANTED TO PROVE THAT I WAS PUTTING THE ONE THAT'S STILL WORKING TO GOOD USE.
WHATEVER THE MOTIVE, YOU WON THE BATTLE. YOU'VE DONE WELL. HERE YOU GO!
THE SYMBOL OF YOUR VICTORY AND PROOF OF YOUR POKÉMON TRAINER SKILLS...
...THE *TRIO BADGE*!

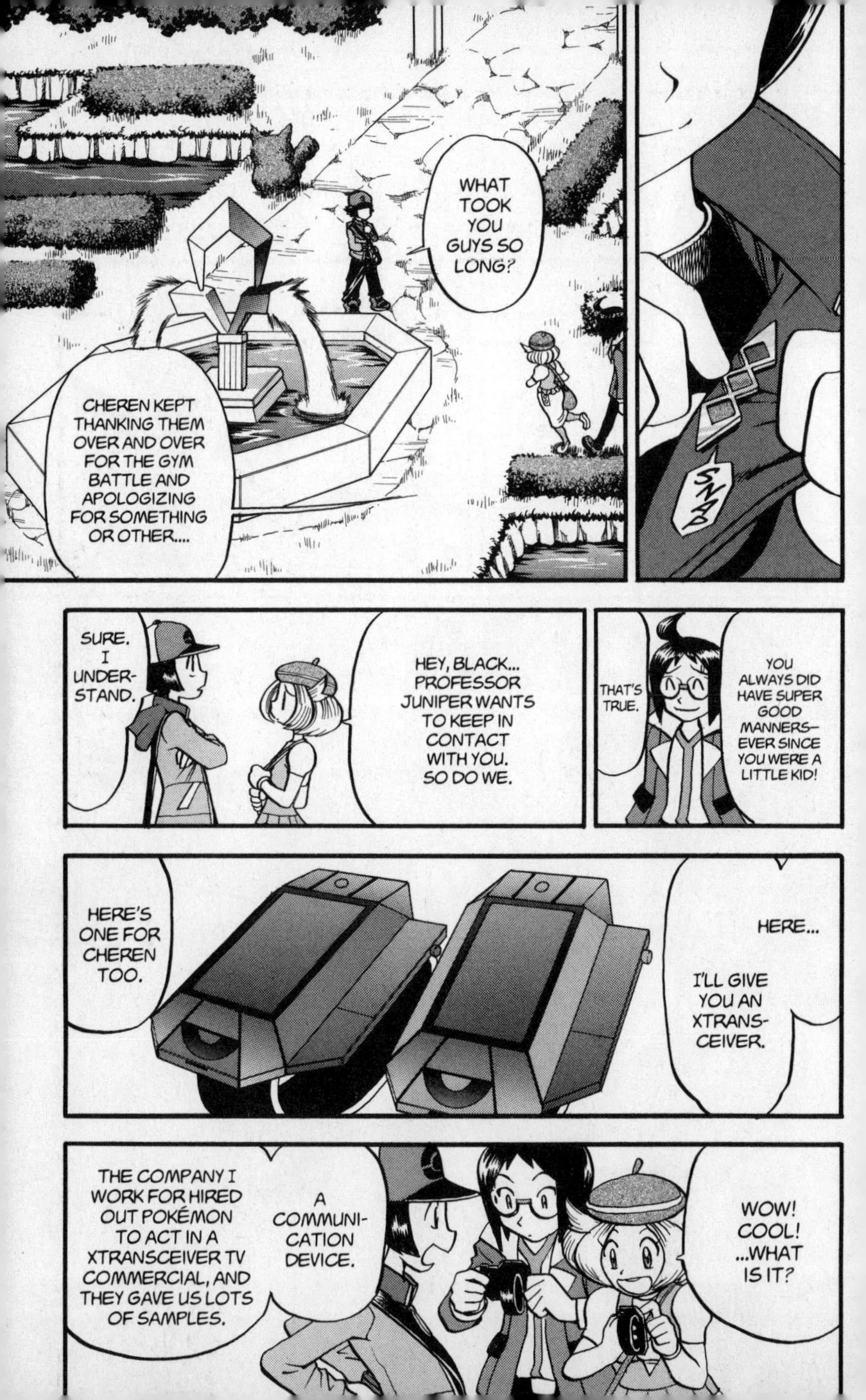
SNAP
WHAT TOOK YOU GUYS SO LONG?
CHEREN KEPT THANKING THEM OVER AND OVER FOR THE GYM BATTLE AND APOLOGIZING FOR SOMETHING OR OTHER....
YOU ALWAYS DID HAVE SUPER GOOD MANNERS—EVER SINCE YOU WERE A LITTLE KID!
THAT'S TRUE.
HEY, BLACK... PROFESSOR JUNIPER WANTS TO KEEP IN CONTACT WITH YOU. SO DO WE.
SURE. I UNDER-STAND.
HERE...
I'LL GIVE YOU AN XTRANS-CEIVER.
HERE'S ONE FOR CHEREN TOO.
WOW! COOL! ...WHAT IS IT?
A COMMUNI-CATION DEVICE.
THE COMPANY I WORK FOR HIRED OUT POKÉMON TO ACT IN A XTRANSCEIVER TV COMMERCIAL, AND THEY GAVE US LOTS OF SAMPLES.

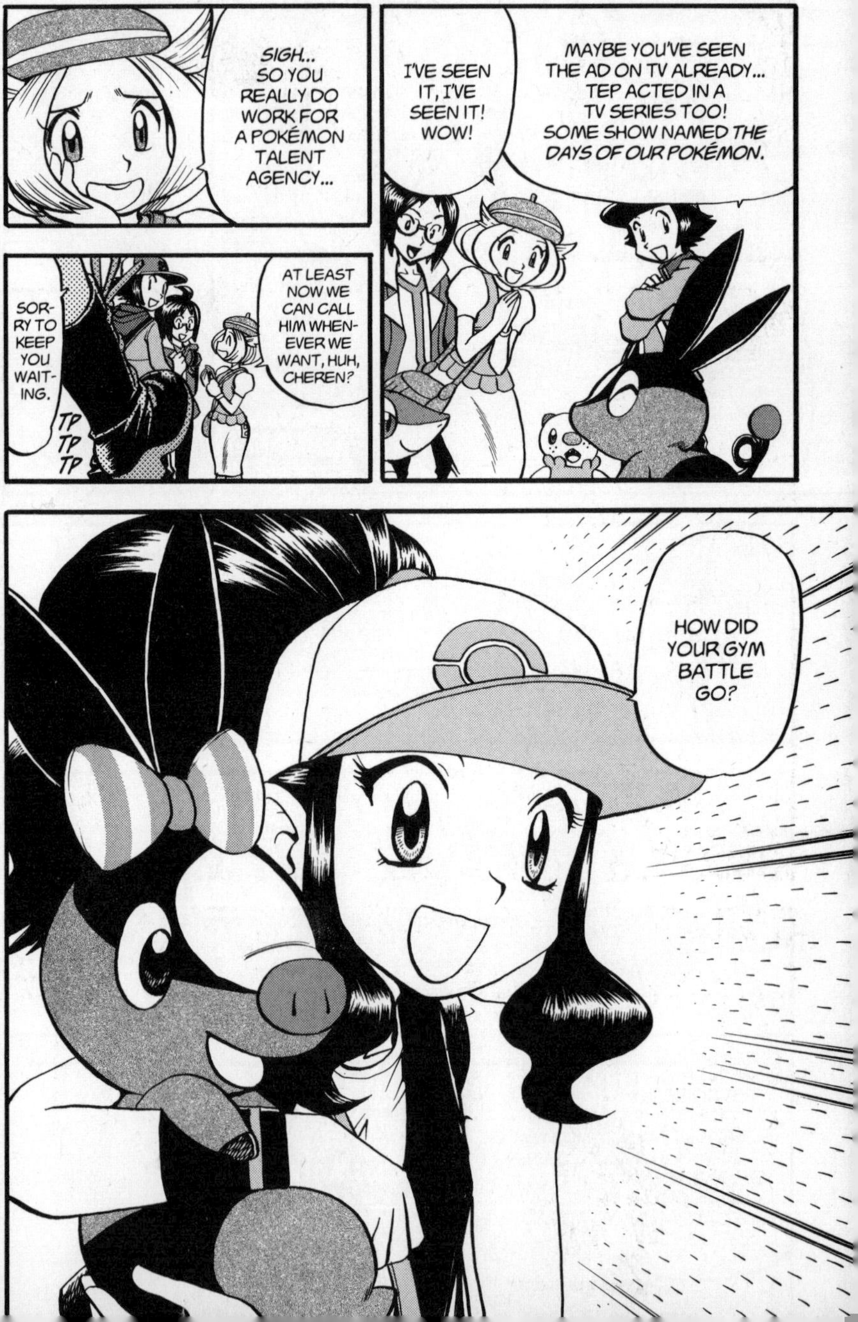
MAYBE YOU'VE SEEN THE AD ON TV ALREADY... TEP ACTED IN A TV SERIES TOO! SOME SHOW NAMED *THE DAYS OF OUR POKÉMON.*
I'VE SEEN IT, I'VE SEEN IT! WOW!
SIGH... SO YOU REALLY DO WORK FOR A POKÉMON TALENT AGENCY...
AT LEAST NOW WE CAN CALL HIM WHENEVER WE WANT, HUH, CHEREN?
SORRY TO KEEP YOU WAITING.
TP TP TP
HOW DID YOUR GYM BATTLE GO?

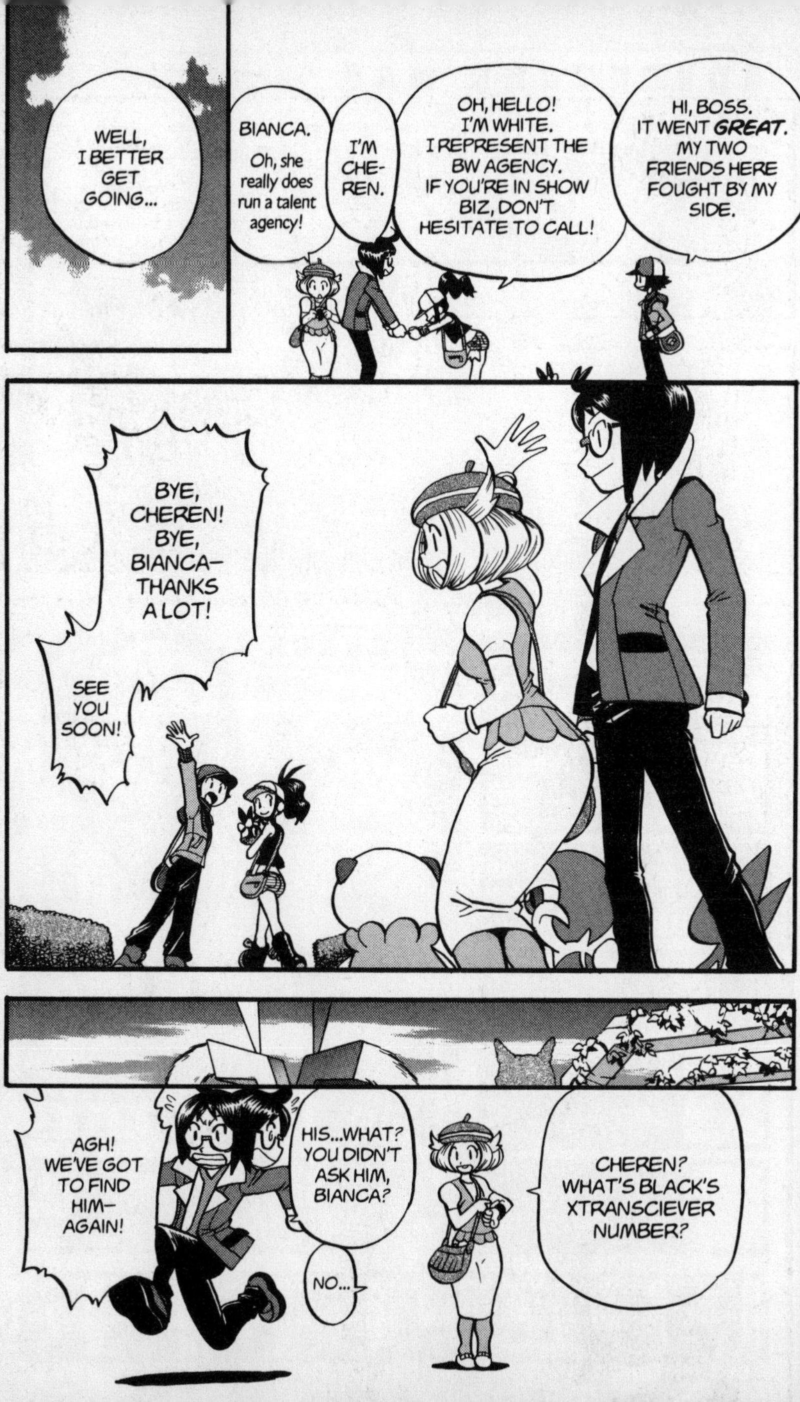
HI, BOSS. IT WENT **GREAT**. MY TWO FRIENDS HERE FOUGHT BY MY SIDE.
OH, HELLO! I'M WHITE. I REPRESENT THE BW AGENCY. IF YOU'RE IN SHOW BIZ, DON'T HESITATE TO CALL!
I'M CHE-REN.
BIANCA.
Oh, she really does run a talent agency!
WELL, I BETTER GET GOING...
BYE, CHEREN! BYE, BIANCA–THANKS A LOT!
SEE YOU SOON!
CHEREN? WHAT'S BLACK'S XTRANSCIEVER NUMBER?
HIS...WHAT? YOU DIDN'T ASK HIM, BIANCA?
NO...
AGH! WE'VE GOT TO FIND HIM–AGAIN!

ADVENTURE MAP

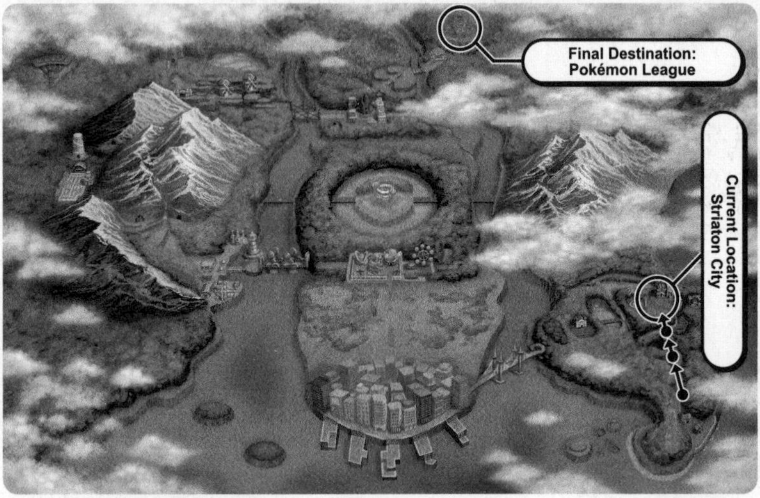

Final Destination: Pokémon League
Current Location: Striaton City

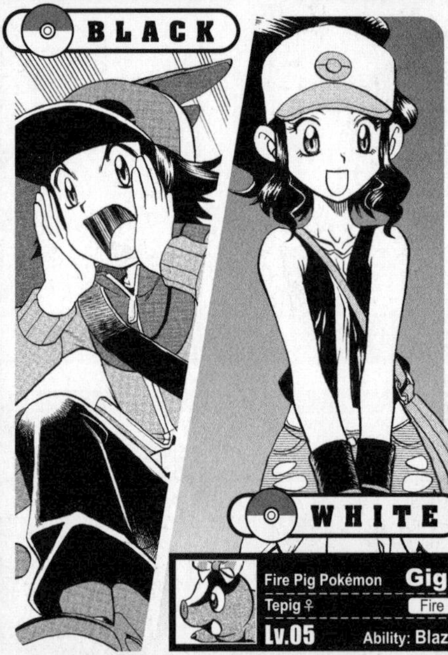

BLACK
WHITE

Fire Pig Pokémon — **Tep**
Tepig ♂ — Fire
Lv.15 — Ability: Blaze

Dream Eater Pokémon — **Musha**
Munna ♂ — Psychic
Lv.36 — Ability: Forewarn

Valiant Pokémon — **Brav**
Braviary ♂ — Normal / Flying
Lv.54 — Ability: Sheer Force

EleSpider Pokémon — **Tula**
Galvantula ♂ — Bug / Electric
Lv.37 — Ability: Unnerve

Fire Pig Pokémon — **Gigi**
Tepig ♀ — Fire
Lv.05 — Ability: Blaze

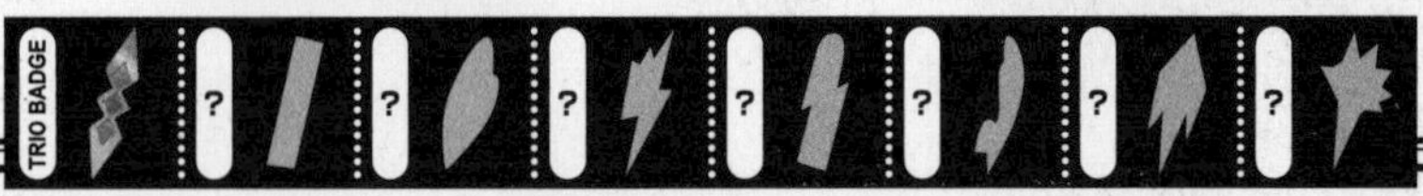

TRIO BADGE
?
?
?
?
?
?
?

POKÉMON ADVENTURES BLACK & WHITE

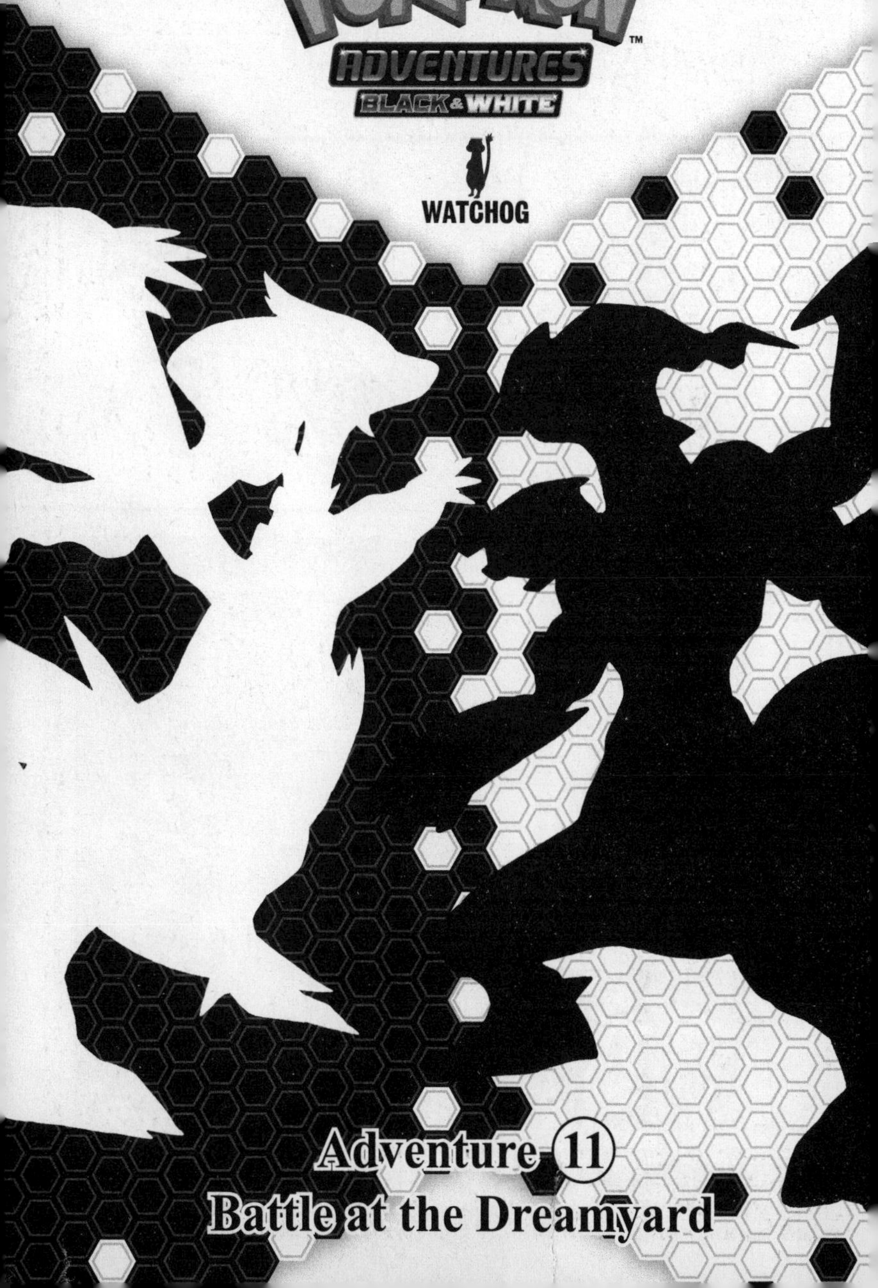
WATCHOG

Adventure 11
Battle at the Dreamyard

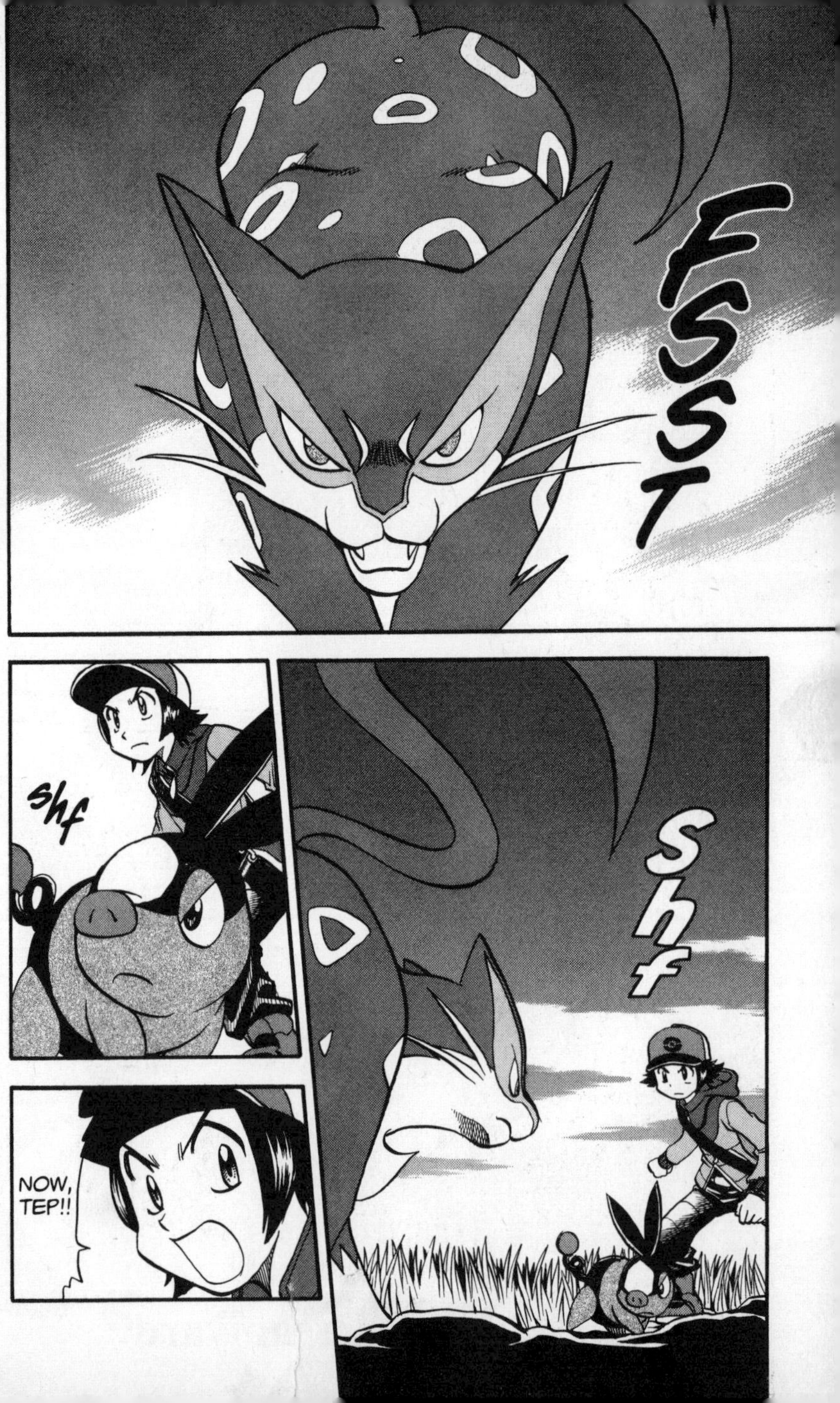
FSSST
Shf
shf
NOW, TEP!!

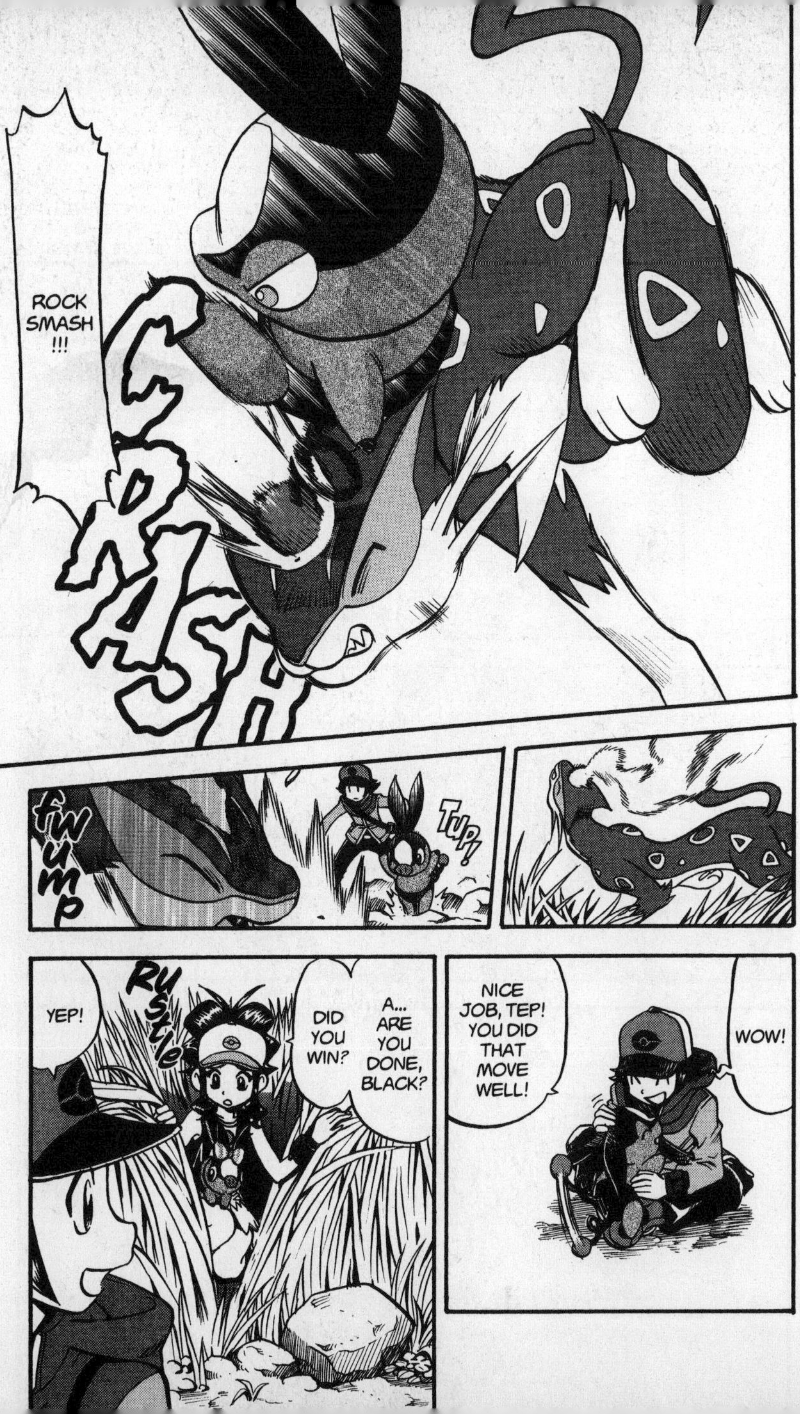
ROCK SMASH !!!
CRASH
TUP!
twump
WOW!
NICE JOB, TEP! YOU DID THAT MOVE WELL!
A... ARE YOU DONE, BLACK?
DID YOU WIN?
RUSTLE
YEP!

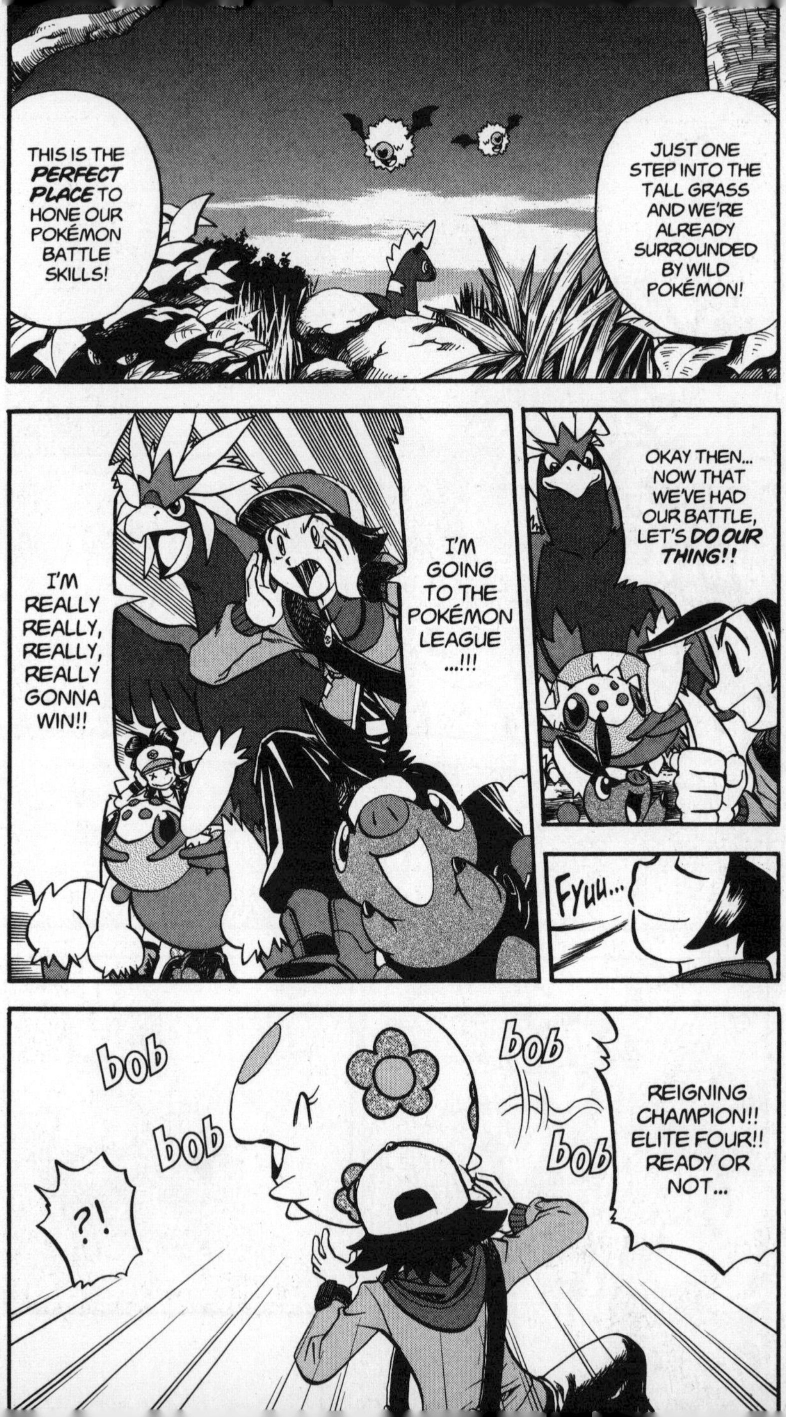
JUST ONE STEP INTO THE TALL GRASS AND WE'RE ALREADY SURROUNDED BY WILD POKÉMON!
THIS IS THE ***PERFECT PLACE*** TO HONE OUR POKÉMON BATTLE SKILLS!
OKAY THEN... NOW THAT WE'VE HAD OUR BATTLE, LET'S ***DO OUR THING!!***
Fyuu...
I'M GOING TO THE POKÉMON LEAGUE ...!!!
I'M REALLY REALLY, REALLY, REALLY GONNA WIN!!
REIGNING CHAMPION!! ELITE FOUR!! READY OR NOT...
bob
bob
bob
bob
?!

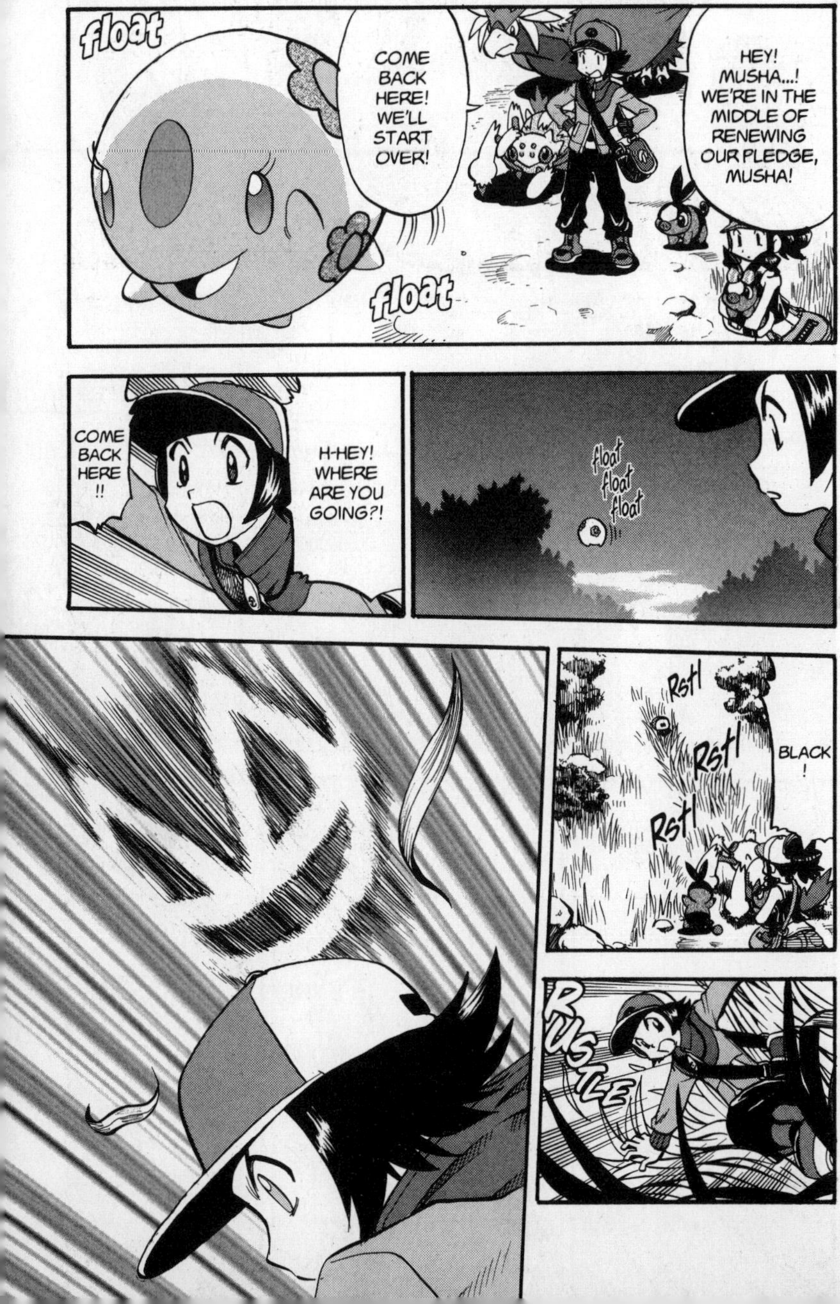
float
HEY! MUSHA...! WE'RE IN THE MIDDLE OF RENEWING OUR PLEDGE, MUSHA!
COME BACK HERE! WE'LL START OVER!
float
float
float
float
H-HEY! WHERE ARE YOU GOING?!
COME BACK HERE !!
Rst!
BLACK !
Rst!
Rst!
RUSTLE

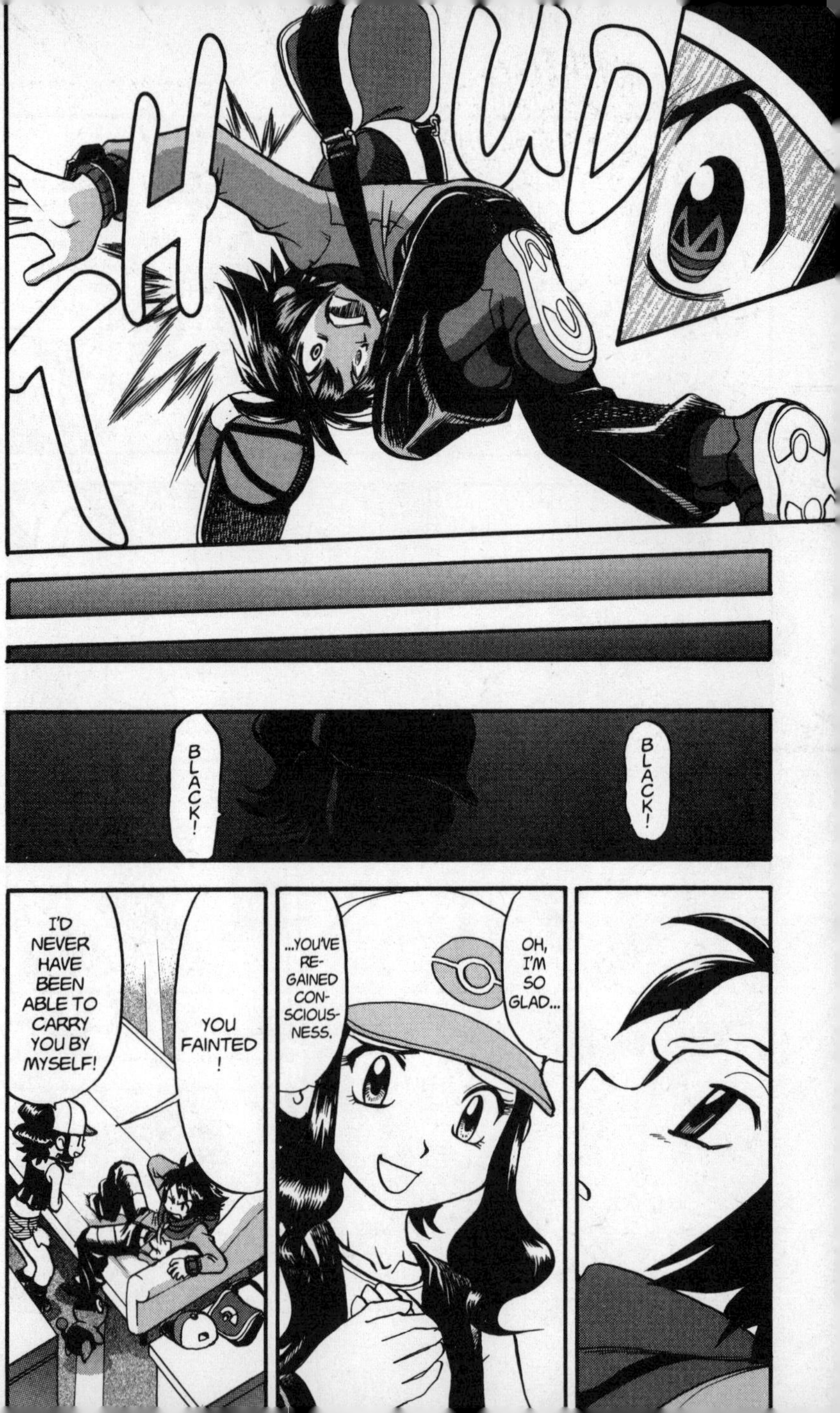
THUD
BLACK!
BLACK!
OH, I'M SO GLAD...
...YOU'VE RE-GAINED CON-SCIOUSNESS.
YOU FAINTED!
I'D NEVER HAVE BEEN ABLE TO CARRY YOU BY MYSELF!

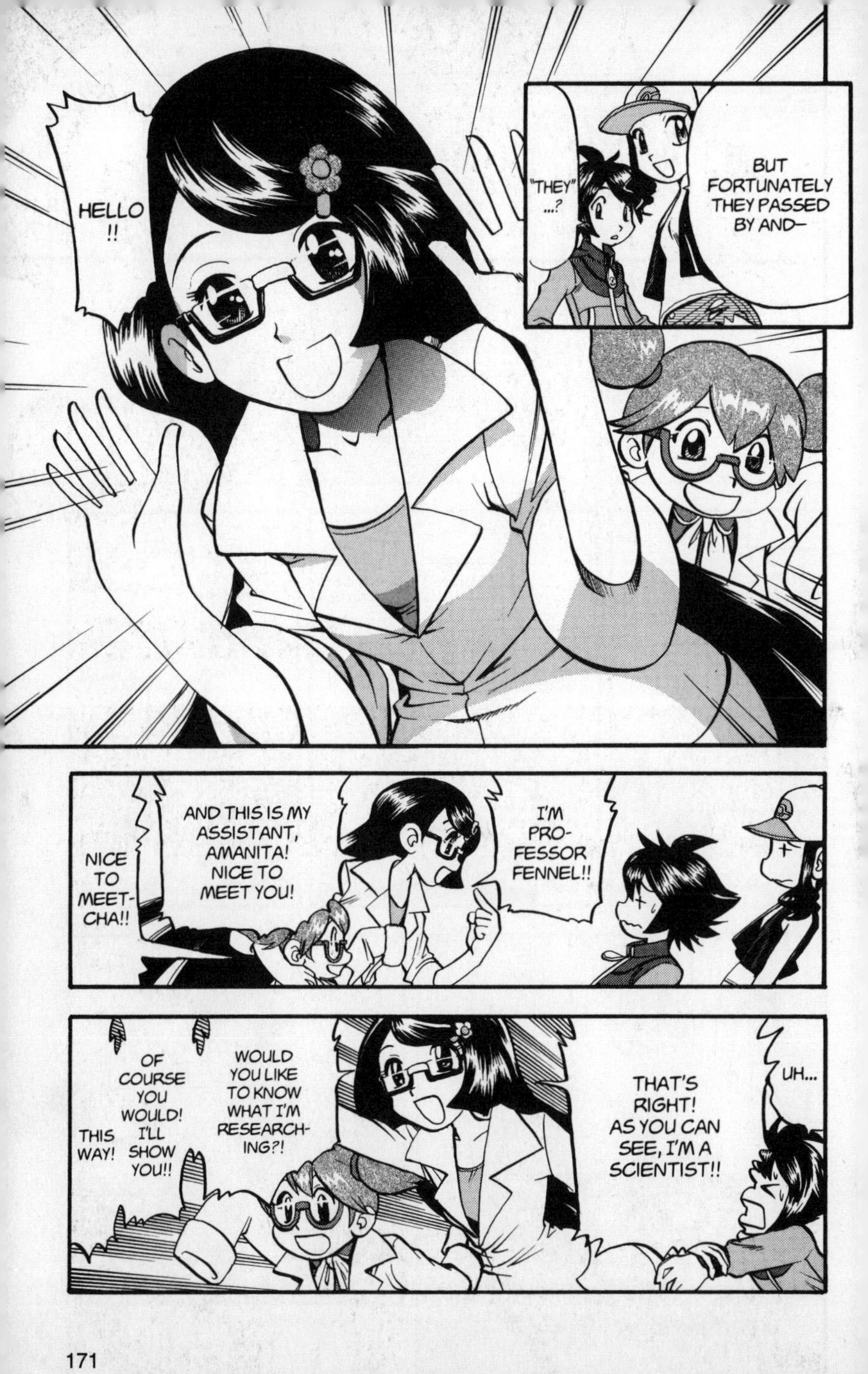

BUT FORTUNATELY THEY PASSED BY AND—
"THEY" ...?
HELLO!!
I'M PRO-FESSOR FENNEL!!
AND THIS IS MY ASSISTANT, AMANITA! NICE TO MEET YOU!
NICE TO MEET-CHA!!
UH...
THAT'S RIGHT! AS YOU CAN SEE, I'M A SCIENTIST!!
WOULD YOU LIKE TO KNOW WHAT I'M RESEARCH-ING?!
OF COURSE YOU WOULD! I'LL SHOW YOU!!
THIS WAY!

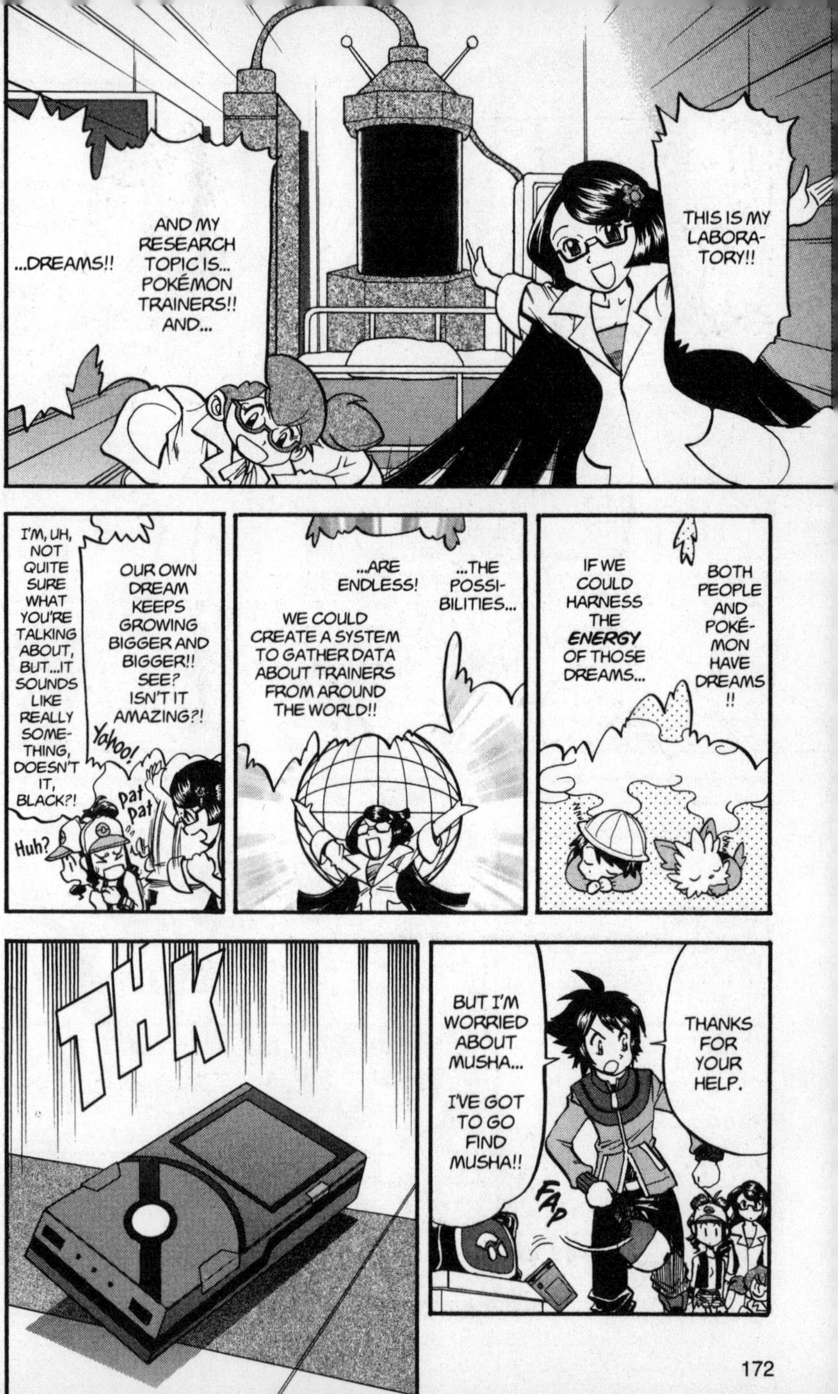
THIS IS MY LABORATORY!!
AND MY RESEARCH TOPIC IS... POKÉMON TRAINERS!! AND...
...DREAMS!!
BOTH PEOPLE AND POKÉMON HAVE DREAMS!!
IF WE COULD HARNESS THE *ENERGY* OF THOSE DREAMS...
...THE POSSIBILITIES...
...ARE ENDLESS!
WE COULD CREATE A SYSTEM TO GATHER DATA ABOUT TRAINERS FROM AROUND THE WORLD!!
OUR OWN DREAM KEEPS GROWING BIGGER AND BIGGER!! SEE? ISN'T IT AMAZING?!
I'M, UH, NOT QUITE SURE WHAT YOU'RE TALKING ABOUT, BUT...IT SOUNDS LIKE REALLY SOMETHING, DOESN'T IT, BLACK?!
Yahoo!
pat pat
Huh?
THANKS FOR YOUR HELP.
BUT I'M WORRIED ABOUT MUSHA...
I'VE GOT TO GO FIND MUSHA!!
FAP
THK

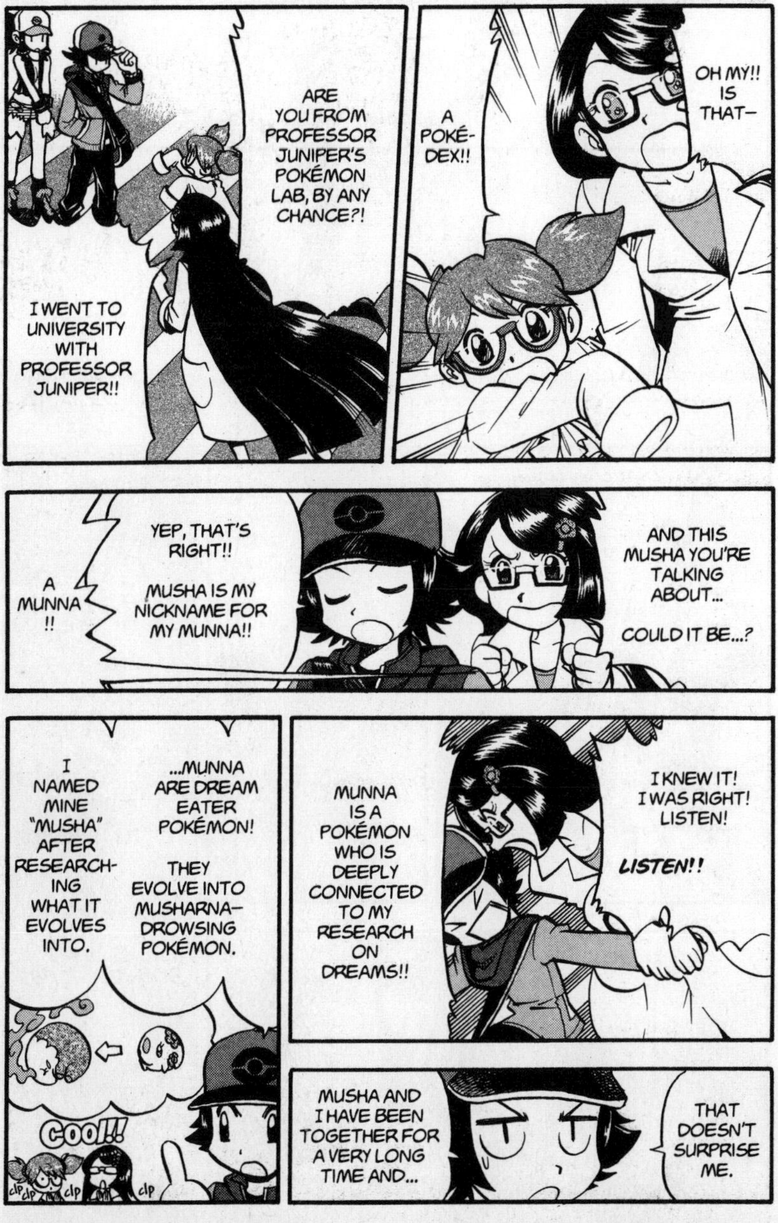
OH MY!! IS THAT—
A POKÉ-DEX!!
ARE YOU FROM PROFESSOR JUNIPER'S POKÉMON LAB, BY ANY CHANCE?!
I WENT TO UNIVERSITY WITH PROFESSOR JUNIPER!!
AND THIS MUSHA YOU'RE TALKING ABOUT... COULD IT BE...?
YEP, THAT'S RIGHT!! MUSHA IS MY NICKNAME FOR MY MUNNA!!
A MUNNA !!
I KNEW IT! I WAS RIGHT! LISTEN! LISTEN!!
MUNNA IS A POKÉMON WHO IS DEEPLY CONNECTED TO MY RESEARCH ON DREAMS!!
THAT DOESN'T SURPRISE ME.
MUSHA AND I HAVE BEEN TOGETHER FOR A VERY LONG TIME AND...
...MUNNA ARE DREAM EATER POKÉMON! THEY EVOLVE INTO MUSHARNA—DROWSING POKÉMON.
I NAMED MINE "MUSHA" AFTER RESEARCHING WHAT IT EVOLVES INTO.
COOL!!
clp clp clp clp

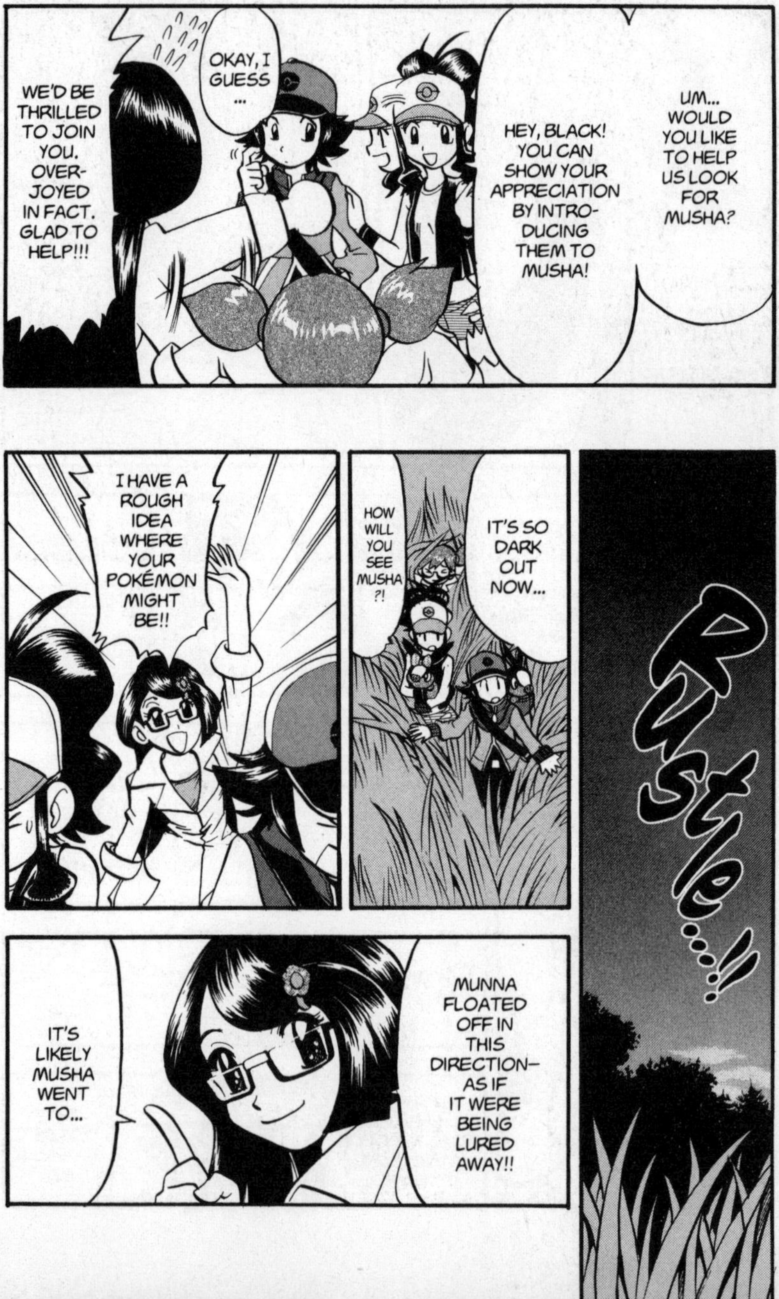
UM... WOULD YOU LIKE TO HELP US LOOK FOR MUSHA?
HEY, BLACK! YOU CAN SHOW YOUR APPRECIATION BY INTRODUCING THEM TO MUSHA!
OKAY, I GUESS...
WE'D BE THRILLED TO JOIN YOU. OVERJOYED IN FACT. GLAD TO HELP!!!
Rustle...!!
IT'S SO DARK OUT NOW...
HOW WILL YOU SEE MUSHA?!
I HAVE A ROUGH IDEA WHERE YOUR POKÉMON MIGHT BE!!
MUNNA FLOATED OFF IN THIS DIRECTION—AS IF IT WERE BEING LURED AWAY!!
IT'S LIKELY MUSHA WENT TO...

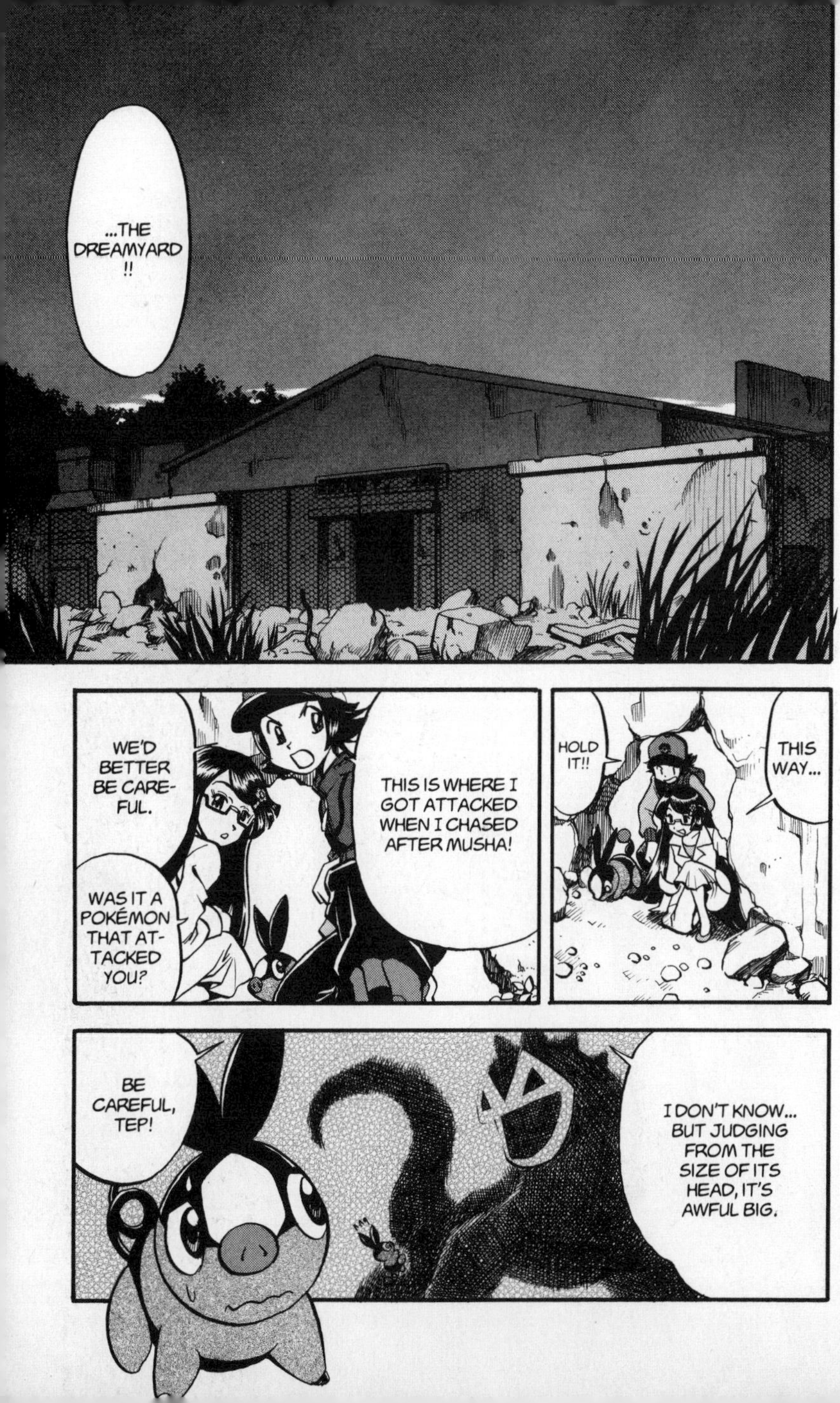
...THE DREAMYARD !!
THIS WAY...
HOLD IT!!
THIS IS WHERE I GOT ATTACKED WHEN I CHASED AFTER MUSHA!
WE'D BETTER BE CARE-FUL.
WAS IT A POKÉMON THAT AT-TACKED YOU?
I DON'T KNOW... BUT JUDGING FROM THE SIZE OF ITS HEAD, IT'S AWFUL BIG.
BE CAREFUL, TEP!

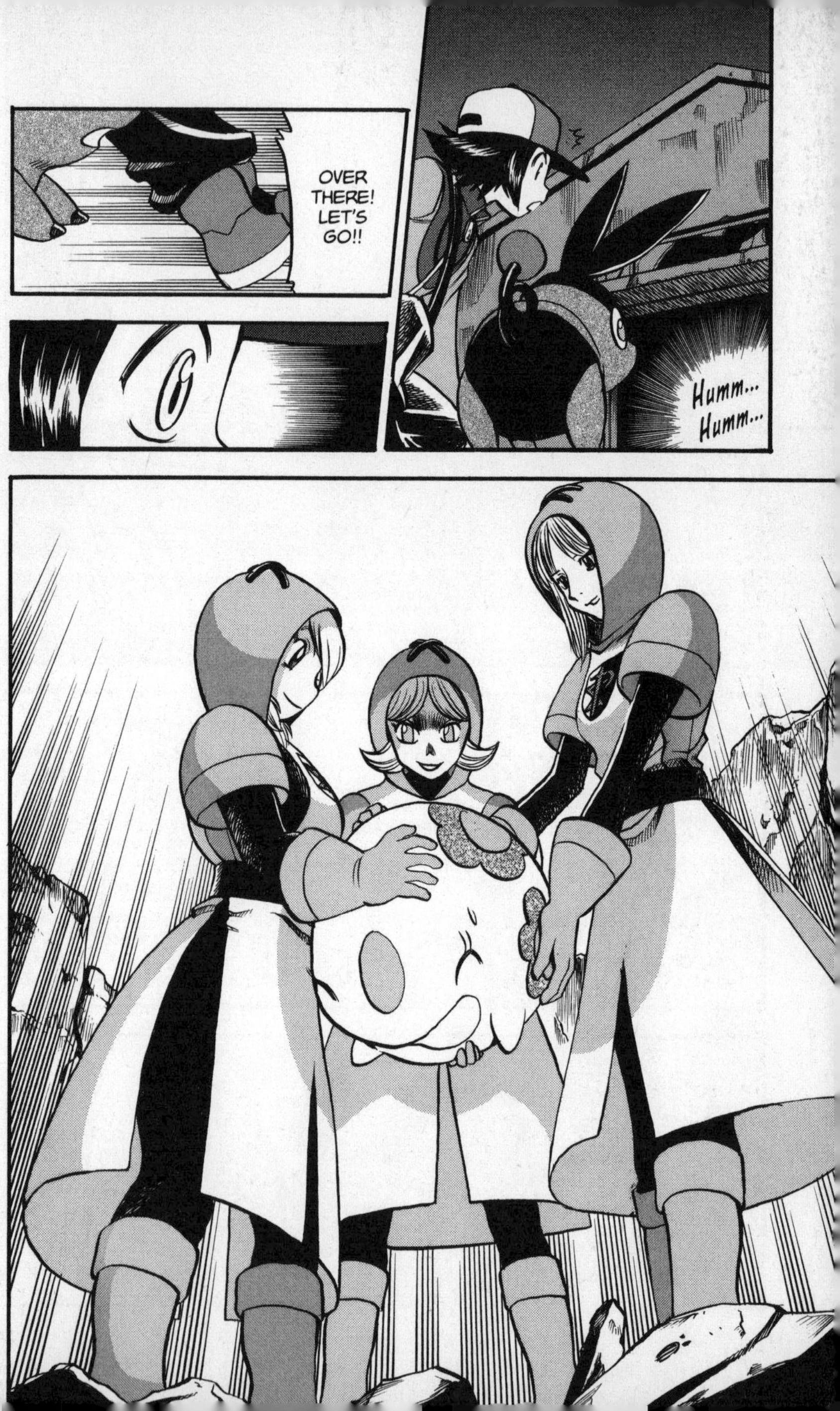
Humm... Humm...
OVER THERE! LET'S GO!!

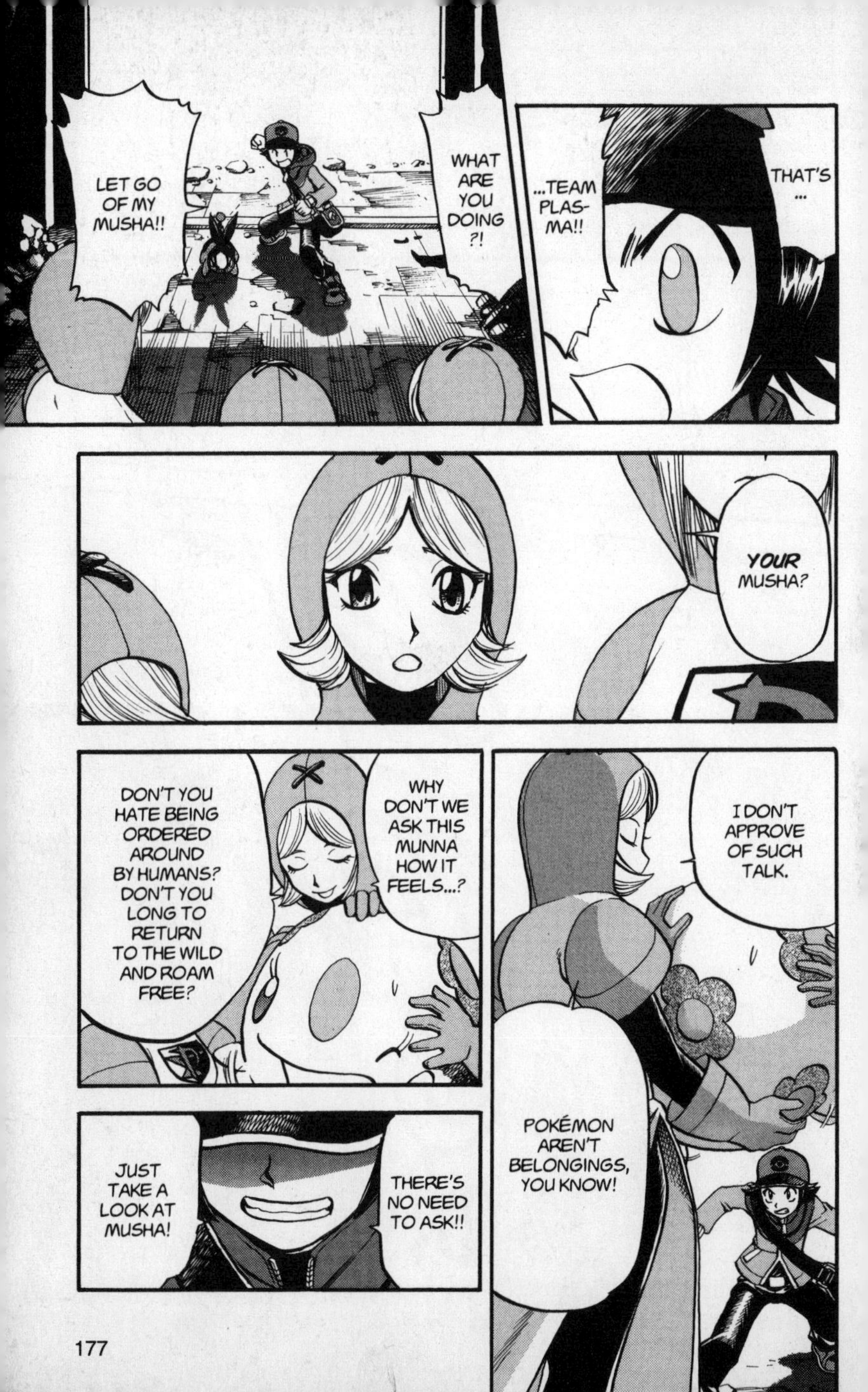
THAT'S ...
...TEAM PLAS-MA!!
WHAT ARE YOU DOING ?!
LET GO OF MY MUSHA!!
YOUR MUSHA?
I DON'T APPROVE OF SUCH TALK.
POKÉMON AREN'T BELONGINGS, YOU KNOW!
WHY DON'T WE ASK THIS MUNNA HOW IT FEELS...?
DON'T YOU HATE BEING ORDERED AROUND BY HUMANS? DON'T YOU LONG TO RETURN TO THE WILD AND ROAM FREE?
THERE'S NO NEED TO ASK!!
JUST TAKE A LOOK AT MUSHA!

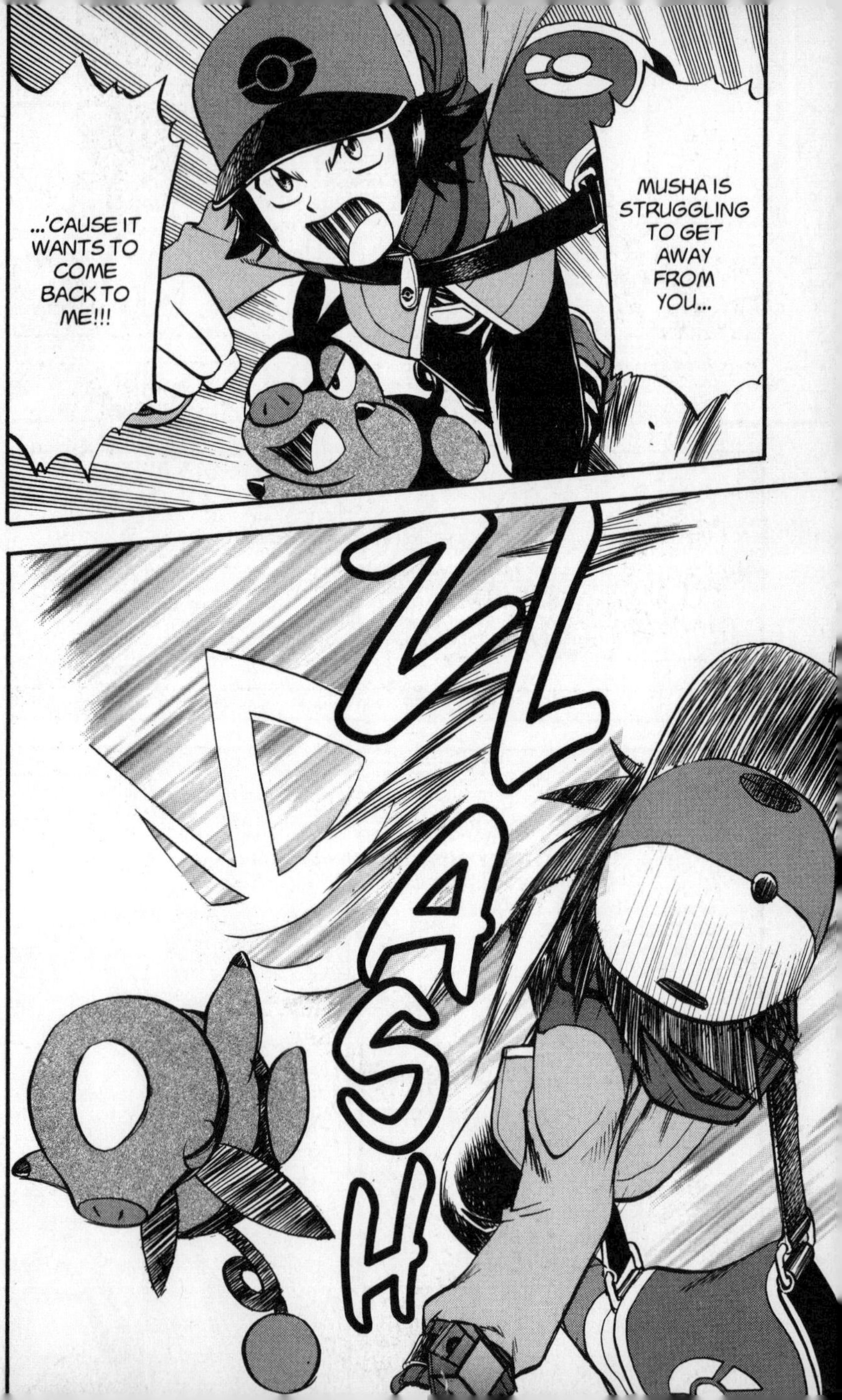
MUSHA IS STRUGGLING TO GET AWAY FROM YOU...
...'CAUSE IT WANTS TO COME BACK TO ME!!!
ZASH

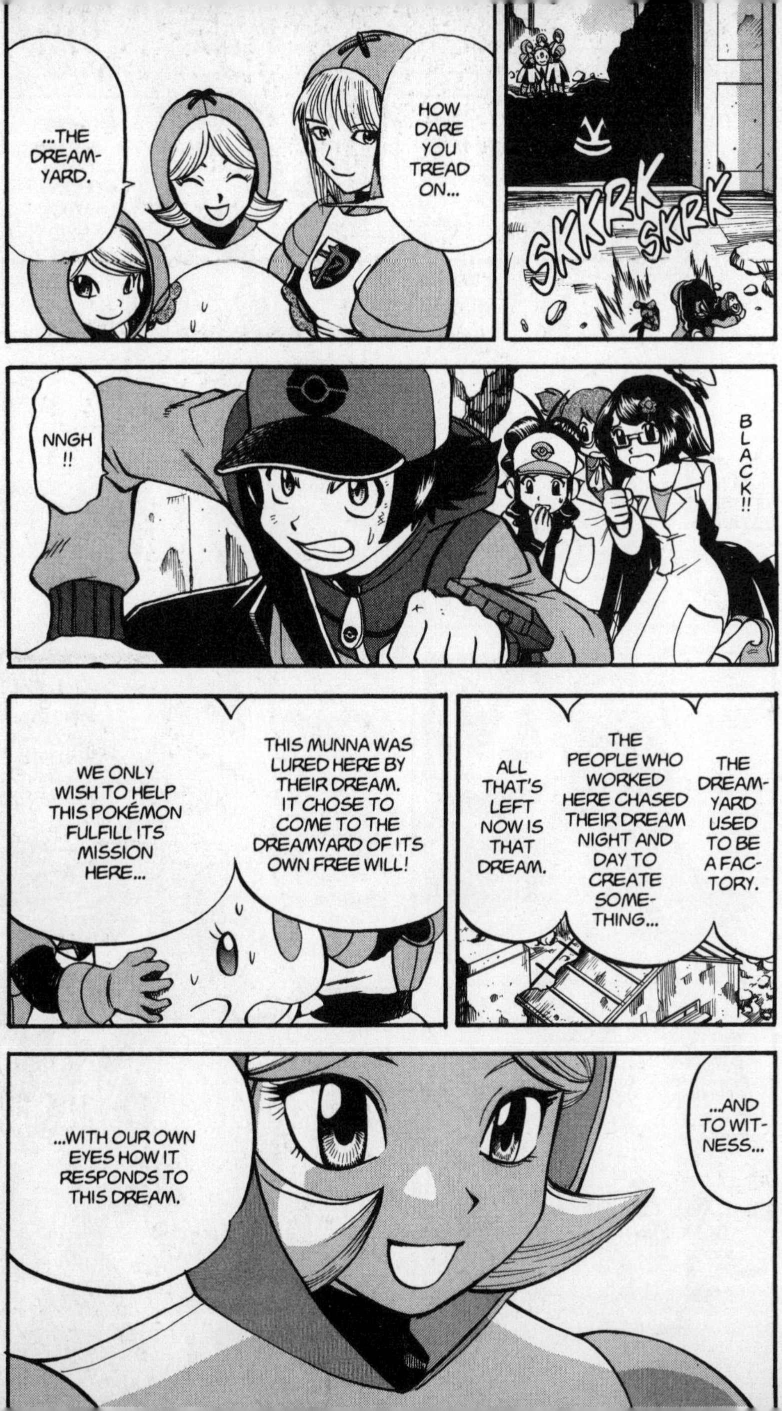
SKKRK SKRK
HOW DARE YOU TREAD ON...
...THE DREAM-YARD.
BLACK!!
NNGH!!
THE DREAM-YARD USED TO BE A FAC-TORY.
THE PEOPLE WHO WORKED HERE CHASED THEIR DREAM NIGHT AND DAY TO CREATE SOME-THING...
ALL THAT'S LEFT NOW IS THAT DREAM.
THIS MUNNA WAS LURED HERE BY THEIR DREAM. IT CHOSE TO COME TO THE DREAMYARD OF ITS OWN FREE WILL!
WE ONLY WISH TO HELP THIS POKÉMON FULFILL ITS MISSION HERE...
...AND TO WIT-NESS...
...WITH OUR OWN EYES HOW IT RESPONDS TO THIS DREAM.

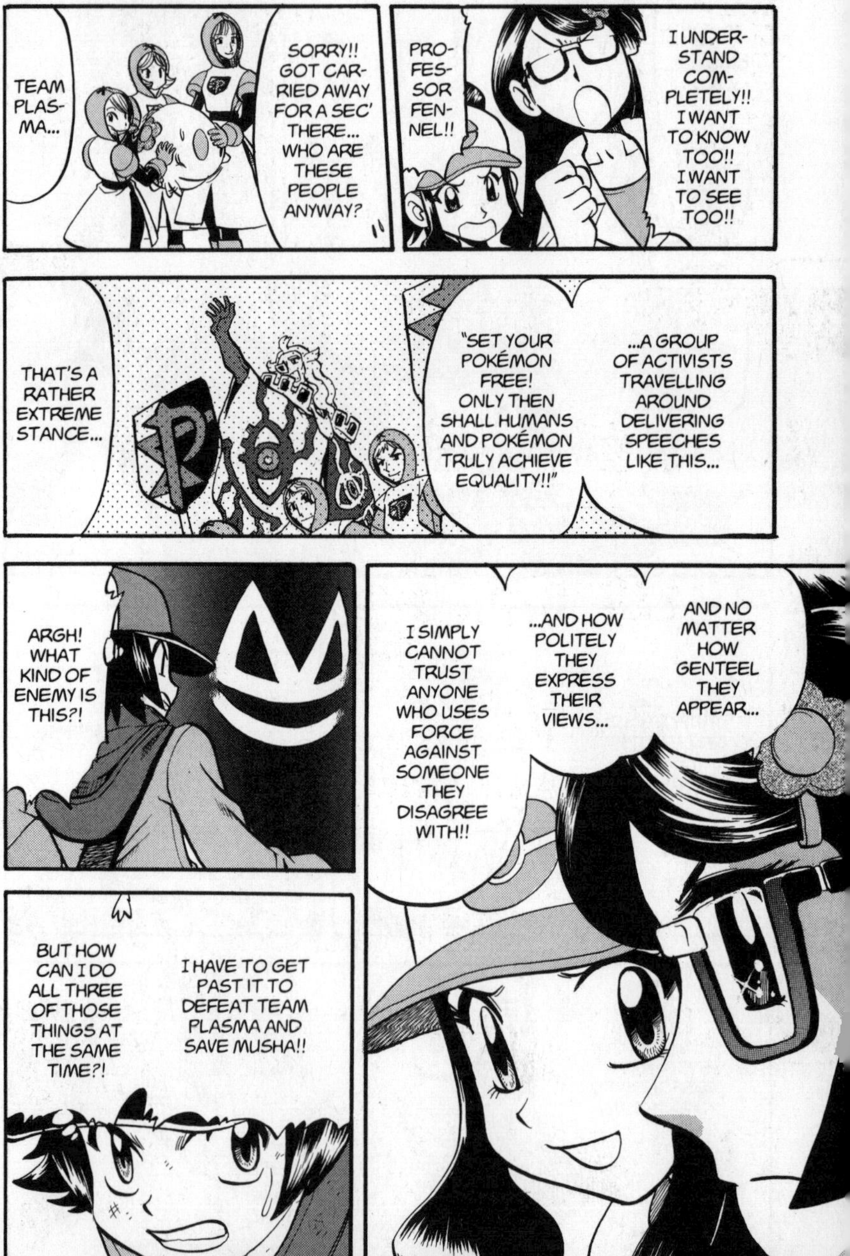
I UNDERSTAND COMPLETELY!! I WANT TO KNOW TOO!! I WANT TO SEE TOO!!
PROFESSOR FENNEL!!
SORRY!! GOT CARRIED AWAY FOR A SEC' THERE... WHO ARE THESE PEOPLE ANYWAY?
TEAM PLASMA...
...A GROUP OF ACTIVISTS TRAVELLING AROUND DELIVERING SPEECHES LIKE THIS...
"SET YOUR POKÉMON FREE! ONLY THEN SHALL HUMANS AND POKÉMON TRULY ACHIEVE EQUALITY!!"
THAT'S A RATHER EXTREME STANCE...
AND NO MATTER HOW GENTEEL THEY APPEAR...
...AND HOW POLITELY THEY EXPRESS THEIR VIEWS...
I SIMPLY CANNOT TRUST ANYONE WHO USES FORCE AGAINST SOMEONE THEY DISAGREE WITH!!
ARGH! WHAT KIND OF ENEMY IS THIS?!
I HAVE TO GET PAST IT TO DEFEAT TEAM PLASMA AND SAVE MUSHA!!
BUT HOW CAN I DO ALL THREE OF THOSE THINGS AT THE SAME TIME?!

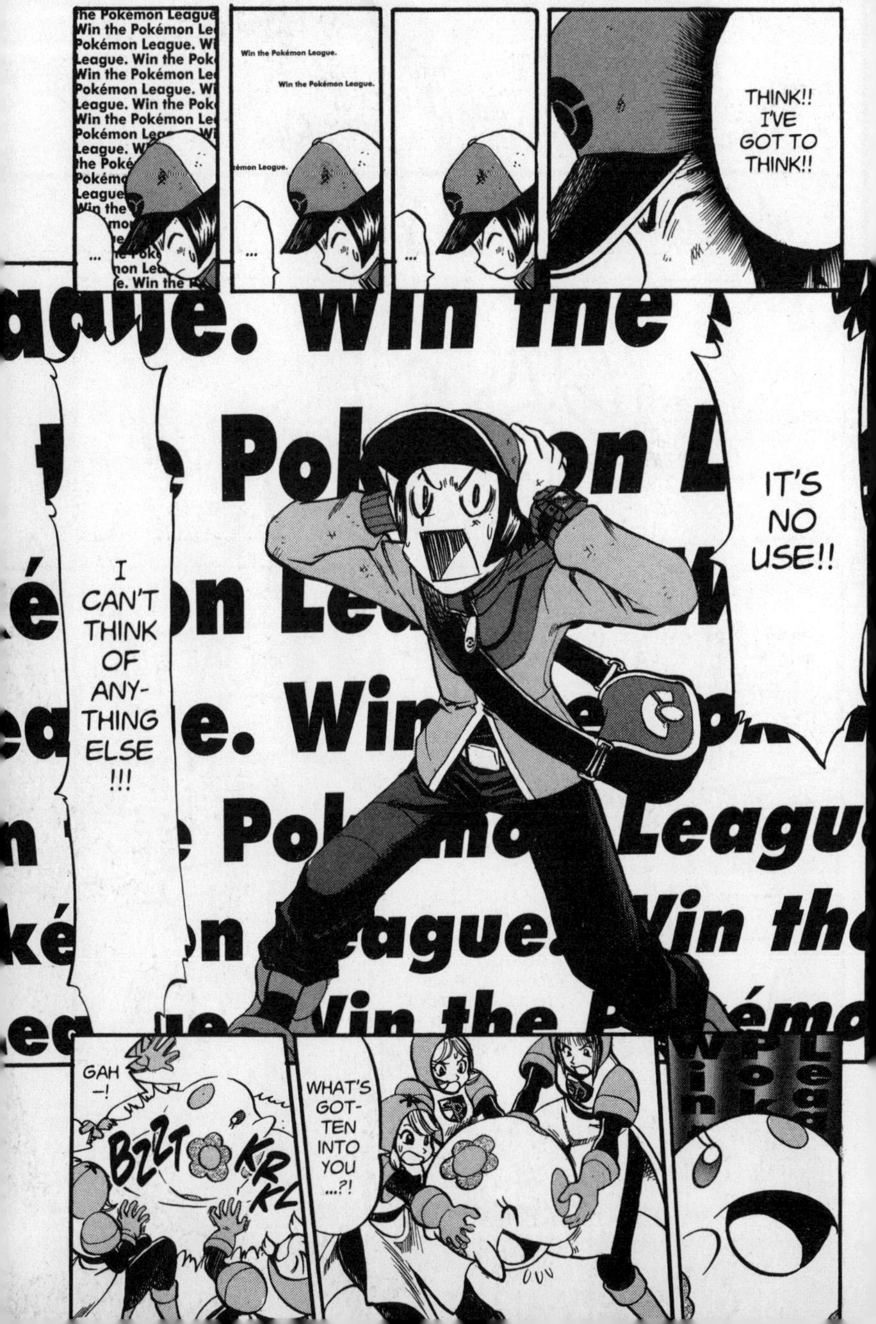
THINK!! I'VE GOT TO THINK!!
...
Win the Pokémon League.
Win the Pokémon League.
...
...
IT'S NO USE!!
I CAN'T THINK OF ANY-THING ELSE!!!
WHAT'S GOT-TEN INTO YOU ...?!
GAH—!
BZZT
KRKL

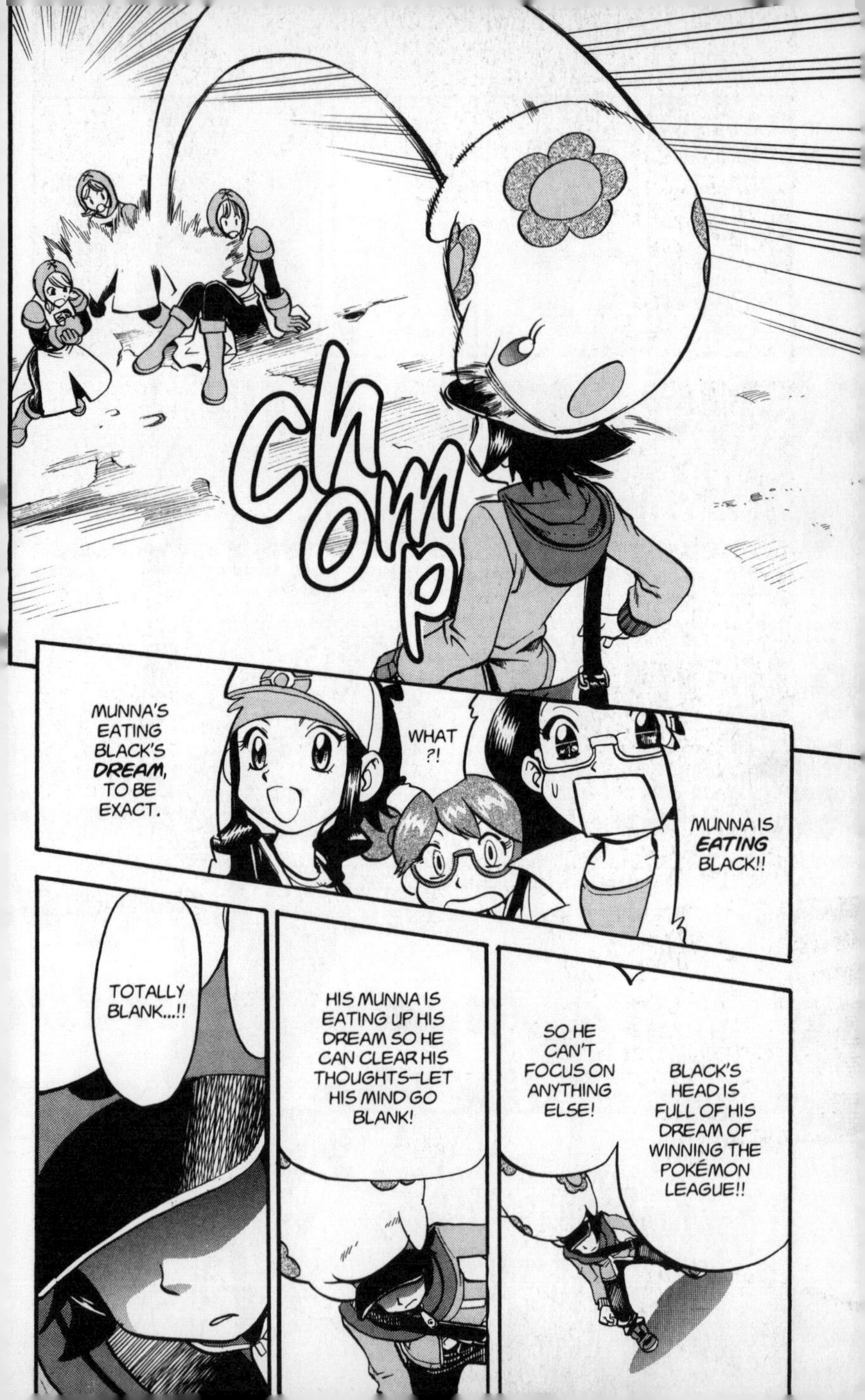
CHOMP
MUNNA IS EATING BLACK!!
WHAT?!
MUNNA'S EATING BLACK'S DREAM, TO BE EXACT.
BLACK'S HEAD IS FULL OF HIS DREAM OF WINNING THE POKÉMON LEAGUE!!
SO HE CAN'T FOCUS ON ANYTHING ELSE!
HIS MUNNA IS EATING UP HIS DREAM SO HE CAN CLEAR HIS THOUGHTS—LET HIS MIND GO BLANK!
TOTALLY BLANK...!!

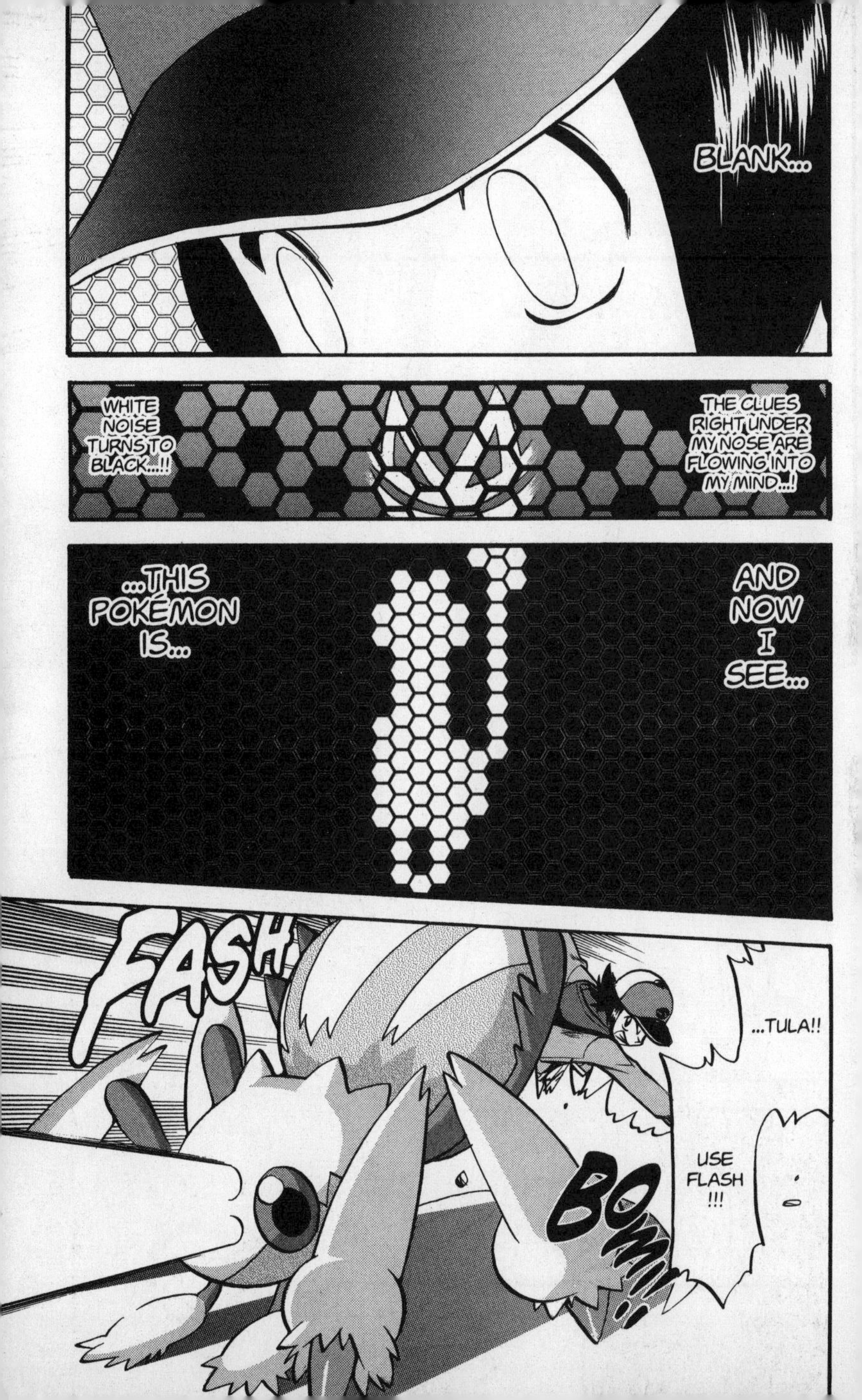
BLANK...
THE CLUES RIGHT UNDER MY NOSE ARE FLOWING INTO MY MIND...!
WHITE NOISE TURNS TO BLACK...!!
AND NOW I SEE...
...THIS POKÉMON IS...
...TULA!!
USE FLASH !!!
FASH
BOM

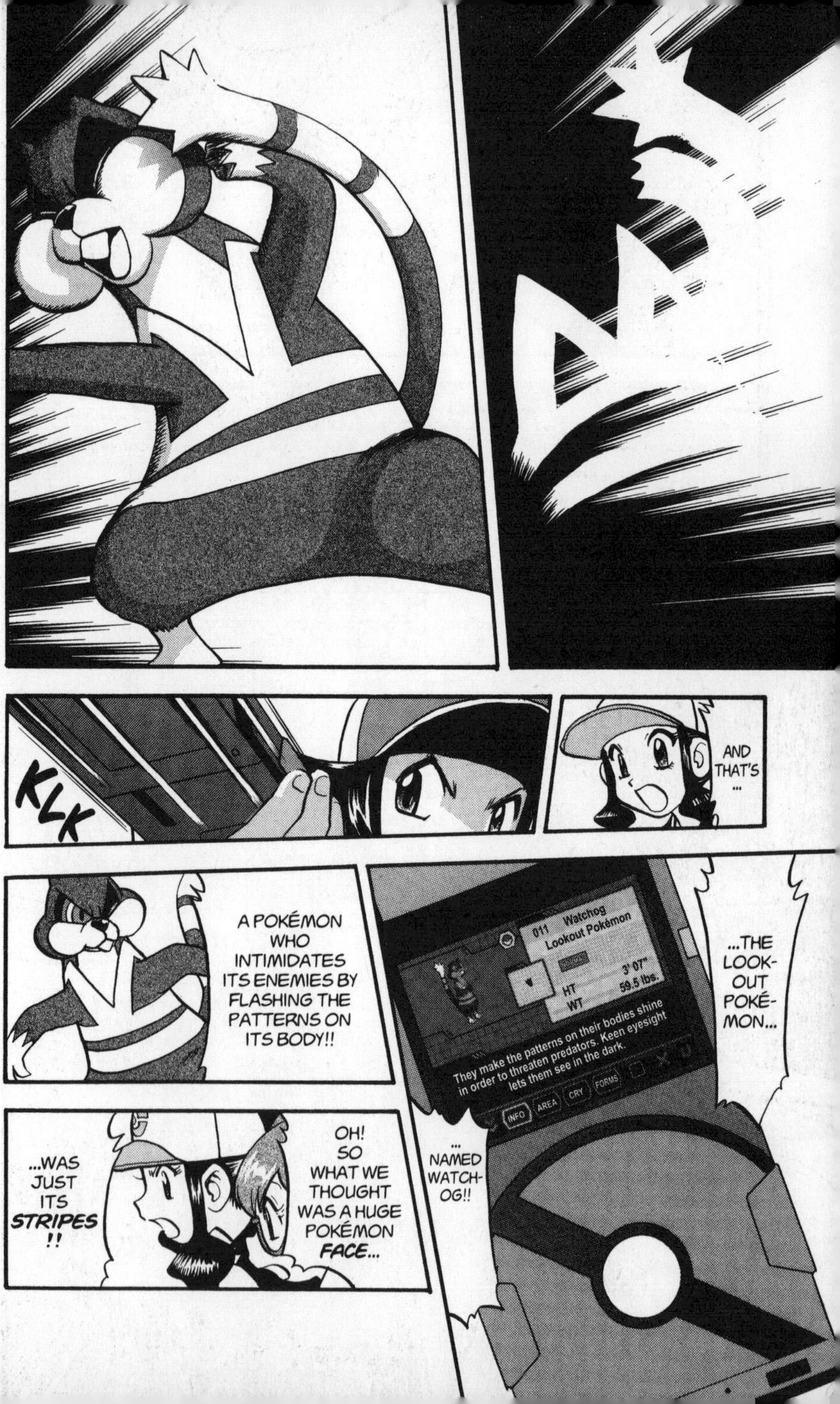
AND THAT'S ...
KLK
...THE LOOK-OUT POKÉ-MON...
011 Watchog
Lookout Pokémon
HT 3' 07"
WT 59.5 lbs.
They make the patterns on their bodies shine in order to threaten predators. Keen eyesight lets them see in the dark.
INFO AREA CRY FORMS
... NAMED WATCH-OG!!
A POKÉMON WHO INTIMIDATES ITS ENEMIES BY FLASHING THE PATTERNS ON ITS BODY!!
OH! SO WHAT WE THOUGHT WAS A HUGE POKÉMON *FACE*...
...WAS JUST ITS *STRIPES* !!

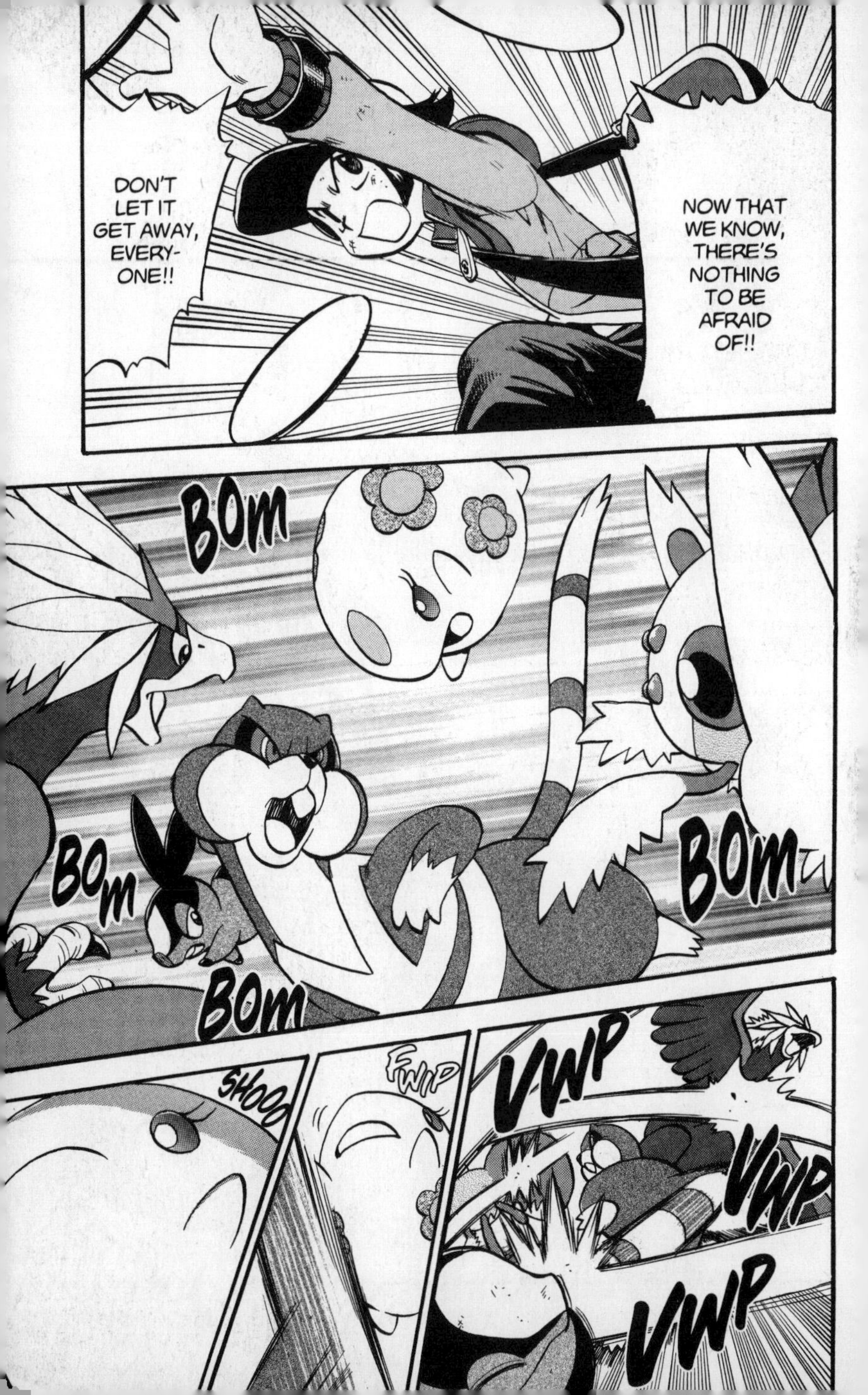
NOW THAT WE KNOW, THERE'S NOTHING TO BE AFRAID OF!!
DON'T LET IT GET AWAY, EVERY-ONE!!
BOM
BOM
BOM
BOM
VWP
VWP
VWP
FWIP
SHOOO

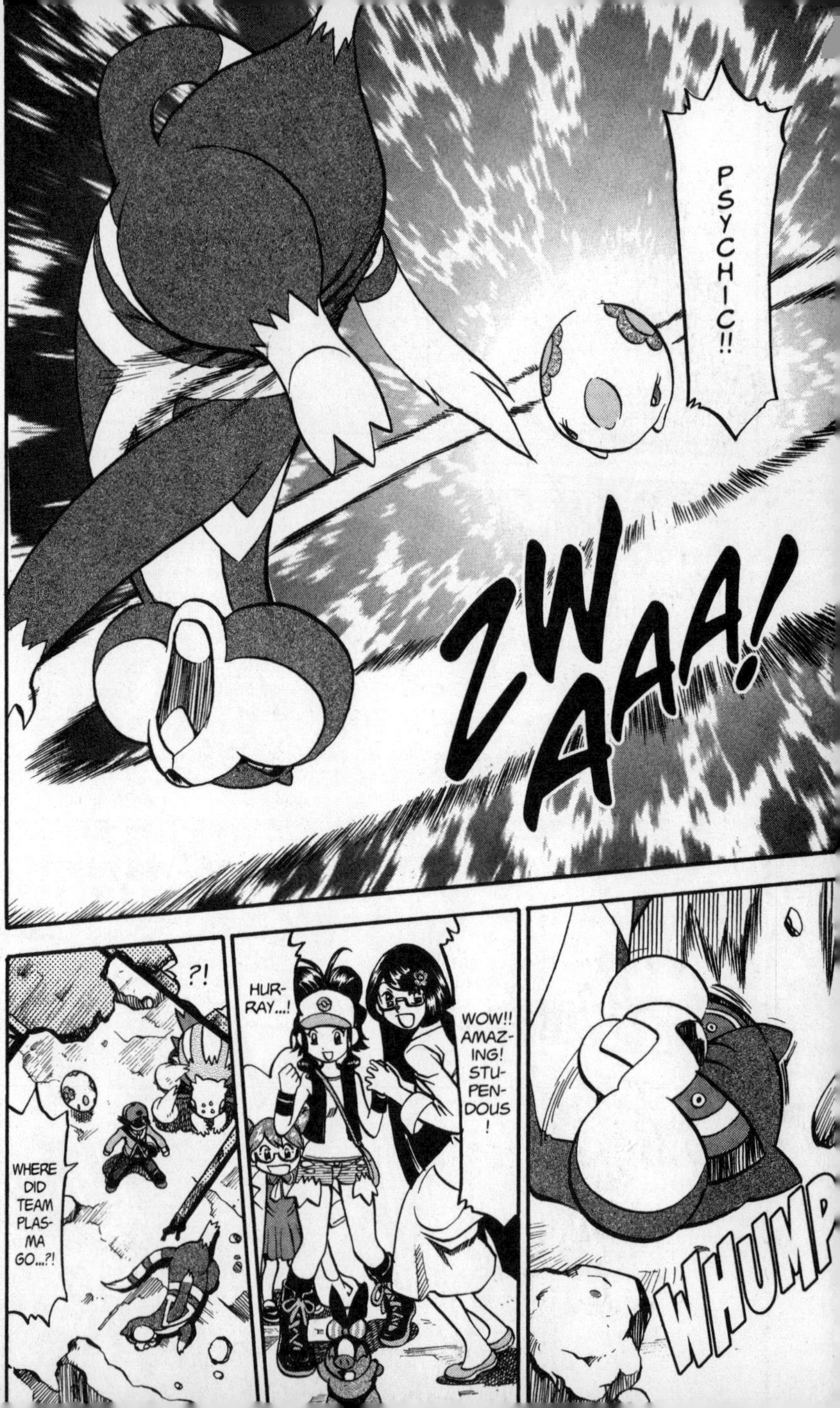
PSYCHIC!!
ZWAAAA!
WHUMP
WOW!! AMAZING! STUPENDOUS!
HURRAY...!
?!
WHERE DID TEAM PLASMA GO...?!

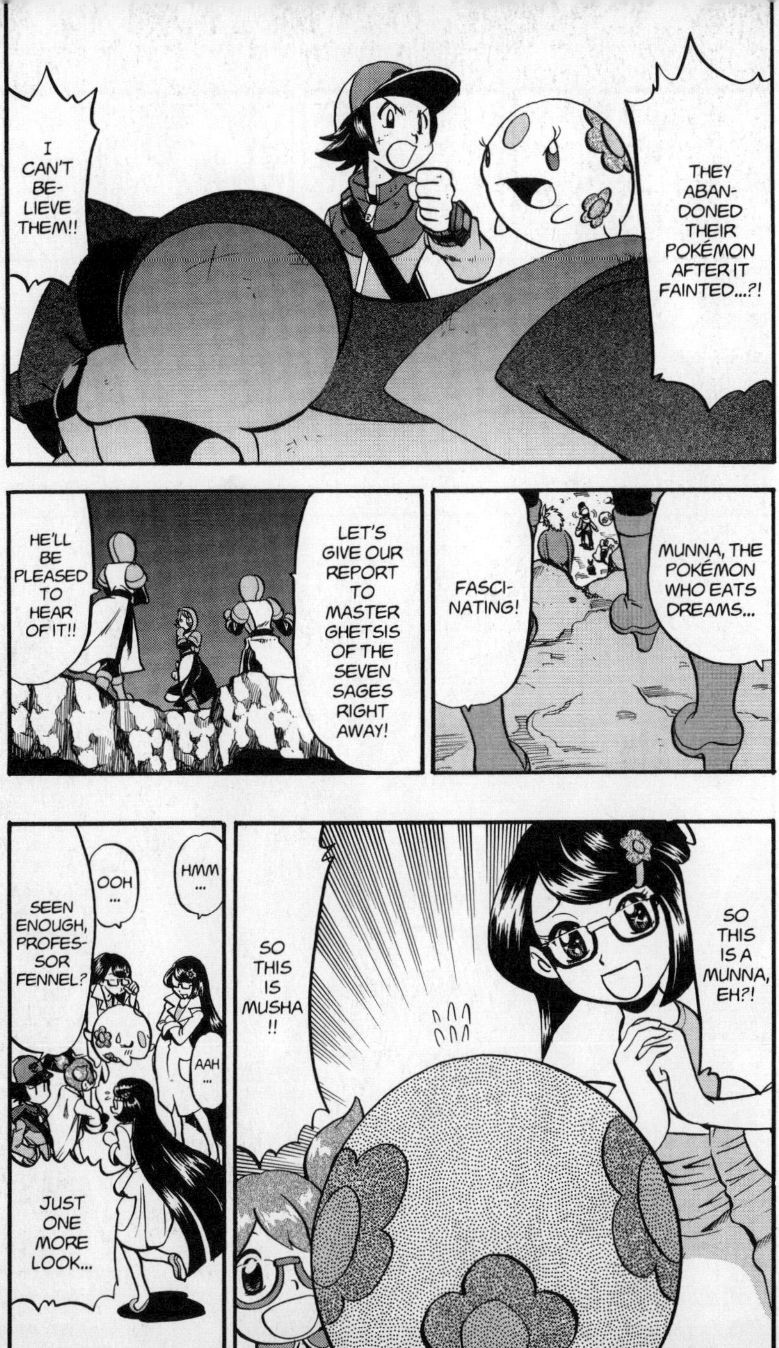
THEY ABANDONED THEIR POKÉMON AFTER IT FAINTED...?!
I CAN'T BELIEVE THEM!!
MUNNA, THE POKÉMON WHO EATS DREAMS...
FASCINATING!
LET'S GIVE OUR REPORT TO MASTER GHETSIS OF THE SEVEN SAGES RIGHT AWAY!
HE'LL BE PLEASED TO HEAR OF IT!!
SO THIS IS A MUNNA, EH?!
SO THIS IS MUSHA!!
HMM...
OOH...
SEEN ENOUGH, PROFESSOR FENNEL?
AAH...
JUST ONE MORE LOOK...

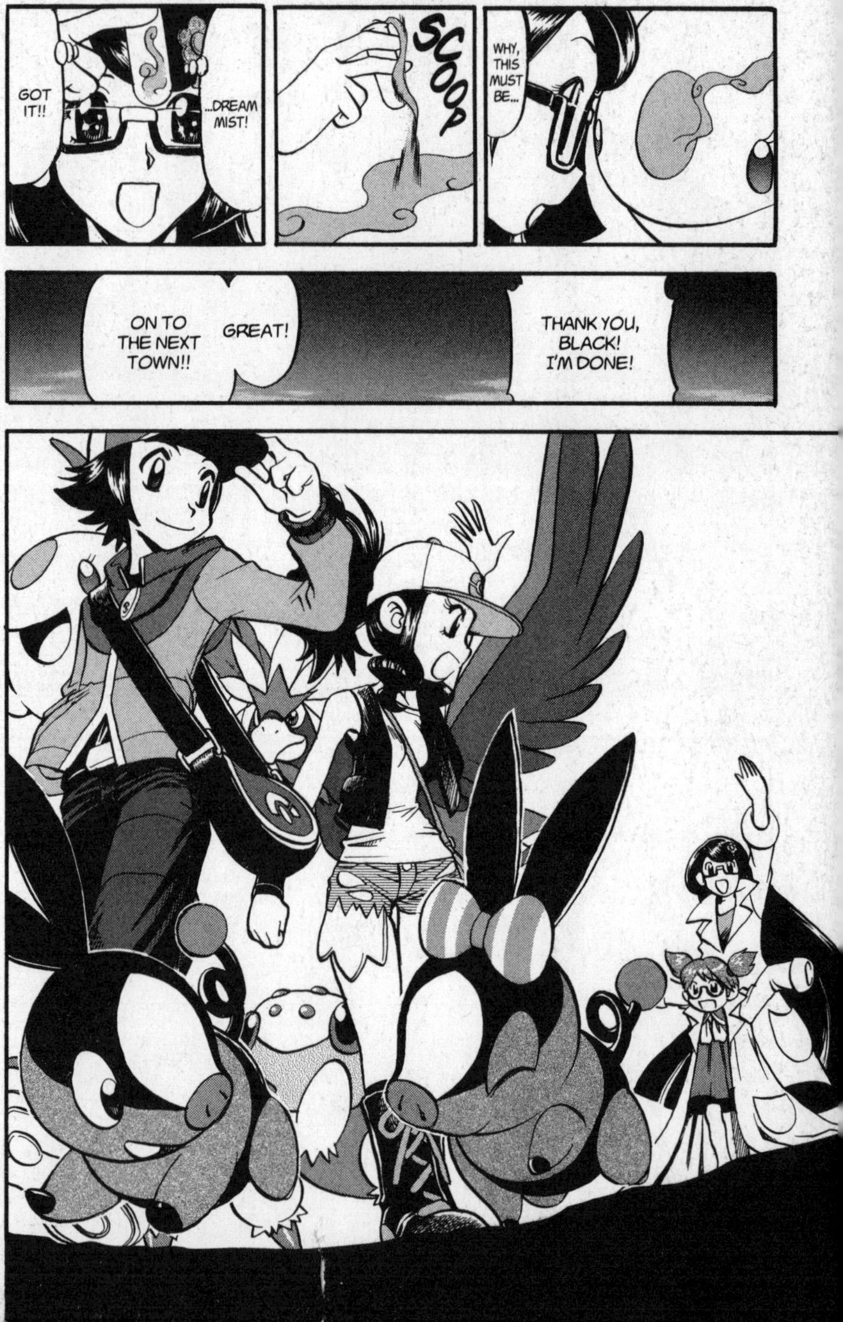
WHY, THIS MUST BE...
SCOOP
GOT IT!!
...DREAM MIST!
THANK YOU, BLACK! I'M DONE!
GREAT!
ON TO THE NEXT TOWN!!

TO BE

CONTINUED

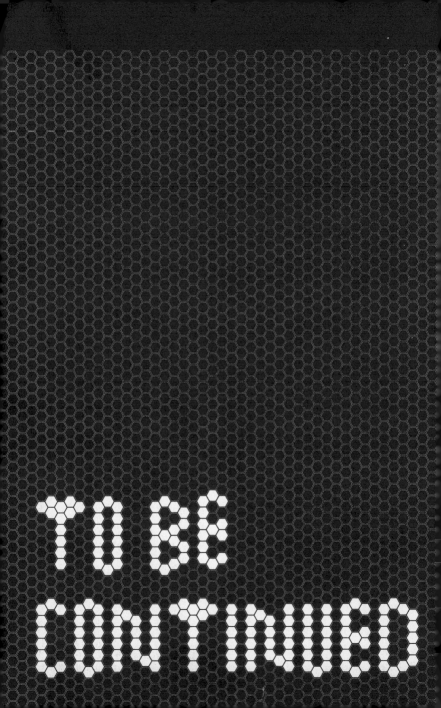

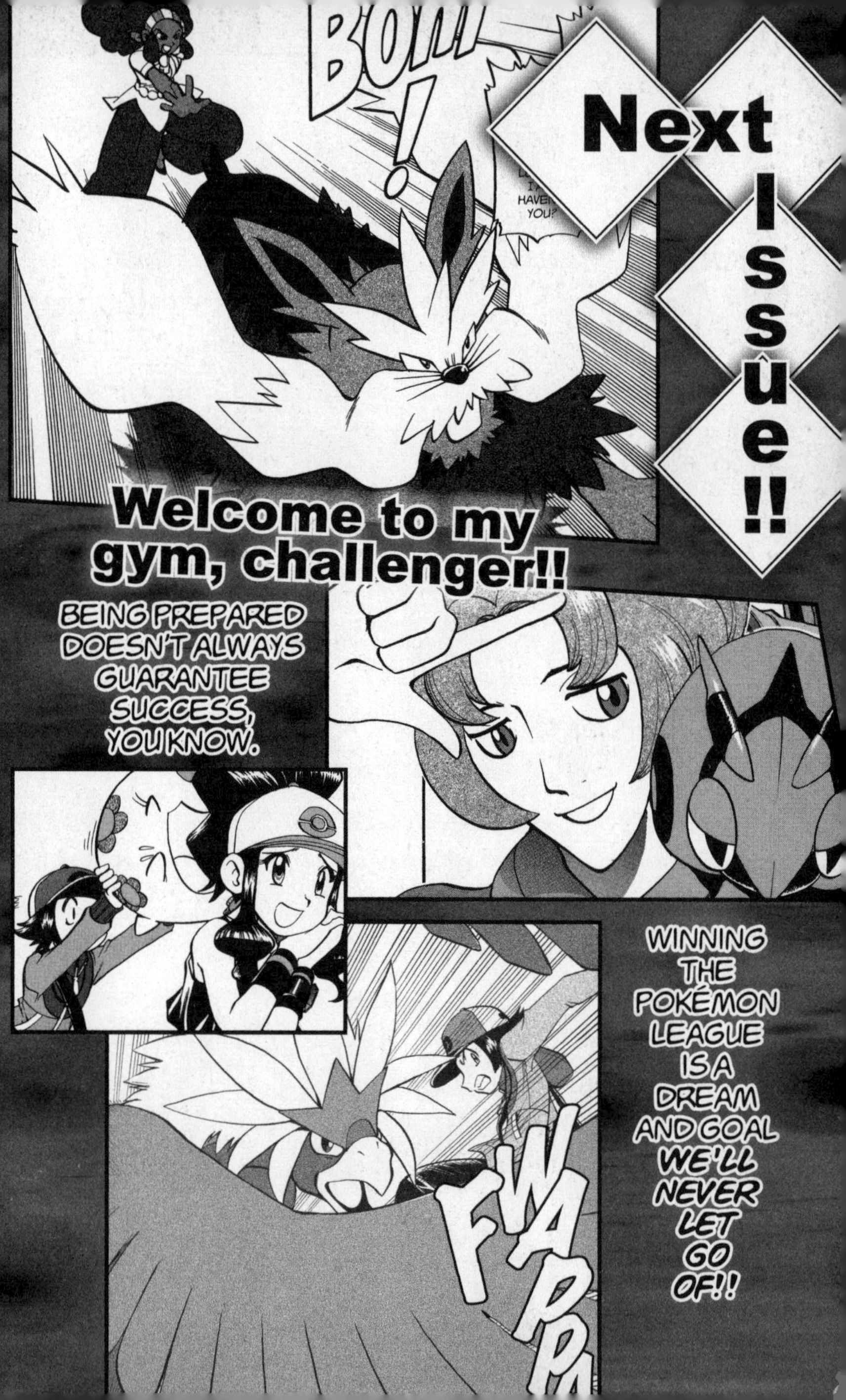

Next Issue!!
BOM!
YOU?
Welcome to my gym, challenger!!
BEING PREPARED DOESN'T ALWAYS GUARANTEE SUCCESS, YOU KNOW.
WINNING THE POKÉMON LEAGUE IS A DREAM AND GOAL WE'LL NEVER LET GO OF!!
FWAP

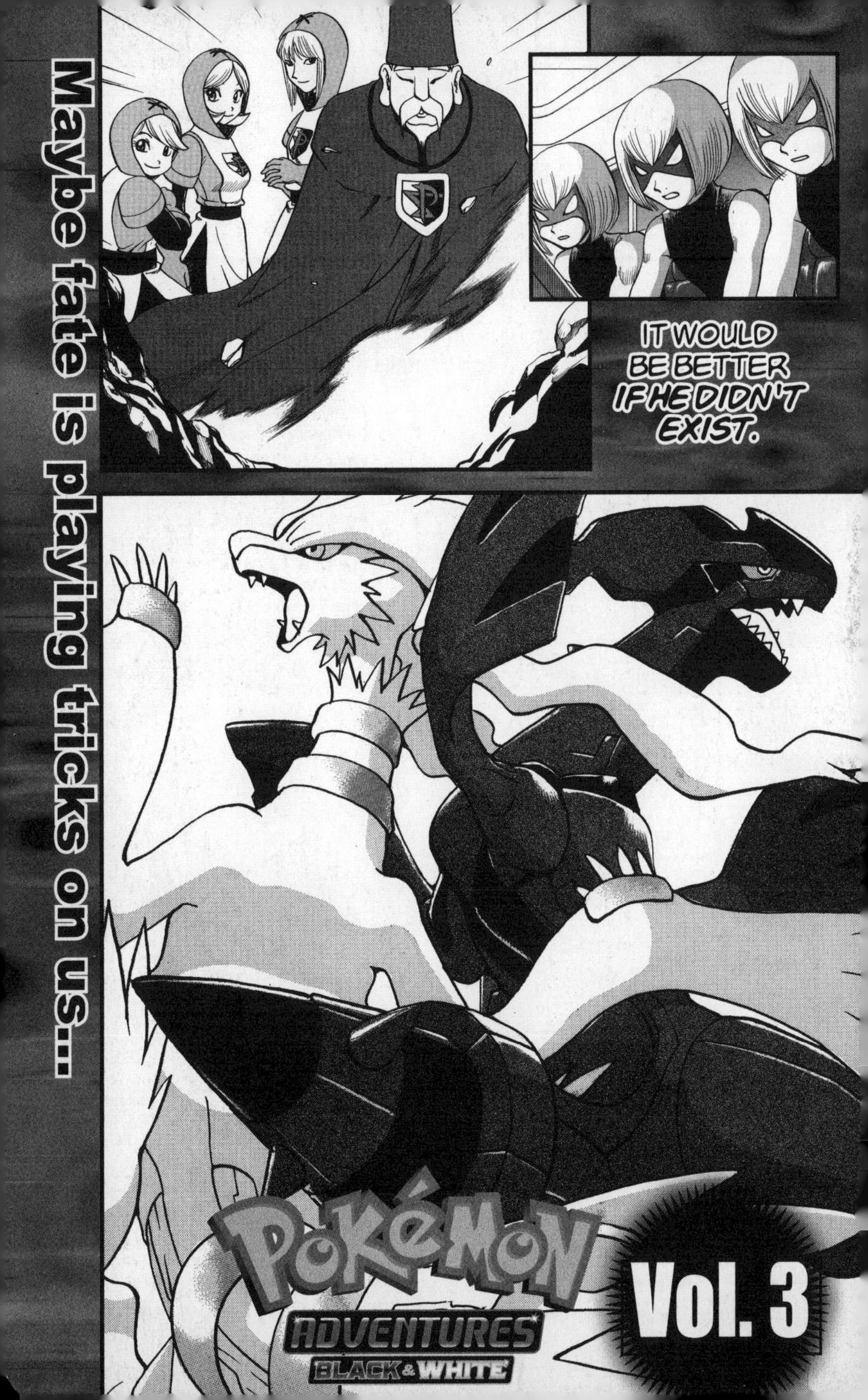
Maybe fate is playing tricks on us...
IT WOULD BE BETTER IF HE DIDN'T EXIST.
POKéMON ADVENTURES BLACK & WHITE
Vol. 3

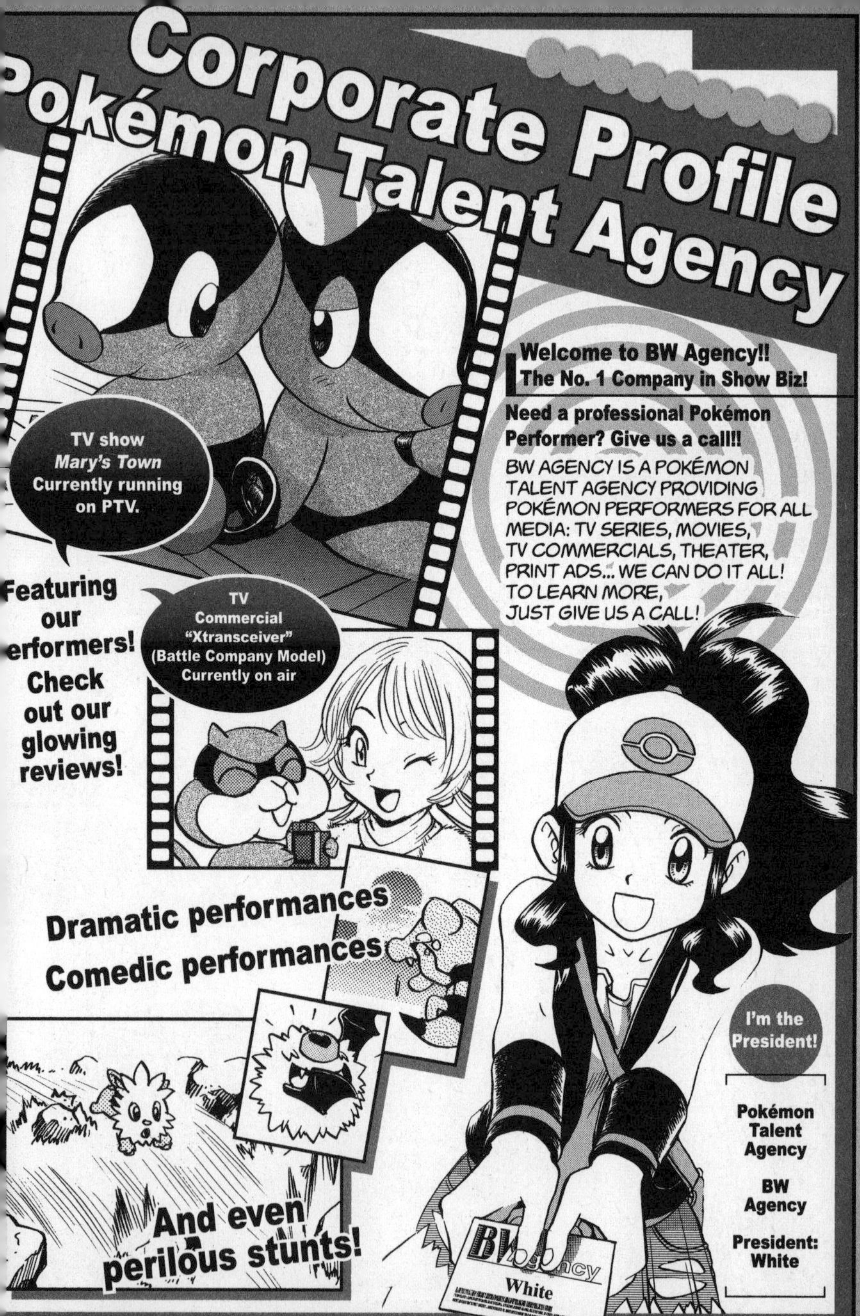
Corporate Profile
Pokémon Talent Agency
Welcome to BW Agency!!
The No. 1 Company in Show Biz!
Need a professional Pokémon Performer? Give us a call!!
BW AGENCY IS A POKÉMON TALENT AGENCY PROVIDING POKÉMON PERFORMERS FOR ALL MEDIA: TV SERIES, MOVIES, TV COMMERCIALS, THEATER, PRINT ADS... WE CAN DO IT ALL! TO LEARN MORE, JUST GIVE US A CALL!
TV show Mary's Town Currently running on PTV.
Featuring our erformers! Check out our glowing reviews!
TV Commercial "Xtransceiver" (Battle Company Model) Currently on air
Dramatic performances
Comedic performances
And even perilous stunts!
I'm the President!
Pokémon Talent Agency
BW Agency
President: White
White

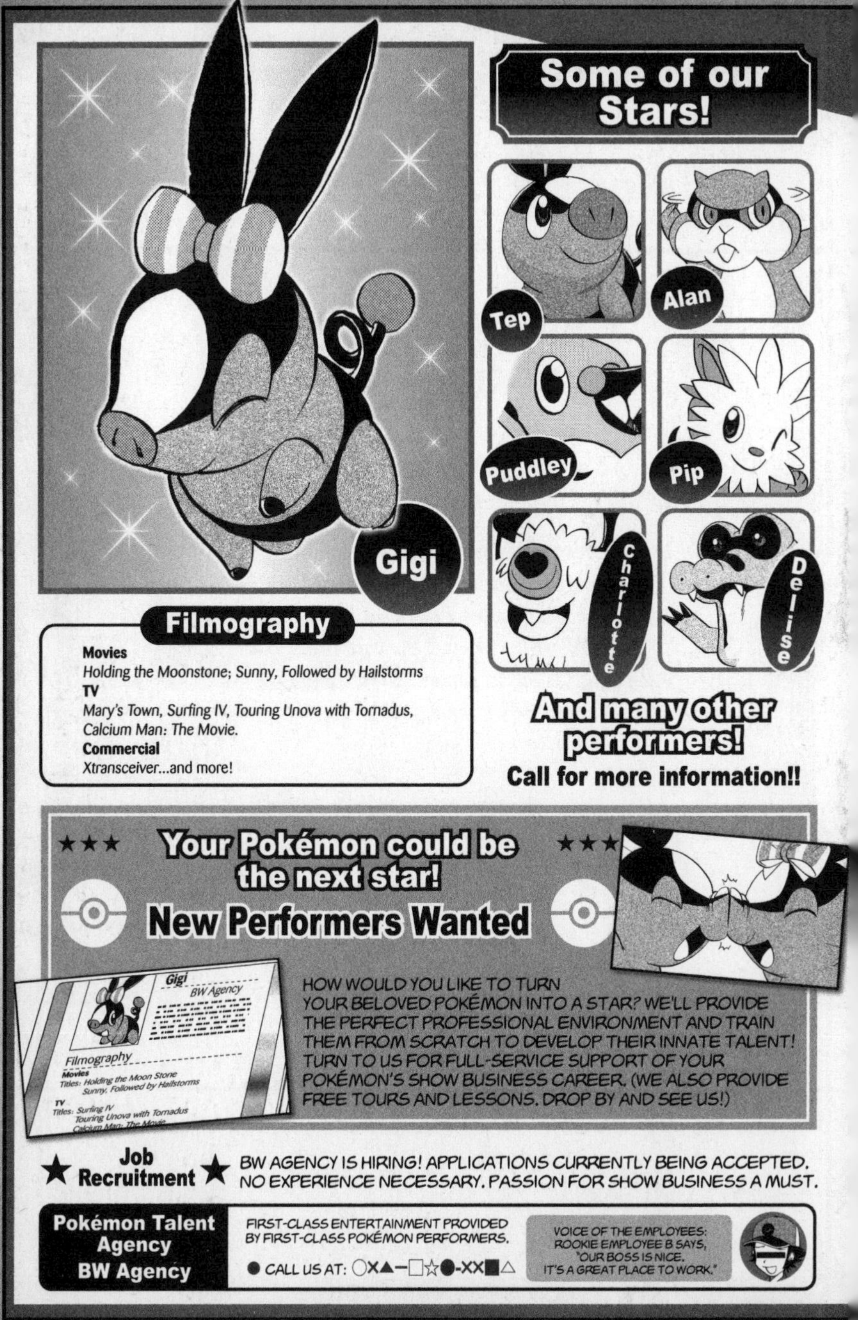

Some of our Stars!
Gigi
Tep
Alan
Puddley
Pip
Charlotte
Delise
Filmography
Movies
Holding the Moonstone; Sunny, Followed by Hailstorms
TV
Mary's Town, Surfing IV, Touring Unova with Tornadus, Calcium Man: The Movie.
Commercial
Xtransceiver...and more!
And many other performers!
Call for more information!!
★★★ Your Pokémon could be the next star! ★★★
New Performers Wanted
Gigi
BW Agency
Filmography
Movies
Titles: Holding the Moon Stone
Sunny, Followed by Hailstorms
TV
Titles: Surfing IV
Touring Unova with Tornadus
HOW WOULD YOU LIKE TO TURN YOUR BELOVED POKÉMON INTO A STAR? WE'LL PROVIDE THE PERFECT PROFESSIONAL ENVIRONMENT AND TRAIN THEM FROM SCRATCH TO DEVELOP THEIR INNATE TALENT! TURN TO US FOR FULL-SERVICE SUPPORT OF YOUR POKÉMON'S SHOW BUSINESS CAREER. (WE ALSO PROVIDE FREE TOURS AND LESSONS. DROP BY AND SEE US!)
★ Job Recruitment ★
BW AGENCY IS HIRING! APPLICATIONS CURRENTLY BEING ACCEPTED. NO EXPERIENCE NECESSARY. PASSION FOR SHOW BUSINESS A MUST.
Pokémon Talent Agency
BW Agency
FIRST-CLASS ENTERTAINMENT PROVIDED BY FIRST-CLASS POKÉMON PERFORMERS.
● CALL US AT: ○X▲—□☆●-XX■△
VOICE OF THE EMPLOYEES: ROOKIE EMPLOYEE B SAYS, "OUR BOSS IS NICE. IT'S A GREAT PLACE TO WORK."

Chapter Title Page Illustration Collection

Presenting title page illustrations originally drawn for some of the chapters of *Pokémon Black and White* when they were first published in Japanese children's magazines *Pokémon Fan* and *Corocoro Ichiban!*.

Let's take a look back at Black and White's journey in pictures...

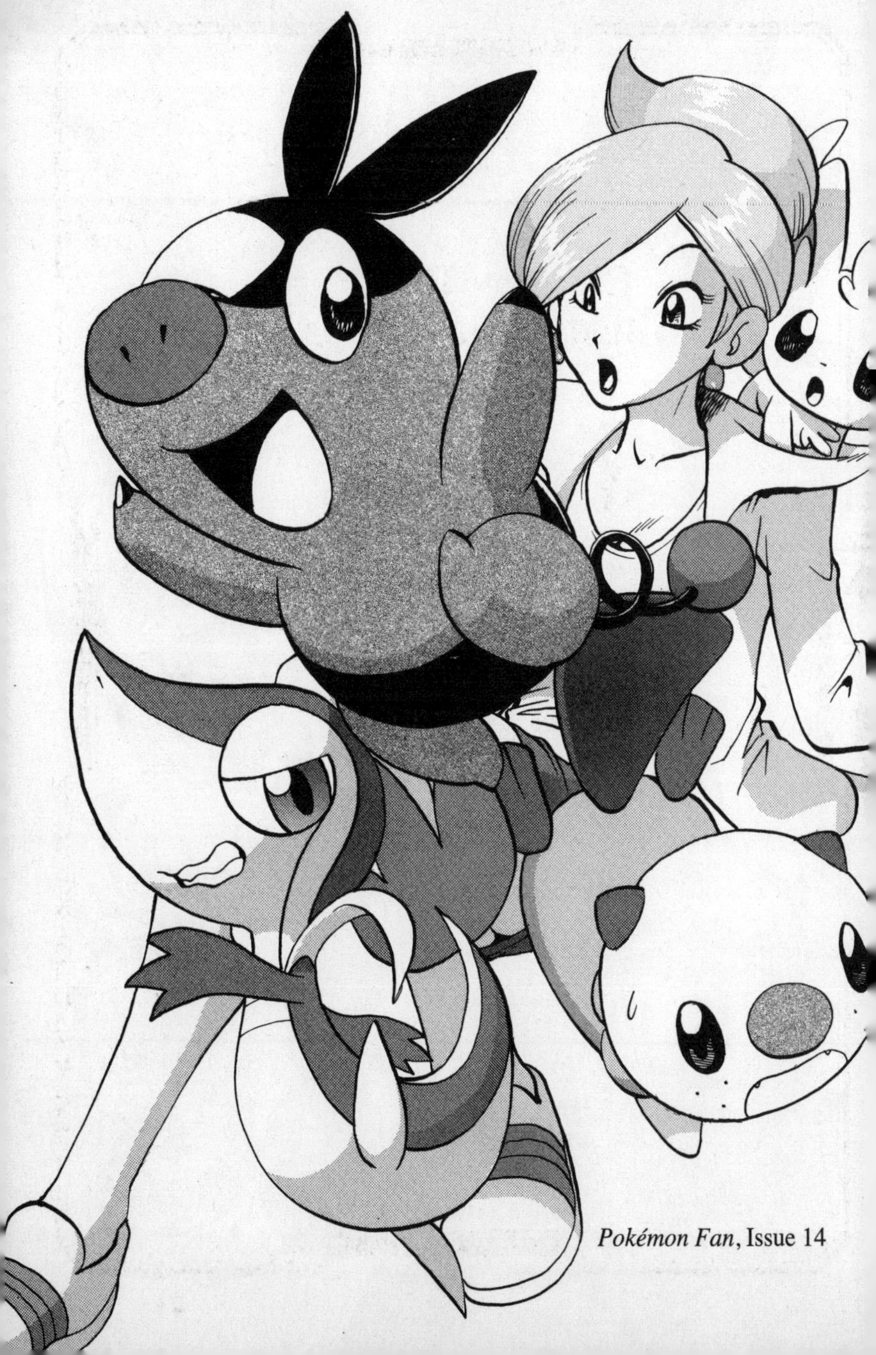

Pokémon Fan, Issue 14

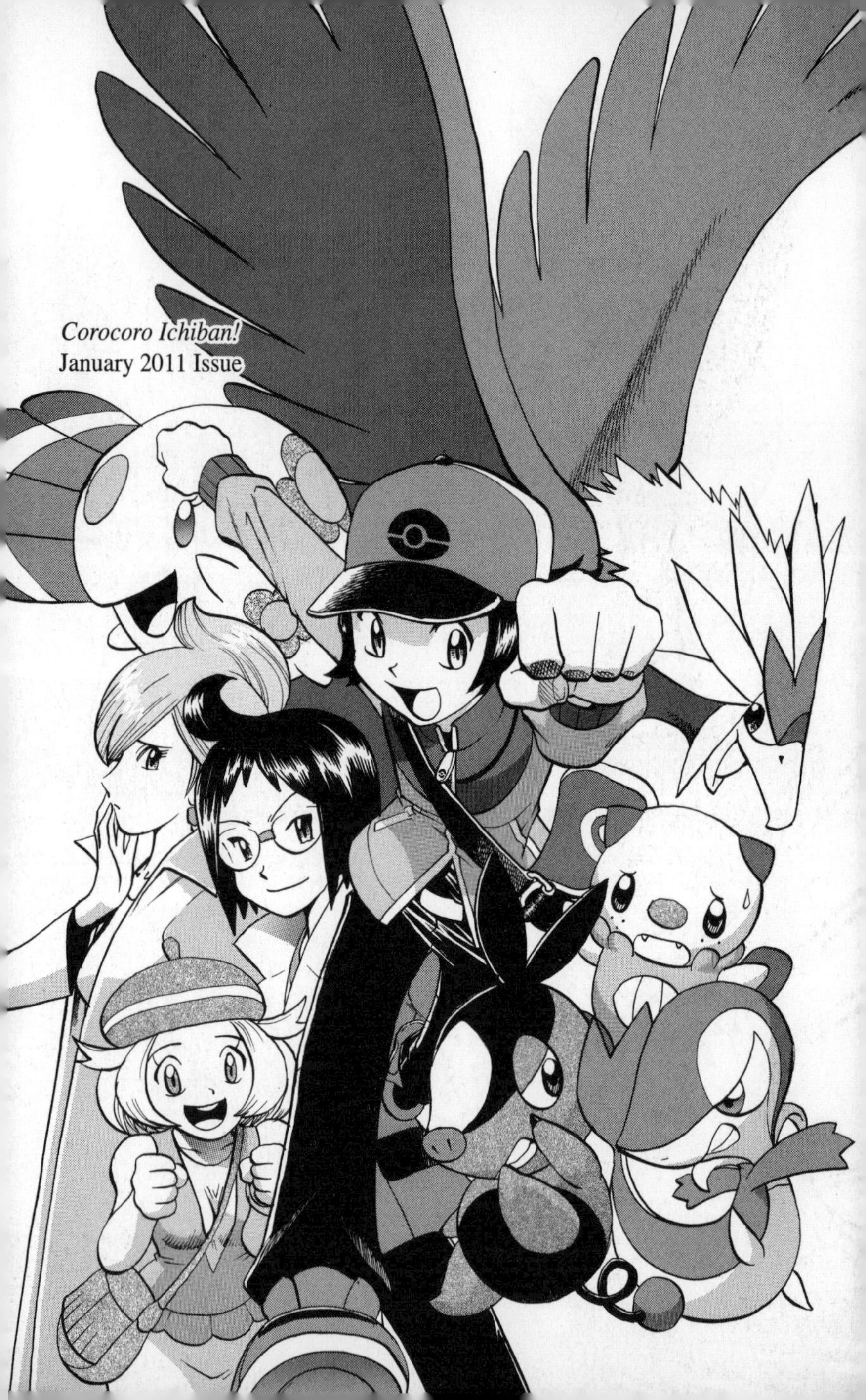

Corocoro Ichiban!
January 2011 Issue

Corocoro Ichiban!
March 2011 Issue

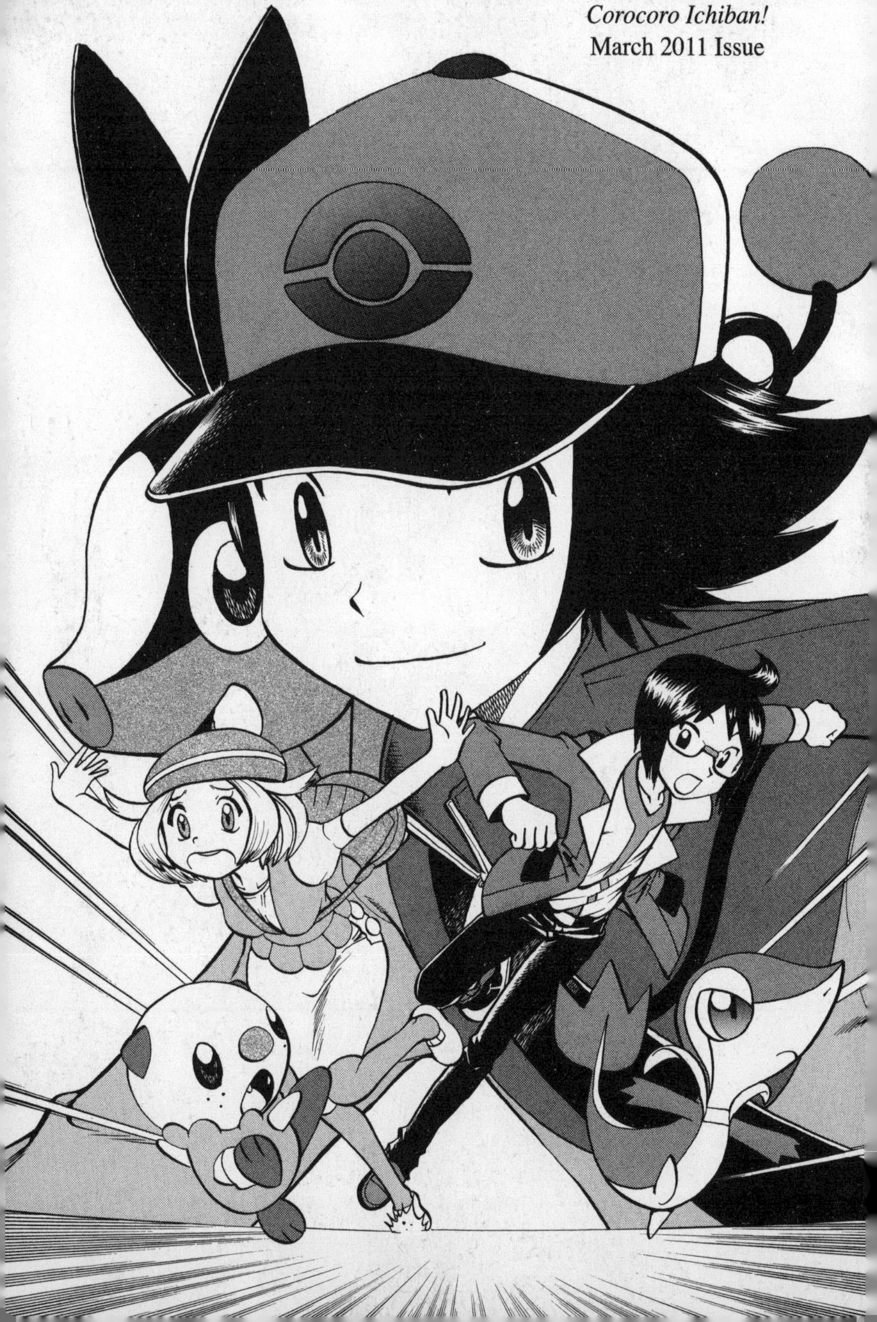

Corocoro Ichiban!
May 2011 Issue

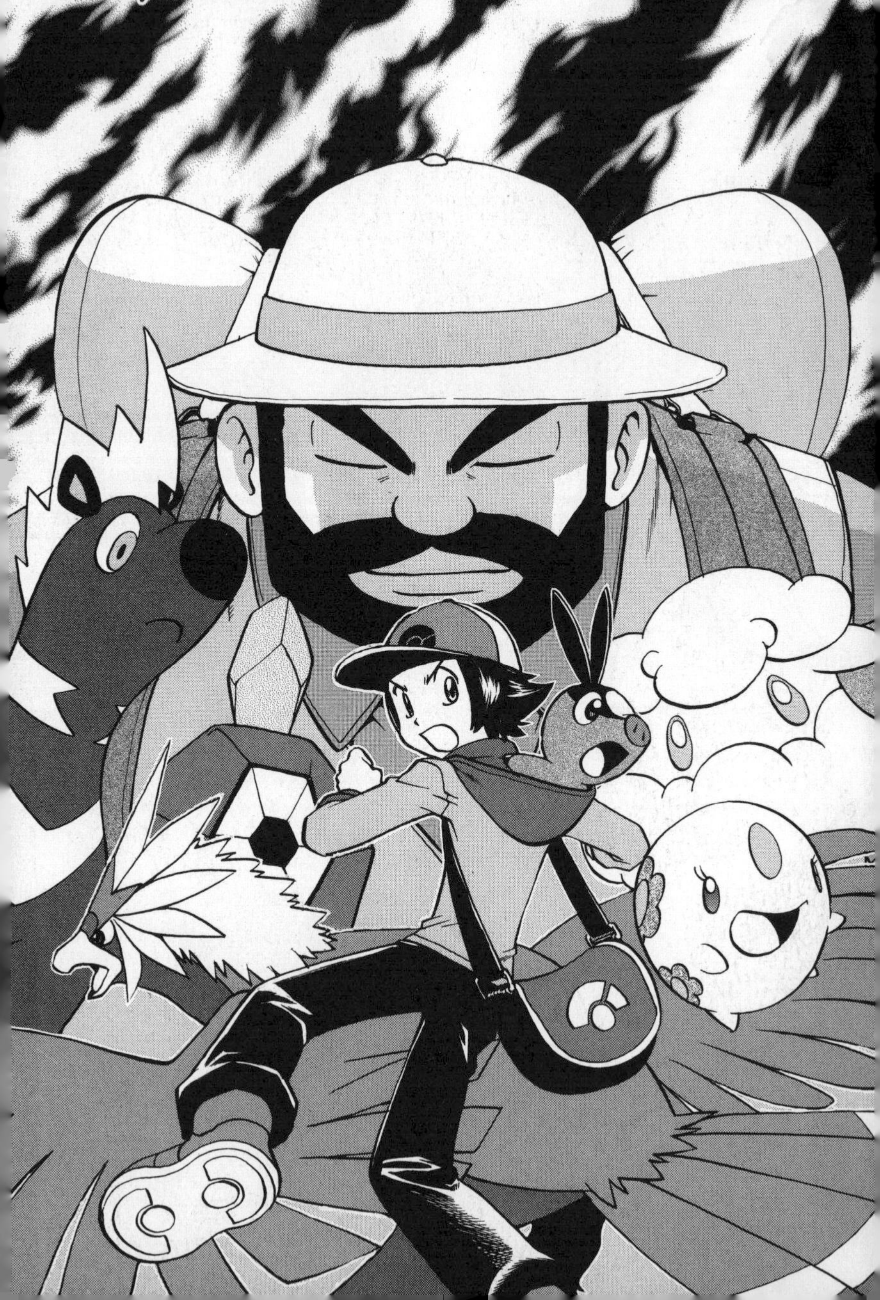

Corocoro Ichiban!
June 2011 Issue

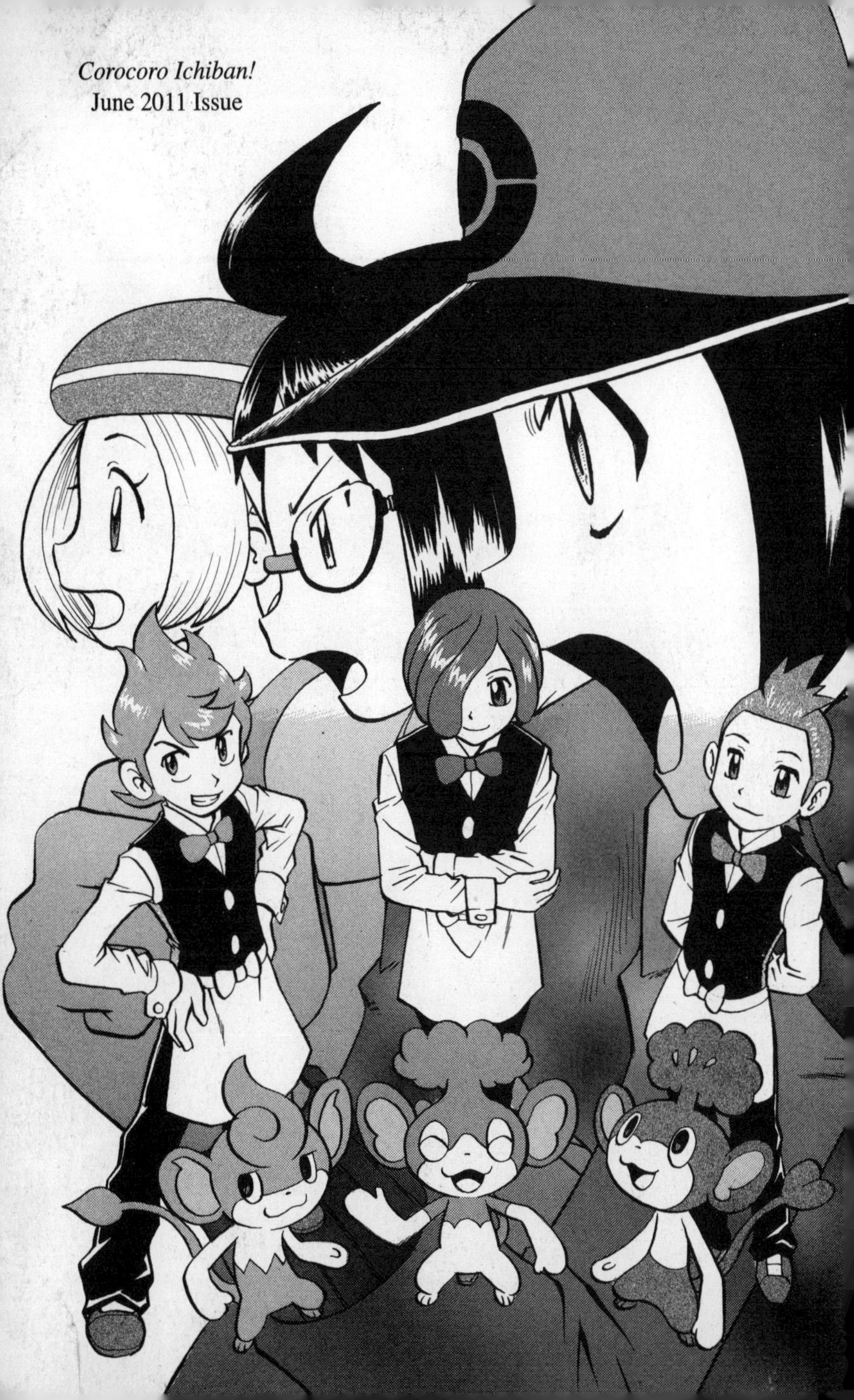

Corocoro Ichiban!
July 2011 Issue

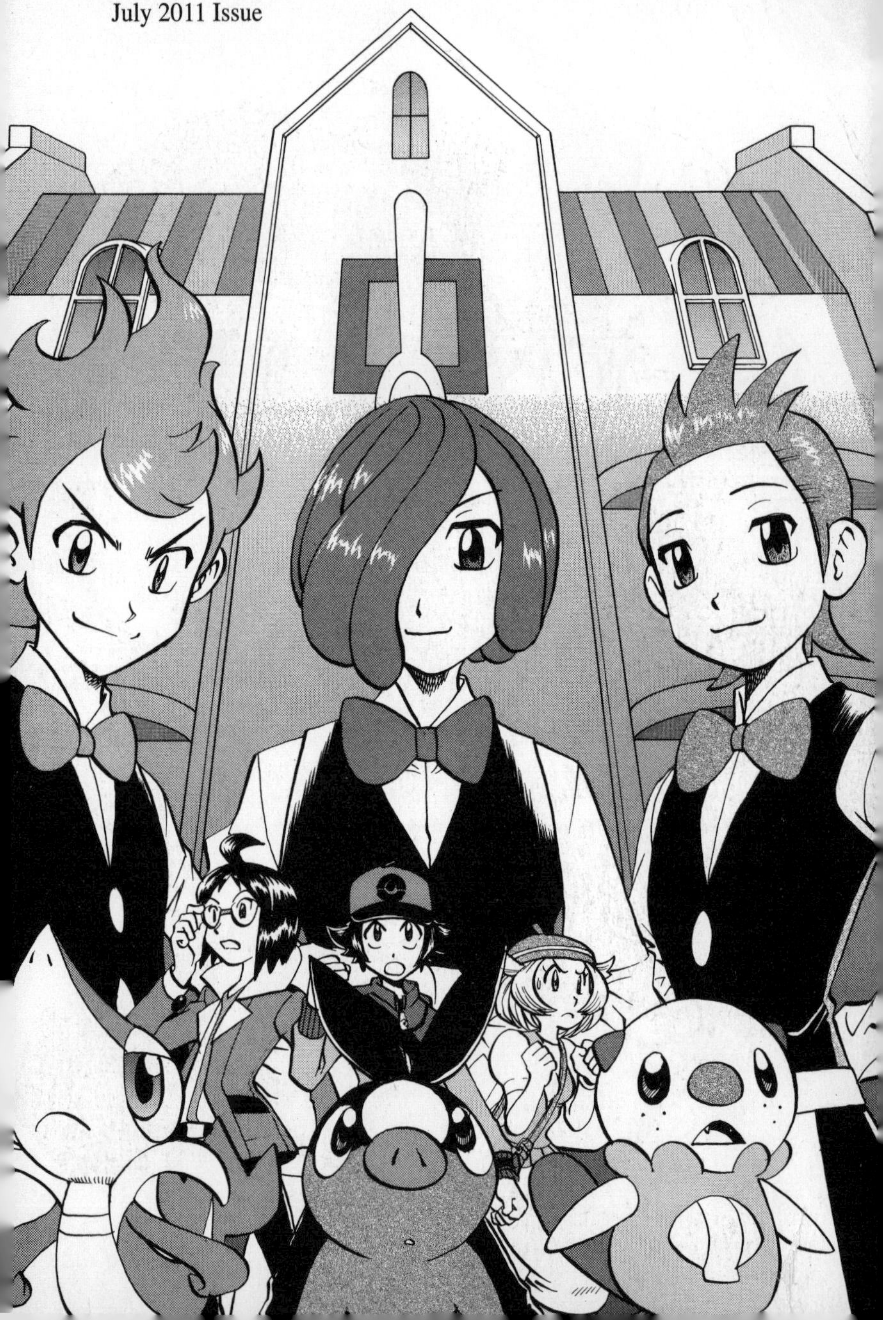

Pokémon Fan, Issue 15

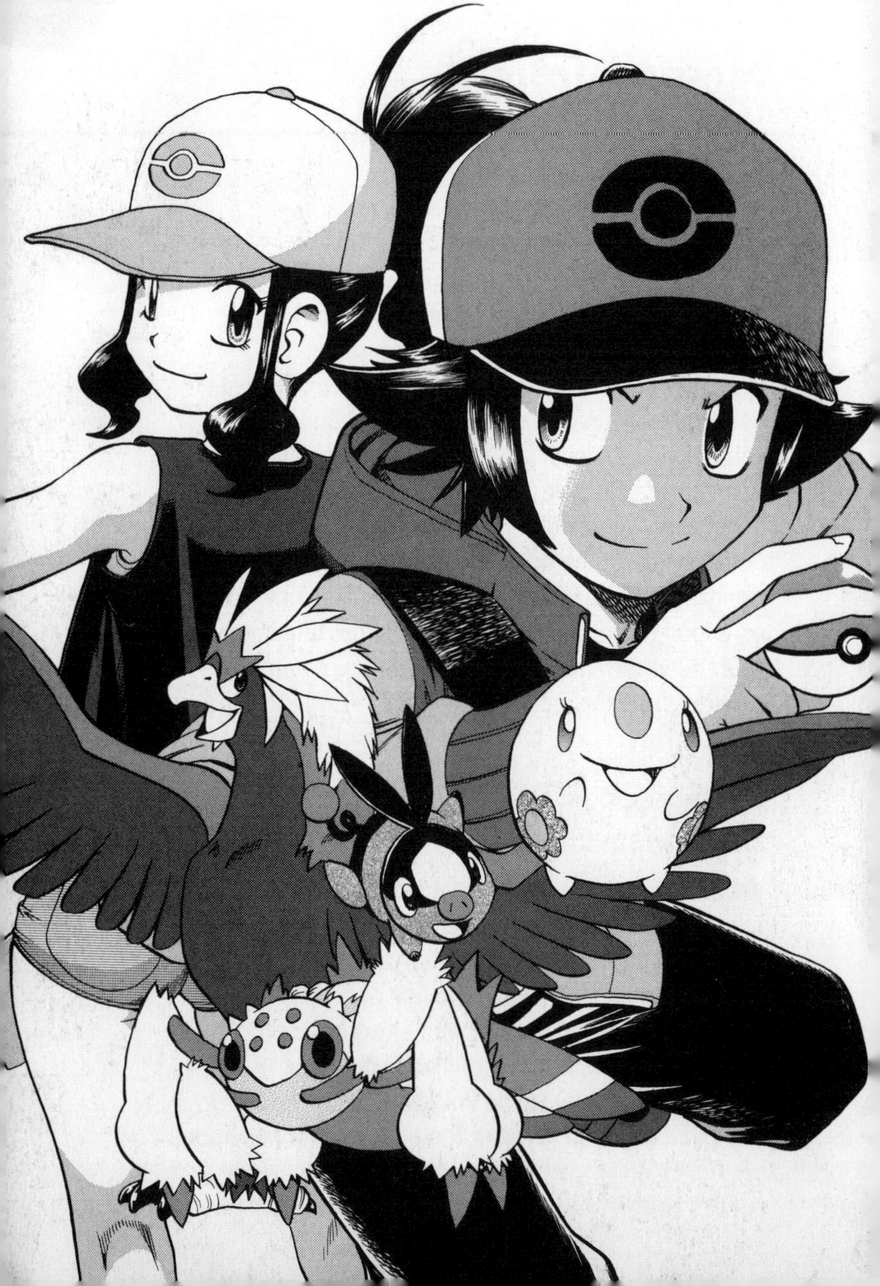

Message from
Hidenori Kusaka

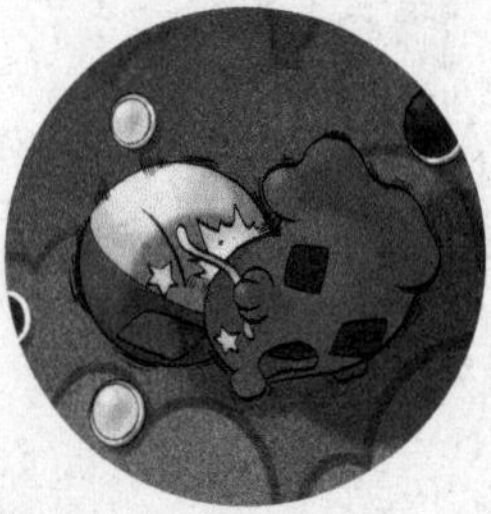

In my straightforward Pokémon stories the relationships between characters have been the boy and the girl, the experienced and the rookie, and childhood friends. And in my somewhat more complex stories we've had relationships like the delinquent and the role model, and the wealthy elite and the bodyguards. I've been trying to think of new contrasting relationships that would work well in the manga. Often I think, "I've already covered pretty much every possibility," but other times I think, "Actually, there are still some possibilities I haven't explored yet." This is one of the challenges of working on a long-running series. But it's also the fun part. (LOL) Anyhow, this time I bring you...the company president and the employee! (^▽^)

Message from
Satoshi Yamamoto

White and N make their first appearance in this volume! I think it's safe to say that now the Black and White story arc truly begins. White is hardworking and clever, so I find it easy to draw her moving decisively. On the other hand, I like to draw N with unexpected motions to surprise readers. I tried to make him look like an orchestra conductor in the Pokémon battle sequences. I hope you enjoy the exciting Tenth Chapter of Pokémon!

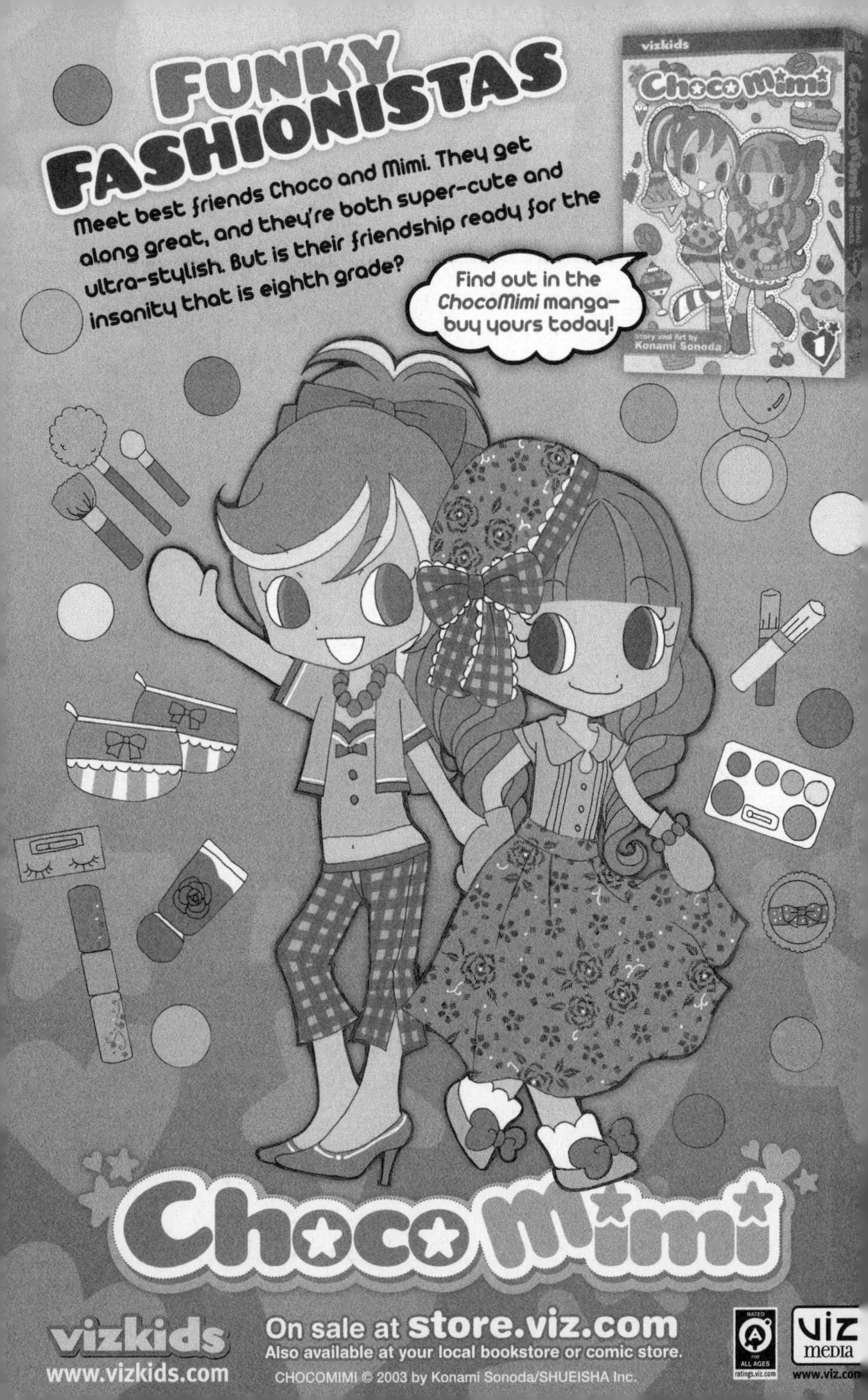

FUNKY FASHIONISTAS
Meet best friends Choco and Mimi. They get along great, and they're both super-cute and ultra-stylish. But is their friendship ready for the insanity that is eighth grade?
Find out in the ChocoMimi manga–buy yours today!
vizkids
ChocoMimi
Story and Art by Konami Sonoda
1
ChocoMimi
vizkids
www.vizkids.com
On sale at store.viz.com
Also available at your local bookstore or comic store.
CHOCOMIMI © 2003 by Konami Sonoda/SHUEISHA Inc.
RATED A FOR ALL AGES
ratings.viz.com
VIZ media
www.viz.com

POKéMON MOVIE

Legend tells of The Sea Temple, which contains a treasure with the power to take over the world. But its location remains hidden and requires a mysterious key. Can Ash, Pikachu and their friends prevent the unveiling of these powerful secrets?

Pokémon Ranger and the Temple of the Sea

Own it on DVD today!

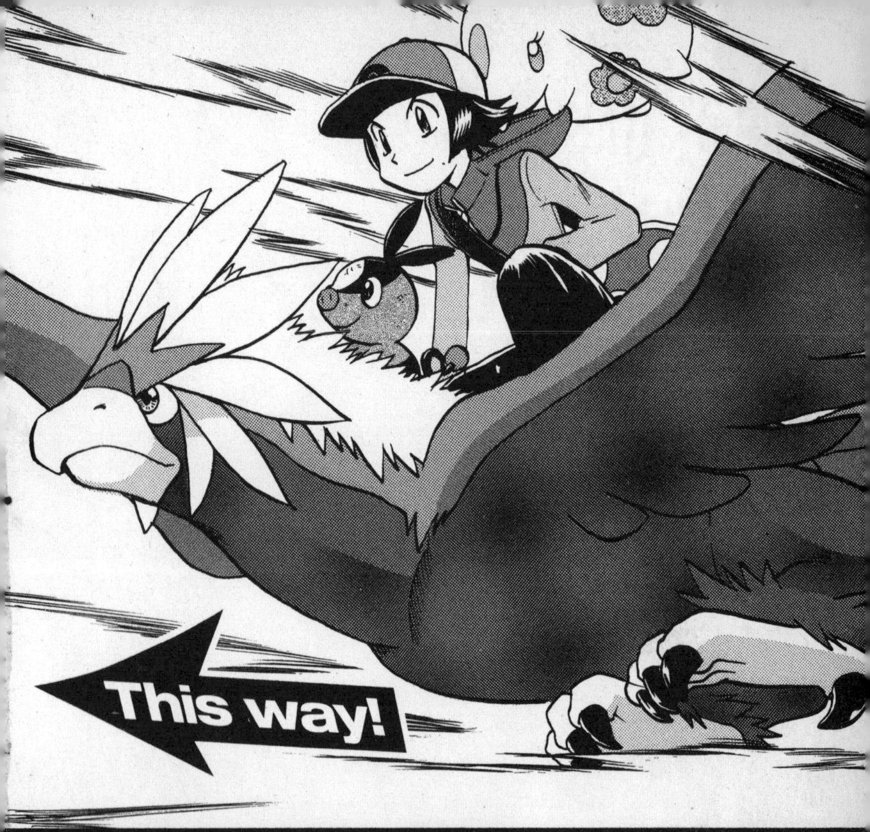
This way!

THIS IS THE END OF THIS GRAPHIC NOVEL!

To properly enjoy this VIZ Media graphic novel, please turn it around and begin reading from right to left.

This book has been printed in the original Japanese format in order to preserve the orientation of the original artwork.

Have fun with it!

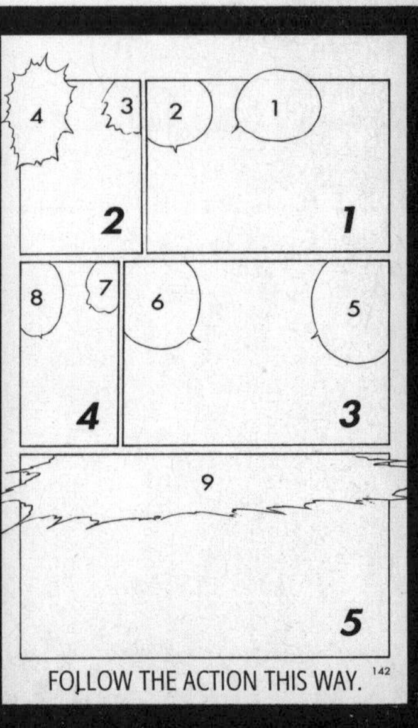
1
2
3
4
5
6
7
8
9
1
2
3
4
5
FOLLOW THE ACTION THIS WAY.
142